One Paper Heart

Donan Berg

DOTDON Books
Moline IL

One Paper Heart
DOTDON Books are published by

DOTDON Personalized Services
514 17th Street
PO Box 1302
Moline IL 61266-1302

Author e-mail: mystery@abodytobones.com

Library of Congress Control Number: 2015908571

ISBN 13: 978-1-941244-09-8 (E-book)
ISBN 10: 1941244092
ISBN 13: 978-1-941244-10-4 (Paper)
ISBN 10: 1941244106

First U.S. Edition: August 2015
10 9 8 7 6 5 4 3 2 1

Donan Berg

To lovers, now and forever,
from the author.

There is a heart of muscle and blood.
There is a heart that guides our soul.
There is a heart that yearns for peace.
There is a heart we search ever to reach.

May the full benefit of all be yours.

Express your love, and pray for
all who have or will sacrifice
to keep this world safe.

Books by

Donan Berg

A Body To Bones
First Skeleton Series Mystery

The Bones Dance Foxtrot
Second Skeleton Series Mystery

Baby Bones
Third Skeleton Series Mystery

Abbey Burning Love

Adolph's Gold

Bubbling Conflict and
Other Stories

Amanda

One Paper Heart

Chapter One

The romantic flames of Alicia Danielson's sweet dreams flared into conscious panic. A sliver of red light from the triple ones on her digital alarm clock oriented Alicia to her bedroom door. Two coughs of acrid smoke convinced her to abandon her search for a robe. On hands-and-knees, she crawled toward her three-room Minneapolis apartment's hallway exit. Sweat drips and the fear of being burned alive snowballed to spur her determination. Yesterday's funk of dying a twenty-six-year-old spinster laminated by a budding hysteria.

A raspy third cough tore at the raw lining of her constricted throat. When her heartbeat amplified the faint hallway doorknob jangle, she willed her butt not to rest on her heels and lurched her shoulders forward. Smoke curled and swirled past her ears.

Unable to hold her breath and lessened the pain of her smoke-irritated lungs, she whispered, "Dam. Hoover Dam." For twenty-three years since age three, she'd deleted the "n" and disguised the profane word "damn" by pairing it with real concrete dams. While at first it was to avoid her mother's soap bar inside her mouth, her

1

quirk blossomed into moments of schoolyard pride. If challenged, her dog-eared atlas proved her prowess to name each and every United States dam. For those itty-bitty dams without names in Minnesota's Hennepin County, she'd rattle off the numbers of highways leading to and across them. It grew to be a crutch to relieve stress.

When her forehead banged the metal hallway door, she shouted as loud as she could, "Help." *Grand Coulee Dam.* "Help me."

Alicia flinched. She sucked the twinge from three right-hand fingertips. "Where are you?" Alicia's throat ached. "I'm here." The door's hot doorknob confirmed that flames, prepared to sear human flesh, lurked inches away. Intensified gray-blackish smoke seeped under her high-rise's tenth floor door. Sirens outside blared. With each blast, Alicia cursed the ditzy blonde rental agent who pooh-poohed fire emergencies to extol the virtue that higher floors muffled late night street noise.

Alicia rejected all worry about makeup. Neither she nor any other woman needed lipstick at two in the morning for firemen in Darth Vader masks. Her three spaced shrieks inflamed her vocal cords. *I'm doomed. Fire engine ladders never extend higher than the seventh floor.*

The medical examiner won't care. With her chest sliced and peeled back, her god-enhanced bar-coded breast assets would wiggle as a synchronized dancing pair on a stainless steel audition tray while her toes dripped water droplets from the corpse washing spray.

Alicia flattened her torso to the floor to breathe in the coolest heated air. Her teary eyes burned. *Don't be hysterical. Gather your wits. Slow your emotions. Lock and Dam No. 4, flow south Ol' Man River.*

A thunderous crash on the other side of the hallway door bounced the floor beneath her body.

"Have the police checked this floor?" The muffled gruff voice goose-bumped her skin.

2

Looters? Alicia held her breath. A second crash flung her rearward. Smoke billowed.

A gloved hand forced her lower jaw into her upper lip and then the pressure subsided.

Alicia screamed. She shuddered as a sprayed callused hand compressed her cheeks. Alien prickled-skin fingers rubbed as if to probe and scrub the innermost recesses of her skin's pores. Her paralyzed vocal cords unable to squeak. Her left instep painfully scraped her threshold's hard lip. Strong powerful hands squeezed her waist.

Alicia wished she could've gazed into her rescuer's heavenly eyes to be smitten forever. His Neil Armstrong bubble helmet temporarily denied her all opportunity.

Muscular arms clutched her tight to connected hoses and the oxygen tank strapped to her rescuer's chest. They dashed to chilly air beneath a street lamppost. A thin blanket warmed her boobs indented by metal tank edges and braided-hose connectors. She expected the crenated depressions to disappear in two weeks if no scars lasted.

Chapter Two

Alicia loved her new South Minneapolis third floor apartment. Macho alpha fireman hero Joel energized her life with her first real dates in two years. True to her Mom's admonition to save herself for marriage, Alicia's dates began and ended outdoors, in daylight, to avoid all suggestion of physical contact encouraged by darkness. Her and Joel's dating length broke her previous longevity record.

It had been a year since her fire escape and Joel's inspection of her new building before she signed the lease had set her mind at ease. Yet, Joel could neither prevent the loss of her third-grade teacher employment nor offer her a solid lead to an elementary vacancy.

Alone in her bedroom, she stretched her fingers above her Dell keyboard to invigorate blood flow. Coy with Joel, she labored in secret to revise her romance novella after a New York City literary agent had scribbled in the margins of her thirty-second rejection letter the first encouraging professional words she ever received. Her fictional fireman, christened Joseph and nicknamed Joe, lived happily ever after with the damsel he rescued from an East End warehouse fire. Alicia prayed the novella would garner the recognition necessary to jump-start acceptance of her full length novel, "A Search Fulfilled."

Atop her frilly bedspread, Alicia's cell phone chirped and vibrated.

Alicia's slipper heels propelled her, without last year's protruding stomach fat, and the computer desk chair rearward. The chair's rollers caught her elongated floral-patterned blue nightgown hem. She grabbed a fistful of flannel and jerked her chair sideways and free.

"Claiborne Lock and Dam, Alabama," she whispered. The shrill chirps stopped; she pressed redial to connect with her Mom. "Yesss, Mom." How many times did she have to repeat herself? "I'm applying for a new teaching position. No, Mom. I haven't given up. Sure, I'll be home Sunday for dinner." Alicia bit her tongue. "No, Aunt Agnes shouldn't bring her card-playing friend's visiting nephew. Love you, too."

Connecticut Dam. Mansfield Hollow Dam. Her quirk soothed Alicia's frustration.

She sighed. Her irritation with Mom had ebbed since her twenty-first birthday. Deep down Alicia realized an embedded uncontrollable grandmother DNA gene governed her mother's actions. Her diminutive aunt last Christmas nearly burst the blood vessels on Mom's forehead by asking Alicia if she'd ever visited Le Adult Toys on East Jervis, off East Hennepin Avenue. Mom's icy glare, and near faint, distracted Aunt Agnes from Alicia's failure to answer.

With her novella revision fresh in her mind, there wasn't time to brood about Mom's latest matchmaking attempt. Mom would never relent. Alicia would bet all the calories in a Dunkin Donut glazed donut dozen, a favorite she'd given up with her diet, that Mom had cajoled Aunt Agnes to bring the nephew.

With her blond hair air-dried from an earlier shower,

Alicia hustled to slip into a brown peasant dress and sandals. Joel would ring the lobby buzzer within the hour. She loved his attention, his sweetness. To protect her diet from the salty French fries Joel craved, she'd filled a picnic basket with tuna fish sandwiches and cut vegetables.

Alicia answered the buzzer. "You're early. I'll be right down."

Neither Joel's puffy gray eyes nor his brief lobby hug lingered. The smoky scent of burnt wood did. Her stomach turned over, over, and over, almost in sync with the fire engine lights she imagined and repressed. A year, and her fire fear never completely vanished.

"I'll carry that." Joel's muscular right arm reached for her picnic basket. "Lake Minnetonka here we come."

As they turned the apartment building's north corner for the parking lot, late morning sun beads twinkled on the complex's swimming pool surface and wherever splashed water collected on the its terra cotta deck. The pool's ambiance didn't excite her. Her agreement to Lake Minnetonka saved her from packing the black Lane Bryant one-piece bathing suit since discarded.

Within minutes they were in luck. No picnic table, but a clean grassy knoll dappled with shade beneath a fifty-foot oak. Alicia straightened the Army blanket's corner after Joel snapped it and allowed it to float to the ground.

"Let's take a walk," Alicia suggested.

Joel's droopy eyelids struggled to maintain the narrowest of slits. "Sorry. Little tired. Fought a four-alarmer into the wee hours."

While she begrudged his audacity, she accepted his apology. Alicia extracted her portable radio from her picnic basket. As she spun the dial, bits of music, most jumbled, permeated the air until she lit upon easy-listening.

Propped against the oak, Joel muttered, "If you don't

mind, I'll eat in a few minutes." He rolled onto his left side.

Alicia bit her lower lip. Her open Harlequin paperback lay upside down beside her. To onlookers, she and Joel appeared to be an old married couple. Like her physician asking her to estimate her pain on a scale of one to ten, she rated her loneliness at ninety-nine. She aimlessly watched two pairs of parading mallards splash into the lake. Nature created romance. How could she write romance if only despair floated through her system?

"Whatcha doing?" Alicia tried to smile through her question.

"Twins baseball is on 'CCO."

Alicia squelched her anger as he switched the dial from music to sports, not her thing. During the between inning commercials she expected at least limited conversation. Didn't happen. In the secret chambers of her heart, where her pride reigned, rational thought of six months of dates with Joel dissolved into emotional nothingness. When Joel snored, she stared at him lying on his back, eyes closed. To be polite, she nibbled on a tuna fish sandwich rather than chance disturbing him with repeated crisp celery bites.

His lips moved. Alicia leaned forward and couldn't decipher his words until he muttered he'd have her sweaty, pinned against the tree. He didn't spelled out "have" and Alicia chose to play it safe and not challenge her assault imagery or the word's definition. She loathed to be a prop to Joel's ego.

When the nearby church bell chimed three times, she jostled Joel's shoulders twice. She pointed out the lengthened sun rays and suggested they leave. With a still heavy picnic basket, she entered her apartment. The tingle of a kiss lingered on her cheek.

Twice in the next two weeks, Alicia declined Joel's date requests. His third week telephone calls she let ring without answering.

* * *

From her bedroom, Alicia called out to Vicky, "Joel still coming at seven?"

Alicia's mortification upon learning Vicky's department store co-worker had paired Vicky with Joel on a double date no longer ruled. Her affection for her roommate superceded any embarrassment Alicia expected.

"Ya sure, you betcha," Vicky yelled. She'd promised Alicia that she'd keep Joel on a short leash and dump him if he ever distressed either one of them.

Alicia groaned. She suffocated the expected chuckle to Vickie's put on Swedish accent. While homesteading immigrant Swedes may have chatted like that on the prairie of 19th Century Minnesota, they'd masked their inbred dialect, if not their coffee drinking habits, in the 21st.

She stared into her bedroom mirror to dab on minimal foundation with a touch of eyeliner and lipstick. After she shimmied into the figure-disguising drapes of a peasant dress, Alicia fit her nyloned-toes into flat-heeled pumps. She joined Vicky next to the breakfast counter that separated their galley kitchen from the open-concept living room.

Alicia paused by the refrigerator. "You cooking for Joel?"

"If you define that as restaurant menu selection, then yes." Above her applied blue eyeliner, Vickie's eyes sparkled, even brighter than the rhinestones on her designer jeans belt.

"Maybe you should undo your top blouse neck button?"

Vicky plucked the last plate from their dishwasher's lower rack. "Why? Can't flaunt my girls like you."

"Didn't mean that. Everyone should see your pretty necklace." Alicia's right hand rubbed her mouth as a distraction to the warmth that escaped her cheeks. "Anyway, you be nice to Joel."

"Strange words considering Joel dumped you."

Alicia wouldn't debate Vicky's misconception, nor admit the imaginary literary fireman hero for her latest short story sprang from a true-to-life Joel. While Joel exhibited home gym virility in his muscle-sculptured thighs and calves and bulging biceps, his gray eyes mirrored a shallow pool. Since the day at the lake, Alicia feared Joel's physical intentions. She considered herself lucky the greatest physical disfigurement he left on her was a non-scarring large indentation he pressed into her left breast while demonstrating a fireman's carry during group horseplay at a bowling alley. The mark disappeared within hours, pushed taut by her expanding lymphatic vessels and fat cells.

Her romantic champion would be dashing, debonair, and virile. Far from Joel's ambitions satisfied by Wednesday night bowling, Saturday televised college football or baseball, and/or Sunday telecasts of the Minnesota Vikings on a local bar's flat screen.

Alicia defended her pride. "He didn't dump me. It was mutual."

"Whatever."

"Mall of America closes at nine. I'll take my iPad and be home by nine-thirty. Don't expect me to wait up."

Chapter Three

Undecipherable and lunchtime conversational words unimportant to Alicia circled her as she sat in the downtown Minneapolis Bunyan Exposition Center lobby. She hoped to be inconspicuous in her muted brown-striped ankle-length cotton dress. Her angled gaze marveled at her iPad's bug-eyed miniature animated paperclip as it clinked and whirled on the screen in her lap. With a light flash and a bell tinkle, the icon winked and froze her cursor on manuscript page thirty-six.

Newburgh, Indiana, Lock and Dam. She blew out her breath, careful not to whistle.

Whimsically she doubted age thirty-six would be her lucky year for no perceived arrows rattled in Cupid's quiver. Fate guided maidens, other than her, to gallop on horseback to romantic bliss. Alicia pondered the digits. She separated and added them to equal nine, the same total as the two and seven in her age. She dismissed the negative thought that a six followed by three also equaled nine. Woe be unto her if she had to wait until her honeymoon could be paid for with AARP discounts.

Distinctive baritone words knifed through the din. "Skipping lunch?"

Startled, Alicia's left hand flicked her iPad closed. She tilted her head up to peer into her boss's face, one Randall Van Gilleran.

"No. Had time for yogurt."

Her right hand reached for the brown paper sack squished between her thigh and the black leather club chair. She didn't know what else to say. Her application to work for him and *New Romance Delights*, a Midwest boutique publisher, had been a last ditch effort for any employment to trickle needed income into her dwindling bank checking account. In her first three weeks, he rarely spoke to her, except to pass on work tasks.

How much had he seen? The sack slid from her grip and tumbled to the slate-tiled floor.

Van Gilleran bent forward to reach the crumpled sack; set it on top of her iPad without a word. His distant gaze validated her surmise that to push a conversation wasn't wise.

Alicia uttered a weak "Thanks" before she squeezed the sack's top.

Not today, but soon, she expected to submit her debut novel to *New Romance Delights*, where all accepted manuscripts required the blessing of Mr. Van Gilleran. How she would present it to avoid ridicule and/or safeguard her job, she hadn't figured out?

The expansive Bunyan Center lobby grouped all leather seats in a center square. All visitors and tenants then had unobstructed access to the elevator banks. Since any person seated during the lunchtime hubbub was easy visual prey, she prayed Mr. Van Gilleran hadn't viewed her title page.

Albeit but ten minutes, Mr. Van Gilleran could've stood undetected behind her. After the frozen page thirty-six, her attention had focused on title page spacing before he announced his presence. Her gaze failed to penetrate his blue eyes. They revealed no hint of what he hid within his mind's recesses.

He unbuttoned his dark-gray suit jacket. "I'll see you upstairs."

"Yes, sir." She doubted he heard her response as his stride joined the crowd's lockstep advance to the right elevator bank. Alicia sighed, then zipped her iPad case. She thanked a courteous gentleman who held an elevator car that whisked her to the twelfth floor after half the occupants exited at the eighth floor. She walked thirty feet to insert her key into the *New Romance Delights* office door lock.

Without a twist of her wrist, the black-lettered opaque glass, framed by mahogany, eased inward. She guessed Mr. Van Gilleran had left the door unlocked. She stepped into an empty reception and paused to glance left and right. On her receptionist desk, she spotted a one-inch synopsis stack, not there when she'd left for lunch. Mr. Van Gilleran's post-it note with the words "Please Process" required no explanation for "process" required her to send out the publisher's standard rejection letter.

She propped her cased iPad against her desk's inner foot well sidewall and logged into the office desktop computer's form letter file. A double click on "rejection" scrolled before her a fill-in-the-blanks form ready for the specific information destined to dash a writer's hopes.

Her desk telephone rang. "Alicia, this is Norma. Haven't received your completed medical questionnaire. I need it to get you signed up."

"Can I bring it in tomorrow?" Alicia worried about how to answer the weight loss question. She didn't know Norma well enough to confidentially ask if she needed to reveal an involuntary weight loss versus her deliberate forty-pound diet success.

"Okay. Don't wait. You're insurance eligible after thirty days and that's next week."

The line went dead.

Donan Berg

Alicia swept her anxiety aside to crank out Mr. Van Gilleran's first six rejection letters. From personal experience, she foresaw the recipient's disappointment upon reading a form letter after months of waiting. The least she could do to ameliorate its dreadful contents was to add a postscript to encourage the writer to hold onto a positive attitude.

At a writer's workshop, the twice-published keynoter had convinced Alicia to forever lock temporary failure out of her consciousness. Her mind's stored negativity spirits sometimes escaped in the middle of the night, but Alicia, with positive thinking, chased the gargoyles into her mind's secret cave and replaced the boulder. A decade ago a high school teacher had repeatedly praised her creative personality. Self-aware that creativity meant change, Alicia remained unsure how to spark it. Like a buoy in a storm, she bobbed at random, moored to her teacher's perception, while she waited for the enlightenment of a new invigorating dawn.

Alicia licked and sealed the last rejection letter envelope. Mr. Van Gilleran had neither peeked into reception nor left the office via the front door.

A tentative push to reception's hallway door caught Alicia's eye before the woman's multi-colored scarf coiled tight to her neck.

"Could you . . . or would it be possible for me to find out if my manuscript has been accepted. My name's Shirley Morrison."

Alicia didn't recognize the name except to know no rejection letter sat in today's pile. "Let me check," Alicia lied. Her right hand dipped to slide out a desk drawer. As the woman rocked on her heels, Alicia peered at a dusty drawer bottom. Her right hand rustled two empty green hanging folders at four and five of her silent ten count. Her uplifted gaze stilled the woman. "It's still under review."

"Thanks."

13

Alicia believed her tactic provided a greater comfort than a vague: "We'll notify you."

Co-worker Carol said good night as Alicia slipped on a light jacket. Four-thirty marked her workday's end. She strode through the Bunyan lobby and squeezed through its rotating door onto Sixth Street to breathe in the cool early September air.

Pleased that her bus, Number 34 orange, appeared at its downtown Minneapolis bus stop on schedule, she drowned out the bus-rider chatter with ear buds and a Neil Diamond CD. Without an accident or other delay, she'd be in her South Minneapolis apartment in thirty minutes.

* * *

"Yo, Alicia, your turn to prepare dinner. I'm starving," shouted Vicky through Alicia's closed bedroom door.

"Eat a cracker. I'll be there in a few." She wouldn't dilly-dally if Vicky had called her Ally. But Vicky used her birth certificate name, the name her mother used when commanding a youthful Ally to sit on a chair and face the living room's wall corner. When either Mom or Dad had been really angry, her full name—Alicia Luann Danielson—echoed throughout her girlhood home. That and the soap bar jammed between her teeth were everlasting memories.

Vicky could cool her heels. Alicia faced a blank computer screen. No energized pixels displayed what was to be the sparkling synopsis for her novel, "A Search Fulfilled."

The reluctant writing god balked. She had to tease him out of his stupor. An ice cube in a washcloth chilled her forehead. She envisioned it likewise caused him to shiver.

A blue jar of Vicks VapoRub loomed within reach to

14

be her second encouragement when she massaged it into his bare, hairy chest. She prayed not to clog her bosom's pores.

The double threat worked. Words magically rippled onto her computer screen. Her fingers danced a-to-z while the pungent VapoRub smell wafted into her nostrils. Times New Roman characters lined up one after the other with an occasional period to let the reader breathe.

There it was—the draft synopsis for her self-polished novel. After eighteen months of starting, stopping, writing, and revising, Alicia bent forward and kissed the paperclip icon. A screen message appeared: "What is this?"

The happy ending not as joyful as she had dreamed—no street waltz in the rain, ala Gene Kelly, heels kicked and arms stretched skyward in exaltation. No multiple hallelujahs sung and chanted toward a glittering ocean in sunset bloom.

Rats.

Alicia rubbed her exhausted arms. Loneliness tugged at her effort to stand. Her fatigued eyes wandered the four sentinel bedroom walls that barricaded the outside world from her written-word journey. She couldn't shake her cloistered feeling. Twisted knots gripped her stomach and stubbornly refused to let go.

No twilight clouds drifted in the sky outside her window. She raised its sash for the chill to encourage breaths of energized life. The intermittent rattle of garbage cans awaiting tomorrow morning's pickup interspersed the evening's still, compressed air.

She fantasized a leap into a new world, like Wendy following Peter Pan. She pleaded with herself. Think good thoughts, great thoughts. *Chocolate syrup. Strawberry swirled ice cream.*

"Yo, Ally. Cracker's gone."

Alicia laughed. Vicky's reality pierced Alicia's

escapist fantasy. She tightened her belt on jeans three sizes too big. A baggy Golden Gopher sweatshirt hung loose at her sides. She slumped her shoulders and rotated her bedroom doorknob.

She shuffled forward and dragged her left leg to ruffle the wall-to-wall carpet.

"Coming master."

Vicky, a *Town and Country* glamour magazine propped open on the armrest, lay prone on the living room sofa with a humming hair dryer. They shared a living room, bathroom, and a small, galley kitchen. A Formica-topped breakfast counter served as a great room divider between kitchen and living room. Two stools provided impromptu counter seating.

Smoke wisps invaded Alicia's nostrils. "Vicky," Alicia shrieked once, then clamped her right hand to her mouth. Smoke sparked fears of flames. She whispered, "Where's the fire?"

"There's no fire. I lit a jar candle in my bedroom."

"Please blow it out. It's freaking me out. I'll buy you scented gel that plugs into an outlet."

"Sorry." Vicky scrambled to her feet and vanished into the apartment's second bedroom.

When she re-emerged, Alicia quit rubbing her hands and asked, "You want salmon cakes?"

Vicky nodded and stretched out on the sofa.

Alicia popped the freezer door, grabbed two Ocean Fresh packages, and rotated the oven dial backward to its bake setting. "We've yesterday's potato salad. How 'bout frozen vegetables?"

"I'll eat anything as long as it's fast."

"Where you going? It's Thursday." Alicia tried to straddle the line between ignorant and nosey. Although she had Vicky's cell number, if the police knocked, she'd feel stupid uttering: "Duh, don't have a clue." Alicia didn't rue her caution inbred by growing up a big city girl. Vicky, two years younger, was more blasé. After a childhood one hundred miles west of the Twin Cities where small-town neighbors routinely left doors unlocked, Vicky was not averse to posting front door notes of when she'd return.

"Joel said he'd pick me up for a movie."

"What about his accountant class?"

"Community college on break."

"Must be serious. Third date this month."

"Oooh, I don't know." Vicky switched the hair dryer angle to blow on her bangs. "He's been really nice."

Alicia hadn't hidden from Vicky her fear of Joel. As long as Vicky entered the relationship with eyes open, she prayed Vicky wouldn't be hurt. Further, Alicia hoped Joel's about-face meant he cherished Vicky and wasn't motivated by revenge to activate Alicia's jealousy.

"Hope it lasts." Alicia stirred the mustard potato salad.

"When you going to spill the beans on all the eligible hunks at your new job? I can just picture those bare-chested romance cover models draped across your desk." Vicky sighed.

"Yeah, right." An oven timer chime signaled Alicia to rotate the salmon. She set two counter places and poured the fat-free milk they always drank. "All those hunks exciting your endorphins live in California. Their photos arrive in FedEx boxes." Alicia waited for Vicky to curl the hairdryer cord. "You wouldn't even be able to smell the scented oil that glistens each one's rippling abs."

"Joel beat his co-workers in a squat competition."

"He could be Hercules doing squats and knee jerks with No. 2 wooden yellow pencils."

"Now you're being catty. Modern accountants use very sophisticated electronic equipment. Plus, Joel wants to specialize in taxes, a very demanding field."

"Touché."

"You must have at least one dateable man at your book office." Vicky sat upright and her magazine slid to

17

the floor. She made no effort to retrieve it.

"What? You think I took a survey?" Alicia switched off the oven and plated the salmon before she added the potato salad and the steaming mixed vegetables.

Vicky swung a leg over a counter stool. "No, silly."

"Eat. You said you were rushed." Alicia's fork cut into her salmon. It flaked. "You going to put on lipstick? Revlon says lips kiss better with lipstick."

"Yes," Vicky hissed. Her fork stabbed at a green bean. "Pry all you want. I'm not saying anything about Joel, kisses or whatever comes next."

Alicia sucked in a forkful of salmon to avoid a tension explosion. In previous months she'd have pushed harder to have Vicky expose her deeper feelings, but not now with the novel completed. No more research needed. But . . . What about a sequel? Alicia swallowed. Forget it. "Now, I know you're serious about Joel. If you weren't, you'd be chirping like a bird, filling me in on all his quirks and shortcomings."

Vicky glanced at their apartment door. She appeared to weigh her words. "You're not going to vicariously live through my boyfriend. You're not a lovesick teenager. Time you got out there." Alicia felt a tear mobilize behind her right eyelid, ready to gush as Vicky continued. "Don't hole up in your bedroom hugging a computer."

A cautious Alicia almost upended her stool in her clumsy dismount effort. She feigned a condiment need. Her rapidly blinking eyes gazed from refrigerator shelves to door compartments. She'd turned the conversation ugly. Her friendship with Vicky had never been strained. She wouldn't let that happen today.

"I'm not going to argue." Alicia closed the refrigerator door empty-handed. "Writing requires a ton of time. I warned you."

Vicky nodded; her stationary lips unmoved by idle vocal chords.

"Remember vacationing in Florida. We'd tie on a

18

teeny bikini, grab a towel, and head for the beach to slather on sunscreen."

"Sure. Pre-Slimfast days."

"And then we tried sunbathing here, halters and short-shorts."

Vicky's face lit up; her ear-to-ear smile radiated. "Yeah, we drove to Lake Minnetonka to relive five-year-old Florida adventures."

"And, what did we get?" Alicia reached for Vicky's dirty plate and glass. A knife clanked on the counter. "Recall two dorky guy waves from a sailboat."

"Wouldn't have surprised me if he wanted us to do all the hard work manning the sail. Then he'd lounge on the bow, a lazy captain, beer in hand."

"Yeah." She stacked Vicky's plate onto hers. Retrieved the knife. "And, his breath probably reeked of pickled herring."

Vicky exploded in laughter. Her forehead touched the counter. With an upward gaze, she stared at Alicia, her laughter under control. "You didn't answer my question. What about the men at your job?"

Alicia arranged the dirty dishes in the dishwasher. "Only one, and he's my boss."

"Wow, sexual harassment."

"C'mon." Alicia's cheek radiated warmth to her eyeballs. "He's not like that." She excused herself to the bathroom. A towel wetted with cold water paled the facial redness once evident in the mirror. When she returned to the kitchen, Vicky had disappeared, presumably into her bedroom. Alicia clicked the living room television to "Wheel of Fortune."

When Vicky re-appeared, Alicia noticed Vicky in dressy black slacks and a multi-colored blouse belted in silver at the waist.

"Is that perfume Target's special collection," Alicia teased. "Have you ever thought of something subtle like a smoky embers fragrance?"

19

"Joel last time said he liked it. You should add it to your novel."

Alicia shook her head sideways. "Out of character."

"How? Your hero's sexy, manly desirable, posing with his Bowflex, and showing off his television Jeopardy contestant invitation?"

"Not my hero. Believe in reality. No bodice ripper cardboard stand-ups. And I think readers agree. So that's how my novel's hero lives and acts."

Vicky stroked a hairbrush through her long, silky brunette hair. "Okay, okay—"

"None of that alien fantasy stuff either. No sixteen chapters of one casual sex encounter after a second, and a third, and a fourth . . ."

"Don't beat a dead horse. You showed me early chapters. Just grateful I couldn't recognize myself in any character description."

Alicia inwardly smiled. Vicky had confirmed Alicia's success in diffusing Vicky's attributes into more than one character. Her roommate's traits incorporated as the fearless one, the lighthearted one, and the unnamed lady who didn't care what other people thought. All these characters Alicia contrasted with her chaste heroine. A heroine who was loosely patterned after her own life's upbringing and sexual experience or "lack thereof" to quote a law student she dated twice three years ago.

After Alicia had showcased her virtues, she deliberately erased all fire-fear mention as her heroine's required character fault. It required three rewrites until Alicia settled on Aunt Agnes's cricket fears, which Alicia expanded to include any six-legged insect. She wove this conquerable insect phobia into her "without-an-Achilles-heel" heroine. With all said and done, she'd crafted her heroine as a female Superhero.

Joel arrived on time without fanfare. After quick hellos, he and Vicky departed. Alicia retreated to her bedroom computer desk and left the room's door ajar.

After a search for a large envelope and a realm of paper, Alicia began her sixteen chapter print task. While the printer labored, Alicia e-mailed her chosen editor notice that the completed manuscript would be hand-delivered the next day. With a drawer full of rejection letters, Alicia had begged sister Elena for a loan to prepay in full the professional editing fee. To hide her chosen pen name—Lady Victoria Dash—Alicia provided no title page. She also kept her roommate—Victoria Hansen—in the dark.

A recheck of her potential publisher list showed but one who hadn't rejected her—*New Romance Delights*. Alicia understood it wasn't a recommendation for she had never submitted any manuscript to her current employer. How loomed as a hurdle. Procrastination prevailed. The manuscript's editing offered her at least a two-week window to plot how to present her initial submission to Mr. Van Gilleran.

Each weekday the letter carrier dumped thirty to fifty large envelopes on her *New Romance Delights* reception desk. The relentless stacks dogged proof of the world's wannabe romance novelists' determination to capture a publisher contract offer. To slip her manuscript in without a postmark invited unwanted scrutiny.

Alicia stacked her printed pages. When she sealed the envelope flaps on her prized creation, her chest constricted. She'd die if Mr. Van Gilleran required her to address a rejection letter to herself.

As the red digital alarm clock numbers that guided her fire escape advanced, Alicia's second life goal required a regular sleep schedule. She wouldn't wait up for Vicky, with or without Joel. Moreover, she'd not embarrass Vicky by opening the apartment door at the slightest noise. Mom had done that to her all through high school, a lit porch light included.

* * *

A seated Alicia kicked her left foot to elevate her dress hem. She stood and let the skirt drape her legs. She strode to reception's hallway door. "Thanks," Alicia said as she reached for the envelope offered by her editor.

"Engaging story. Call me if there's any question."

"I'll have to look at it tonight."

Alicia bade her editor good-bye and added her manuscript to the extra large handbag she had carried to work for this very purpose.

Anxious to read her editor's suggestions, Alicia hurried to her apartment elevator after her seventy-year-old neighbor, stationed in the lobby, coaxed her to sign a protest petition. Upstairs, Alicia threw open her bedroom window. Pungent horse manure vapors, spiraled three stories from a foundation flowerbed, gagged her. Alicia slammed her window shut, comforted by the scent of fall mums. The bouquet was Vicky's gift to celebrate Alicia's novel completion.

As evening darkened into night, Alicia labored to accept and reject her editor's suggested revisions. Weary eyed, she put off the critical proofreading until the next evening.

Satisfied with her punctuation and story tweaks, she decided to mail her manuscript submission and have it appear like any other writer submission. She telephoned her adoptive parents to inform them she'd be using their suburban Minneapolis/St. Paul New Brighton, Minnesota, address. Alicia explained a publishing guidebook tip suggested the benefit of a residential street address to indicate the author's stability and maturity. Alicia also happy the address choice further disguised her authorship from Norma, Wanda, Carol, and Mr. Van Gilleran.

While Alicia didn't divulge her pen name, she explained to Mom and Dad that publishers often confuse and/or mangle author's names so if any letter or package arrived, no matter to whom addressed, they were to accept it and telephone her immediately. Alicia inhaled until her stomach pressed her spine. She crossed her fingers for luck that all her deception didn't confuse.

After she hung up, a steeped small fear grew into a dull headache. How would she easily identify her three-chapter submission from the other mailed envelopes received? Alicia dared not deviate from standard white or manila. A gaudy pastel would be a submission faux pas rewarded by immediate summary rejection.

She rummaged through a bedroom dresser drawer where she'd stockpiled classroom supplies should she ink a new teacher contract. A pad of leftover Valentine Day paper hearts hid under an eraser package. Alicia's fingers traced the round heart edges to their points.

The brilliant red color, shaded to imply depth, exuded cuteness, well, Alicia thought, cuteness for an eight-year-old.

Inspiration struck. Each heart's adhesive presented a definite plus.

One paper heart would be an inconspicuous corner addition to her envelope to identify her manuscript submission from the multitude.

With her rubber-banded story pages, a synopsis, and a SASE reply envelope tucked inside, she sealed her envelope after her umpteenth recheck. On the exterior, Alicia affixed a typed New Brighton return address and a completed mailing label. Onto the lower left front corner, her fingers pressed her one paper heart doubly hard.

With her submission mailed, she dared not leave her *New Romance Delights* reception desk even for a minute. When Aunt Agnes telephoned Tuesday morning with an offer to buy lunch, Alicia tried to put her off and failed. The best Alicia did was to get a persistent Aunt Agnes to agree to postpone lunch to Thursday.

Later than usual, the letter carrier dumped two huge envelope piles with an untypical groan. Alicia estimated three dozen. After a hand swipe into his leather pouch, he and Alicia traded good-bye waves. She quick-stepped letter-sized correspondence to the in-office mail center. Startled when a co-worker said hello from behind, a jumpy Alicia responded with a curt, "Hi, must get back to the phones."

When Alicia glimpsed her paper heart point peeking out from the left pile, third envelope from the bottom, she tried a normal breath. With both reception doors closed and no one waiting, Alicia leaned forward to separate her manuscript submission from the others. She considered it inane to be holding her breath. Her left hand lifted the envelopes above hers as her right hand tugged it free and laid it front and center on her desk. Her stuck fast red paper heart marred by a black streak.

Alicia maneuvered to tuck her knees and the desk chair's front casters beneath her desktop. Her red heart had admirably fulfilled its mission to easily identify her manuscript's arrival. Prepared to say good-bye, she reached her right hand index finger forward to slide its nail under the heart's right edge.

A male voice interrupted. "Let me take those slush pile novels."

Alicia froze, her right arm in midair six inches above her affixed paper heart.

The speaker, one Randall Van Gilleran, acquisitions editor for *New Romance Delights*, stood three feet from her arm, his manicured hands outstretched at the waist. The interior office door edged shut behind him.

Caught red-handed, Alicia's constricted throat blocked all larynx efforts to utter even a grunt.

"Oh, you saw it too." Van Gilleran chuckled. His intense and intelligent eyes bypassed her presence to scan reception's empty chairs.

Alicia's heart thumped to conquer her brain's suspended animation. "Saw what?"

"That paper heart." He advanced a step. "Some

wannabe author is so foolish."

Alicia pressed her lips together to force her lungs to breathe slower. Why didn't her hand drop faster and hide her paper heart? No answer came to her. "Oh, that." The two words uttered whispery and hoarse. Yet, she wasn't ill, not yet anyway. Was she frightened by what Mr. Van Gilleran might do next, absolutely?

He lowered his hands to his sides. "He or she must think romance publishers are impressed by envelopes with cutesy red hearts." No compassion encircled his words.

Her paper heart became the electrical spark to race her chest's heart. Alicia prayed for a visitor or a telephone ring. No Luck. Her gaze darted to the ceiling and then to Mr. Van Gilleran.

"Don't you agree it's foolishness?" He charged on without giving Alicia a chance to respond. "It deserves to be tossed without reading."

Alicia's hands sunk faster than gravity's pull to squish the last remnants of trapped air out of her envelope. Her left shielded the return address from Mr. Van Gilleran's view; her right obscured her red paper heart. "What . . . what," she stuttered. She forced her voice to increase its volume. "What if . . . what if there's a postcard or reply envelope inside."

Her left hand slid off the New Brighton return address. She twisted her face to Mr. Van Gilleran. The animated facial gayety of his first chuckle absent. His pressed together eyebrows and pursed lips forged horizontal parallel lines.

He snatched the heart manuscript from her desk.

Not until he'd completed his swiping action did she realize her right hand rested on his left forearm's white shirt sleeve. Alicia pleaded. "We request submitters to send us a way to tell them we received their submission." She glanced at her manuscript clamped in her boss's hand. "Shouldn't we honor that? Our website promises authors that courtesy."

Alicia retracted her hand from his arm. She couldn't bear to gaze at his face.

Mr. Van Gilleran walked to the front of her desk. With her white envelope still gripped by his left hand, his right pawed through both desk submission stacks.

In a moment of panic desperation, Alicia envisioned a dash around her desk, a grab of her manuscript, and a hallway run to catch the lobby elevator. If she were lucky, an Orange No. 34 bus awaited. If not, Plan B was a jog to disappear into one of the Nicollet Mall shops.

She dismissed the asinine Rambo exploit as foolish and impractical. To have her manuscript published remained her cherished goal. If she didn't expose herself as Lady Victoria Dash, Alicia foresaw her flash drive backup copy reprinted and mailed under a second pen name.

That is, if an angered Mr. Van Gilleran didn't mount a crusade to unearth Lady Dash's identity. Alicia breathed easier. She'd built a firewall to hide her connection to Lady Dash. There existed no listed telephone, Facebook page or Google search listing. Alicia's bliss dissipated in three seconds. Her *New Romance Delights* personnel file contained her parents' New Brighton telephone number and address for emergency contact. He could easily check. Connect the dots. She needed to divert his attention.

In her three-week tenure, Alicia garnered one Mr. Van Gilleran habitual tidbit. He always planned his every move. He wouldn't lower himself to walk into reception to collect and carry unprocessed manuscript submissions to his office. She crossed her two right hand fingers behind her back. *Be consistent, please, please, please.*

"Was there something else you came out here for?"

"Right." He glanced at her desktop.

Alicia's eyes followed his. His unwillingness to lift his head or speak provoked an impatience in her brain incapable of release.

"Wanda said she gave you a statistical report." He tucked Alicia's manuscript under his right arm. "You were to double-check her calculations. Have you completed that?"

"Yes." The nerve-racking suspense that coursed her veins excised, for now.

Alicia reached to her left for a manila folder, transferred it between hands, and balanced the folder atop a manuscript pile. Wanda Swanson, Mr. Van Gilleran's personal secretary, had been the first office person introduced to Alicia. An office friendship blossomed.

To support the opened calculations folder, Mr. Van Gilleran slid her manuscript envelope beneath it. While he read, Alicia's hands in her lap fidgeted.

When he closed the folder. Alicia's slightly relaxed body tensed. She gasped. *He's taking the manuscript with him.* Her right hand stifled the sound of a second gasp.

Mr. Van Gilleran stopped two steps from reception's interior employee-only exit door.

"Perhaps you're right." His right hand tossed her paper heart manuscript onto her desk corner. "Guess I'll have to at least skim it. Process it along with all the others."

Alicia quietly sighed. "I'll do that."

She gazed at the black-streak scarred red paper heart.

"Expect it'll be below our acceptance standards, although we're more liberal than the industry giants in New York City."

A light blinked on Alicia's phone. Intercom. She ignored it. *Please hurry, leave now.*

"Another thing, has a Mr. Jackson Grant stopped by?"

Alicia didn't recognize the name. Her fingers tapped her manuscript, but she didn't have the courage to slide it further from Mr. Van Gilleran. "Only morning visitor was the mailman."

"Jackson's a good friend, collaborated on a

27

documentary that won an Oscar." Mr. Van Gilleran's
facial features softened, especially his sharp, taut
forehead lines.

"Impressive. I'll ring Wanda if he shows." Alicia
rotated her chair a quarter turn.

"Thanks. I'm trying to enlist his help."

Alicia stretched her left arm to grab three envelopes
to stack atop the paper heart. "What kind of drama does
he write?" After the words emerged, she realized her
question delayed his exit.

"Doesn't really. He's more involved in screenplay
promotion."

Alicia sat quiet, hands folded in her lap. The
connection between screenplays and novels seemed
simple enough. A dozen seconds, each silently counted
by Alicia, elapsed as Mr. Van Gilleran leafed a second
time through the manila folder he carried.

"Later."

After the interior reception door closed behind his
departure, Alicia crossed her palms across her chest and
audibly sighed. Her entire body shivered with the
memory of her boss's cruel suggestion that her
manuscript be tossed into the trash without reading.
She'd heard stories of boorish, egotistical, and sadistic
editors. Although Mr. Van Gilleran had been brusque,
she wanted to believe he harbored no callous mean streak
proven by tossing a manuscript unread.

Writers labored untold days and weeks, sweating
profusely at times, to create a memorable work. For most,
including her, success wasn't the money, but the pride of
a published book. Authors mimicked actors. Both desired
to have their name blaze forth: authors from bookseller
bookshelves, actors from the Carnegie Hall marquee.

The prior week she'd witnessed an author in the
lobby coffeehouse slam a book closed and mouth the "f-
word" at the mention of Randall Van Gilleran. The
following day Wanda surprised her by a casual mention

that her boss received high school salutatorian honors three, maybe four, years prior to Alicia's similar graduation from another Twin Cities high school.

His extended reception stay and comments mobilized her brain to think, catalog him in her memory. The habit an exercise learned from her high school English instructor.

Mr. Van Gilleran impressed Alicia as being ten years older, even if she knew he wasn't. Perhaps the inch of receding scalp hair enhanced the perception of his added years. Still, he lacked the image of a stooped, short-tempered, grouchy, white-haired editor she'd expected.

If he'd appeared similar to one of her writing professors who critiqued student efforts with the air of condescending Shakespearian superiority, she definitely would have skipped her round two interview. She never detected a speech accent in Mr. Van Gilleran's first interview despite his European, Continental-sounding name. Nor had she spotted, to answer Vicky's question, a calabash pipe on his person or anywhere in the office.

His reaction to her paper heart exhibited a personality trait harsh in its extreme. Alicia recalled Wanda's advice to ignore him if he acted rude. In this same conversation Wanda mentioned her boss would go bonkers if writers submitted manuscripts ripe with typographical errors. Initially he, according to Wanda, would repress the frustration until the anger resembled volcano lava erupting skyward through a crater fissure to flow over the rim. Alicia's unexpressed fear calmed and comforted when Wanda informed her Mr. Van Gilleran confined and directed his ire at the anonymous transgressors and not toward his office staff.

Alicia refused to characterize his actions today as personally rude unless he latched onto the New Brighton address quicker than she realized and meant to taunt or scare her.

Wanda didn't mention it, but Alicia's casual first

week glance confirmed he didn't wear a wedding band. Neither did his left hand finger expose a pale ring of one recently removed.

Okay mind, snap out of it. Enough about him.

Alicia began to worry. She hadn't developed an action plan B for that stupid red, paper heart she'd pasted on her envelope. She cast off all inclinations to discard it. Her boss had seen it. Office processing instructions required all postmarked-envelope content to stay with manuscripts, secured with a rubber band.

She tried to think positive. Alicia couldn't allow her author's journey to be scuttled, not by an imperfect or dull story idea, but because she'd decided to identify her arriving manuscript submission. In her defense, the left side of her brain countered with how could she have known this would be the precise morning for Mr. Van Gilleran to visit reception minutes after the mail arrived. She surmised the writing god desired to extract his revenge for her applied forehead ice cubes, smeared greasy chest ointment, and feet tickled with her fluffy mental feathers.

Irony gripped her soul. She mused that her publisher's reception desk position would thwart her published author vision. The job had been taken as a last resort after her failure to land a teaching contract and the apartment fire and to forestall her forced move to live with her parents.

"Alicia, those manuscripts ready?" Wanda peeked around the door that separated reception from the employee office/work area. "Mr. Van Gilleran said they were on your desk."

"Still working on them."

"Needed a breather." Wanda strode to the side of Alicia's desk. "Don't know what ticked him off," Wanda said in a hushed voice.

Alicia wiped her right hand on the coarse robin-egg blue cotton material of her ankle-length dress. "Don't

Donan Berg

have a clue," Alicia lied.

"Of course. See you later." Wanda exited and closed the door behind her.

Alicia slit the last large envelope flap fifteen seconds before Wanda revisited reception. "He's circling his desk talking out loud, composing a letter to an unknown author who sent in a manuscript with what he called an audacious and stupid red paper heart. If the story was sweet, his words aren't. Give me a minute. Never seen him like this."

"Doesn't a heart epitomize romance. Hearts enflamed by Cupid's arrow."

Wanda retreated to hesitate with her right hand on the exit doorknob. "Right."

Alicia ignored the sarcasm in Wanda's reply. "I'll buzz when I'm done."

"Great." Wanda twisted the doorknob and glanced furtively into the office area. She gazed rearward toward Alicia. "You going out for lunch today?"

"Hadn't planned on it." Alicia disregarded her computer's new e-mail pop-up.

"What about after work?"

A second e-mail notification flashed without commanding Alicia's attention. "Where?"

"Three or four of us girls plan to stop by the Nicollet Mall's newspaper-themed restaurant. Have a drink. Catch-up on gossip. You game?"

"Okay, maybe not so much on the gossip part."

Wanda left.

Alicia mentally counted thirty-eight large envelopes. A light day, especially for a Wednesday. Why so few? Now the red paper heart stood out brighter than the lighted downtown Minneapolis Foshay Tower on a cloudless summer night. She hustled to complete logging in each submission.

When finished, Alicia's fingers traced the heart's outline. Her fingernail stretched the paper heart's

31

adhesive, raising its left half from the Lady Victoria submission. With a thumb flick to the forefinger, her paper heart would be unceremoniously buried in her wastebasket.

She stopped.

If she removed it, she could expect Mr. Van Gilleran to visit her and ask which envelope had the heart to provide a name and address for the letter Wanda said he dictated.

She'd have to be truthful and tell him. Alicia's human heart renewed its thumping.

Thinking tormented her. She could . . . no, no, she mustn't . . . why not? Third graders jumped and never looked back. When was the last time she'd been spontaneous? She failed to remember. Wasn't her responsible instinct dependable?

Alicia prayed her parents would forgive her. She'd been brought up to be honest. Perhaps she could explain the paper heart was rubbed off by another envelope when the stack tumbled to the floor after a gust of wind, generated by a visitor's hallway door push, hit her desk. She mulled the idea as her right index fingernail stretched the paper heart's adhesive. Careful not to rip or otherwise damage her paper heart, she lifted her finger higher to strip the scarred red paper heart from her envelope.

One paper heart rested on Alicia's fingertip ready to be flicked.

The wastebasket yawned wide.

Chapter Four

Alicia lifted her gaze from her paper heart to scan the
envelopes arrayed across her reception desk. At random,
her left hand selected the nearest white envelope that in
appearance matched hers and dropped it, address side up,
in front of her.

She positioned the paper heart on the lower left front
corner of her chosen envelope. Her thumb pressed her
heart onto the same envelope location that had carried it
from her apartment to *New Romance Delights.*

A tinge of remorse not strong enough to reverse her
conscious and dastardly design coursed through her
veins. A left and right lower-eyelid tension surge
indicated a sinus headache on the way. Alicia's stomach
muscles twisted when her brain scolded her for marching
an innocent and hopeful writer onto the rejection
scaffold.

She buzzed Wanda to pass on the manuscript
submissions. After Wanda strode into reception, a guilt
surge gnawed the edges of Alicia's soul. She lied to
Wanda that she'd missed processing two submissions and
sent Wanda away empty handed. When Alicia chided

herself for the lie, she realized her latest lie uttered with less reservation then her first to Wanda earlier.

While complete submissions went to Wanda, incomplete submissions stayed with Alicia for a form letter reply and eventual shredding. Alicia weighed the incomplete form letter creation. She could finesse the form letter but had no control of the shred process. Mr. Van Gilleran still expected to see an envelope with the red paper heart. *It can't be mine.*

Frightful images of whirling steel shredder blades blinked her eyes. She steadied her gaze through the eye holes of a fantazied invisible black hood and left her transferred paper heart where it was. She rationalized her secret thumb press within a publisher's sanctuary wouldn't mark her as the writer's executioner.

The longer she procrastinated her all-consuming dread escalated. She dismissed a coin-flip solution. Alicia finally convinced herself no harm would come with the paper heart pressed to another envelope.

She peeked into the office and found Wanda and Mr. Van Gilleran absent, presumably at lunch, and piled the submissions on Wanda's desk and left the office to window-shop the Nicollet Mall. The savory aromas from a cafeteria convinced her not to eat. Her queasy stomach threatened to wreck unrelenting havoc on her digestive system if food cascaded in.

At mid-afternoon, Wanda, unannounced, entered reception. She abruptly stopped. "You look ill. Anything I can do?"

"I'm okay." Alicia's smile attempt didn't change Wanda's somber expression. "Really."

"You can cancel attending tonight. I'll take notes on the juicy stuff."

"No need. I'll be there."

Wanda continued through reception and into the hallway.

Alicia returned to her incoming e-mail sort duty.

When Norma delivered Alicia's employee insurance documents, she stuffed the bulky packet into her purse unopened. She doubted there'd be enough time to file a not-yet-existing claim before her firing voided her enrollment.

The uncharacteristic parade of employees into reception continued when at four p.m., thirty minutes before quitting time, her lateral gaze caught Mr. Van Gilleran stride into reception. Alicia kept her eyes on her keyboard until his stare infused her left cheek's pores. *Why doesn't he say something?* She didn't wish to raise her head to ask. If he said a word, he'd be the executioner this time. With left and right hands pinched to her keyboard's outer edges, she tilted her head left. "Can I help you?"

"Broke down and read the red paper heart manuscript."

Alicia's arched glance noticed his calm eyes, no other facial expression. What made it so important he interrupt his day to report to her? Did he have it dusted for fingerprints? "That's good."

"Absolutely terrible." His right hand brushed his chin and his upper lip rose. "Horrendous plot. Infantile. No writing craftsmanship whatsoever."

"Sorry, I didn't read it," Alicia muttered. She rotated toward him. The arrogance that sprouted in his eyes snuffed out self-pride haughtiness.

He smoothed his tie. "Most disturbing, others weren't much better."

"Oh?" She longed for her novelist career to be launched, not transformed into Thomas-the-Engine-stalled-in-the-station. She dared not pound the keyboard space bar multiple times or replicate Tarzan's forest yell while Mr. Van Gilleran stood there. All she could do was keep her head high and noiselessly grit her teeth while an escalating fear twisted her stomach muscles as a vendor bent pliant dough into a figure-eight pretzel.

One Paper Heart

No Rambo dashes played out in her skull. Worried she couldn't outlast his stare without confessing, she allowed her upper torso to cogwheel toward her blank computer screen in small jerks. Her thoughts drifted toward confusion when he didn't explain his submission review in greater detail. Why couldn't e-mails arrive when she needed one, maybe ten?

Alicia watched Mr. Van Gilleran from the corner of her left eye. He stood motionless. Was it good he had no manuscript submissions or shredded paper strips in his hands? Or, had he already trashed them and forgotten her rejection letter task?

Again, she dared not ask. Her one keyboard space bar press didn't bring e-mails.

Mr. Van Gilleran cleared his throat. "After years of experience, I'm beginning to believe that submissions postmarked Saturday or Sunday should be rejected unopened."

Her eyebrows arched and her head twisted his way.

"We might miss one considered worthy, but we'd save a ton of time and grief." He fixed his gaze on her as his shoulders swayed three times front and back, never threatening his collapse.

Alicia marshaled her courage and corralled her wits. Someone had to defend authors. She'd followed the rules, well, almost. "Don't you have an obligation . . . an obligation to use every effort to discover the one novel that will forever advance the publishing world?"

"Not with romance."

Hypocrite. Why did he belittle romance? He deposited a paycheck from publishing romance novels? Millions of devoted readers bought romance novels or novels with strong romantic elements. She paid Romance Writers of America dues. Their latest facts extolled increased readership. Nielson figures couldn't be paranormal fantasy. Information she garnered from the University of Iowa Writers' Group supported and confirmed statistics and anecdotal evidence circulated on the Internet.

Alicia returned her gaze to him. "How can you say that?"

"We solve no great mystery. Nor unveil hidden scientific truth."

"What about a blockbuster novel to vault us to stardom?" Alicia hesitated. Her question using the word "us" troubled her. Was she too forward? This out-of-the-blue conversation started by him. Except for his earlier surprise visit, he'd never visited twice in a day or paused this long or chatted.

Could it be he fished for information about her manuscript? Would her wrong response justify his firing her? She needed her new medical insurance. "Shouldn't we evaluate every manuscript for its potential to make an indelible mark on the reader?" Alicia thought of Mother Theresa.

"In theory, you're right." He smoothed his tie. This second effort accomplished without his eyes following his right hand. "That's my acquisitions editor job. However, I prefer my writing."

"What's that?"

He frowned.

Had her exposed ignorance insulted him?

"I forgot." He began to pace. "You're new. I also secretly write novels we publish."

"Really?" The shrill inflection she gave the word waned as she continued. "Haven't seen your name as an author."

His square jaw intrigued her. She tried to determine if he wore contacts. She'd seen a solution bottle on Wanda's desk last week. Wanda said he'd left it.

With a sense she'd stared at him too long, Alicia glanced at her computer screen. She'd overheard him mention he would on occasion play tennis. If he stayed to talk, should she ask if he has a club membership or what kind of tennis? No. She shouldn't get personal. "May I ask, what's your pen name?"

"Beatrix Smothers."

"Thought no publisher would allow that." She excused herself to answer the telephone. After she easily transferred the caller, she re-affixed her attention on Mr. Van Gilleran.

He ceased pacing in front of her desk. "Oh, it's one of the hush-hush little secrets within the publishing world. We can hire four or five writers cheaper and with less hassle than acquiring marketable freelance stories. In the long run we save on residuals, control copyrights, and pocket reprint profits."

"I had no idea." She waited. He kept his eyes riveted on her hands. She quit rubbing them. "How can you do both jobs?"

"Easy. I know the formula." A glint flashed in his eyes. "There's either a change in the heroine's name, locale, or a plot variation. Significant details or character motivations can be mixed or strung out with a series. Presto, a new romance tale ready for our printing press."

Alicia refused to believe his explanation. "You're kidding, right?"

"Absolutely not. Each story takes about two weeks, a week if one's really charged."

"I've read several novels by author Charlotte Webb."

"Know her."

Alicia's tensed muscles softened, relieved her romance writer research at least recalled one author multi-published by *New Romance Delights*. "You're not going to tell me she's a fictitious person are you? Or a man?"

"No. Charlotte's one of our most beloved and successful writers." He hesitated.

"And?"

"And, what?"

"Woman or a man?"

Donan Berg

"Sorry." His gaze rotated from her face to the floor. "She's very much a woman. One day when Charlotte drops in from San Diego I'm sure you'll verify."

"Then, that's great." Alicia lifted her right hand and placed it on her desk. Her voice filled the lull. "Don't mean any disrespect. But impersonating a woman who rewrites prior stories sounds awful close to cheating the buying, reading public? If I were to write a novel—" Renewed tension piggybacked Alicia's deep inhale. Convinced she'd strung enough rope to hang herself, she tried to regroup. "Sorry. Meant read not write. I want to believe that each book I've read was original and creative and not a rehash." She sat quiet, her integrity bolstered.

"That's idealistic." Mr. Van Gilleran glanced toward the front door.

Alicia didn't respond to his monotone delivery of what she characterized as a polite rebuke.

"I'm not embarrassed, nor cheating the reader. Readers of our romance novels desire to be transported into an exotic life or shielded from their common, every day existence, and my stories help them enjoy the fantasy."

She slid her chair rearward and clasped her hands on her lap. If publishers rehashed tried and true stories by hired writers, how would she gain entrance into the published-author arena? There had to be a greater opportunity than reading obituaries or holding a vigil candle outside a hospital emergency room door waiting for news that an accomplished, well-known author passed away.

Alicia wasn't encouraged his stoic expression left her unexposed and off the hook. She grappled with how to indicate common ground if none existed. "In an odd way, don't disagree. But really can't fathom every reader wants to revisit worlds they've already experienced."

"We offer different characters, a new world in each book—" He renewed his pacing.

Characters? How naive was she? If she kept her ears open, how many unearthed secrets would she hear? Did that include the mysterious Mr. Grant sought by Mr. Van Gilleran earlier? Hadn't he connected this Mr. Grant with screenplays? She didn't remember the mention of romance novels, but why should she care?

In what ways did Charlotte, the author, differ from her story characters? Did it make her successful? Alicia, unwilling to be confused by the divergent and salamandrian wiggles of her thoughts, put aside her internal questions about romance author authenticity. Mr. Van Gilleran's revelation he wrote romance dispelled her belief all romance authors were women.

Mr. Van Gilleran stared across the crest of her hair and resumed, "When readers buy our books, we offer value matched to what they desire. There's no exploitation with sadistic or sexual violence or erotic voyeurism."

The lack of facts swimming in Alicia's knowledge pool blunted her ability to comment.

"Other publishers may pass that off as quote romance unquote, but we don't." Throughout his exposition of romance philosophy, he appeared to list. His shoulders slumped left and his eyes flattened.

Alicia had expected her author path to be strewn with rocks, not her vision deceived by boulders. Even if her receptionist job was a way station until she nabbed a teacher position, she wished to enjoy it. Yet, she'd been deceitful herself by shifting her paper heart to another writer's submission. A writer whose name she didn't recognize and a person obviously unintroduced. A stranger who'd never know he or she had been cheated by Alicia's selfishness. Alicia, unwilling to confess her dirty trick, realized she'd entered a pressure cooker world alien to her prior teaching positions. Tangled yarns, once spun, unyielding until unraveled. She returned her gaze to his blue eyes.

He pushed his left shirtsleeve toward his elbow and glanced at his wristwatch. "I overheard Wanda planning to join other women for drinks."

"Yes. She mentioned it earlier." After her words came out, Alicia feared she'd confirmed a get-together and violated an office confidence.

"Well." He grinned for the first time. "If you talk about me, don't tell me." In a stop and start gait, he ambled to the office door.

Alicia watched his back until the door closed without a response to his gossip quip. She reverted her attention to unanswered e-mails and found none humorous or earthshaking.

While her conscience retained doubts about her women's confab attendance, she assumed, since Wanda had given her the address, the women left singly and met at the agreed location. She stopped in the restroom to apply a touch of rouge. All the other office women arrived at work every day very stylish. Alicia wore ankle-length, loose-fit dresses that had been snug before she chose to lose fifty-one pounds.

She'd built her self-confidence by keeping the pounds off. The security deposit for her post-fire apartment stretched her finances and depleted her new wardrobe budget. An advance for her novel would be a godsend.

Alicia jabbed at the down elevator button. She replayed Mr. Van Gilleran's comments that none of that day's novel submissions excited him. Her odds calculation of being protected from office shame by her pen name, if she remained employed, rifled a shiver up her spine.

Chapter Five

Randall Van Gilleran sat in his office at four-thirty-three
disappointed that longtime friend and collaborator
Jackson Grant hadn't returned his call. He stuffed his
briefcase with his graded student essays necessary for this
term's final class on the University of Minnesota's
Minneapolis campus. The shrill wind whistled between
skyscrapers. He wrapped his unbuttoned topcoat tighter.
Soon, snow would encrust the entire Twin Cities.

While the harsh winters were why he demanded
heated seats in his Lincoln, in tolerable weather he tried
to undo the lethargy of sitting in a chair all day with a
walk. He also disliked crowded rush hour buses packed
like sardine cans and University Parking issued no
Frazier Hall permits to part-time volunteer instructors,
such as himself, teaching adult classes, even if an alum.

Leg shivers forced him to hasten his University
Avenue pace.

In a steam-heated Frazier classroom, he tossed his
topcoat on a student chair and unclasped his briefcase as
it rested on a table outfitted with a wooden lectern.

"Hello, class."

42

Only Jose in the front row mouthed an audible greeting. "Buenos noches, senior."

Randall rapped on the lectern. He was content his universal gesture quieted all but the last row couple whose bowed heads were close enough to be kissing.

"Tonight's our last class this session. Eight weeks ago we started with fourteen students. I'm happy to congratulate the twelve of you here tonight. You should applaud your dedication to learn how to write English essays."

A raised hand in the back row waved for his attention. "Yes."

"Will we get grades," asked a young woman in a food server uniform.

"Final pass/fail, not letter, grades will be posted by next Monday. This assumes your final essay is turned in tonight. One of you, and I won't mention a name, is in danger of an incomplete. I'll accept makeup essays left by this Thursday in the Dean's office upstairs. Extra credit deadline for topics distributed last week is also this Thursday. Si, Jose?"

"Senor Gilleran. When is final exam?"

Randall ignored the muffled snicker uttered behind Jose.

"Jose, no final exam. Last essay equals half your grade; prior essays combine for fifty percent. Shown improvement can add a ten percent bonus toward a passing grade." He scanned the class for raised hands and other questions. Seeing none, he continued, "Tonight we'll review sentence punctuation, especially the semi-colon, comma, and exclamation mark."

He wrote examples on the blackboard. Student whispers ended when he finished and pivoted to face the class. At the conclusion of his last example and answered question, he collected a stack of essays for grading.

A handshake and verbal congratulations to each student exhibited his pride in each. The majority

43

struggled to earn English credit for their high school GED equivalency and others, like Jose, strove to learn a second language to help their kids graduate high school or attain personal employment.

The official course curriculum stated all essays were to be typed or printed. Except for the final essay, he allowed legible handwriting. He credited this leniency for his high student retention and completion percentage. His strict-rule colleague, who taught a companion Thursday course, registered a forty percent dropout rate in each session's first two weeks.

After he packed the essays into his briefcase, he switched it between gloved hands as he scurried back to his Lincoln parked in the Bunyan building underground tenant garage.

He fought off his stomach growls as he drove to his mother's monthly book club meeting.

* * *

The intermingled chatter of feminine voices allowed him to enter the back door of his parents' Northeast Minneapolis home without fanfare. He tiptoed to the entrance arch of the spacious first floor family room of the upscale three-bedroom, two-story home located off St. Anthony Blvd.

"Hello, Randall," welcomed his mother. She posed momentarily at the fireplace before she strolled toward her son.

She hugged Randall, and with a pride-broadened smile, rotated toward her guests. "Ladies, your attention please. Anyone who desires can finish the extra dessert. Then we'll hear from tonight's guest speaker."

Randall's cheeks warmed. He surmised they were no less red than his mother's crimson lipstick. As he sheepishly waved to Mother's next-door neighbor, who stood and clapped, he recognized all but one of the eight Columbia Heights Library Mystery Book Club members seated around the room.

He waited while two women carried dirty dessert plates with dark crumbs past him to the kitchen. His empty stomach craved a piece of his favorite chocolate cake he hoped his mother had saved. He rubbed his stomach muscles. Conversation fragments dotted the family room as several paperback copies of *A Body To Bones* rested on chair arms, tables, or the floor. When his mother passed him, she whispered that he should start when she returned.

"Good evening, ladies." Randall's two forward steps gave him command of the room. "Nice to visit with you all again. For anyone who might have forgotten, I'm Randall, second son of Charles and Ann Van Gilleran."

He glanced sideways to see his mother's beaming reflection in the room mirror she'd positioned decades ago to help her spy on him and his older brother growing up.

"Must confess I've not read the well regarded mystery you've been discussing. From the Internet reviews I understand it includes a romantic subplot. That's my specialty at *New Romance Delights*." Four heads nodded.

"Did you bring any new releases?" asked Gloria Johnson, seated in an armchair to his left. Mother had warned him to expect Mrs. Johnson's question.

"Sorry. Not this time. To be here for your club's first fall meeting required I come here direct from the class I teach at the university."

Randall ignored Mrs. Johnson's gossamer frown.

"Rather than me ramble on about things you're not interested in, let's start with your questions."

He acknowledged Sophia Crandall's raised hand. "Why aren't we seeing as many hardcover books as we used to?"

"Simple answer, economics." He discerned from their faces his audience desired an extended answer. "Readers hunt value. Also, younger readers don't feel a need to save books. I'd venture a guess most of you have books displayed around and above a fireplace, or in a study, like this room. Libraries, affected by dwindling revenue these days, maintain extensive circulation collections by shelving more paperbacks."

His second audience glance indicated he'd lose their attention if he elaborated. "It's a sign of the times. Books are becoming disposable, not heirloom classics."

"Is that why we're seeing more trashy stories?"

He didn't see who asked. "Maybe. But not at *New Romance Delights*. Pardon me for the self-serving plug."

"Do you recommend any new writer we should look for?" Luann Hitcher asked. "As president it's hard to find a new suitable author. After years of meetings, favorite big-name authors have died. This group's not into science fiction, vampires, or, oh yes, trashy stuff."

"Start with the library bestseller list. I'm always telling people to check out Beatrix Smothers at *New Romance Delights*. He, excuse me—" Randall's right hand covered his mouth. "She seems to release a new book every two to three months." He gritted his teeth at the hidden self-promotion. However, getting new readers for the books he wrote under his pen name remained of critical importance, no matter the deception.

"A member suggested a question earlier." His mother's voice and smile shifted the group's focus. "What is your advice on what to look for when reading any story."

"Yes, yes," said Mrs. Hitcher. She nodded vigorously to the lady seated next to her.

Randall raised his right index finger. "Please don't read the ending before you read the beginning. Yes, I know you want to have an inkling of how the story turns out. Nevertheless, you'll lose the tension and suspense the author builds into the plot." He ignored Mrs. Johnson's glum facial expression. "You won't enjoy the twists and turns your mind creates and develops, many of which the book's author never thought of."

Two ladies began to gather their belongings until Mrs. Hitcher glared at them.

He raised two fingers. "I'd be misleading you if I told you not to expect a heroic or a near happy ending, especially in romance. All may not be Horatio Alger stories, but when has Sherlock Holmes not solved the crime with Watson's help? Americans love happy endings." He watched his mother in the mirror indicate a yes with a head nod. "The triumphant cowboy, on a white horse, rides into the blazing glory of the setting western sun. The space traveler overcomes flying asteroids, weird-looking aliens, and hazardous gases or exploding planets to find peace in the galaxy. So again, if you know this, I ask, why peek at the ending."

"What about characters?" Mrs. Johnson asked.

"Good question. Look for interesting characters besides the main ones. For characters with substantial page time, track them to see if they change attitudes or a life perspective or the author leaves them in limbo. As an aside, not every character has a beginning and an end. Butlers, maids, or a visiting plumber show up and disappear with the assumption they arrive and depart in going about their normal lives. They're only important to great a guest, serve a meal, or fix a leaky pipe. The latter so that the hero can fight the villain after a good night's sleep undisturbed by the drip, drip, drip of a faucet."

Mrs. Johnson waved her hand. "What if one of those characters returns?"

"Right. Sometimes a character appears minor at first glance, but is not. The plumber who fixes the leaky pipe may be the villain in disguise. He's casing the hero's house for an upcoming burglary or to hide a bomb triggered by a remote detonator. The author should leave clues. Something is not quite logical. The plumber's truck may have no logo on it. He may not have the proper wrenches. Or, the heroine gets a blank look when she asks him if he uses a certain brand of tools. It's a tip-off the author is hinting the reader shouldn't believe outward appearances."

Additional questions led him and the women into a lively discussion on whether or not the hero should be male or female. After several minutes and no consensus, Mrs. Hitcher rose to her feet to express the club's thanks for his coming.

He sensed the club's allotted time had expired, not that he'd been yanked by a vaudeville hook. He exchanged well wishes with each club member departure. Next to him, his mother declined three offers to help with the dishes.

Randall pulled out a kitchen table chair and sat.

"I've saved you a piece of chocolate cake. Let me start the dishwasher first." She set a dessert plate with fork in front of him.

"Thanks, Mom." He swallowed a large forkful. "Delicious. Love the raspberry frosting."

His mother poured herself a cup of coffee. "Would you like coffee?"

"No thanks." He rose to fill a glass with tap water. Then sat.

"When are you going to have that writer you mentioned visit us? What's her name, ah yes, Beatrix Smothers."

He shuffled his feet. Stood, and hung his suit coat over the back of a nearby chair.

"Saw one of her books at Lund's Supermarket. There wasn't a picture of her, but inside the cover she was described as twenty-six, a graduate of the University of Minnesota-Duluth, and now living in St. Paul. You must have met her."

"I know her, Mom. Don't think she goes out much."

"Sounds a lot like you."

He audibly gulped, a momentary reflex as he tried to finish the swallow of cake frosting then halfway down his throat. He grabbed his water glass. His fingers fumbled to align the glass to his lips. A sip. Water drops slid diagonal from his lower lip to his chin. The water flushed the frosting to his stomach. "M-o-m!"

As melancholy graced his mother's expression, the back door hinges creaked. Randall wiped his chin with the back of his right hand.

"Hi, Son."

Dad had arrived to save the day. Not a white knight slaying the fairy tale villain, but a respite from another round of his mother's questions on why he didn't have a social life.

"Dear, did you save a piece of cake for me?"

"There's one last piece in the breadbox," Mom replied. "I wouldn't let Randall devour the last piece." She glanced at him and winked.

Randall stretched his mouth muscles into a smile. One day the breadbox, its every use contrived to keep things out of sight, might even have bread in it.

Dad kissed Mom on the cheek. If true to form, Dad wouldn't dilly-dally in the kitchen. His dad, a chemist, had converted a basement corner into an office stacked high with work manuals. To his chagrin, Dad's routine consistent for nearly three decades until Randall moved out.

When, with cake in hand, his Dad rose and excused himself, Randall expected Dad to eat in his office. Randall traced his introverted demeanor to his Dad's genes for quiet solitude. That made his writing enjoyable. He doubted he'd inherited a full measure of Mom's social genes. He would've liked to follow Dad, but that option would devastate Mom. He always hated to act like he chose one over the other. Mom's book club invitation tilted his attention to her. When football season arrived, he'd visit Dad to view a game together.

"You've got to not hide from people."

"Mom, what are you talking about?"

"Before your Dad arrived you said this Beatrix doesn't go out much. Remember?" He nodded. "Every time I ask what you're doing since the divorce it's all work-related."

He bowed his head. *Please, Mom, don't drag up the divorce again.*

Mom drew out a chair and sat next to him. "You've got to get past the divorce. Erase it from your mind. Sometimes I think you and Mia weren't destined to be together. Not like your dad and me."

Randall expected that if history repeated, so did his mother's comments. Not vicious, just unrelenting. While divorce after any length of marriage was regrettable, his divorce after two years demonstrated to Mom a premature marriage. He raised his defenses to deflect Mom's religious and personal belief admonitions that only death broke a sacred marriage vow.

The early days after his breakup with Mia represented the worst. Vague generalities frustrated Mom, but he refused to elaborate. Dad perceived Randall's sexual problem during a conversation within the confines of his office, however, Randall wouldn't confirm.

He tuned out Mom's glorified family silver and golden wedding anniversary history. As a ruse to avoid speaking, he alternated his fork and water glass to his lips. The mention of Mia's name vibrated his eardrum.

"Mia impressed me as a lovely young woman."

Randall agreed Mia turned male heads. His fraternity brothers at the University of Minnesota-Duluth and then at the Minneapolis campus his senior year envied him. If God had reincarnated a mythical Scandinavian goddess, the beloved creature lived as Mia Johansen. He'd used Mia's physical qualities as the heroine's description in Beatrix's *Love Divines a Goddess* romance novel—

shoulder-length blond hair, blue eyes, five-foot-seven, one hundred twenty-two pounds, small cheek dimples, and a smile capable of melting an Alaskan glacier.

"Not only beauty, but intelligence, too."

Randall agreed with a head nod. Mia's School of Nursing graduation program listed Mia's B+ overall grade-point-average.

"Any coffee left?" He felt an impulse to short-circuit their one-sided conversation.

"Sit." His mother rose to pour him a cup from the percolator on the kitchen counter. "You know, you'd be celebrating your seventh wedding anniversary if you'd not gotten divorced."

"Newspapers don't publish divorce anniversaries." Hot fresh coffee splashed his tonsils. He shut out the vivid recollection of the day he'd been served his divorce papers. He had stood devastated as the deputy sheriff strolled away. His twirl of the cherished gold wedding ring placed on his ring finger twenty months prior hadn't reversed the deputy's stride. He and Mia had tried two months of counseling to no avail.

Fueled by five champagne toasts, their one night of intimacy before the final divorce decree hadn't mended their conflict. His manual-driven foreplay lit a glowing fuse, hot and ready to ignite everlasting passion. It sputtered and fizzled to an inglorious extinction without a puff of vapor. His plan to bring he and Mia to nirvana had been what dynamite safecrackers cursed as a dud.

Mia's shrouded eyes expressed disappointment. He'd been ready to cry. Yet, his eyes remained dry. His expected miracle didn't come to pass. Cupid snapped love's arrow. Eros covered her eyes without a peek.

Against all odds of belief, Randall said, "I'm over the divorce, Mom." Yet, his ears detected the underlying hostility of his words, a tone not reflective of a child's love. "I'm sorry. Let's say goodnight with the realization no life's perfect and mine does harbor happy moments."

One Paper Heart

"If you say so." His mother's affectation insincere.
"Before you go, your brother Charlie agreed to bring
Mary and their two kids for Thanksgiving. You're
invited, too. You should bring a guest."

"That's a long way off." Randall stood, cup and plate
in hand. "Two months at least."

"This year I want to advise you of the plans ahead of
time." His plate clinked the kitchen's porcelain sink and
Mom twisted on her chair toward him. "Last year you
came alone because you said you didn't have enough
advance knowledge. Well, now you have." She smiled. "I
won't expect a repeat."

"Last year was fine. Charlie's son, an electronic-
wizard, loved beating me at that juvenile video game. I'm
a worthy foil for a four-year-old."

His mother lowered her voice. "And, you shouldn't
be as critical as you were last year when Mary asked you
to help her with a recognition speech she had to give at
work."

"C'mon, Mom. I was nice. If one of my adult students
had turned in a writing like what Mary prepared, I'd have
given a D grade without hesitation."

"You must radiate a special gamma ray that causes
problems with women."

"Where'd you get that? Oprah?" He leaned against
the kitchen counter.

"Heavens no."

"There wasn't a problem earlier tonight. Women, not
one man, filled the family room." With a sense of anguish
that his words would kindle an argument and delay his
departure, he stopped.

"Okay. I'll be more specific." Mom rose from her
chair. "You must transmit a unique invisible beam that
causes problems with women your own age."

"You know, your cake was exceptionally delicious.
Every crumb."

"Go ahead, change the subject. The best way to

reverse divorce pain is to fill your heart with another's love. You know I don't think it was entirely your fault."

"Thanks, Mom." He stiffened his abs to stand erect. He'd not be rude. His love for Mom anchored his feet in the world's reality.

"I don't believe society's recovered from the 1960s women's lib jolt of Helen Gurley Brown, Betty Frieden, and their ilk. As a country, we should've learned the importance of women staying home. I won't tell you who to get married to. That's your choice. However, I believe you'd be happier sharing life with someone."

"I know, Mother." His voice projected no enthusiasm.

"From your reaction, my words must've bounced off a wall." She tipped an empty cup.

"Sorry. You know I love you. It's been an exhausting day."

"All I'd like you to remember is to bring a guest this Thanksgiving."

"I will, Mom." He leaned forward to give his mother a kiss. "I love you."

"Why don't you invite that writer . . . Beatrix?"

Mom's thunderbolt request struck him square. He stumbled for a response. "She . . . Beatrix may have a . . . a . . . boyfriend." He gazed toward the family room, satisfied he blunted his Mom's desire to search his eyes, a window to his soul. "Or, . . . right, she may be required to attend her own family Thanksgiving."

"Well, I don't think she has a boyfriend." Mom pressed her lips together.

"Why?" Randall realized this conversation extension represented stupidity, but he shouldn't raise his Mom's expectations any higher than necessary in case he arrived alone at Thanksgiving.

"That book cover with no picture said she lives with two Humane Society cats. Our book club long ago discovered the way you publishers write. If she had, what do you call it, a significant other, it would've been phrased different."

Randall shifted his weight from his right foot to his left. "For tonight, let me tell Dad good night. I really need to be going."

He returned to the kitchen to wrap his mother in a big hug.

"Thanks, Son. Thanks for being the book club speaker. I'm sure the ladies appreciated seeing you again."

"You're welcome. I'll check my suit coat pockets tomorrow morning to see if any of your friends slipped in a paper scrap with a woman's name and phone number." His mother's lips parted in a coy smile. "You might know how publisher's write, but I've experienced how you and your accomplices try to play Cupid."

* * *

The yellowish-orange-tinted security light illuminated the outside parking lot of Randall's condo. His early investment in a five-story, thirty-unit condominium building nestled amongst converted warehouses undergoing urban gentrification hadn't yet attracted assessor attention to inflate taxes. He loved living within a two mile summer hiking distance of downtown Minneapolis and a mile and a half from his parents in the opposite direction.

His footsteps failed to raise an echo on the second floor's hallway carpet. Inside his unit, he tossed two handfuls of class essays on his kitchen table. The folded used envelope he discovered in his right suit-coat pocket he added to the closest pile.

Secured by a pizza delivery magnet, his three p.m. Thursday doctor appointment reminder hung above his refrigerator handle.

Chapter Six

After a sip to taste, Alicia lowered her second cocktail, a fancy red concoction The Front Page server referred to as a cosmopolitan. She slid her sour cranberry drink inside an upright menu, confident her co-workers, engrossed in animated conversations, would fail to notice her drink evaporate without leaving a ring stain on the wood plank tabletop.

Dizziness had snuck up on her.

Timid and not wishing to leave and earn a wet-blanket label, she listened to children exploits and news of upcoming church programs unrelated to her life outside of *New Romance Delights.*

Wanda leaned near her. "You okay? This group can be intimidating. I know I felt that way the first time I came."

"I'm doing fine." Alicia's ears listened for a tidbit here or there, which, if distilled or embellished, could inspire a new literary character.

"Good. You appeared paler this afternoon."

Alicia anticipated she could trust Wanda with her question. "When do we order food?"

"Not yet."

Alicia bit her lower lip while she counted six women, including her and Wanda. The restaurant décor with its newspaper page reproductions, linotype slug enlargements, and metallic typeface artifacts impressed her as unique. While acquainted with the Nicollet Mall, its pricey stores and eating establishments limited her periodic trips to discount sales and seasonal holiday window-shopping. She hadn't expected the two-for-one mid-week drinks or her invitation to last longer than two hours. A mural above the bar reminded her of the hard-as-nails reporter who tried to out drink the speakeasy mobster, and failed. She wouldn't go that far.

She tapped Wanda on the shoulder. "Is the entire female office staff here?"

"Yes. We're the newest." Wanda reached across the table for the refilled popcorn basket.

"Thought you were an old-timer?"

"Only two years. I've heard you're the first receptionist hired that's earned a four-year college degree." Wanda abruptly pointed her right index finger toward the restaurant's front door. Alicia surmised she should gaze that way. Her lower jaw dropped. To hide her gape, she lifted her left hand to her lower face.

The hypnotic swirl of the group's conversation dove into silent astonishment. Their attention captured by a curvaceous, statuesque brunette who stood immediately inside the restaurant's entrance with an outstretched arm pointed their way. Intrigued, Alicia fought her inclination to characterize the woman's outfit. There was the hideous forward-tilted black velvet hat with the raspberry-colored feathers. The dark tweed wool suit with the powder-blue scarf portrayed conservative taste. Together with heels, the woman radiated either the snooty attitude of a stuffy blue-blood or the designs of an ambitious status seeker with naughty thoughts who sought to latch onto her next sugar daddy.

The woman's shrill "Hello, darlings" shattered any pedigreed high-society image.

"Whoooo is that?" Alicia asked Wanda.

"Ms. Charlotte Hauser, one of our romance writers."

Before Alicia could ask a clarification question, two co-workers started clapping. The newest guest, deliberate in her every step, sashayed toward them. Male heads turned to gawk. Men, seated at tables with women, snapped their eyeballs to their companions.

"Darlings. I'm sorry to be late. Is Randall here?"

"No, Ms. Hauser," said two voices in unison.

"It's just the office staff," Wanda added.

Alicia sat quiet. She anticipated Ms. Hauser's hat to hit the floor.

"So sorry to hear that," Ms. Hauser replied. "It's unfortunate I've scheduled conflicting appointments this trip. Please accept my most gracious apology if I don't hoist a drink with you. You're all so nice at NRD. Next time, I'll host. Good night all."

With a pivot on her left heel, Ms. Hauser appeared to control her head's swivel to survey adjoining tables. Her right hand squished her hat's flowers as she departed without the hip sway flourish that highlighted her entrance.

"That was strange," Alicia said aloud to no one in particular.

"No. Not really," Wanda replied. "Charlotte only stopped in to see if my boss attended. She must've heard there was an office party, construing that to be everyone, not just us girls. Sorry, I meant women."

"Help me, Wanda. I've read an author named Charlotte Webb, not Charlotte Hauser."

"Same person."

"What?" Alicia reverted to her confused understanding from that afternoon. Mr. Van Gilleran had intimated there existed an author by the name of Charlotte Webb. She didn't remember his mention this

57

Charlotte also used a pen name. If both were the same person, Alicia couldn't deny that Charlotte, whatever her last name, was indeed a woman.

"Why would Ms. Hauser only care if Mr. Van Gilleran was present?"

Wanda put her hand near her mouth. "She's one of four regular romance writers. Was one when I started." Alicia curled her fingers around her cosmopolitan's glass stem, but didn't raise it. "At that time she was married to her third husband and now he's history. Of late she's been gushing around Mr. Van Gilleran. Those of us who see her in his presence think it's either funny or pathetic."

Wow! Alicia hadn't been prepared to hear gossip about Mr. Van Gilleran. Should she honor his comment to tell him what she heard? No. He'd been kidding. What if he found out and she'd kept quiet. No. The women present wouldn't put her in jeopardy.

Alicia faked a cosmopolitan sip and reached for a menu. "Ms. Hauser must be in her late forties?" Alicia based her age estimate on the amount of foundation makeup evident.

"Yeah. Forty-eight. Saw her birth date on a novel contract." Wanda followed Alicia's clue and grabbed a menu.

At the risk of sounding catty, Alicia asked, "Surely, Mr. Van Gilleran can't encourage her attention?"

"Well." Wanda lifted her menu to shield her face from all except Alicia. "Yes and no. He's between a rock and a hard place. He can't be responsible for getting her upset and lose the book buying public she brings to NRD. Then also in her favor, she's rumored to have inherited millions after her second husband died."

"Interesting."

"And, you've probably read about all the art and symphony fund-raisers she hosts. The *St. Paul Dispatch* once quoted her as saying she's honored to promote community charities and be able to say hello to her reading public—all at the same events."

Before she accepted her job, Alicia envisioned
publishers had favorite authors. A publisher obviously
loved, if not adored, an author who garnered bestseller
honors with each book. However, to learn of writers on
staff surprised Alicia. The arrangement seemed plausible,
but how entangled did the writers become with the editor
supervising their work? What about non-writing
enticements to get their works published? If Ms. Hauser
dangled her high society connections, was that an
unethical inducement or good business?

"Hope I'm not out of line," Wanda said, "but are you
seeing anyone or otherwise attached?"

"My only attachment is to a little girl I've fallen in
love with."

Wanda's raised eyebrows formed long forehead
wrinkles. "You have a little girl?"

Alicia realized in an instant she'd been too cryptic.
Wanda's facial hint of embarrassment said it all. Alicia
had never imagined her peasant dresses would be
interpreted as post-maternity wear.

"Yes and no. Three or four years ago I signed up to
sponsor a child. Picked out a black-haired infant girl with
a polka-dot ribbon and the cutest blue eyes. They
reminded me of my Scandinavian grandmother." Wanda
nodded. "However, the agency said she lived on a
Southwestern U.S. Indian reservation. Hold on a minute."

Alicia reached into her purse and removed her
billfold. She opened it to a picture. "Here's my little
sweetheart."

"She's beautiful." Wanda continued to gaze at the
picture. "But I'm always leery that these solicitations are
scams or shams to make someone rich. For example, Jim
Baker was always on television with his wife and her
ungodly makeup. Last I heard he'd been jailed."

Alicia returned the picture and billfold to her purse. "I
know. A former parish pastor I trust told me he visited

the reservation and came away convinced everything was legitimate. That helped calm my fears. Made me feel comfortable."

"Good to hear you investigated."

"Georgia's every now and then letter fills my heart with joy. In that respect it's money well spent."

Alicia swallowed hard to quash the sentimental pang in her chest. She didn't want to expose her adoption at age eighteen months. She had resisted the urge to search for her "real" mother, content to accept her adoptive parents' word that they didn't know. Her research into successful search techniques uncovered several examples where children adopted as infants unraveled court-ordered secrecy. More often than not the discovery of biological parents horrified the child.

Creation of her heroine's successful search for her novel character's biological mother satisfied the real life curiosity bottled up within Alicia's soul. She left the heroine's father and her own biological father forever lost.

"You want kids of your own?" Wanda asked.

"Someday. At least one boy and a girl."

"Excuse me, may I slide over and join in?"

Alicia gazed at Wanda for guidance. Wanda motioned the woman in a gray pants suit and a red silk neck scarf to move closer. Wanda introduced Carol as a proofreading and book-block formatting staffer.

"I'll be forward." Carol's eyes twinkled. "Overheard mention of children." Alicia swiveled her knees right to prepare to leave for the restroom whether or not her body physically required the trip. "Have a younger brother who's single. I'd venture a guess he's about your age."

Alicia's lip muscles curled her lower lip above her upper. A deep inhale relaxed them. "I've never had much luck with blind dates." She flashed her right index finger to her lips to forestall Wanda's anticipated matchmaking comment. "Not to say your brother isn't nice."

Wanda wasn't stifled. "He'll have to stand in line."

* * *

Alicia dared not let her fingers smudge the extra foundation applied beneath both eyes after she'd seen the dark circles in her bathroom's mirror.

She attributed Carol's cheerier reception greeting to their attendance at the staff's night out. Alicia's good morning uttered through a tensed jaw. Her muscles relaxed when Carol left without a mention of her bachelor brother.

Alicia expected the letter carrier when a puff of stale hallway air struck her face. She elevated her gaze to a disheveled man in an unbuttoned rumpled tan suit, creased blue shirt, and loosened paisley tie. His scuffed brown shoes matched the scratched satchel he carried.

"Good morning. Is Mr. Van Gilleran in? I think I have an appointment?"

"Whom may I say wants to see him?"

His eyes surveyed reception and its empty seats. "Mr. Grant. Mr. Jackson Grant. Don't know if we've met. Perhaps if you gave me your name I'd remember."

"Sure we haven't since I'm new. I'm Alicia." She purposefully withheld further information.

"Then I wouldn't remember."

She would've preferred Ally, but this after all was a business office. Her nameplate, overturned by previous manuscript submissions, did say Alicia, but she'd never flipped it toward visitors. "Mr. Grant, please have a seat. I'll check on Mr. Van Gilleran's availability."

He retreated to a chair near the hall door as she buzzed Wanda on the intercom.

"Mr. Grant." Alicia inched her body erect. He rose with his eyes fixated on her. His gentle gaze, not a leer or an ogle, traveled from her head to the desktop. "Mr. Van

Gilleran's not in, but is expected. If you follow me, you can wait in his office."

"Thanks. Lead the way."

Mr. Grant hesitated until she'd stepped past the end of her desk. If he had expectations of viewing her legs, he'd be disappointed for her skirt hem touched her shoe tops. A right hand twist and a doorknob pull allowed them into the office area.

With a dozen steps, they stood, Alicia in front, before a bright and cheery Wanda who displayed not a hint she'd toasted the night away. Alicia stepped aside when Mr. Grant said, "Hello, Wanda. How are you this fine day?"

"Fabulous," Wanda replied. "I telephoned Mr. Van Gilleran on his mobile phone. He'll be here shortly. He suggested you wait in his office."

Mr. Van Gilleran's office, located without exterior windows in the office's center, sported a huge picture window and a wood-framed glass door. Wanda's desk guarded the window's front. With the interior office blinds opened, Alicia scanned two walls of floor-to-ceiling bookcases.

"Holy Cow!" Mr. Grant exclaimed. "Since when has Randall displayed that Oscar statuette we won three years ago? Think my last landlord stole mine."

Alicia had never noticed the statuette before. She'd only sat in Mr. Van Gilleran's office once, her second job interview, and her recollection was hazy. "Was that for a romance novel?"

"Screenplay," Mr. Grant answered as he stepped into her boss's office. Alicia and Wanda followed. "We were a fantastic team. Randall, Andy Shaw, and I. Randall's brains led the team. Boy, those were the days." His gaze rested on the statuette for several seconds.

Alicia wanted to pick up and hold the golden icon. She experienced a magnetic pull toward the left bookcase. It had to emanate from the statuette. Then her brain's neurons overpowered her fantasy. "What screenplay?"

Either annoyance or apprehension skittered across Wanda's face. Although uninvited into Mr. Van Gilleran's office, Alicia didn't feel uncomfortable.

Mr. Grant appeared to enjoy Alicia's attention. His dimples deepened as he buttoned his sport coat, which didn't camouflage his wrinkled shirt. "Alaskan documentary. Trekked the frozen tundra of native Indian tribes and poked around in historical Eskimo settlements."

"What an adventure." Alicia felt the corners of her mouth defy gravity.

Wanda shook her head from side to side.

Mr. Grant sucked in a deep breath. "Never could eat before a bush pilot flew us to a remote landing strip." Alicia's face must have registered her hangover. "Sorry to mention that."

Wanda slid her feet left until she stood between the office doorjambs. Her eyes peered the length of the office's interior corridor and toward the employee entrance. "He's here," Wanda whispered. Alicia hustled after Mr. Grant to be aside Wanda's desk.

Mr. Van Gilleran scurried towards them. The corridor's wall-to-wall red carpet bordered with a golden diamond pattern sucked in the noise of his elongated strides.

Within six feet of the threesome, Mr. Van Gilleran called out: "Jackson, great to see you. How's California?" His pearly whites broadcasted his animated smile.

Alicia's chin lifted. Without an expectation of this reunion emotion, she glanced at Wanda. Wanda shrugged and burst into a smile as the two men hugged.

Mr. Van Gilleran disengaged his arms. "Expected you yesterday. What happened?" He didn't acknowledge either Alicia's or Wanda's presence. His right hand on Mr. Grant's left elbow nudged his friend through his

63

office's doorway. After the door closed, Alicia watched Mr. Grant on the opposite side of the office's picture window drop his satchel on Mr. Van Gilleran's oaken desk before the two men plopped into visitor chairs.

Wanda turned to her. "I saw the way Mr. Grant sized you up."

"Huh?"

"You must have noticed. Well, maybe not from behind. So, what do you want me to tell him if he later asks about you?"

"W-a-n-d-a!" Warmth rose in Alicia's cheeks.

"Shush. We'll attract eavesdroppers."

Alicia glanced the corridor's length. No staffer visible. She waited for Wanda to continue.

"Last year when Mr. Grant visited he asked about the former receptionist. Caught me off guard. Only trying to be helpful. That is, if I can."

Alicia, her lips ratcheted tight, stared at Wanda. She hadn't really given any thought to Mr. Grant as a potential suitor. He definitely hadn't heeded anyone's advice on how to present a dress-for-success appearance. Then, with an Oscar on his resume, he'd already scaled the success mountain.

Alicia's jumbled mind remembered her sixth sense sensation, confirmed by Wanda, that Mr. Grant had scanned her body: first in reception, and later outside Mr. Van Gilleran's office. She worried if an unfastened bodice button spurred his attention. She glanced at her chest. No. Was her slip showing? Nah. From a belted waist her dress fabric hung a foot longer.

"Well?" Wanda tapped her right foot. "What do I say if he asks about you?"

"Think up something." Alicia halted her pivot to return to her receptionist desk. She twisted her head to whisper, "Say something nice."

Wanda winked.

Seated at her desk, Alicia wondered if she'd done the

proper thing. She sighed. If her proverbial toe was now dipped in the ever-expanding pool of office relationships, she had to trust Wanda for there was no one else. Only once before, as a first year elementary teacher, had Alicia experienced anything similar and the hurtful consequences reverberated. Her ex-boyfriend ended up not having his teacher contract renewed and the bitterness overflowed into the fall as his male friends snubbed her and planted promiscuous lies. It was true she hadn't dated much, but to be labeled as only interested in women scaled cruelty's heights and the harder she fought to disavow the lies the stronger the backlash. She hated every co-worker and the vicious lies.

Only her insomniac fire nightmares stole a greater number of her night's sleep hours.

If Wanda had short-circuited Carol's younger-brother matchmaking, why would she trouble herself about having an answer for a question Mr. Grant might never ask? When Alicia saw the letter carrier had left two large envelope piles, Alicia buried all office romance qualms under the now familiar, and boring, routine of processing submissions. *Must be close to fifty.*

On a lighter day she looked forward to filling idle minutes by reading four to six submissions to broaden her knowledge of competing writers. She doubted Mr. Van Gilleran favored the weird tale of a Medieval lady-in-waiting who hid an egg in her bosom with the goal of hatching it within three days only to be distracted by a young squire's kisses on day two. Alicia didn't desire to read on to discover if the egg hatched.

A half hour later she heard the door behind her open.

A silent Mr. Grant smiled and paused at the hallway door. Mr. Van Gilleran stopped aside her desk. "Mr. Grant and I are going to lunch. Will you be here at one thirty?"

"Yes, yes, sir." She craved to ask the why question. His abrupt turn toward the door left her eyes plead with his back for an answer, which wasn't forthcoming.

Alicia noticed Mr. Grant didn't carry the brown satchel evident on his arrival.

Although the manuscript pile would've daunted her three weeks ago, she completed her tasks by noon. After she unloaded the second batch on Wanda's desk, she joined Wanda and Carol for lunch at a small oblong table next to the office pop machine.

"I'd get bored with yogurt five days a week," Carol explained.

Ready to set the microwave timer for a one-dish meal, Wanda interjected, "Me, too."

A defensive Alicia replied, "I change sandwiches, but love yogurt."

Unsettled by ascending stomach butterflies that tickled her throat, Alicia longed to ask Wanda if Mr. Grant had quizzed her. However, with Carol present, Alicia dared not and the three ate in companionable silence until Carol excused herself. "So, did he ask?" Alicia's hands packed used food containers into her new insulated lunch bag.

"No."

Alicia exhaled a sigh of relief. "Good." Her stomach butterflies collapsed their wings against their abdomens and left hers calm. "Do we have time? Can I see the Oscar up close?"

Wanda smiled and led the way to her boss's office. "Mind you. It's only a replica."

Alicia's hands trembled with anticipation. "I've never been so close to even a replica." She tried not to sound like a giggling, enthralled, teenager with front row seats to a rock star concert. "Wow!" She caressed the statuette handed to her by Wanda. "This is heavy." With one hand under the statuette's base, the fingers of her second hand traced the crossed arms. "Where's the real one?"

"Mr. Van Gilleran locked it into a safety deposit box."

"That's good thinking." Alicia scanned the bookshelves for an award presentation picture, but couldn't locate one. The one framed eight-by-ten photo showed a five-member family posed in front of a studio's mountain backdrop.

"Yeah. You heard Mr. Grant. He had his stolen. He should've taken advantage of the Academy's official offer to purchase a replica."

Alicia tapped her right-hand fingers along the golden curved surfaces. She'd never subject Oscar to the torment she visited upon her writing muse. "If I were awarded one, it wouldn't sit out." She caught Wanda's quizzical glance. "Didn't intend to be critical."

"Do you have hopes to win your own?"

"Oh, yeah." Mock enthusiasm dripped from Alicia's words. Her mouth puckered like a bag's tightened drawstring. No one outside Vicky needed to know she'd written and submitted a romance novel. She handed Wanda the Oscar. "Why did you even ask if I hoped to win an Oscar?"

"Because. Everyone who's applied to work here the last two years seems to clutch tight a published-author dream. Merely assumed you'd be no different." Wanda wiped a shelf with her right hand and placed the Oscar on the shelf from whence he came. "You majored in what? English? Right?"

"English and elementary education."

"That fits with what you said last night."

"What?" She'd said so many things. Unremembered words had drowned in the sipped gin and orange juice, Carol's ordered replacement for the sour cranberry cosmopolitan.

"Wanting children. Caring for that cute little girl."

"Guess so."

Alicia's clock glance told her she needed to unlock the hallway door. Fat chance persons were lined up to enter. Then too, she'd promised to be available to Mr.

Van Gilleran in forty minutes. Within her stomach the re-energized butterflies flapped their wings. She wanted very much to believe that Wanda's diversion to children would forever distract Wanda's intuitiveness into Alicia's ambition to become a published author. A need for income to avoid living with her parents gave Alicia a compelling reason to accept the receptionist position, not to obtain an inside position to worm her way onto bookseller shelves.

Other non-teaching jobs within commuting distance hadn't offered medical insurance benefits and sharing a bus-route apartment meant she could get by, if she counted her pennies.

"I should return to reception." Alicia retrieved her lunch bag. "Thanks, Wanda."

"Quick question. Why aren't you teaching?"

"Bad decision. Tried to land the most prestigious position. Failed. Ignored other good teaching jobs until it became too late to apply. And, I wasn't ready to move out of the metropolitan area."

"I hear you there."

"Never could be lured to live in far off places like California."

"Well, you ever been asked?"

Alicia perceived a devilish twinkle in her co-worker's eye. Had she treated Wanda's earlier remarks too lightly? Or, did Carol's brother live out of state. Would she have an interest? Vicky pestered her to get a life.

"Easy to understand both points: indecision and having roots." Wanda's words weighed heavy and somber on Alicia's ears. She listened closer. "I got so anxious to find a job after I married that I abandoned college. Of course, becoming pregnant changed my world, too." Wanda's coy smile teased Alicia.

"You have a lovely family, Wanda. Last night's photos and this one here on your desk?"

"Thank you."

"Let's leave this Oscar to his winners." Alicia pointed to Wanda's desk. "Enjoy your stacks. The front door lock calls out for me."

Alicia stepped into reception and then peeked to confirm that Wanda hadn't remained at her desk. Alicia calculated she had two or three minutes to sneak a peek around the boss's office for any hint or evidence of her manuscript. She found Mr. Van Gilleran's office door locked. The slanted blinds allowed Alicia enough light to see her boss's desktop clear of manuscripts. One corner file cabinet appeared to have its top lock cylinder pushed in.

While she risked discovery by a co-worker, she suspected non-authors didn't spend time to ogle the ten framed Beatrix Smothers' book covers hung opposite the shelf with its Oscar statuette. The replica gave her a new awe-inspiring perspective on her boss. Even if the office had no official red carpet, maybe she should placate Vicky and buy at least one fashionable dress or a stylish pants suit with an extra frilly blouse. The clothes an apt acknowledgement she'd passed her thirty-day probationary period.

Alicia refused to breathe easy for doom still hovered. Her red paper heart switch represented good cause for her firing. Seated behind her NRD desk, her manuscript location worries still plagued her. She bookended a twenty minute interval to stand, rotate her hips, and stretch her shoulder muscles. Undisturbed by the typical lack of reception visitors, she flinched when the intercom buzzed.

Relieved it was Carol, Alicia sat. Alicia unclenched her fists and apologized profusely when informed she'd misdirected three e-mails. Alicia reviewed her sent e-mail box to find a fourth misdirect. Embarassed by her first-caught mistake, she e-mailed Norma an apology and attached the unforwarded e-mail.

Caught up with work tasks and bored, Alicia had no

choice but to wait for Mr. Van Gilleran. She flipped the lid on her compact. The mirror's image confirmed her applied foundation hadn't flaked or cracked to expose either last night's dark eye circles or the puerperal that dotted her neck. Each doctor's theory different why it remained below her ear and rear jawbone since the fire and disappeared elsewhere. If to be beautiful a woman had to feel beautiful, she didn't.

Alicia's muscles tensed when the shadow outline of a person lingered beyond the hallway door. If Mr. Van Gilleran, she expected he wouldn't hesitate. Her left hand lifted her hem while her right slid her compact into her purse before she grabbed its two straps. If caught before she reached the interior office door, it's swing offered her little defense, but better than none.

Flung wide, the door exposed Mr. Van Gilleran. Alicia's throat throttled a sigh of relief.

"Thanks for being here." He laid his doubled-over topcoat on a visitor chair. "Don't like to be late for appointments, especially ones I request."

Alicia, puzzled why he lingered in the hallway to create the door shadow, dismissed asking. A person outside her vision could've waylaid him.

"Fifteen minutes is no big deal. Wait longer at the—" She pressed her lips together. No need to expose her fixation with her ugly skin discoloring.

"You ever been to a professional football game?"

A pen dropped from her right hand. "No . . ." Her why question remained unasked.

"Mr. Grant's a long time Chicago Bears fan. The Bears play the Minnesota Vikings Sunday, October 18, at the Metrodome . . . and he said before lunch he has four tickets."

Beneath her cheek foundation, Alicia's skin stretched taut as a deer hunter's bow. She dared not drag out her compact for a peek at her neck.

He started to pace in front of her desk. "Would you

want to go?"

A lump formed in Alicia's throat. Her brain froze without any inkling of who would actually be going. She assumed Mr. Grant because Mr. Van Gilleran said he had the tickets. But, her mind whirled, he lived in California. Something else had to be happening next month.

She contemplated her immediate rejection would be impolite. To give her brain time to develop a response outside yes or no, Alicia tilted her head sideways and reached her right arm to the floor for her purse. The collision bang of two chairs jerked her head toward Mr. Van Gilleran. His coat lay folded across his two forearms.

"I can understand you may need to check your date book. The game's weeks away."

"Right—"

"Think about it overnight. I'll call Jackson in the morning."

"Mr. Grant's left town?" Once she spoke, her brain's logic cells hustled to divine a need for her interest in Mr. Grant's whereabouts.

Mr. Van Gilleran elevated his left forearm to balance his coat. "Yes and no. He's at the airport for an afternoon flight to California. Should be checking in about now."

"Only asked because he left for lunch without his briefcase."

"You're very observant. His briefcase contains our latest joint project. He distrusts delivery services." Mr. Van Gilleran paused to toss his topcoat over his left shoulder. "He'll fly back for the Bears/Vikings weekend. He thinks he can deduct his trips as a business expense. Please don't mention my belief that the IRS may think different."

It wasn't much of a confidence, yet, like Mr. Van Gilleran's earlier longer conversation, it represented a further thaw in his initial persona.

"Okay. I'll give you an answer in the morning."

"Anything else happening?"

"Wanda has today's submission arrivals."

He nodded, strode past her, and departed reception toward his office.

Unable to contain the news, Alicia buzzed Wanda. They plotted a restroom rendezvous an hour later at three.

"Were you asked to attend the game?" Alicia asked Wanda.

"Don't expect to be."

"Did Mr. Grant ask about me?"

"Never left my boss's office."

* * *

Seated on the No. 34 Orange bus as it circled the Metrodome, Alicia stared at the huge letters spelling out Mall of America Field. As the bus circled before the driver gunned its engine to speed up the I-35 entrance ramp, she marveled at the huge, puffed up, unfrosted muffin top that created its roof. To attend a baseball or football game under the stitched together Teflon roof panels had never interested her.

If she didn't wish to go, could her ticket be given to her brother? Alicia channeled the question to the rear of her mind for the bus trip home. At her apartment she used her key and bypassed a buzzer push to alert Vicky to let her into the elevator lobby.

Alicia's courtesy not to trouble Vicky transformed into self-conscious discomfort when she saw Joel next to Vicky on their living room sofa. He wiped his face with a white handkerchief and tucked it into the rear pocket of his jeans before she could speak. Alicia perceived telltale red smudges that matched Vicky's lipstick shade.

A timer chimed. Vicky dashed to open the oven door. "You want to share pizza?"

"If no anchovies. Hi, Joel."

"Hi," he replied matter-of-factly. His gaze dipped to the coffee table and the TV remote.

Vicky slid a deep-dish pizza off a wooden paddle onto a wire cooling rack centered on the breakfast counter. Alicia sidled up to Vicky and said nothing about her roommate's smeared lipstick. They joined Joel in the living room.

Alicia shoved Vicky to the sofa's middle cushion, next to Joel. She settled in on the sofa's end nearest the kitchen. When Vicky angled her body to face Alicia, which blocked Alicia's full view of Joel, he made no effort to change his position. That suited Alicia.

"You'll never guess the invitation I got this afternoon?" Alicia's words reverberated with nervous undertones. A pepperoni aroma invaded her nostrils. "Or, what I found out?"

"You're going to a tropical island for a photo shoot weekend?" Vicky guessed.

Joel interjected. "Disneyland?"

"You're both wrong. But Joel's closer in a way."

Joel leaned forward and clasped his hands above his head like a winning prizefighter. Vicky twisted her upper torso to glare at him. She unwound to again face Alicia.

"Today, the office received a visit from a Mr. Jackson Grant who—with Mr. Van Gilleran—won a real, honest-to-goodness screenplay Oscar years ago. Didn't know until today there's a statuette in my boss's office." Her words rose in pitch. "He was out of the office when Mr. Grant arrived." Alicia ignored Joel's rise from the sofa. "I got to hold it."

"Like you see on TV?" Vicky asked.

"I'd estimate the replica I held weighed more than a pound."

"Didn't he receive a real gold one?" Kitchen utensils rattled and Vicky glanced at Joel. "Wrong drawer. One to the right." She gazed at Alicia.

"It's squirreled away in a safety deposit box

73

somewhere."

Joel, a pizza cutter in hand, sliced the circular crust into serving pieces. "Who's this Mr. Grant fellow?"

"Comes from California," Alicia replied. She wondered if Joel planned to stay all evening. "Looks slovenly. Clothes wrinkled and shoes scuffed."

Vicky joined Joel. "Bet he boasts a great tan coming from California."

Alicia stood. "Not a remarkable one." She doubted Mr. Grant lounged on a spread ocean-beach blanket. Her first office impression had struggled to determine which personality scale polar extreme he landed at. She judged by his appearance he either lacked self-esteem and social skills or had extreme self-confidence and didn't care how others reacted.

Vicky conscripted Joel to peel carrots and chop celery for the packaged iceberg lettuce she retrieved from the refrigerator. When he whistled an untitled ditty, Alicia shook her head. On a date, his whistling had irked her by attracting unwanted stranger attention. She stifled her negative thoughts. He'd rescued her. Nothing tainted his heroics.

Alicia excused herself to change into a sweatshirt and baggy jeans. Upon her return she swung her right leg over a breakfast counter stool. "Mr. Van Gilleran surprised me today."

"How?" Vicky asked, her eagle eye on Joel until he dropped the peeler.

"I've never seen him show any kind of emotion except an occasional small smile. He acts so stern, stoic, and formal. And then today he flings open the employee entrance and scampers to hug Mr. Grant. Not a hesitant hug, but a big, manly hug. His grin beamed."

"That doesn't sound so unusual," Joel muttered. "Firemen hug . . . well sometimes."

"That's not all. After lunch, he comes to my desk and asks me if I want to go see a professional football game at the Metrodome."

Joel pivoted. The chef's knife in his right hand swung through the air.

Vicky gasped and leaned backward.

Joel lowered the knife. "I wanna go to a Vikings game." His expressed desire hung in the air, ignored, and unanswered as he offered Alicia a large pizza slice. She chose a smaller one and filled her plate with salad.

"Who asked?" Vicky inquired. "Mr. Grant?"

"Mr. Van Gilleran. He asked if I wanted to go October 18."

Vicky bent forward. "What . . . what did you say?" Vicky's squeaky voice no louder than a whisper. Anticipation exuded from each syllable she uttered.

"He saw me hesitate and then suggested I check my date book." Alicia felt her cheeks warm at the repeated "date" word mention.

Vicky's right forefinger touched the tip of her nose. She spoke through parted fingers. "He actually used the words: date book?"

An embarrassed Alicia nodded. "Can't forget those words."

"C'mon. Tell me you said yes." She stared at Alicia. "I'd say yes."

Joel's voice interrupted the silence. "I'd say yes just to see the game."

"Shush, Joel. I'm waiting for Alicia."

"Agreed with his suggestion to think about it overnight. Give him an answer tomorrow."

"You've got to say yes." Vicky implored in a loud voice. "Do you good to get out."

Vicky's words stung and beat a familiar drum. Alicia's repressed anger prickled her skin. *Sometimes people do things because they want to, not because someone else forces.* Alicia's clenched teeth left her words unsaid. Alicia was proud of her novel. She'd sacrificed for it. It provided her a way to express feelings never expressed to friends or family. In her heroine, she'd conquered all imagined obstacles, except publication. Would going to the game help her attain publication? She wouldn't compromise personal values to attain publication. She preferred to remain an unpublished unknown rather than be how she envisioned Charlotte Hauser—a cartoonist's caricature in high heels.

As if Alicia hadn't heard her, Vicky repeated, "Yes must be your answer."

"It's not just him. He said Mr. Grant had four tickets. Don't know who all is going."

"Doesn't matter. He asked you."

Joel waved his hands. "He might just be the wingman."

Vicky cried out. "Joel!"

Joel recoiled until his buttocks bumped into a kitchen cabinet.

"Put a piece of pizza on a plate and eat it in the hallway," Vicky ordered. "When it's time for you to come back in, I'll open the door."

When he passed her, Alicia recognized his lips formed a small pout. She felt a twinge of sadness. When the hallway door closed, she asked, "Wasn't that harsh?"

The firebrands in Vicky's eyes cooled. "He'll learn not to interrupt. We've had this conversation before."

"Because we didn't hit it off doesn't mean I wish to get between you and Joel."

Vicky chewed a pizza bite. "You won't."

"Guess Mr. Van Gilleran, who yesterday said he desired Mr. Grant to join *New Romance Delights*, doesn't want a peon to willy-nilly refuse an invitation to Mr. Grant's face."

Vicky swallowed a second pizza bite. "Keep talking."

"Mr. Grant may be the nicest person, but I don't want any long-distance relationship nor to move to California. I'll gladly settle for annual Winter Carnival ice sculptures and family picnics with summer lake breezes."

"Forget the Winter Carnival." Vicky's facial features, sharper than Paul Bunyan's axe, reminded Alicia of an unmoving, frozen in time Winter Carnival ice sculpture. "You said Mr. Van Gilleran displayed positive emotions. Now you're sprouting motives to justify your saying no without proof they're real. You said he doesn't wear a wedding ring."

Alicia's right hand grazed her sunken cheeks.

"Take a chance. Fall down if you must, but get up, and try again. No Mr. Right will wake you up in the middle of the night to say, 'Here I am.' There'll be 64,000 fans at the game. What is it—four hours? You'll survive even if it's horrendous."

"Okay. I'll tell him in the morning I'll go."

"One more thing."

"What?" She'd caved in to Vicky's push. What more could there be?

"You have to promise me that you'll tell Joel that going to the stadium is no big deal."

"Huh?" Alicia bit into a lukewarm pepperoni.

"I want him to believe that it's more fun to watch the game on the sofa with me. With television timeouts and instant replays, game interruptions at home can be more fun."

"Agreed. Now please invite Joel back. This pizza's getting cold."

Vicky nodded, followed Alicia's suggestion, and trailed Joel to the breakfast counter.

"You going?" Joel asked in a subdued tone.

Alicia reached for the lo-cal salad dressing. "Yes. I'm going."

Joel's face lit up. "Good. For luck I'll loan you my Vikings jacket. It hasn't been worn since the cleaners."

Vicky shrugged.

* * *

77

Aunt Agnes waved to Alicia from a Ruthie's Restaurant booth window. Alicia dodged the Thursday Hawthorne Street foot traffic, swelled by lunchtime locals and passengers headed to and from the Greyhound terminal. Inside the arched doorway, Alicia breezed past tables to clasp Aunt Agnes's extended hand.

"Auntie, have you been camped out since daybreak or did you bribe the owner?"

"Shush."

Alicia scooted into the booth seat opposite her aunt. "Can I say I adore your new knit cap before you begin the third degree?"

Aunt Agnes wrinkled her nose, small like the rest of her. She resembled the tune, "Five-foot two, eyes of blue," while her family stature mimicked Queen Elizabeth. "Please let's order, my treat, and then we can talk, my darling."

This had to be serious. What had Alicia done since the family's summer barbecue? While her anxiety rose, Alicia picked at her chef's salad doused with balsamic vinegar.

"Your mother, upset and crying, telephoned me last month about your giving up teaching."

"Haven't done that." Alicia jumped past an explanation she'd placed all her hopes on one job and lost three others. "Just failed to get a desired position."

"Can't understand it." Aunt Agnes dabbed her mouth with a napkin. "Your being a receptionist undervalues your talents, but that's not what really troubles your mother?"

"Has mother's depression taken a turn for the worse?"

"Don't think so. It's just that she always compares you to Elena."

Alicia bristled. "Mother doesn't compare any of us."

"You say that, but it's not true. Well, maybe for George and Alan. Regardless, Elena has given birth twice and my sister offers fervent daily prayers you will know the joy God has denied her. She's dismayed you don't seem interested in children and the years pass. I see in your mother's eyes the hurt that eats away at her soul."

"I've dated. Brought a guy home so Mother knows I've tried."

"Let's not discuss that hippie."

Alicia clenched her teeth. Aunt Agnes could be so sweet if she desired. Cross her and her words wielded an edge sharp as any surgeon's scalpel. She'd raised six children; learned how to read a child's devilish mind. Alicia lower her gaze. *Lord knows I've prayed hard for God to bless me with what Mother considers to be my life's role.* She nodded assent for the server to top off her water glass. "What did Mother say?"

"She's concerned you'll end up miserable and childless without a strong husband."

"I've always been able to support myself. Been that way since high school graduation."

Aunt Agnes clasped her hands on the table. "That's your problem."

"Huh?" Aunt Agnes confused her.

"Do you have a job?"

"You know I do."

"How about a car?"

"Yes."

"A house?

"Well, not exactly, but I pay my half of the rent on time."

"Clothes?"

Alicia wouldn't leech off others. "What's your point?"

"I'll assume your testiness is a positive. What about food?"

"Of course."

"Now think. You have all the things society commands men to provide. If that's so and the man sees

79

that he can't be a breadwinner, head of household, or, heaven forbid, satisfy his male ego he'll search for another woman."

"What about love? Intimacy? Hearts and souls joined together to challenge the world."

"Not important. Men consider themselves providers. You've got to respect that and do nothing to undermine it."

Alicia pondered if she'd been destined to be alone. The children in her life to be those she taught in the classroom or an orphan or two she supported with cash contributions. "Oh, I don't know . . ." Alicia gazed into the street. She doubted all the men in her sight were consumed by the desire to dominate women.

"Don't be headstrong. Your mother and I wish to see you happy. It means the world for her to see you and Elena as respected women in the community."

Alicia tried not to be rude. "I'm sorry I have to rush. Thank you for lunch." The greater truth was she required medical insurance. She surmised Aunt Agnes had included benefits within her having a job question.

"You'll consider your Mother's point of view?"

Alicia didn't wish to offend either Mother or Aunt Agnes, even if their views were old-fashioned. "Tell her I will."

Aunt Agnes waved off Alicia's offer to leave a tip and adjusted her knit cap.

Chapter Seven

The sterile, dull, two-tone gray, medical clinic reception area failed to wallpaper a happy facial glow onto Randall's a.m. hangdog expression reflected between the backward letters on the room's tinted glass entry door. He counted the wall clock hands jerk and click ninety times after his nine a.m. arrival. His stomach growled. Three sips of requested iced water hadn't eased the hunger of his thirteen-hour fast.

If he'd been fruitful and desired a snip to dam energetic sperm, then maybe his avalanche of sorrow wouldn't suffocate so.

He toyed with an old idea to scribble notes to capture his escalating discomfort. *What use?* No romance reader enjoyed mundane suffering. Other than his brain's manufactured heartache, no body part throbbed or burned.

Randall's memory reverberated with Jackson's grousing throughout their Minneapolis lunch and then their evening follow-up telephone call. No matter how persuasive Jackson's argument, no way he would edit a third documentary. He'd convinced himself, if not

Jackson, that documentary films were passé. All niche cable channels including PBS, The History Channel, and The Travel Channel broadcasted endless dust storms, countless animal skeleton excavations, and cute birds falling from nests ad nauseam.

Jackson had harped on his grand image of three February weeks on a Pacific Ocean island ala Margaret Mead. Randall scored it so-so. He had gritted his teeth when Jackson justified the sun tan a welcome contrast to Randall's howling-winter-wind pink and freezing cheeks.

After he had guzzled a Hamm's longneck beer as a last pre-fast act, Randall telephoned Jackson to apologize. Relieved the big lug took no offense, Randall had argued they needed a fresh, outside-the-box inspiration to jack up their faded Hollywood presence. Jackson agreed in principle, but said his idea-gauge-needle pointed to empty. Randall pitched his friend on buying a novel to craft the plot into a screenplay. Jackson pooh-poohed an adaptation effort and offered to search his mind's back roads for an original screenplay idea.

Undaunted by Jackson's flights of fancy, Randall extolled a *New Romance Delights* manuscript received from an unheralded author with an aristocratic name, Lady Victoria Dash. Although exquisite punctuation starved his pet peeve, his contextual summary to Jackson downplayed the novel's jumbled syntax, stilted dialogue, and purple prose scenic descriptions. With gusto, he described a main feminine character who effused intrigue with physical attributes from the pages of Vogue magazine. Her carefree, fearless actions sparkled in the face of other's frustration and indifference.

A sheepish Randall had confessed to Jackson he wouldn't mind a date with the real life individual the author recast into a fictional character. However, Randall's and Wanda's every attempt to reach Lady Victoria Dash had ended up a dead end.

Randall sighed when he overheard the receptionist

inform a gray-haired senior gentleman that the doctor was still at the hospital. His mind wandered. After Mia, he'd acted like a beached turtle in a PBS Nature documentary. He'd withdrawn into a shell to protect against all feminine hurts and potential attacks.

If this continued, he'd join the frightened turtle's isolated world. His ego de-emphasized the fact that the turtle's salvation required it to poke out its head, decide on a direction, touch its feet to the sand, and move, regardless of direction.

Randall scribbled the turtle analogy on a paper scrap as fodder for Beatrix Smothers's next novel. His called name enjoined his scribbling.

"Mr. Van Gilleran," a young woman in scrubs repeated. She stood with a clipboard inside the waiting room door.

The gray-haired man flashed him a thumbs up. Randall waved a thank you to the man's random act of kindness.

"Please follow me." The woman's shrill voice belied a position of authority. Led into a corridor, each door a gateway to an examination room, Randall won no prize behind the Room C door she selected.

"The doctor will be right in."

Right. Randall's expectation blown by a five-minute wait.

"Mr. Van Gilleran, please stay seated. I'm Doctor Chester Jones. I see by your chart Drs. Campbell and Halverson referred you here. Your problem's not uncommon. Are you married?"

He gazed at the doctor's round face, a flesh-colored globe atop a six-foot white column. *What a question.* "Not today. Divorced."

"Seeing anyone special? Expect to get married soon?"

His mother would applaud this doctor's approach. "No."

"Have a need or desire to be a sperm donor?"

83

"Doc, why all the questions?" Two months ago, Randall had gone in for an annual checkup with Doc Campbell who, until then, had expressed no great concern about his low sperm count. After his divorce, he'd learned secondhand that Mia had given birth. Family rumors hinted at a girl. Since Mia hadn't contacted him, he assumed all the long-shot odds ruled against him being the father. Nonetheless, Doc Campbell had convinced him to undergo a complete fertility clinic workup. The Doc cited statistics that of every hundred low-sperm-count men tested one was diagnosed with testicular cancer. A seated Randall squirmed on the exam table until his back muscles tensed..

Dr. Jones flipped a page in the chart folder he held. "There's good news."

"What?"

"Cell and lymph node test results show no present cancer."

Randall's sigh bounced off the nearby wall and his shoulders slumped.

"However, long term concerns exist."

Randall, unable to gaze at the doctor, stared at the wall. His lower back muscle spasm pinged nerve energy upward. It's spinal trajectory collided with his brain launched apprehension. *Tell me.* He rotated his face toward the doctor. "What concerns?"

"Our tests confirm Dr. Campbell's low-sperm-count diagnosis."

Randall tuned out the doctor. He'd heard the speech before. While not by much, he'd disproved Dr. Campbell's day one suspicion he shot blanks. Mia had passed her fertility tests with flying colors, her inside baby track as perfect as her outside.

He'd declined artificial insemination. He wasn't available to have anybody stick a suction tube below his belt. His decision had added tension to their marital difficulties. Mia called him bullheaded. Maybe so, but he retained his macho pride.

"Do you want me to continue?" Dr. Jones asked. "Your choice?"

"Sorry if I'm lightheaded." Randall had fretted nine weeks for this appointment and a redo was the last thing he wanted. "Still waiting to have blood drawn."

"Not necessary."

Randall didn't know if he should feel relieved or distressed.

"Let me summarize."

Dr. Jones's words overjoyed Randall's craved-for-lunch stomach.

"A man's expected to produce millions of motile, kicking sperm. A woman, one happy egg. On an importance scale, sperm quantity ranks higher than quality. Man's role mimics mosquitoes—hatch millions to guarantee a few will survive to carry on the species."

Randall understood the analogy. He wanted to hear how the long-term concerns affected him. "You going to say I can't be a dad."

"No, no, no. I read where Dr. Campbell prescribed medication to boost your count. If you took it, it hasn't produced the desired result. That's not uncommon. Let's give your body time to react. I'd suggest you stop the medication and return in six months. You can have sex, no problem. I'd remind you to make it safe sex."

"Anything else?" Randall resigned himself to listen.

"No. You're in good health. I'll be sending a copy of my findings to Dr. Campbell within the week. My pleasure to have met you." Dr. Jones clapped his folder closed and departed.

On his way to the corridor exit, the nurse shot Randall an uneasy smile when he squeezed up against the wall to let her pass.

Randall called Wanda to inform her he'd be at home to write a *New Romance Delights* investor report. Eager to calm his hunger pangs, he tossed his briefcase with

Wanda's research and calculations onto his living room sofa.

While he microwaved a frozen turkey dinner, he straightened his refrigerator magnet reminder that Alicia had said yes.

* * *

Randall, two nights later, punched in cell phone numbers to give Jackson a shout. He figured enough time had passed for Jackson to forget his anger about Randall's refusal to hop a Pacific Island flight. If criticism ever penetrated Jackson's skin, Randall's experience demonstrated it never hitchhiked to his memory cells.

If only Randall could emulate his friend. How could he explain to the romance reader that an improperly placed comma threatened to destroy the world? Well, he couldn't. But correct punctuation usage still mattered to him. He'd written in an essay that words separated by small marks; a pen's dot, a squiggly line, or a bold stroke existed to make clear the meaning of time, place, and people. From the depths of his soul, he believed that.

"Hey, good buddy." Jackson's greeting culled from CB lingo. "Sky's sunny and the wind's calm here at poolside. How's your north wind tan?"

"Serious?" Randall heard a chuckle in the background. "I'm having a hard time contacting this Lady Victoria. I'm ready to chuck her entire manuscript into the river."

"Won't the ice bounce it back?" Randall heard large, boisterous, belly laughs interlaced with speakerphone static. "I'm still willing to applaud hula girls shaking South Pacific grass."

Jackson couldn't see Randall's head shake no. "That's water under the bridge."

"What if we took this story, risked a lawsuit, and

Donan Berg

proceeded full speed ahead?"

Randall stretched out on the couch and planted his stocking-covered feet on its arm. "Hollywood frowns on plagiarism and we need not risk our reputation."

"All I'm hearing is a bunch of nos." Jackson elevated his vocal pitch. "Enough business. How you doing as Charlotte's latest boy-toy?"

Randall swung his feet to the floor. "I'm not her boy-toy," he said through clenched teeth. He stood to regain his inner composure.

"Could have fooled me."

"Drop it." Randall buried his indignation in the mausoleum of unspoken words. One of these days he'd tell Jackson of Charlotte's confidential offer to help him start his own publishing company. She mentioned no strings, however, he'd be naïve to believe no strings attached to a risky and substantial investment. His medical history would be a non-issue. He imagined the older Charlotte harbored no inner desire to nursemaid a child and crimp her lifestyle.

"Yo, Randall. You still there?" Jackson repeated his shout out a third time.

"Yeah. Had trouble with a beer cap. You know those foreign brews."

"Flimsy excuse. No intent to upset you by mentioning Charlotte. Better you than me."

"What?" Randall didn't comprehend what Jackson referred to.

"Based on what I've heard, being her boy-toy has risks. Count her husband funerals. She fits any black widow definition to a T."

Randall coughed. "Have read nothing suspicious in her past marital relationships."

"Dude. Think. Not one but three husbands dead before old age."

"Let's not talk about Charlotte. I've kept my distance. Soon she'll be wintering south of you in San Diego. Does

87

she have your address?"

Randall chuckled. *Him, Charlotte's boy-toy? Never.* Even if his address comment was snarky, Jackson needed to be kept on his toes.

"Truce?"

"Until next time, Jackson. Remember, I find my own dates."

"Yes, boy-toy."

Randall tightened his jaw and refused to respond to Jackson's dig.

"A dip of my little piggies in the pool might inspire a new project. This life without promotion kills me. 'Til the Monsters of the Midway trounce your Vikings."

"As my neighbors would say, ya sure you betcha."

* * *

Alicia exited the downtown Minneapolis bus into a football fan fervor an hour before Mr. Van Gilleran's expected arrival. The Bunyan Exposition Center towered above her. Her blue jeans, wool sweater, and calf-length black boots insufficient to warm her October-chilled bones without Joel's shoulder-to-thighs official Minnesota Vikings' NFL jacket. On any day not a Sunday game day, she'd stick out like a lost tomboy. Today her to-and-fro pacing blended in, steps invisible in the purple and white blur.

She eased her jaw line. Even if she still owed Joel a post-fire rescue favor, she satisfied Vicky's request to humor Joel by wearing the heavy-duty hooded-jacket.

A distant blue speck, perhaps three blocks away, advanced toward her. In a minute it would be too late to change her mind. Around her the exuberant chants, painted faces, and Chicago Bear taunts filled the air. The excitement a thousand times greater than she had ever experienced before her parents' TV.

Alicia's pulse rate spiked when she spotted a late model, midnight blue, Lincoln ease into the posted fifteen-minute delivery zone. She waved, focused her eyes straight ahead, and strode forward. The gaiety in Mr. Van Gilleran's eyes loosened her taut nerves. His frown and deep brow furrow evident Friday after she'd declined his offer to pick her up at home no where seen. He circled his car's hood and stood ready at the rear passenger curbside door. His left hand gestured for her to slide in.

Alicia ducked her head to hear "Hello, darling."

A stunned Alicia dragged her eyeballs from Mr. Van Gilleran to mutter "Good morning." She sank into the rear leather seat before she gazed at Ms. Charlotte Hauser. Alicia first noted the absence of a feathery hat, however, Ms. Hauser impressed her with an outfit of leather slacks, silk blouse, and a waist-length, faux-leather coat. On closer inspection, Alicia decided the coat was authentic cowhide, not a manmade leather imitation. Her suede leather mid-calf boots sported two-inch heels.

Mr. Grant from the front's "shotgun" seat twisted his head rearward. "You ladies comfortable? Hope so. Us'ens here in the front seat don't need to have our butts toasted by dialed-up heated seats. Right, Randall?"

"Sorry," Mr. Van Gilleran said. "Seats preprogrammed for January's Super Bowl Sunday."

Alicia didn't believe she could add anything intelligent to the front seat banter. It reminded her of not butting in when her brother George entertained his male friends at home. Ms. Hauser shrugged and displayed her hands, palms up.

"Hey, good buddy." Mr. Grant pointed to the rearview mirror. "You didn't tell me we had to ring the football re-education class bell today."

He shifted his torso right to glance past his left shoulder. His gaze bored in on Alicia. She grasped that Mr. Grant's jacket, with its blue and orange colors visible at the shoulders, probably had a Chicago Bears tie-in. Her

89

sleeves radiated purple and white. A golden Vikings logo adorned her parka's breast pocket.

Alicia perceived no chill in Mr. Grant's stare, but his prior eye twinkle hibernated. He must have considered her traitor for he shifted his gaze and conversation to Mr. Van Gilleran. "Bears need a victory today to salvage a terrible season. Their new quarterback, Cutler, the Bears shelled out big bucks for, won't play to equal an injured Favre. Rex's flop leaves a bad taste."

"Why should these nice ladies know, or care about, any of that? If they spoke up, I bet they'd say forget the stats and strategy. And don't ask. Let's wait and enjoy the game."

Caught between siding with Mr. Van Gilleran and offending Mr. Grant, Alicia internalized her thank you that Mr. Grant hadn't asked her a question to expose her deficient football knowledge. A silent Ms. Hauser gazed left out the Lincoln's side window until she poked Alicia's shoulder. "We're here," she said.

Charcoal fumes and an array of mingling food aromas bombarded Alicia's nostrils as soon as she pushed her car door away from her seat. Brats and steaks sizzled, hissed, and sputtered on grill grates. The smoky haze may have warmed the stadium's forty degree parking lot, but Alicia's exposed pores failed to notice.

Unzipped coats exposed both men to be wearing blue jeans topped by official, numbered jerseys—one Vikings, one Bears. While glad she opted for jeans, Joel's parka hid her bunched waist cinched by her new smaller belt.

Alicia considered Ms. Hauser, who clung to Mr. Van Gilleran's side, overdressed.

When Mr. Grant shed his parka and zigzagged in his No. 23 Bears jersey toward the stadium, the three of them followed. Alicia struggled to avoid collisions with tailgaters chasing each other or thrown footballs. Mr. Grant slowed twice to wave to two Chicago-fan clusters .

Alicia voiced no displeasure with the decision not to

tailgate. Her right hand thumb pressed her ticket to her fingers unsure if she'd be asked to display it again to a lower concourse Metrodome usher. Charlotte squeezed between her and Mr. Van Gilleran to rest her hand on his shoulder as Mr. Grant asked each what they wished to eat and drink. Alicia's head swiveled to absorb the event's spirit, even if unconnected bits and pieces of conversation swirled.

Ms. Hauser's tilted head blocked Alicia's eye contact with Mr. Van Gilleran. Rather than be rude and interrupt, she listened to Ms. Hauser's impressive knowledge of community figures and organizations. Mr. Grant's return with a drink carrier stacked with wrapped burgers and fries signaled the start of their pilgrimage to their thirty-yard-line seats. He requested the women sit in the two outside seats.

Mr. Grant, at her right elbow, kept imploring her to call him Jackson. She replied in kind and requested he call her Ally. While surprised at Mr. Grant's attention, she appreciated his game explanations and Joel would be impressed she had a direct view of the Vikings' bench. If Vicky limited her distractions to timeouts, perhaps Joel saw his parka on TV. A now and then glance occasioned by a long pass on the field found Mr. Van Gilleran's hand clasped by Ms. Hauser. Twice Ms. Hauser leaned close to whisper into his ear.

Alicia tried to root for both teams. The seesaw game caused Alicia to be yelled at by a Vikings' fan when she cheered a Chicago TD. Mr. Grant's glare in the shouter's direction quelled the incident. He jumped and hollered along with Bears fans throughout the stadium as the fourth quarter expired with Chicago leading the Vikings 24-22.

A jubilant Jackson high-fived Bear fans all the way through the concourse and into the parking lot. Mr. Van Gilleran muttered over and over: "We'll return the favor at Soldier Field. Wait and see."

One Paper Heart

Mr. Van Gilleran's bypass of the I-35 downtown exit revived Alicia's jitters. No one had mentioned after-game activities. When he asked her for her home address, Alicia hesitated. *Will it expose me as Lady Dash?* How could she be so foolish? She didn't need Mr. Van Gilleran digging through her personnel record.

"Take the exit to South Minneapolis. Second stop light, turn left."

Mr. Van Gilleran parked curbside at her apartment building's lobby entrance. Alicia noted his gentleman courtesy to open the rear door for her. He surprised her with a friendly hug while he said thank you at least twice. Alicia's thank you words stuck in her throat until a raspy rendition finally emerged. A split-second wink graced his emergent smile until he whispered, "You shouldn't have cheered so loud for the Bears."

His remark conflicted her. Did he think she favored Mr. Grant? Her seat next to Mr. Grant hadn't been her decision. She'd tried to be neutral, fair to each team even though she wore Joel's Vikings parka. Her widened lips uttered no words; her heart-pumped blood gorged and warmed her cheek's capillaries. Mr. Van Gilleran's pivot to circle his car's rear bumper gave her no chance to steady her complex emotions. Alicia halted her two-step retreat to wave good-bye to Mr. Grant and Ms. Hauser.

It didn't trouble her she saw no hand movement behind any Lincoln window. Neither did she wish to dwell on the warmth buildup trapped beneath Joel's parka. She twice flapped Joel's unzipped parka on the elevator ride to her apartment. Her failure to lower her skin temperature attested to her realization she didn't require Joel's parka to warm her.

Alicia let the parka hang loose as she crossed her apartment's exposed threshold. Vicky jumped up from the sofa. "Tell me about the game?" Vicky's balance shifted from her right foot to her left and back again as she swayed. "The TV cameras didn't catch you."

92

"It was fun." Alicia slipped her scanned game ticket from Joel's lower parka pocket. Unlike the woman's office party, she'd stayed with Coke while Ms. Hauser and the men drank beer. Yet, the bottled-up energy required not to let it slip she was Lady Victoria Dash left her feeling half-tipsy. For the first time since Mr. Van Gilleran's game mention her nerves relaxed.

"C'mon. That's limp. Spill the beans. So, who was your date?"

"Don't know and that's the truth." She fit Joel's parka on a hanger, hooked it on a rod inside the front closet and trailed Vicky to a breakfast counter stool. She explained her excitement from the Metrodome parking lot to the game's end, which included her sitting next to Mr. Grant. To her surprise her voice didn't creak when she added Mr. Van Gilleran's drop-off hug.

Vicky slid forward on her stool. "That's a good first step."

"What?" Alicia's right hand gripped the counter's edge.

"The hug."

"He was just being nice. Lots of people hug. It's a conditioned reflex in many families."

Vicky smiled coyly. "He wouldn't have if he hated you. Significant that Mr. Grant never left the car. You said he was in the car, right?"

"Yeah. Texting buddies in California about the game, I think."

"Joel loves football, but he wouldn't totally ignore me."

"Where is Joel anyway?" She expected his repeated visits made him their newest fixture.

"Said he has an early morning report. You can fill him in later." Vicky winked. "Remember your promise. Was the fourth one of those buxom cover models?"

"Dream on. It was a woman who's written novels for *New Romance Delights*." Alicia rose to reach into a kitchen cabinet for a water glass. "Seems pretty close to my boss." She filled her glass from the tap. "Her name's Charlotte Hauser."

"I've heard of her. She's old." Alicia raised her eyebrows. "If you put your mind to it, you can edge her out. Besides, you're to be a published author soon yourself, right?"

"Don't know." Resignation edged Alicia's words. "Ms. Hauser's awful rich."

"And wrinkled. Don't you forget that."

"Stop it. It's not nice to be catty."

"Chill. You gotta think positive. From what you've said about this Mr. Van Gilleran he's probably awash in strong swimmers. He'll give you that thirteenth chromosome you'll need to diaper those multiple kids." Alicia grabbed a dishtowel to hide her face as Vicky continued. "This next week we're going to Dayton's to get you fitted for one or two wow outfits. The world will notice your new curves."

"Oh, I don't know." Alicia's weak protest didn't square with her desire.

"Yes, you do. You need a book cover photograph. Think business expense."

* * *

A Thursday edition of the CBS Evening News cast streaks of light on Randall's stockinged feet as he stirred a one-dish microwave entree. He muted his condo's TV to listen to the first of four phone messages, a reference request by Jose. Randall hit the redial button and promised Jose he'd do it within the week. He reviewed and deleted the three solicitations.

His disquiet raged. He retrieved and plunked his aspirin bottle on the kitchen table next to his half-eaten dinner. Four hours hadn't elapsed since he'd swallowed two 200mg pills. He paced and debated without resolution whether his headaches were transient or symptomatic of an underlying illness undiagnosed by Dr. Jones.

He pressed his cell's contact list and selected Jackson. "Good buddy. What's up?"

"Office gossip today said you sent Alicia a Chicago Bears football jersey. You trying, behind my back, to subvert my receptionist when she showed great taste in football apparel?"

"I'm confused about her."

"How?" Randall plopped into a dining table chair.

"In your office she's dressed like a peasant. At the game, it's not high-society clothing, but she showed class—jacket excluded—with a figure I wouldn't have believed she possessed. She treated me nice. The jersey only said thank you. Why did it offend her?"

"Not that I know. When I mentioned the game in passing, she evaded all mention of either you or Charlotte." The back of Randall's left hand shoved his entree dish aside. "I'd guess she took your gift to be more than a thank you."

"Why, you eyeing her? You invited her; used me as a decoy?"

"Quit it. I'd never on purpose subvert our friendship." Randall hoped he hadn't been misunderstood. Limited to office females and no outside date options, Wanda, his last resort, would've been awkward.

"Now you're being coy. This is Jackson, remember? The Jackson who boasts of ESP. I picked up on your words 'on purpose.' We've known each other too long."

Randall eschewed teasing his friend. Their screenplay stakes escalated with each passing week and he'd not cracked the nut of finding Lady Victoria. Nor had Jackson suggested a viable original idea. He still waited for a reply to his Thursday letter to Lady Victoria's submission envelope's return address. "Alicia also

impressed me at the Vikings' game. Sorry, Bears' game."
He had to be straight with Jackson. "First time I've seen
her outside the office. Will agree Alicia dresses like she's
hiding herself and doesn't, like Charlotte, talk fashion
past boring."

Jackson laughed. "I lost Charlotte's invitation to one
of her charity functions."

It reminded Randall he'd escorted Charlotte to her
fund-raiser for disadvantaged kids. Lucky for him
Charlotte believed his migraine headache excuse to beg
off a nightcap at her place.

Satisfied his disclaimer convinced Jackson he
harbored no designs on Alicia, Randall hung up. He
forsook two aspirin to uncap a Hamm's and channel
surfed until boredom drove him into his pajamas. When
his landline phone rang, Randall crossed his right fingers
into a sign language R that Jackson would buoy his spirits
with an original screenplay idea.

A dejected Randall sank into his sofa cushions. "Yes,
Mother. Haven't forgotten your Thanksgiving Day
invitation." He separated his ear from the receiver on her
third repetition of his need to bring a guest. He
understood by implication his mother meant a young
woman of marriageable age and disposition. "Said I'd
try."

"Excuses won't do. You must do more than try."

"Yes, Mother." He again promised Mother his
determined effort to bring a guest before he rattled his
phone's handset into its cradle.

Stretched out on his mattress, Randall tossed and
turned. He didn't have the heart to tell his mother her
desire for him to remarry and bless her with
grandchildren likely wouldn't happen now that the
medical specialists had confirmed his pencil lacked a
little lead. A stronger fear engulfed him when Dr. Jones's
long-term cancer prognosis surfaced from his
subconscious like pinpoint hesitant bubbles in a pan full

of water resting on a burner dialed to boil.

* * *

Distracted by worry pangs and the fatigue of mind numbing submissions, Randall initiated a midmorning coffee shortcut through reception. An unexpected vision reined in his step. He gawked at a bent forward Alicia near the far wall visitor chairs. She wore tight-fitting white slacks and a tucked in psychedelic, multi-colored top. From the rear her hairstyle reminded him of former First Lady Jackie Kennedy.

"Alicia."

She jumped. A magazine dropped to the floor. She faced him. "Mr. Van Gilleran, didn't hear you enter. Needed to switch last month's magazines." She gazed at the floor.

Perhaps Jackson sensed something he failed to see. "I know this is the office, but if only you and me, please call me Randall." He watched her eye her desk without a hint of what concerned her. "If you would, I'd appreciate it very much."

"I haven't been a receptionist long. Only wish to do what's proper."

"Don't worry." Wanda had repeatedly praised Alicia and he trusted Wanda's judgment. "From what I've heard and observed, you do a superb job. You were gracious to accept the football game invitation. If not a total football nut, Jackson is easily classified as a Chicago Bears fanatic." Alicia's miniature smile exposed white teeth at the center of her mouth's red lipstick but no words. "And, you handled it very well." Randall strained to be more profuse in his praise. While Beatrix Smothers was glib in print, rigidity controlled his interpersonal conversations.

Alicia's hands fussed with her wrists. She crossed and uncrossed her arms. First at her sides and then behind her back, he wanted to tell her to be calm, but didn't.

She mumbled, "Cannelton, Indiana, Lock & Dam."

"What?"

"Nothing. I tried to be polite. Never been to a professional football game." She glanced at her desk. "It's something I'll always remember . . . cherish."

Randall couldn't decide if he should leave. His stomach muscles cramped as he listened.

"Don't know how I can ever repay Mr. Grant for the ticket. Certainly can't send back the number fifty-four Bears jersey he FedExed." A mist clouded her eyes.

Could she be ready to cry? The answer evaded him. "You don't have to. It's his generous way to say thank you. However, if you wear his Bears jersey in my presence, you might cause me to rip it off you."

Alicia trembled at his words.

Randall regretted his word choice in an instant. It wasn't his desire to scare her. He readied his arms to hug her. No. That would create greater embarrassment. "I'm sorry." He lowered his hands to his side. "Nothing will happen to you. I only wanted to emphasize my being a Vikings' fan."

"I know." She sidled to his left, within an arm's length of her desk.

He retreated a full stride and sensed she hadn't relaxed. He'd have to tiptoe on eggshells. "Can I ask you a question."

"Yes." Her voice sounded barely audible.

Randall tried to mobilize his courage not to high-tail it to the elevator or slink away to the sanctity of his office. Conflicted, he hesitated.

Alicia alternated her stare between him and the office door.

His right hand fingers puffed his front pocket. He pondered a retreat. Any delay wouldn't be a capitulation as he surmised the future would offer another opportunity to speak to Alicia in private. At the worst, he'd end up eating Thanksgiving Day turkey at Charlotte's, if she didn't have a Radisson fund-raiser. He harbored no doubt his eating at Charlotte's would send her the wrong impression and ruin his life forever.

Alicia gazed at him; her lips stretched and the corners of her mouth drawn back.

"Do you remember my telling you I write books under the name Beatrix Smothers?"

Indecision flitted between Alicia's eyes. Her lips quivered when she said "Yes."

Randall stretched his shoulders to right his posture and avert the slump engendered by the hundred-pound boulder his mind lashed to his back. His every breath lapsed into a slow and labored gulp of perfumed air. "My parents don't know I do that." How childish he must sound.

Alicia's eyes widened to remind him of a Northern Minnesota doe caught in his vehicle headlights. She seized the lull that engulfed them to maneuver behind her desk. She stood relaxed, her hands steady. All hesitation clues now absent from her face. Her limp arms rested against her sides. Why hadn't his deductive powers realized Alicia felt more comfortable with a barrier between them? He added this to his collection of personal failures as Alicia answered the telephone and directed the call to Norma.

"My request may seem strange, even weird, but hear me out before you answer. Please?"

"Okay."

Randall relieved the taut muscle spasms that wrapped his spine and shoulders by a backward plop into a visitor chair. By the extra distance and his seated position, he hoped to signal Alicia he entertained no design to attack. He strived to be extra careful in how he phrased his question.

"Like most families at Thanksgiving, our family has a meal with turkey and all the trimmings." When Alicia sat, his buoyed spirit steadied his resolve. "My mother suggested I invite Beatrix Smothers." Alicia half-smiled. "Obviously, that's impossible since Beatrix and I are the same person. If I go alone, my mother will be shattered."

He watched his imagined frost curlicue melt from Alicia's face. "What about Wanda?"

"Won't do. Mother's met Wanda. All this may sound convoluted, but I'd appreciate it if you'd agree to accompany me to my parents' Thanksgiving Day dinner as Beatrix Smothers." Randall's slow exhale released his trapped tension. He thanked God no one had entered reception.

"You want me to lie to your parents?" Her voice gained more strength and volume than necessary to traverse the increased distance between them. That wasn't the spin Randall desired. He discarded his practiced twisted syntax to flat-out deny her honest interpretation. Alicia didn't lack common-sense intelligence, and he'd insult her if he responded as if she did.

"Perhaps a superficial reading casts that meaning." Alicia's eyes kept their cool. Her hands didn't grip a heavy object to be tossed at him. "However, I'd like to think of it as helping an officemate out of a jam, or a day on the theater stage." His right hand rubbed his cheek. Laughable villains on Matlock reruns tried to convince viewers of their innocence by stronger rationales. "It won't hurt anyone and you'd make my parents jubilant."

If Alicia asked why his mother demanded he bring Beatrix, there was no torture or wily inducement on earth strong enough to make him reveal the real truth. Anticipation's electrical charge sparked his heartbeat to new heights as Alicia's gaze painted the ceiling with languid brushstrokes. The panic in Randall's chest expected Alicia's elongated silence sealed his doom. Four times he held his breath and doubted his survival if he tried a fifth to await her eye contact.

Donan Berg

Alicia's lips twitched. "The only thing I would have to do is . . ."

Yes, but what could she be thinking?

Her lips twitched again. "Impersonate . . . impersonate a female author with the name of Beatrix for a two-hour dinner?"

"Yes." The word raced off the launch pad of his tongue. His heart skipped a beat. Had he sounded sincere? Would she accept his idea? Or, was her calculation how to be nice and say no. He was at her mercy, her total and complete mercy.

"But I know nothing about what she's written or published." She clapped her right hand to her mouth and let it drop. "Sorry, guess you'd know that."

He accented her halted chuckle with a polite laugh. His Hail Mary request required he bolster Alicia's charm and composure with the confidence necessary to pull off his charade. Was she teasing him? Getting even for his criticism of her cheers for Jackson's Bears? His choice to expose his need left him vulnerable. Boxed in by his desire to appease his mother, he let Alicia know he lived as a thirty-one-year-old mama's boy. He choked his pride. "I'll get you the latest three novels. To help you feel at ease, I'll type up a two-page outline to distill each novel's storyline and to highlight the pivotal characters."

Alicia rubbed the back of her left hand with her right. "What about her book picture?"

Boy, was she smart. "None's ever been published on any book flap. She's always been described as twenty-nine, attractive, and extremely talented. You'd be a natural."

Alicia blushed and gazed left.

She must think I'm a flirt at best or a kook at worst. Why had he thought this a good idea? If he showed up stag to the family Thanksgiving dinner what could his mother really do? His low sperm count remained a medical pity card option. No. Mother fawned over

101

grandkids and needed to maintain her hope he'd catch up
with his brother.

"What about Beatrix's prior life, where she lives,
etc.?"

"If you're positive about doing this . . ." Randall
chastised himself for letting his anxiety escape.
"Misspoke, not you, but I'm positive we'll figure
everything out. With Beatrix's books you'll be able to
read what scant information has been written about her
personal life. It's all very generic. Since you've lived in
the Twin Cities, you're familiar enough to . . ." He caught
the word "lie" in his throat. "Ah, . . . adlib an answer to
any question. With my Dad or brother you can talk about
watching Vikings football at the Metrodome."

"You told your parents we went to the football
game?" She renewed her stare.

"Heavens no." He tried not to overreact to her frown.
"Used the Metrodome as an example of how easy your
conversation can be. Dad loves . . ." Randall bit his
tongue. He had no intention of a second jersey faux pas in
forty minutes. "Dad'll talk football for hours if you let
him. You'd not have to say anything."

A smile crept onto the edges of Alicia's lips. He'd
exaggerated his father's willingness to speak about any
topic except paint formulas. Randall regretted his lapse
into white lies. They weren't supports to his belief in
Alicia's ability to excel in his charade. She didn't have to
be put on guard against his greatest fear—Mother's
efforts to entangle their lives?

"If you swear to me here and now that you've not
mentioned this Beatrix to your parents, other than being a
writer here, I'll agree to help you."

Randall grabbed the arms of his chair lest he tumble
to the floor. He prayed her acceptance would last. "I
swear." His right hand executed an X on his chest. "Cross
my heart and hope to die." His heart raced, banged his rib
cage twice before his hands pushed his body erect. "I'll

get those books for you."

"Just so you know. I won't back out, but I've never done this kind of thing before. I might rue my saying 'yes' for the rest of my life." Alicia swiveled in her chair.

Randall forgot about coffee and sauntered closer to the reception exit door that led to his office. "I'll do everything in my power to protect you."

"Another question. You won't push food down my throat all Thanksgiving Day?"

He failed to understand the question's importance. Mother's Thanksgiving always meant food, lots of food. "You can eat as much or as little as you like. I'll make it a point to stand between you and my mother. What can I say? She's a typical mother. She guilts people to eat."

"It's agreed. I'll be Beatrix Smothers . . . for this Thanksgiving Day. Don't expect an encore. And, swear it's only between you and me. If I hear even one word of office gossip, the deal's off, absolutely no deal."

"This is definitely between you and me. I'll forever be in your debt." Randall ran his right hand over his hair. A greater power blessed him this day. He blurted out, "You really look nice today."

"Thank you." Alicia avoided his gaze. "Okay if I ask more questions later?"

Renewed panic rained on him head to toe. Randall's right hand rubbed his eyebrows lest his anguish be exposed. He'd been selfish not to ask a question that, if it came to Alicia, would likely crash his entire plan. His gaze floated past the crown of her head. "Will you be missing out on your family's Thanksgiving?"

"No. Our family always celebrates on Friday. Someone always had to travel. To delay the turkey carving one day has become our logical alternative."

"I'm relieved. I should've asked first." He shifted his gaze to reception's office door. "Better get back before Wanda sends out a search party." Pleased Alicia again smiled, he departed.

103

Later that afternoon, he left three books, all authored by one Beatrix Smothers, on NRD's reception desk with no explanatory note. He would've liked to thank Alicia, but it wasn't to be.

Randall closed his office door ten minutes before the office closed when his cell's caller ID listed his mother. "Mother, I can't understand a word you're saying."

"It's all so horrible, horrible, just horrible."

"If you continue babbling . . ." He halted his chastisement for he understood it wouldn't stop her crying.

"Mrs. Johansen telephoned. Mia's been murdered in Phoenix."

"When? How?"

"Don't know. It's all so horrible . . ."

Randall offered his sole alternative. "Call me tonight. I'll be home."

Mother promised and Randall punched "end."

He pressed his forehead to his desktop. His eyes remained dry. He started a silent "Our Father who art in heaven . . ."

Chapter Eight

Alicia groaned to ward off the reality of her blaring bedroom radio: "Everyone needs to bundle up for the morning commute. Ladies, it's a skirt alert day. Expect wind gusts to thirty miles per hour. Light snow blowing and drifting."

Half awake, Alicia heard Vicky stir, or rather, bang an aluminum kettle with its lid—unofficial signal Alicia had better hustle to the bathroom or lose her turn. She grabbed her dangling robe belt and tapped her right hand fingers on the breakfast counter as she passed. Vicky, her hands filled with a roaster pan and its lid, asked, "You free this Saturday?"

Alicia challenged her roommate. "You know the answer to that."

"Good. We can double date. Joel wants to introduce you to a friend. Nothing fancy. Movie at the mall, and something to eat after."

"Tell me more tonight. I'll be awake by then." Alicia closed the bathroom door.

She ignored the apartment telephone ring.

"Ally," Vicky shouted.

One Paper Heart

Alicia cracked the bathroom door. "What?"

"Your father's on the phone. He says it's important."

She refastened her robe and picked up the handset left by Vicky. "Hello, Dad."

"Had hoped you might visit. Two or three letters addressed to a Lady Victoria Dash arrived here. Two from *New Romance Delights*. Your mother remembers at least one call."

"Hold on to the letters." Alicia tried to restrain her excitement. "I'll take the bus after work to pick them up, if that's all right?"

"Of course it is. Everything okay at work?" Foreboding tinged Dad's voice.

"Fine, just fine." She hadn't anticipated a letter from her employer raised the specter her parents would assume bad things.

"Don't eat. We'll set a supper plate for you."

"Thanks, Dad. I love you." She racked the handset into its kitchen cradle.

From behind her, Vicky's plaintive voice asked, "Everything okay?"

Alicia turned. "Fine." Her response insufficient to ease her roommate's lower eyelid tension. "Parents received letters in response to my novel. Told Dad I'd visit after work." Vicky's eye corners remained drawn back. "The bathroom's yours in a couple minutes."

"What if it snows?"

"Dad will give me a ride if it's too late for the bus. If the snow's bad, I'll stay with them."

Alicia hated to wear her heavy snow boots. It meant she'd have to carry an extra pair of shoes in a bag. Vicky always claimed a shoe bag provided mugger protection. She referred to it as a double pump punch. Alicia hustled to wrap herself for the outdoors.

A gusty wind buffeted her outside her apartment's lobby door. Her long dress and high boots protected her legs from exposure. On the walk to the bus stop, a bowed

106

head shielded her face from the sting of miniature wind-driven ice particles. From her frost-edged bus window, she read a TCF Bank sign flash twenty-eight degrees.

No messages left with the three Beatrix Smothers novels on her desk generated a healthy sigh of relief. She locked two novels and her purse in a lower right drawer and went to Wanda's desk to say good morning.

"You'll probably feel like you're on vacation." Wanda's eyes twinkled.

"Huh?"

"Boss won't be in. No rush today to get the submissions processed."

"Mr. Van Gilleran ill?"

"Out of town, family matter."

Alicia left it there. She trusted Wanda, ten years her senior, like a sister. A silver framed picture of Wanda, a taller husband, Dale, and two, darling grade-school-age girls sat propped at an angle on Wanda's desk. "I'll keep my reception celebration quiet and subdued."

"Great idea to read the boss's work." Wanda flashed a right thumbs up. "Sure you have no gene mutation to be a novelist?"

"Nooooo. See you at lunch."

Alicia set Beatrix's novel aside to bore herself with e-mails and telephone answering. Greetings to the letter carrier split her morning's boredom. She read Beatrix's first chapter. If an author fictionalized his real life experiences, Randall's words weren't those of D.H. Lawrence. But then, she had no interest other than to rattle off Beatrix's words to a Thanksgiving audience she expected may not have read more than the first.

She added the unfinished novel to the other two. Alicia paused at Wanda's empty desk on her trip to the office lunch table. Her heart skipped a beat.

A queasy feeling twisted Alicia's stomach into knots.

She spied a single, red paper heart point exposed at the bottom edge of a thick manila file folder next to

Wanda's family photo.

This can't be my heart.

She hadn't seen her submission since the morning of its arrival nor been required to create a rejection letter. Childish willies and gigantic streams of negative energy crashed against her cranial walls.

Her legs didn't move. Didn't Dad mention receipt of more than one letter? Alicia rejected a telephone call to her mother. *Calm down. Think positive.* She released a cleansing breath.

Alicia convinced herself that worry lacked the power to solve anything.

Silly to believe a red paper heart ruled her life. Better to forget it. Who's to know? The paper heart on Wanda's desk might not be hers. Didn't Hallmark and Wal-Mart shower the world with paper hearts like hers? Coincidences occur every day. Yet, she didn't, like now, experience a bout of light-headedness every day.

What if Wanda saw her? How underhanded had her silence been when Wanda expressed the belief that only wannabe authors applied to work at *New Romance Delights?* How many lies transformed a pure soul into pitch tar?

Right! Her heart's black scar.

Alicia stretched her torso forward, careful not to knock over Wanda's photo. A black metal clip along the folder's side secured its contents. As far as she could see, no visible mark existed on the red heart. Had the black mark been higher? Alicia's memory collapsed without an answer.

"You joining us for lunch?"

Alicia gulped. The fear of being exposed red-handed cascaded in a tumultuous rush from her throat. She eased her rotation toward Wanda's voice. "You really have a great family. Give me a second. I'll meet you at the table."

Alicia sat silent and conversationally isolated from

Donan Berg

Norma, Carol, and Wanda as they tried to best each other with the funny antics of their children. She stabbed and devoured pickled beets to prevent their reddish juice invasion into her tuna fish mound.

"You must like beets to have that many," Norma said.

"Not really. Refrigerator this morning resembled Old Mother Hubbard's cupboard. These emptied my roommate's jar."

When Wanda touched on Thanksgiving, Alicia said she'd be going to her parents as usual and passed the table discussion to Norma. If Alicia was to be fair to Mr. Van Gilleran about her threat to cancel if there was office gossip, it was a second reason she didn't dare speak of her duplicate Thanksgiving Day plans.

Her plastic knife pushed her last tuna fish tidbit onto a rye crisp. She glanced at the red heart folder on Wanda's desk as she retreated to reception. Her workday couldn't end soon enough.

* * *

Alicia's chill subsided when she boarded the jam-packed red No. 25 bus at Ninth Street and the Nicollet Mall. Her what's-in-the-letters anxiety crested when she approached her childhood home. She loved the one and a half-story house her adoptive parents brought her to as an eighteen-month-old infant. From its big upstairs bedroom dormer, she had watched the front street maples bud and green in the spring and again bare their branches when Mother Nature and snowplows buried parked cars. The big green script D on the living room's white metal awning always sparked her joy of a homecoming welcome.

"Mom, great to see you." Alicia dropped her shoe bag on the dark green vestibule carpet square to give her mother a big hug before she slipped out of her boots.

109

One Paper Heart

Alicia's parents, John and Myrna Danielson, and her younger brother, Alan, seventeen and a high school senior, lived in the house. Older brother, George, thirty-five and a career U.S. Navy petty officer, sailed the high seas. Her older sister, Elena, thirty-eight, lived with her husband and two youngsters in Shakopee, a Twin Cities suburb. All had been adopted although not informed until age sixteen.

The kitchen door creaked—a distinctive squeak Alicia never forgot. With ease she skirted the eat-in kitchen's table. The two expansion leaves for the table that sat eight removed and stored in the basement until needed for holidays and family celebrations. She reserved Dad's hug until he placed a pan of Lund's carryout lasagna on a counter. Fresh snowflakes clung to his green parka-clad shoulders like epaulets.

"Great to see you, Precious." As long as Alicia could remember, Dad called her and Elena precious. She attributed his brief extended-arm hug to his not wanting to drip snow on her neck.

He gazed at Mom. "Plant tension's rising. Falling car sales threaten more layoffs. Say a prayer President Obama's stimulus works."

Mom gazed at her and shrugged. Alicia suspected Mom had heard Dad's worry many times.

"Dear, Alicia's hungry. Wash up and we'll set the table for supper."

Alicia excused herself to shove her stockinged feet into shoes and hang up her coat. She wanted to rush to Dad's office desk to find her letters. The first floor room had once been Alan's bedroom until her departure for college. He then moved into the larger upstairs bedroom she had shared with Elena. Alan's old bedroom transformed into Mom's sewing room with Dad's desk moved up from the basement. Alicia couldn't be selfish. She returned to the kitchen. Mom loved to have her there, even if Alicia didn't stir a pot or add an ingredient. She rattled an oven rack and accepted the lasagna from Mom's hands.

"Where's Alan?" Alicia envisioned her brother, like her, to one day be a college graduate. As with her, she expected her parents to bridge the shortfall between student loans, scholarships, and part-time jobs.

"Basketball practice. I'll save him a plate in the oven once the lasagna's heated. George wrote last week that the Navy's activated new communication setups for sailors to e-mail and send pictures via the Internet. Don't mention it to Dad."

"Why?" Alan still used her old Packard Bell computer with Windows 3.1 and no updated browser for his school writing projects.

"He's not keen on either a new computer or paying for Internet. You should call him for supper."

Alicia did and Dad strode into the kitchen in khaki trousers and a blue plaid shirt. He hugged her. "Do you need a ride after supper?"

"Would be nice. Rode the bus from downtown." Alicia set a place setting in front of her father plus three others. She sat, lasagna spatula in hand, while her mother sliced aromatic warm garlic bread.

"You find any teaching job?" Dad asked. Mom picked a lint piece off his flannel shirt shoulder seam. His eyebrows lifted, but he stayed silent and poured milk.

"After Christmas I'll be putting together a new application package for next fall, or summer school, if there's an opening that will carry forward."

Mom carried the lasagna from the oven. "How's your job downtown?"

"Like it so far. I've met nice people. Publishing on the inside isn't as glamorous as it looks on the outside. Never would've believed the number of writers trying to get a book published."

"Your mail's on my desk," Dad said.

"Thanks. I'll take it with when I leave. Any big

111

envelopes?"

"One. Said calendar inside." Dad's two hands balanced a full plate handed to him by Mom.

Dad's news made it easier for Alicia to eat. "Can I ask about next week's Thanksgiving?" Neither parent spoke. "We still celebrating with turkey on Friday?"

"Nothing's changed," Mom said. "I've gotten notes from Uncle Frank, Aunt Agnes, and a couple of Dad's cousins. They're all coming as usual. Don't you get the day off?"

"Yes. I'll be here. On Thursday I'm invited to a coworker's holiday dinner. I agreed on the condition it didn't conflict."

"We going to meet this guy sometime?" Dad asked, a twinkle in his right eye. Alicia raised a napkin to hide her face. Her peek caught Mom's glare at Dad.

"You ignore your Dad. He wants you to bring home a new guy so he can forget the one you last brought home three years ago. You accept your friend's invitation. Meet new people. It's good for you to get out."

Dad chuckled. "Yeah, he was some hippie."

Mom shook her head and busied herself eating.

"He wasn't a hippie," Alicia retorted. "Any guy with head hair that touches his ears you label a hippie. He taught humanities."

"Where's he now?"

"Last I heard he received a Harvard scholarship to study for his PhD."

"Didn't get good vibes from him. Half the time I couldn't understand those big words he used and he knew nothing about sports."

Alicia ignored Dad. She passed Mom the bread with the hope the silent interval avoided further parental prying into her social life.

"Aunt Agnes said you and she enjoyed lunch."

"We did, Mom." Mom's comment confirmed Mom played at least a supporting role to Aunt Agnes. Alicia sucked in her stomach muscles. Her try abandoned when the muscles failed to touch her spine. "Every server at the restaurant seemed to know her."

"Her second son, Edward, works as a late night cook there you know."

"She didn't mention that."

"Not even Edward's bowling team friend. The friend's a teacher."

Alicia tightened and relaxed her stomach muscles. In cahoots. Ever connivers. That's what Mom and Aunt Agnes were. "No Edward, no friend, no teacher. Let's drop the entire subject."

"Your mother wishes only the best for you."

Mom cleared her throat and then rose. Her frown, at Alicia's glance, transformed to a smile.

"Me, too," Dad added.

Ready to refuse dessert to maintain her diet, Alicia relented to a two-inch square of blueberry cobbler, her favorite. Not to be rude, Alicia, knowing that a second piece would feed three to four, permitted Mom to wrap a piece for Vicky. Her mother added it to the plastic bag Dad brought in from his home office.

The three then retired to the living room to watch "Wheel of Fortune" until Alan's arrival.

Alicia's fingers itched to untie the plastic bag. By its weight, she knew it didn't contain her Lady Victoria manuscript. She speculated it had to be somewhere in the *New Romance Delights* office, separated from her red paper heart.

Trapped in the purgatory of her own deceit, Alicia's brain flunked the TV game show puzzles. She rejoiced when Alan's update on his basketball exploits amused her well past eight. When Dad offered to warm up his Taurus, Alicia excused herself for a bathroom visit.

Alicia gaped in horror at the red-tinted toilet bowl water. She hadn't cut herself and it was way too early for her period. A shout for Mom wasn't an option. Three deep breaths calmed her nerves. No abdominal pain racked or rippled her midsection. She hurried to powder her upper lip sheen, nose, and cheeks.

She hugged Alan and Mom good-bye in the vestibule and carried her cobbler and mail toward Dad's Taurus parked at the front curb. The car's whitish exhaust cloud foretold a temperature rise since her walk to the bus. The street glistened, streaked yellow by the sodium street lamps. Alicia counted the wetness a welcome blessing. Her father faced no ice-glazed pavement.

Once she and Dad were on their way, Alicia tiptoed into questions about Mom's health. She left unrepeated his recent fears about leaving Mom alone in the house. A decade previous Alicia had surreptitiously heard Dad and Aunt Agnes talk about her mother's near breakdown after the family doctor had explained she and Dad could never birth children. Alicia had asked her mother the why question while home for a college spring break. Mom had sobbed. Alicia swore off the subject forever. Dad hinted that his suggestion they adopt helped Mom cope.

"Your mother's having a hard time again. She shows more energy and thinks less of crying when she expects your visit."

Alicia bit her lip. Sister Elena, worried Mom would attempt a second suicide, had last month suggested they adopt a visit schedule. It had yet to be finalized. Alicia read Dad's furrowed forehead as an outward manifestation of his inner worry. "Has Mom quit her volunteering?"

"She still goes to the Ann Society Circle at church."

"What about sewing? You encouraged that."

"Most days, however, she'd rather entertain Elena's two children."

Alicia understood Mom's grandma status as a double-edged sword. The healthy grandkids brought immeasurable joy and a dark reminder to Mom of her repressed personal failure. "That's good. How's work?"

"Try to remember the good-old days."

Alicia tried to think of another subject to fill the last half of her trip home, but couldn't.

"Order came down from Ford's Detroit headquarters to layoff four."

She tried to be positive. "People will buy new cars."

"It's not only that. Robots have invaded my paint application department and outsourcing to Mexico lurks on the horizon. Lucky for me I'm closer to retirement than most."

"Isn't it easier to supervise a robot?" Her attempt to lighten the conversation bombed.

"There's no joy. But I'm old; you've your whole life ahead. I remember you loved teaching. You need to go back. Or, be like Elena and find yourself a good man."

She nodded. The exit off I-35 meant she needn't switch topics. Experience taught her Dad's dating advice limited to one mention per conversation. "Park and I'll walk myself to the lobby."

He leaned toward her. "Enjoy your Thanksgiving Day. Mom and I will expect to see you Friday morning."

"Thanks for the ride, Dad. Love you." She unbuckled her seatbelt.

"Come early. I'm sure Mom will appreciate your help. Each year it gets harder and harder for her. Her pride won't allow her to ask for help."

"I will. Have a safe trip. Give my love to Mom and Alan." She waved from the lobby entrance until his taillights disappeared. She gazed skyward. *Thank you, God, for a loving family.*

Alicia used her apartment's door key so as to sneak past Vicky to the privacy of her bedroom. She failed.

Vicky sat at the breakfast counter. Her face erupted with excitement. "Show me your acceptance letter. C'mon show me."

"Mail's unopened in the plastic bag with your cobbler dessert from Mom." Alicia scanned the living room. "Is

Joel here?"

"You must have missed him. I sent him out with the garbage." Vicky smirked. "He should be good for something."

Alicia aligned her boots next to the front door; hung her coat in the closet. She laid the bag on the breakfast counter and slowly tugged at its plastic knot.

Vicky peered over Alicia's shoulder. "Hurry up, I gotta breathe."

Alicia cast aside two letters as obvious junk mail. Two business-sized envelopes with a *New Romance Delights* return address remained. A last-month postmark stamped on both. She handed Vicky both letters. "You open them; I'm too nervous."

Puzzlement floated from Vicky's eyes. "Who's Lady Victoria?"

"Don't sweat it. Read the letter."

Vicky tore open the flap of the oldest postmarked letter and flattened the one-page, accordion-folded letter. She read aloud:

> *Dear Lady Victoria Dash,*
> *We have received your manuscript submission and, after an exhaustive reading, find it may have potential.*
> *As with many manuscripts, even by well-established authors, additional editing and formatting may be required.*
> *Please contact Mr. Randall Van Gilleran at your earliest convenience.*

Alicia's heart swelled with excitement. "Tear open the second envelope."

Vicky ripped and read aloud:

> *Dear Lady Victoria Dash,*
> *In follow-up to prior correspondence, we regret to inform you we have determined after a further review of "A Search Fulfilled" that your manuscript will not be in the spring*

quarter's publication schedule.

"Don't . . . don't read anymore," Alicia stammered. "They've rejected me." The weight of rejection number thirty-three slumped her shoulders. Alicia lowered her head and the breakfast counter chilled her forehead. She welcomed the discomfort.

Vicky's hands squeezed her shoulders. "Wait a sec. Don't cover your ears. Listen to this:

> *However, our acquisitions editor, Mr. Randall*
> *Van Gilleran, desires to speak with you at your*
> *earliest convenience, preferably at our*
> *downtown Minneapolis offices, to discuss*
> *a contract for the purchase of an exclusive option*
> *on your submitted manuscript.*
> *Mr. Van Gilleran hopes to hear from you soon to*
> *schedule a mutually convenient time to meet.*
> *Please telephone the above number.*

Alicia shivered and then shook. She pressed both her hands on the breakfast counter edge to steady her muscle twitches. She gasped for breath as her heart raced. She didn't know whether to cry or raise her arms and shout hallelujah to the seven seas. If she ran outside to grasp the streetlight post and kick up her heels, she'd scare the neighbors. Alicia continued to rest her head on folded arms. The counter no longer chilled her exposed skin.

A soft knock echoed from their apartment door. Vicky let Joel in.

"Alicia's going to be a published author. She got a letter from her boss."

"That's fantastic," Joel exclaimed. "We can celebrate Saturday?"

Alicia's right hand fingers rubbed her forehead. "No, absolutely not. This leaves nobody's lips. We can't celebrate something that's not final."

"There's concord grape wine." Vicky opened a cabinet. "The three of us should at least raise a small toast to Alicia's success. This milestone deserves recognition."

Joyous chants of "Cheers" followed by the clink of glasses filled the apartment.

After two sips, Alicia gathered up the letters and excused herself. Sprawled on her bed behind a closed bedroom door, she read and reread the second letter until almost memorized. Wanda's initials at the letter's bottom foreclosed questions to her one office confidant. She tucked the letter beneath the saved teacher supplies in her top dresser drawer.

Alicia cracked open her bedroom door to peek into the dimness beyond. She saw neither Vicky nor Joel then or as her quick strides ended in the bathroom. A fainter red showed in the toilet bowl. Neither cold water nor her writer's exuberance subdued her trepidation.

Restless fits marred her repeated attempts to fall asleep. Shivers punctuated every thought that tried to predict what she'd do at work.

Foreboding gnawed Alicia's insides from the moment her foot stepped into reception Friday morning. Each door handle rattle, hallway door silhouette movement, or mechanical ring tone startled her hyper-sensitive nerves. *Cowans Ford Dam.* No employed trick calmed her. Her reading a Beatrix Smothers novel failed to distract her.

Alicia gave thanks Mr. Van Gilleran hadn't popped into reception. The office door creaked and Alicia flipped her paperback.

"Aha, caught you."

Alicia couldn't decipher which office secret Wanda unearthed. "What?"

"Reading the boss's work won't get you a raise this soon after probation."

"Oh." Alicia chose the minimalist tactic. If it worked for Hemmingway, why not her?

"You're safe," Wanda said.

Alicia sighed with relief.

"Mr. Van Gilleran won't see you read on the job today, or even tomorrow. He'll not be in. Stack the processed submissions on my desk." Wanda, headed for the office door, flashed a coy smile. "If you dare."

Alicia assumed Mr. Van Gilleran's absence related to the prior day. While she didn't wish grief upon the Van Gilleran family, Alicia seized her opportunity. She waited and then peeked into the office area at ten minutes before ten a.m. Wanda's desk was unoccupied. *So far, so good.* She returned to reception to grab a telephone message pad. This time the deception she planned generated no internal qualms. She filled in the pad's blank lines with the information that Lady Victoria Dash had telephoned Mr. Van Gilleran in response to his letter. Alicia checked the form's box to indicate there'd be a later attempt to contact.

Alicia folded the message into the palm of her right hand. To avoid an awkward moment should Wanda return, Alicia's left hand carried three letters addressed to Mr. Van Gilleran. She exhaled a deep breath and a second when no one lurked near Wanda's desk. Her glance into Mr. Van Gilleran's office showed it to be dark and unoccupied. Alicia patted her contrived message facedown next to Wanda's telephone.

Second thoughts crowded Alicia's mind with each quickened step to her desk. She fidgeted with an aspirin packet until the memory of her recent bathroom visits cautioned her to avoid all medication. She forced a smile for the letter carrier. When the lunch hour approached, it helped that Carol wasn't at the office lunch table. Alicia steeled herself to face Wanda.

"Needed to ask something about that telephone message you left."

A shard of bone-deep fear sliced through Alicia. Had she messed up? Given herself away? Alicia remembered Hemmingway. "Which one?"

"The one this morning. Did Lady Victoria Dash give you a contact telephone number?"

"Sorry. If it wasn't there, I forgot to ask. Please

forgive me."

"Let's eat. Mr. Van Gilleran won't be seeing it for days and, I doubt, it's on his mind today. Can you keep a secret?"

"Absolutely."

"Mr. Van Gilleran's in Phoenix. He told me a former family member died."

Alicia blanked the anxious thoughts battering her brain. The main one being: *Should I ask?* She tried to frame it with a touch of concern coated with aloofness. "Will he be back by Thanksgiving Day?"

"Don't honestly know."

Alicia tiptoed onto hotter coals. "Heard Carol talk about publishing options. So I'm not stupid, what are they?"

"Publisher pays an author money to obtain rights to publish a manuscript."

"That's all?"

"Oh, there's more. Although there's money paid, publication isn't guaranteed. The option exists for a negotiated period of time. If the time expires and the publisher hasn't printed the book, the author retains the option money with the right to shop the book elsewhere."

"Thanks." Alicia couldn't fathom why a publisher paid money for a manuscript never to be printed. Was her agreement with Mr. Van Gilleran to portray Beatrix Smothers like an option? If he didn't show, was she off the hook?

Alicia piled her uncertainty atop the worry that Thanksgiving Day arrived in less than a week and she hadn't finished Beatrix's third book. She pulled it out of her desk drawer and propped it open on a stack of unprocessed submissions. If he didn't fulfill her expectation he'd return in time, she'd drop in on her parents a day early.

Beatrix's words formed an unintelligible jumble in Alicia's mind until she quit reading and doodled on a paper scrap. How would she handle the request for a meeting with Lady Victoria Dash. She didn't believe she could saunter into Mr. Van Gilleran's office and announce: *I'm Lady Victoria Dash, surprise!*

She pondered the hire of a local attorney to represent Lady Victoria. The attorney to meet Mr. Van Gilleran and claim she'd embarked on an extended European book tour. Problem was she neither knew an attorney nor had the bank account balance necessary to finance further deception. Without an inkling of the option's dollar amount, the attorney's retainer could exceed the option's value.

An exhausted Alicia cast out all uncertainty to relish her success. Whatever the shame, the glory of her having created a novel deemed worthy of a publisher's option would remain in her heart forever. She contemplated her willingness to forego the option with an unfound Lady Dash. Did she have the strength to do so. Yes, but this path also crushed her publication fantasy.

Mr. Van Gilleran probably acted like all men. Offer one wondrous seductive inducement and then later renege. Waving a white flag or turning tail weren't her choices eighteen months ago.

Her heroine had conquered all.

I'll do the same.

* * *

Vicky stared into Joel's rearview mirror until Alicia, preoccupied with how she'd act as Beatrix Smothers, if she had to, waved. Along for the ride was an apt description of Alicia's Saturday night double date. Joel had championed an Embers Restaurant supper, the special-effects movie, and Rick, who sat stiff on her rear seat's far side.

"A fireman eating at an 'Embers' restaurant. Who

would have guessed?" Alicia quipped.

Joel extinguished his nervous laugh without further comment.

Alicia waited until Rick popped her car door. Without physical contact, he escorted her into the restaurant and helped her be seated.

Joel jump-started the conversation by saying he and Rick attended the same accounting classes. When Vicky blurted out, "Alicia is going to be—"

Alicia interrupted. "Did . . . did see a Vikings game." Rick's eyes lit up. They glazed over when Alicia mentioned literature or the arts. Fortunate for her, the mouthfuls of fast-served food and the theater darkness eliminated all requirements for extended conversation.

Joel dropped Vicky and her off at their apartment building. On the three-floor elevator ride, Vicky started their conversation. "You spent more time at the restaurant gawking than usual. Is there anything wrong other than a dull and boring Rick?"

"Please tell Joel I thought Rick was nice. He definitely acted courteous."

A beeping telephone answering machine slowed Alicia's accelerated rush to her bedroom. "It's for me. My Aunt Agnes." *Dating Pushers Inc. struck again.* Her aunt wished to help cousin Edward introduce his friend.

Vicky kicked off her shoes and sprawled across the sofa. "Heard anything more about your book?"

Alicia plopped into the living room's chair. "Mr. Van Gilleran has been out of town."

Vicky's blank gaze indicated she didn't understand the fix Alicia now found herself in.

"You see that guy who sent you the Bears jersey?"

Alicia filled a glass with water. "He's not been in the office."

"You're on a no streak if I hear you right."

Alicia cut short her chortle. She'd been tightlipped to Vicky all night. That wasn't fair to her best friend. "I'm sorry. Life should be fun, not gloom. How can I make it right with you?"

"You were brave enough to go out with one of Joel's lame friends. I must scout the department store where I work to see if there are any eligible, college-educated, hot, handsome men panting to meet the next superstar author."

They both laughed.

Alicia felt her eyelids close. Her day's activities, coupled with the worry, left her exhausted, which unfortunately recurred daily. "You and Joel seem to be getting closer. You're both carefree spirits. Wouldn't presume to make your decisions, but from the outside he seems to make you happy."

"We have great moments. You will, too. Go to bed before I end up having to carry you."

* * *

A boredom-cloaked Monday in a short Thanksgiving-Day-week dovetailed with Alicia's lowered anxiety begot by non-red toilet bowl water. While caution dictated her vigilance, she counted thirty hours of clear flushes.

Diffused lamplight scored the loosely drawn drape's center seam to hint at Mr. Van Gilleran's return. Wanda, tight-lipped about new absence details, cautioned Alicia not to interrupt her boss's office sequester. Alicia obliged. Her idea to take advantage of a reduced holiday staff to search his office thwarted by his return. She retreated to reception.

Mr. Van Gilleran surprised Alicia Tuesday morning with a lunch invitation. She hesitated and then agreed. At noon, he entered reception to escort her to a first class restaurant on the top floor of Gregg's, a Nicollet Mall department store. He selected a back booth.

"You still okay with Thanksgiving Day dinner?" he

asked after they ordered.

"Yes. I've read two of the books I supposedly authored." His flashed smile broke his stoic expression, but only for a split second. "Never knew a writer before who injected so much drama into a kiss between two people." Her cheeks warmed. Her writing observation meant to draw out the conversation, not be a bellows for her self-conscious blush.

"It's all fantasy." The deep furrow that pleated his brow remained. "Need to mention something before Thursday."

Alicia squirmed on her chair. Below the table's edge, she clasped her hands.

"I'm sure it'll enter the conversation. My ex-wife was murdered last week."

Alicia gasped. *Chapman Dam, Pennsylvania.*

"Her name was Mia. Police found her in a suburban Phoenix alley. Multiple stab wounds. They theorize the killer abducted her from a mall, killed her, and dumped her where discovered. That's why I was absent from the office last week."

"Dreadful . . . horrible . . . I'm so sorry." Uncertain of what else to say, Alicia searched his eyes and found only pain.

He fiddled with his fork. "I'm only mentioning this because my parents really liked Mia. They felt hurt by the divorce."

"Any children?" Alicia breathed three times before he exhaled his one deep inhale.

"That was my second reason for going to Phoenix."

"Your child okay?"

"Don't know."

"How terrible. What did the police say?"

Before he could respond, the server appeared with their orders. Alicia had ignored Mr. Van Gilleran's urgings and stuck with a chef's salad. His fork flaked a salmon filet. The server filled both water glasses and departed. Alicia strived to soften their discussion subject.

"If I'm Beatrix, do I know Mia?"

"Let's see. No. Beatrix came later. You can say you never knew Mia."

"That's easy to remember." Alicia scrapped the high caloric salad dressing to her plate's edge. Lettuce and vegetables, staples for her latest diet, doubly important as she expected Thursday and Friday to both be tempting excess calorie days. She declined dessert. "Wish there were soothing words I could say to ease your pain. Please accept my sincerest condolences."

His fork shifted his plate's filet from side to side. "Thank you."

"Will the police contact you about the children?"

"There was potentially only one."

Alicia sipped water; food didn't interest her. "Don't understand."

"It's complicated. The divorce proved difficult. We'd been married little more than a year." He lowered his voice to a whisper. "I understood Mia became pregnant near the end, but child support never surfaced. My lawyer advised me not to mess with things Mia didn't raise."

"Surely the police checked out where she lived."

"They did and I did. No clue or sign a child lived there."

Alicia said little thereafter, either in the restaurant, or to interrupt their strides to the office. After a buckle of noise cascaded down five stories of green-tinted glass with a second wind gust, Mr. Van Gilleran lent her his gray cashmere scarf. The fuzzy fibers tickled her stung face from the bridge of her nose to her chin. Opulent animated mannequins, festooned blinking Christmas lights, and jeweled tree ornaments in mall store windows failed to ensnare their footsteps or generate the ohs and ahs heard from others.

In the Bunyan lobby, she unwrapped and returned his scarf and, on the elevator ride to the twelfth floor,

thanked him for lunch. He said he'd pick her up
Thursday, one p.m. at her apartment. His mother planned
dinner for two o'clock.

* * *

Thanksgiving Day frosted the lobby exit door of Alicia's
apartment building. She fretted if wearing snow boots
would be déclassé. Tuesday and Wednesday afternoon
above freezing highs had left icy patches on city streets.

Alicia sucked in her abs when Mr. Van Gilleran's
blue Lincoln stopped within view. She worried her outfit
would expose her charade. Wednesday she'd asked
Randall what he expected Beatrix to wear. His business
casual reference had confused her. Nice sweater, dressy
slacks, and shined shoes she understood. She carried her
Sunday church shoes.

She hopped into the Lincoln's front seat to pre-empt
his exit. Under his woolen topcoat she glimpsed a dark
blue sport coat, white shirt, but no tie.

He gazed at her, his hand on the gearshift.
"Nervous?"

"Should I lie?"

His sheepish smile endured until she waited for him
to open her car door at their destination. When halfway
up the concrete walk, a pair of eyes peeked through a
front door windowpane. Her amped nerves triggered an
army of goose bumps beneath her sweater and slacks.
The door swung out when she and Randall neared the
bricked front stoop.

"Mom, Dad, this is Beatrix Smothers."

Alicia's vestibule sidestep allowed Randall to squeeze
in alongside her. "I'm so please to meet you both," Alicia
said. "I've heard such wonderful things from—" She
extended her right hand. "From . . . Randall."

Mrs. Van Gilleran hugged Alicia. Randall's father

clasped her joined hands and requested she follow him into the family room. Counterclockwise, she met Randall's brother Charlie and his wife, Mary, six cousins, and one uncle. Randall whispered he anticipated Charlie's two kids to race in later. The corner television, its volume lowered, broadcasted a football game. Alicia recalled the Chicago Bears helmet insignia. A cousin, surprised she voiced an interest in football, identified the second team as the Detroit Lions.

Alicia, under her breath, asked Randall if Mr. Grant was at this game.

"Not likely. The game's in Detroit."

Alicia tried to restrict her helpings as she passed dishes from Randall to his father. Her confidence grew as she fielded easily handled news and weather banter. When Randall's mother announced that dessert would be served later, everyone retired to the family room where Alicia learned the Lions had defeated the Bears 21 to 17.

When Randall's mother entered, he lifted his right foot at the last moment to avoid tripping on his father's extended left foot as he crossed the room to sit next to Alicia.

Mrs. Van Gilleran sat in the seat vacated by Randall. "Beatrix, how do you come up with your ideas for the people and places in your novels?"

"Combination of past and present travel, movies, books, sometimes TV."

Randall's mother smiled. "What about formal writing education?"

Alicia pushed a blond hair strand off her forehead. "Most at the University of Minnesota."

"That's right. I recall one of your books saying you went to the U of M at Duluth."

Alicia's brain froze. She'd forgot the university had multiple campuses. She jettisoned a clarification lest it be disastrous. "I give a lot of credit to Randall for his expert editing. He infuses so much emotion into my stories.

Gives them depth and sparkle." She gazed at Randall. He fidgeted.

"Did he mention he was the featured speaker when the Columbia Heights Library Mystery Book Club met in this very room in September?"

Charlie and Mary shifted chairs to start another conversation across the room.

"Mother, please," Randall objected. He wrung his hands.

"And, he told all the members to go out and buy your books."

Alicia winked at Randall. His right thumb rubbed his left hand knuckles. "That was extremely nice of him. I hope he does that for other authors who have or will have their books published by *New Romance Delights*. I doubt the book buying public really appreciates how much energy and research goes into writing a book."

Randall's father rested his left hand on his wife's knee and then spoke. "It must satisfy you to see stacks of your books displayed at the bookstore."

"I'd rather see empty shelves," Alicia said, "after the books have been delivered."

Randall grinned at her and his father's lips parted in a smile.

Alicia relished the family room cousin invasion that broke her direct sight line to Randall's parents and splintered the conversation. Those nearest her focused on upcoming Christmas parties and festivities, especially the annual St. Paul Winter Carnival. If spoken to, she joined in, otherwise she concentrated on constant side-glances toward a calmer Randall.

His back arched when his mother stood. "Beatrix, you're so pretty. Why don't they put your picture on your book jackets like so many other authors?"

Randall's lips parted, and then he gazed toward the fireplace and stayed silent.

Alicia's fingers stretched her sweater's collar. "That

was a conscious decision." Her mind whirled. She and Randall hadn't rehearsed his mother's question. Alicia relied on her own history. "My name isn't my real birth name. I was adopted."

"Couldn't you use a pen name?"

The melodic sing-song of Lady Victoria Dash pulsed through her consciousness like sweet, debilitating truth serum. "I'm afraid that wouldn't help." Alicia scanned the intent faces within earshot. They expected a revelation. She masked her history. "There's a man out there I fear. He tried to kidnap me as a teen and stalked me my senior college year. I can't risk having my photo spread across this country on library bookshelves, in bookstores, and interstate gas station book racks to advertise my whereabouts. Randall is kind enough to not require book signings."

Randall's father interrupted, "Can't the police help?"

"Not really. What's important is that I have the opportunity to make a living at what I know best . . . and that's writing. Thus, my book bio confers basic truthful information, but also obscures my real life identity by not including a photograph."

Randall's mother seemed engrossed by Alicia's explanation.

"I'd hope any snapshots taken today that include me stay off the Internet and within your family." She glanced to catch Randall's reaction. He'd rotated his head toward the TV.

"Don't worry," Mrs. Van Gilleran replied. "Our family will protect your privacy. Your safety's important. Isn't that right, Randall dear?"

"Mother, the second football game has reached the final two minute warning. I believe it's time I depart and make sure Ms. Smothers gets home safe."

His mother reached out and clasped Alicia's hands. "It's such a joy to finally meet you."

"Mrs. Van Gilleran, may I first help with the dishes?"

One Paper Heart
"Darling." Alicia cringed at hearing Ms. Hauser's favorite word. "You're our guest. The dishes aren't a big deal. We'd love to have you visit again. Isn't that right, Randall?"

Mrs. Van Gilleran riveted her eyes on Randall without a movement of her head.

He gazed her way. His shallow voice said, "Yes, Mother."

At Randall's repeated announcement of their departure, Alicia treasured each moment when all adult family members rose to extend gentle hugs and gracious good-byes.

In his Lincoln, Randall spoke first. "Beatrix, I mean, Alicia, thank you so very much. You can't imagine how much you helped me."

Alicia tugged at the seatbelt to twist toward Randall. "Your family was very welcoming. I think only twice did I catch myself ready to say the wrong thing."

"I didn't notice any. Your comment about empty shelves was exceptional."

"The three books you gave me to read were interesting. Your heroines acted a little frilly, often distracted or consumed by wardrobe, but the plots had no scatterbrained maiden tied to the railroad tracks or 'bodice-ripper' front covers."

He braked for a red light. "Where'd you learn the trade's 'bodice ripper' term?"

"Came up in college English to categorize all the early twentieth century novels where the terrorized heroine, typically bound, had her blouse strategically torn to reveal enticing cleavage, but not too much flesh. In my estimation, modern movies have duplicated the novels."

"Why say that?"

"A woman, either fully clothed in high heels or scantily clad after untying bondage ropes or pulling off duct tape, runs down a dark alley flashing glimpses of dark nylon hose, loses a shoe, if one's originally present,

130

with a suspicious, not shown, person, or beast, in threatening pursuit."

Randall shrugged and accelerated the car forward. She caught him shift his eyes from the road for a glimpse of her sitting there with both hands on her lap clutching a purse. She unsuccessfully tried to recall what started her heroine literature prattle.

He broke the consuming silence when slow cars ahead limited his acceleration. "Let's try a different topic. And, it involves none of what you talked about. I take pride in my personal honesty, my author role as Beatrix excepted."

Alicia dreaded what she might hear. Her car seat warmth uncomfortable. What else?

"I asked Wanda if you were involved with anyone. Now . . . don't blame Wanda. I didn't know who else to ask."

"I won't." Alicia held her breath, not positive what might follow. The chill in her cheeks confirmed her facial blood drain until her stored adrenaline triggered her heart's left ventricle to fight her uncertainty and gorge her veins and internal organs.

"Wanda suggested I had to act before Jackson Grant came back to town."

His statement puzzled her. She refused to acknowledge his glance at her from the corner of his right eye. She recalled Wanda had said Mr. Grant hadn't asked about her. Where or how would Wanda determine that Randall had to battle his friend for her favor? Why had Randall prefaced his words with his "honesty." Liars did that. *Why was she so judgmental?* What did she lose if she listened?

"So . . . I'd be honored if you would go with me to the Guthrie Theater a week from this coming Saturday for their scheduled performance. It's either *Tartuffe* or *The Merchant of Venice*." He kept his gaze straight ahead, hands at ten and two.

She shifted her purse to her side to cloak her slowness to accept or reject his requested date. "I . . . I'd . . . be happy to." She'd caught herself before she uttered "love to."

"Fabulous." Randall's car horn honked. "Sorry, my hand slipped. Hoped you'd say yes." He glanced at her with a grin that radiated extreme elation. "I'll check the tickets in my office desk drawer. We could go early. Have dinner first."

"After your family's heaping meal, I can't think about food."

"It's not tonight." He corrected a lane sway after his extended glance in her direction.

"If it's all right with you, let's not plan on dinner before the theater." She hoped her dinner regrets didn't crush his expressed joy.

"Don't feel bashful if you'd like to change your mind."

Her awkward feeling subsided when her apartment building loomed ahead.

He eased his car next to the curb. "Here we are. I'll see you to the door."

His Lincoln idled as they walked to her lobby entrance. Her exposed face caused her to believe the temperature dipped below freezing.

Outside her apartment's exterior door, Alicia, alongside Randall, said, "Again, thank you and your family for a wonderful Thanksgiving." Her arms and hands hung limp at her sides.

Randall pivoted in front of her, leaned forward, and his hands clasped her shoulders. Without a word, he softly kissed her closed lips. His arms slipped around her for a brief hug and, before Alicia's eyes reopened, he'd backed away.

As after the Metrodome game, her paralyzed vocal cords trapped all sound. She willed the words "thank you" to glide past her lips and float across her visible exhaled breath. She prayed her two words would reach the nape of his neck before Randall's sidewalk strides circled his Lincoln's rear bumper.

When he did, she waved.

Randall waved in response. Within moments his car's taillights disappeared into the darkness.

Alicia buzzed her apartment. No answer. She searched her purse to find her key.

Lady Victoria Dash trembled, not from the cold, but passion's spark and lightening bolt.

Her impersonation adrenaline continued to circulate as she tugged free of her boots and calf-length nylons, hung her coat, and tossed her shoes into the foyer closet. The apartment's closed door left her in darkness.

Rocky Gorge Dam! Why didn't I leave the stove light on?

Alicia flicked on the kitchen light and bent forward to rub her stubbed right big toe. The dime-sized toe bruise strung. Neither a dent nor blood marred the breakfast counter's lower side. Alicia refused to coddle herself to search for a Band-Aid. Unlike the scheduled doctor visit for the mystery cause of her toilet water's red tint, she alone would cope with her toe. She sat on one counter stool and rested her right foot on a second. Alicia enjoyed the quiet, content not to have to answer Vicky's questions about Thanksgiving with Randall.

Her hyped red blood cells, incited by his strong, not rough, warm lips, competed with the ignited sparks of emergency white blood cells that rushed to her big toe. If Randall had accurately recounted what Wanda said, her office friend indeed earned conniver honors. Alicia didn't need to be convinced of Randall's gratefulness for her first-run Beatrix debut. While his first hug after the Metrodome had been respectful, his Thanksgiving Day kiss exploded, coursed her veins, and activated a dormant longing she'd always tried to hide.

If he had acted on impulsive, it didn't concern her.

One Paper Heart

Despite her historical heroine recitation, she submerged no conscious desire he grab her and rip her clothes. Their car topics flowed naturally from her research into romance writing and the conversation with Randall's mother. Three years since she had last kissed her "hippie" boyfriend marked a long exile.

Enough schoolgirl daydreaming. A second Thanksgiving Day turkey meal waited at her parents. She spotted a saltshaker, used as a paperweight, next to the kitchen sink. Vicky's scribbled note explained she'd be home Sunday after a holiday trip to a cousin's home.

Alicia sighed. She wouldn't be awakened by Vicky. Alicia's excitement, from the time her head touched her pillow, was slow to dissipate. Rehashed memories propped her eyelids wide-awake for an hour until sleep arrived.

The early morning red No. 25 New Brighton bus required a downtown transfer. On her lap Alicia carried a cranberry dish. She balanced it atop her left hand when she knocked on her parents' front door.

"You're early," brother Alan said after he opened the door.

"Nine isn't," Alicia replied.

"It is if it's not a school day."

"Are you going to let me in?"

Alan stepped to the side. Dad waved as he carried a grandchild piggyback toward the basement door. After Alicia laid her coat in the small bedroom, she carried her cranberry dish to the kitchen counter. Mom hurried to dry her hands on her holiday apron. She gave Alicia a big hug. Alicia ignored the muted living room conversation bursts to spot a kettle filled to its brim with steaming boiled potatoes and, without a request, grabbed a metal masher.

"How was your friend's Thanksgiving Day?" Mom asked.

"Wonderful. Lots of food." She grasped her Mom's

134

Donan Berg

right hand. "I like it best to be home."

"Go talk to everyone in the living room. They'd like to see you."

Dad entered the kitchen without a child clutching his forehead. He hugged Alicia. "You look livelier today." He freed her and stepped back. "Last week's worry wrinkles gone."

"That's because I'm seeing you more often."

Her dad beamed and led her to face uncles and aunts who cut sentences short to greet her. Brother George entered the living room from upstairs. She rushed to embrace him. "Didn't know you'd be here."

"Neither did I. Touch and go when the Navy misplaced my original leave request." Aunt Agnes gave them the sofa's near end. Alan sat crossed-legged at Alicia's feet. "Dad said you saw the Vikings in person. I'm jealous."

"The Metrodome's so huge inside." George and Alan's wide eyes never left her. Alicia focused on the game and the parking lot tailgating. She passed over how Charlotte hung onto Randall. And, she said not a word about Mr. Grant.

Uncle Frank interrupted. "You still teaching at the same school?"

"No." She didn't need to grovel in front of the cousins about her failure.

Aunt Agnes came to her rescue. "She's working downtown. The Bunyan Center. Isn't that right, Alicia?" She nodded. "Freddie's friend is looking to show her the town's nightlife."

"C'mon now," Alicia murmured. Uncomfortable to divulge Joel's double date, she pursed her lips.

Alicia rose first when Mom broke in with her call to dinner. The kitchen table, expansion leaves inserted, seated all adults. Elena's kids smeared food on the card table Dad had set up in the living room.

Her dad bowed his head and recited a Thanksgiving

135

One Paper Heart

Day prayer. Dishes laden with food passed Alicia left to right. Her gaze lingered on Mom. She prayed Mom kept a future focus. In the last two years Alicia had noticed faint changes. Dad had never purchased carryout lasagna as she witnessed last week. Mom's right hand trembled. Dad never took his eyes off Mom.

Alicia's full heart overflowed, especially with all present at the holiday table. No one had to explain to her or any of her siblings they were blessed to be one loving family. She didn't know why her parents never conceived a child. The older Alicia had gotten the brighter her parents' love shone. Not in fancy gifts or grand vacations, but in everyday caring, hugs, and endearing words. If only she could be so blessed.

George's tales of exotic Mediterranean ports continued to Dad's Taurus when George volunteered to drive Alicia home. She teased him he wouldn't escape a return to romantic Greece and Italy without the purchase of a wedding ring.

Alicia flipped through Vicky's *Town and Country* magazine left on the coffee table. The classy feminine photos didn't buoy her. She willed herself not to fret about the hereditary roots of what inflicted Mom. Alicia's adoption eliminated all direct blood or DNA links. Worry shuttled her to be troubled she lacked knowledge of her own biological pedigree. Goose bumps convinced her she exercised no control over when, or if, the red-tainted toilet water would return.

She rubbed her forearms as she paced three circles from the television to the kitchen sink and back. Her English professor loved to reference the mythical Scylla and Charybdis. Mom fashioned a better way of stating Alicia's Lady Dash dilemma. It's the frying pan or the fire.

Vicky's holiday absence allowed Alicia to mumble without castigation, avoid unsolicited advice, and/or to be shooed off the sofa. Her head rested on the sofa's arm;

her body stretched across its cushions. Alicia's mental anguish heightened by her stomach's painful digest of her second Thanksgiving Day feast. Randall's unsolicited Thanksgiving Day ride comment he prized honesty floated distinct and powerful across her memory. If he hadn't walked into reception when he did, she wouldn't have been dishonest to switch her red paper heart to another envelope.

She chastised herself a fool for not writing down the envelope's return address. Her actions had made her one with the three characters Dorothy met in the Land of Oz. Alicia lacked courage, a heart, and a brain.

How'd her heroine react? Alicia had no clue.

She began to sob.

Her absent writing god of no help. She envisioned her computer paper clip icon winked and asked: "What is this?"

Alicia, en route to the bathroom to commandeer a tissue box, wiped tears with both hands before she threw herself upon her bed.

Her fears of Mr. Van Gilleran battled the warmth of Randall's stolen kiss the night before. Indecision swallowed her joyful anticipation of a Guthrie Medieval play date. Beyond the initial trepidation of impersonating Beatrix Smothers, the Van Gilleran holiday experience exposed a new Randall. He had exhibited a depth of humor and a love of family.

She assumed he'd not hid the real Randall beneath the hero's cloak snatched from one of his novels. His family hadn't chided him for play-acting. His displayed restaurant's hurt, on the verge of depression, weren't Mr. Grant's Hollywood.

A punched bed pillow failed to ameliorate her anxiety.

Alicia sulked into the kitchen. She rummaged through the utility drawer until her right hand forefinger and thumb clasped the last two red paper hearts.

One Paper Heart

Alicia tossed both into the trash.
She still felt helpless.

Chapter Nine

Randall stared at his apartment's bedroom floor and shrugged. His grand plan to free his mind of all earthly cares and world-created guilt-trips doomed by two piles of soiled underwear.

To a man's man, this Friday-after-Thanksgiving-Day laundry chore humiliated all bachelors. He rationalized the condo's basement washer/dryer amenity as a chance to eavesdrop on feminine conversations to add juicy, if not authentic, dialogue tidbits to his next novel.

He plugged quarters into two washers. Tempted to quote Robert Burns's reference to mice and men, he opted to leave the unoccupied laundry room and return to his unit. Piece by piece, he tossed a week's junk mail stacked on his kitchen counter into whirling paper shredder blades. A University of Minnesota alumni solicitation jogged his memory to complete his syllabus for the upcoming January-to-March quarter.

His living room filing cabinet, disguised as an end table, coughed up his prior syllabus and a saved computer flash drive. He revised deadline dates and modified two essay topics. Within thirteen minutes, he logged off his computer to figuratively thumb his nose at academia's egotistical requirements. He perched himself on a sofa cushion edge to stash the syllabus hardcopy and the saved flash drive into his filing cabinet.

His condo's landline rang. He scooted backward and picked up the portable handset. Mother's voice inundated his ear canal with unbounded Thanksgiving visit praise. And, she didn't stop with him. Beatrix received a whole truckload of positive, glowing compliments. Mother listed Beatrix's courtesy, manners, intelligence, and willingness to help with the dishes.

"What about Mary?" The question marked Randall's first words since his hello.

"She helped your sister-in-law with wording for an appliance complaint letter. Beatrix's such a lovely girl," Mother gushed.

"I'm happy you're pleased." Randall tried to sound gracious and noncommittal. He suspected Mother may have an ulterior motive so he attempted to divert her without being caught. "You deserve kudos for your great hospitality."

"One thing didn't seem right though?"

Oh, oh, Mother wasn't fooled.

What little known fact had he misstated that mothers ferret out with their well-honed in-bred intuition. He pressed the receiver to his shirt for the cloth to block Mother's perception of his fear. His standing aggravated his unease as a dizziness wave struck. He stammered to excuse himself to obtain a drink of water.

"Sorry, Mother, what were you saying?" He braced his back against the refrigerator, ready to offer a profuse apology.

"I was going to say . . . she looks so young."

He placed his free left hand over his receiver's mouthpiece and exhaled.

"M-o-m." He feigned disbelief. "How can I ask Beatrix for a certified birth certificate?" It was a ridiculous question and he knew it.

"Guess you're right. She probably visits a spa to keep her skin so soft."

"That . . . that could explain it. You're very observant." Randall brushed his left forearm across his forehead.

"Second reason for my call."

Randall's shoulders slumped against the refrigerator. If he uttered a few "uh-haws" at the appropriate intervals, he'd survive all further discussion of Alicia. He'd then hang up with the knowledge he'd dodged Mother's expectations. His Beatrix worries relegated to the past with her exiled to California to join Jackson. He'd enjoy Alicia's company without family drama. She and he required only to be circumspect at the office. As the isolated receptionist, he figured that keeping their secret would be a piece of cake.

"Sorry, Mother, what was that?"

"Mia's parents plan a memorial service in Edina or Eden Prairie. You might want to extend an invitation to your entire office."

Oh, Mother. Why do you do this to me? How could he explain to the office attendees why Mother addressed Alicia as Beatrix Smothers? "Don't know, Mother. It's been a long time."

"The service will be non-denominational, a weekday at five thirty. If you don't invite the office, you could invite Beatrix. We'd all go out for supper afterwards."

"M-o-t-h-e-r!" Exasperated, Randall's constricted throat refused to articulate a second word. If Mother didn't understand the nuance of his one word reply, she'd not take to heart harsher words. He latched onto a subtle silence, a tactic that had worked well since his teen years.

"You'll bring Beatrix for Christmas dinner, won't you?"

Randall groped for his glass and a third water gulp. His strong-willed Mother loved to crank up the pressure.

141

She, he calculated, hadn't heard what he said. Or, more likely, ignored it to focus on her own desires for his life despite her repeated avowals to the contrary.

"Hadn't planned on it."

"Well, I didn't hear her talk much about having any nearby family. Christmas is such a depressing time to be alone, away from family."

Randall struggled to deflect Mother. His "no" required a reasonable explanation for why Beatrix couldn't be available. He didn't want to lie. A weave of half-truths to cover-up his deception likely to backfire if he wasn't careful.

"Beatrix's promised a new book by January first. Since I haven't seen any proofs, one must presume she'll be busy to meet her *New Romance Delights* deadline."

"Randall Charles."

Mother's tone and the use of his first and middle name shouted her disappointment. He allowed the two words to sink into oblivion without a response.

"Are you sure?" questioned his mother. "Sure you're not making up excuses so you don't have to ask her? Ask and let her make up her own mind. I saw the way she looked at you. Trust me. She radiated interest in you more than just as someone who works for the same company."

"M-o-t-h-e-r!" He recognized his exasperation again fell on deaf ears.

"You have to be open to a new relationship. As heartbreaking as the news about Mia was, there's, sorry to say, closure and all my hope for reconciliation extinguished."

Mother's truthful words struck him as a hammer does an anvil with a resounding "Dragnet" TV show thud. "Let's not go into that." Randall shifted the handset to his left ear.

"I prayed you two would annul the divorce. I never told you because I didn't want to interfere or appear to be pressuring you. That's why I've kept in contact with her parents. Mia's mother required a sedative when police authorities broke the news."

Although Randall felt queasy in resurrecting all the emotions he experienced in Phoenix, he didn't desire to be insensitive. "Please call me with the church and service details. Right now the clothes washer buzzer tells me I need to add bleach. Thank you again for yesterday. Tell Dad I love him, too."

"Bye, son. We love you. Think about Christmas." Static filled the line.

Randall walked to place the telephone handset into its charging cradle. His claim he heard the washer buzzer was a white lie. Love. Marriage. Neither should be a lie. Why had Mia hid the child?

He skipped every other stair tread in his two-flight rush to the basement laundry room. He'd witnessed where a tardy tenant found his or her dripping clothes tossed on a nearby table to free a washer. That had happened to another guy's red boxers, including a pair faded to pink. Building tenants snickered for a month thereafter. He'd not suffer the same table-of-shame fate.

Randall breathed a sigh of relief to find his underwear spun tight against the washing tub sides. He mulled Mother's statements as he transferred his wet clothes to a dryer. She said she didn't want to interfere in his personal life. Ha! *He bet all mothers say that.*

He didn't question she wanted him to be happy. And, if his happiness fathered grandchildren, she'd deplete her Forever Stamp stash with ecstatic joy and overload the household e-mail server with cutesy birth announcements and newborn pictures. Randall closed the large commercial dryer drum door with both his washer loads inside. A competitor's romance novel rested on a nearby chair along with a frilly-pink-change purse. He hoped that this precise moment blessed Alicia with family Thanksgiving celebration warmth.

Randall chose the chair next to the novel to wait. He and his father had grown apart. His father's on-site research and client seminars had separated the two since Randall's teen years. Then, at age eighteen, Randall accepted an Ivy League college scholarship. The fragile closeness bond severed when he never entertained pursuit of his father's chemist vocation. Although Randall never doubted they both, deep down, loved each other, he reconciled himself to the cordial, superficial relationship he and his father practiced.

His glance at the cast aside novel cover artwork showed two heads with barely the width of a litmus strip between their lips. A remorse pang attacked. He shouldn't have kissed Alicia. Prepared to shake her hand, her closed eyes drew him in. Not even a date, and still he kissed her.

When he had hired Alicia, he'd expected to challenge her skills with a less public position. However, he couldn't transfer her to a proofreading vacancy that never materialized. Her initial figure-less peasant dresses made reception a gamble, but her drive and work qualifications impressed Wanda. Reception's few visitors lauded Alicia's personality and professional warmth. He discounted Jackson's praise as self-serving.

Randall's throat buried a chuckle. Woe be it to him, a man with four dark suits, to compare Alicia's lackluster office wardrobe to Charlotte's flamboyancy.

He cocked his head toward the dryer when two females entered, one in cut-off blue jeans, tank top, and flip-flops and the second in brown slacks, white blouse, and sneakers. He feigned a hello to the forty-ish woman in slacks. The younger one, whose sharp nose mirrored the elder woman's, flipped her ponytail and picked up the change purse. She tinkered with washer dials. The older woman watched until she rotated her entire body toward Randall.

"Hello." The woman's scant wispy, short-clipped

black hair piled mop-like atop her round face. "I'm Olivia. We've walked past each other in the lobby."

"Think you're right." He struggled to keep his eyes focused on her face, as her right eye never seemed to move. "I'm Randall." His brief stare convinced him her eyelash didn't blink.

Olivia pointed to the ponytail. "My daughter, Greta."

Randall acknowledged with a nod.

She lifted the novel and sat where it had rested.

Oblivious to him, the daughter began to ridicule a guy she dated the week before. Randall cringed when she said the dude deserved to be slapped for an attempted kiss. When she said her life didn't require a "dippy-do," Randall, without a clue to her slang's meaning, took note. Maybe his life required a "dippy-do."

"Excuse me, is that novel a good story," Randall asked.

"Greta says no. Why?" Olivia asked.

"I work for a book publisher downtown."

Long wrinkles formed across the woman's forehead. "That's a come on, isn't it?"

He regretted his conversation starter. After a moment, he continued, "Do you think all guys are forever on the make for pretty females?"

"I do," the daughter said. A rock step and a pivot swished her ponytail. She glared at Randall. "That's what my mom says to me all the time."

Olivia folded her arms.

"Well, I'm not." Randall focused his attention on the daughter who, with her right hand on her hip, jutted out her elbow. "If you would please, answer me one question. If a guy I'll call A told you he knew that his friend B was interested in you, would you agree to go out with A?"

"Sure. Ya." Greta twirled the coin purse by its finger loop.

"If you found out that guy A lied, what would you do?"

"Dump him faster than smelly socks." Greta popped her bubble gum.

"You bet I would," Olivia interjected.

"Oh." He'd stretched God's truth when he told Alicia that Wanda had mentioned Jackson's interest. Now the jaws of a trap he set threatened to wipe Alicia's kiss from his lips. *Trouble did come in threes.* Jackson's inability to think outside the box for a new documentary project, his inability to locate Lady Victoria Dash, and Phoenix authorities unable to locate a child Mia had hid. When his dryer timer clicked off, he tossed unfolded dry clothes into a basket.

"Thank you, ladies."

Randall shifted his basket to his right hip when the sound of a ringing telephone greeted his second floor arrival. He slid the laundry basket onto the dining table and picked up the landline receiver. As he expected Mother, he listened before he spoke.

"Hello, darling."

"Charlotte, Happy Thanksgiving." Randall didn't recognize the caller ID area code. "What sunny state are you calling from?"

"California, Randall darling. I'm visiting Del Mar Downs racetrack in San Diego. Lovely. Gorgeous. You should be here."

"You know I couldn't. Family tradition." His answer not tinged by shades of gray.

"Did you know that for decades women honored a tradition to wear fashionable, often outrageous, hats to this racetrack on opening day? I've seen pictures in the local museum."

Last thing he sought was a women's hats discussion. "Didn't know that."

"Without knowing it, I've lived to carry on a glorious lifestyle in fashionable hats."

"You're always a trendsetter." White lies had re-emerged to litter his feminine conversation. Was it he or the women? Men didn't evoke this tendency in him.

"Sorry to say there are few of us left in what used to be an Easter tradition. I e-mailed Aretha on how nice her hat looked at the last Inauguration."

"You're always considerate." After his praise, he realized he paced his living room. Could he shorten this conversation without being rude? Charlotte had to suspect a closed office left him with nothing scheduled.

"Thank you, darling. Heard about your dear Mia. Shocking. Absolutely dreadful. I think I know how you must feel."

A tongue-tied Randall's labored for a response. Charlotte lived a widow times three. Any question about her upcoming novel stymied by the fact that her story synopsis and character outline lay locked in his office desk. He relied on his tactic with Mother. He kept silent.

"You need to have a change of scenery. Will do you good. I know it did me wonders when overwhelmed with grief."

"I'm fine." He clenched his jaw with the expectation Charlotte schemed to launch into her own agenda, like his mother. "Appreciate your concern." He relented to fill the silence. "Don't you have a manuscript due here next month?"

"Hoped there might be a rain check."

Randall breathed a sigh of relief. He'd steered Charlotte toward work. "You still searching for character ideas? I vaguely recall you whispered that to me during the Metrodome football game." His shoulder muscles relaxed as he concentrated on characters that populated Charlotte's novels. If given an inspiration, Charlotte would run with it, flesh out character strengths and weaknesses. Her success in selling NRD books feathered his hat. He chuckled at his cliché's irony when applied to Charlotte's attire.

"I've been thinking about the virile, animal-skin clad Viking mascot."

One Paper Heart

"You can't redo a fantasy/romance keyed to a hero's bulging biceps."

"Darling, you take all the fun out of hero research. You could be my hero."

Randall contemplated relief from his renewed tension by swift bangs of his head on the refrigerator. Charlotte, a vixen known for subtle sexual innuendo, would want him to piece together her California invite and her hero reference. He stifled a hang up and waited for her.

"I need closer inspiration."

Right on cue, Charlotte.

"I was thinking your visit here could be a life's tonic and do us both good."

Charlotte's thinly veiled ulterior motive exposed, he countered. "My leaving the Twin Cities isn't in the cards. Next year's publishing schedule review must be finalized in two weeks."

"Warm breezes stroke tired brain cells and e-mail never leaves you unconnected."

"Can't, just can't." His tone flat compared to Charlotte's sultry enunciation.

"Why? On my last book our being together gave you the inspiration to suggest deletion of the suave town banker so as not to confuse the readers on who competed for the heart of my poor, impoverished heroine."

Randall strived to distract Charlotte. "Try this. Walk to the Gaslamp Quarter. Watch people parade pass Sixteenth and George. You're likely to see at least two heroines and three or four heroes or a clinging-vine couple you can craft into your next romance story narrative. Your imagination will bubble onto the page, believe me."

"You sure?"

"If not, check out the rowing crews on an inlet practicing for the next Olympics. You've never done an Olympic hopeful. Interview an aspirant. One of those muscular rowers must have a treasure trove of stories to

148

tell about conquests or shutdowns. Your choice whether the rower is male or female."

If Charlotte didn't bite, he'd capitalize on his idea. A vision of sitting under a palm tree with a laptop, synchronized to the trunk's shade, flitted behind his eyeballs.

Charlotte's modulated voice compressed the airwaves. "You want me to do research. Interview? Randall, why don't you tell me what your heart desires. Could camouflage it in a best selling novel and fulfill it in real life."

Randall gazed at the refrigerator. Boy, Charlotte presented a perpetual challenge. Innuendo escalated to brassy. Had she flipped, dived off the deep end?

"You know—" Randall's voice conquered by his swallow. "I truly idolize and adore your writing." He weighed each word as he strove to be careful and express his rejection with the innocence of Little Bo Peep. "Even if you exaggerated my mundane life, I'd be too embarrassed. *New Romance Delights* readers crave your imagination, your unique grit and grime portrayal of everyday emotion, and your climatic, feel-good hero and heroine as they conquer death-defying roadblocks to live in their everlasting happiness."

"Wow, you sure do know how to make a writer feel good, really good. Okay. I'll go to the Gaslamp Quarter as I've heard there's a really superb Hispanic eatery with live salsa music."

He perceived a high-note end to their conversation. He crossed his right hand fingers that Charlotte would forget her proposition the next time they spoke. "You're one-of-a-kind."

"And, darling, don't you forget it."

Whew! He'd succeeded. "I'll look forward to receiving your manuscript."

"Tell me when your plane arrives. I'll pick you up."

Like a successful salesperson, a relentless Charlotte

tried to close the sale.

"Good-bye, Charlotte."

He'd teetered, but not fallen off the Charlotte
tightrope.

His life each day transgressed into one deception after
another. He deceived his mother as regards to Beatrix. He
deceived Charlotte as to his future intentions. He
deceived Alicia about both his underlying feelings and
contrived a story to enhance his chance to get a date. If he
believed the women in the laundry, his slap would be
forthcoming.

Alicia's complexity flustered him. Her ill-fitting
clothes were a shadow of what she was not. No
irresponsible blithe soul exhibited the drive to obtain a
college degree in four years as she did. Yet, she settled to
be a receptionist. He couldn't fathom why. She, unlike
her predecessor, didn't drop a manuscript on his desk
upon completion of the probationary period. Perhaps a
plausible explanation existed. He hoped so.

* * *

Randall dove into his post-Thanksgiving week
manuscript backlog well rested. He'd slept in both
Saturday and Sunday. Jackson's new screenplay
telephone call Monday scraped old scabs. Randall tired of
spouting excuses Lady Victoria Dash had gone
underground.

Preoccupied with his upcoming Saturday date with
Alicia, he avoided eye contact with her every time
another employee ventured near them and once jumped
when a shadow crossed the hallway door with him and
Alicia alone in reception.

He ignored Jackson's midweek calls until a panicked
Friday message.

"No, Jackson, we're not doing Pacific grass skirts."

"Hell, then, what? You're not helping if you get stuck on a manuscript who's author you can't find."

"Let me get back to you. I'm making progress." He lied. Deception no longer raced his pulse. He peeked into reception to find Alicia alone.

"Last chance for dinner."

Alicia in her beige peasant dress didn't complete her twist toward him. "Rain check, please."

He didn't argue. "The Guthrie's *Merchant of Venice* curtain rises at eight. I'll be outside your apartment tomorrow at six-thirty."

Through his Lincoln's frost-edged windshield, he gazed at Alicia's brisk stroll. She braved the freezing temperatures in a white ankle-length, down-filled coat. He rushed to open the front passenger door, it's seat-warmer toggled to high, like his always was.

A bulky hood ringed with faux fur hid her face. Her voice, without visible lips, intrigued him. Without her expression to guide him, he skipped talk of football, work, and Beatrix Smothers.

That changed to Randall's glee in their Guthrie lobby conversation. A two-to-two dead heat existed in number of nieces and nephews. He strived to remember her relaxed mien. She spoke with pride of the accomplishments of her brothers and sister without identifying any by name. Alicia anticipated seeing all at Christmas. Randall kept his mouth shut about a Beatrix encore.

Should he hint at a second date or play it cool? He was befuddled, uncertain of Alicia's potential response. Tonight wasn't the time to disrupt a real, honest-to-goodness date—a first date. *But didn't women want to asked, even if they said no?*

Randall couldn't wait for the unique and entertaining stage performance to end. He finished his topcoat buttons before Alicia. He asked, "Can we find a place to continue our conversation. I so enjoy your company."

"I'd like that."

Randall suggested a fondue eatery located two blocks off the Nicollet Mall that offered privacy. On the trip there, Alicia repeated her preference for unbuttered popcorn. He tried not to guilt-trip her and said she could enjoy the unadorned fruit and not dip any into the chocolate.

He found the Dip'n Eat crowded with one corner table available. Soothing jazz from a two-piece combo filled the room. Alicia surprised him when she pointed to a cranberry cosmopolitan, served straight up. He ordered a pedestrian seven and seven.

As they sipped, Alicia detailed how nepotism derailed her teacher hiring. It confirmed his suspicion that her receptionist acceptance was stopgap employment. His ears perked up when she casually mentioned a Vicky.

"Is this Vicky a relative?" He had no words to describe her facial countenance.

"It's short for Victoria, my roommate."

"Okay." He filed this interesting information in a memory bank for later follow-up.

"You must be proud of that Oscar in your office."

"It's been three years, a long time in Hollywood. Two others and I wrote and filmed an Alaskan documentary. You've met Mr. Grant—" Randall cut his reference to Jackson before Alicia could respond. "Perhaps you have another question?"

"What are the five most important things it takes to be a romance writer?"

He parried, "You interested in becoming an author?"

"Oh, I don't know."

He judged her reply to be unconvincing. Maybe she desired to help her roommate? Her silence offered no clue. She jolted him by a subject change.

"Manuscripts come across the reception desk never to be seen again. Several months later a new novel appears. Don't understand."

"We're experimenting. Scanners image paper manuscripts for our computers."

"You mean digital files? No paper manuscript sits on your desk?"

"Right." She reverted to the facial expression he couldn't decipher. He obviously missed something. "You said your roommate's name was Vicky?"

"Yes." She sipped her drink.

He ventured an initial probe. "Is she a writer or an author?"

"Not that I know of. She works at Northern Marks, the famous department store."

He sensed little resistance. "Would you describe her as carefree with a devil-may-care approach to life?"

"I enjoy living with her. Her boyfriend and I have issues and he pals with dull friends."

The server brought a fruit tray with a pot of melted chocolate.

"You sound like you've stockpiled negative experiences."

"Not really. We attended the same university. Been roommates for five, six years."

"Sorry. My question referred to Vicky's friends." He believed Alicia knowingly avoided his question's most important part. Whether or not she knew Lady Victoria, he didn't know. Since she'd gone out with him, he had a chance even if there existed another man.

"My fault to get carried away." She sliced pineapple chunks with her knife. "It's not Christian to gossip about other people. Even niceties get misconstrued."

He posed his remaining question. "What's Alicia looking for?"

Alicia hesitated and gazed at the chocolate pot for nerve-racking seconds. "Don't consider myself any different than most people. Want to achieve goals I've trained for." He met her upward gaze. "I'd like to be part of a family like the one I grew up with, except I'd prefer

153

not to adopt."

"You saying you're adopted?" He'd never considered that.

"Yes, my two brothers and an older sister." She bowed her head.

"That had to be hard." Randall dipped a strawberry and ate it.

"Not really. As kids we never knew until age sixteen. You see other kids who don't look alike. You think that makes your brothers and sister normal. What's important is how your mom and dad treat you. If they love you, nothing insurmountable exists."

"My mother always told me it's important to raise your own children." A brief frown curled Alicia's lips. "My dad considers adoption praiseworthy, but not preferred."

Alicia's eyebrows furrowed at his last statement. Her eyes became fixed on him. "Don't know what happened to my biological parents." He steeled himself for whatever would come. "They may have been killed in an accident. I could've been conceived and been unwanted. Just don't know." She set her knife on a napkin to allow her right hand fingers to grab the table's edge. "I've learned you don't live on what might have been. You appreciate what you have. I have two loving parents. They aren't stepparents or anything hyphenated."

From the corner of Alicia's left eye, a tear trickled across her cheek.

Never before had he experienced a debater's eloquent rejoinder so understated and gut wrenching. He'd been shamed. If a rock existed nearby, he'd have crawled under it.

"I'm sorry. I didn't intend to offend."

She grabbed a napkin. "You didn't. Kids strike an emotional chord, especially when I hear about parents who have kids and then abuse or abandon them."

"I agree." His ears filled with the combo's soulful

melody, a request not his.

"No child in this country deserves to suffer." Alicia pulled a tissue from her purse, the napkin discarded. "That's why I donate to a children's group with a mission to provide food, shelter, and medical help to orphaned infants."

"I've heard about that, but *Sixty Minutes* frequently airs an expose about contributed money that never reaches the children. I'm sure you thought about that." He noted a good sign when she picked up her fork. "I applaud your caring." He refolded his napkin. "I'd like to learn more about you." He gazed into her now dry eyes. "Perhaps we can go out again?" He held his breath. His lips touched.

"I'd like that . . . very much I'd like that." She smiled.

His throat relaxed and saliva lubricated his dry mouth. He'd caused her to cry on their first date and his ignored second thoughts prompted him to wait. He hoped she hadn't thought he required her acceptance for continued employment.

In front of Alicia's apartment building, he didn't idle his Lincoln. He escorted her to the lobby where Alicia flipped the fur hood from her face.

This time he didn't kiss and run. Words weren't necessary. He desired his enchantment to sail to infinity and beyond and retain the physical warmth ignited by Alicia's kisses.

As he turned his ignition key, he lost track of his whereabouts. His gaze to the building disclosed no shadow behind the frosted door. He didn't remember his footsteps on the walk.

The heat of his front seat was a constant.

The sweet taste of Alicia's kisses loitered along his upper lip's cupid's bow.

Chapter Ten

The great joy jet-streaming through Alicia's ectodermic skin layer triggered a spasm. She kicked her bed's warm comforter to the floor. Her shoulders pressed into the mattress as she arched her back and stretched her crumpled top sheet taut from her toes to its upper hem tight to her throat. An unending loop of her Guthrie date memories convinced her she hadn't slipped to give away Lady Victoria Dash's identity.

Happy her alarm clock, primed to buzz at seven, hadn't interrupted, Alicia's time reversal transported her into Lady Victoria Dash's fictional world. Her chest heaved and cascaded to stillness after a trinity of jagged-length sighs.

Lady Victoria's hero and heroine clinch. The hero's sensuous fingertips trace the heroine's neck contours. His thumbs uplift her chin. She caresses his muscular shoulders.

An Edwardian mansion's darkened interior hallway extends behind them. Gilded candlesticks fitted with two slender lit candles cast a soft glow from a marble pedestal. Delicate black and white ceiling light patterns flutter in harmony with the oblivious couple.

Lady Victoria's imaginary lovers kiss and kiss—long, breathless, and passionate.

Alicia, infused with the emotion Lady Dash gave to her characters, allowed the memory of Randall's kisses to initiate trembles above and below her waist.

The fictional hero releases the heroine's chin. His hand calluses glaze the heroine's clavicles to fondle her swan-white shoulders. With a tortoise's speed, his kisses become a traffic jam along the curvature of her jawbone. When he pauses to breathe, she lands her moist lips on his left cheek. He twists his head to nibble her right earlobe before his gentle push guides the heroine into the sitting room.

He haphazardly piles his waistcoat and knickers upon the heroine's rose-taffeta tea-gown that lies on plush wool carpet dyed maroon. His gracious nudges leave the heroine supine on the divan. A slit in her dressing gown exposes alabaster right-leg skin.

Early morning winter sunrays slither across the top of lapped window valances. The room's motionless air captures a suffocating heat, unreleased prisoner embers from the night's two fireplaces. The heat intensifies the heroine's dreamy mien. A glistening sweat drop slides from her brow to her nose.

Alicia's right forefinger flicked the wetness from her nose.

An emboldened light streak penetrates the closure seam of an east window's velvet curtains. Neither hero nor heroine are troubled by the streak's bright stripe that divides the glistening polished caramel oak hardwood floor and twinkles the sideboard's glassware.

With all household servants dispatched, no hearty front door knock would summon either undressed lover. Neither expects bloody-fisted neighbors nor a nobleman or messenger intrusion. Yet, the heroine fears that a trail-weary rogue, rather than walk away from an unanswered locked door, will, in search of treasure to plunder, peer through a window curtain's crack. She clutches her bosom. The wry gaze of the hero quickens the lovers' high-pulsed flirtation.

The heroine's pleasure sigh anticipates her hero's revitalized vigor. She rakes her fingernails across his Herculean chest and desires their love to be consummated without delay amidst the burgundy velvet curtains, ornate gilded furnishings, and under the steely portrait eyes of a mustached patriarch she despises.

The hero fantasizes a wedded eternity on a Greek island beach. His powerful chest muscles glisten, and his warrior-forged biceps bulge. The heroine's soft feminine arms and shoulders overpower his creative fancy for hot sand and lapping waves. His fingers slide the white lace off her shoulders. He caresses the heroine one body curve at a time. His languid finger movement so sensuous it doesn't indent.

The heroine closes her eyes. Her nerve synapses tingle.

The imprisoning power of her lover's tenderness radiates to her soul.

Her ears capture his endearing words: "Dearest" and "Forever, Love."

Her body adopts the rhythmic rise and fall of shore-seeking ocean waves. They lap against the reef of desire, her desire. The sun's wider shaft of light touches her thigh.

A stone's clink vibrates a windowpane.

Torsion afflicts Alicia, her exhilarated heart ready to burst.

Rattle, crash, thud, clang. Alicia's horizontal shoulders bolted vertical.

"False alarm," Vicky shouted.

Alicia landed her bare soles on the floor. She cinched her robe's cloth belt and shuffled her slippered feet to the kitchen. She tiptoed past pot lids and a skillet. "What happened?"

"Tried to grab a pot behind the roaster. The roaster and its lid hit the floor." Vicky pointed. "See the dent. Let's hope the landlord considers it normal wear and tear."

Alicia hated when the klutz in Vicky surfaced. Yet, her irate outburst wouldn't improve Vicky. "No problem. Accidents happen." She reached into the refrigerator for the orange juice carton. "Have to tell you. I'll be gone this afternoon."

Vicky smiled and sorta blushed. "Why? Big date, huh. Secret rendezvous."

"I've invited myself to my sister's in Shakopee. She'll feed the kids and me. Then I'll baby-sit so she and her husband can enjoy a kid-less dinner out."

"Last night's date must have zoomed off the charts so you're now ready to practice how to take care of kids."

"V-I-C-K-Y!" Alicia's OJ glass tipped; liquid pulp dotted the floor in six spots. "I had a good time. The Guthrie Theater looked a little shabby." She dropped a paper towel to soak up the OJ and bumped the refrigerator door closed with her left elbow. "Afterwards, Mr. Van Gilleran took me for chocolate fondue near the Nicollet Mall. There was music. We were lucky to get a table."

Alicia inserted wheat bread into the toaster.

"Forget the boring stuff. Did he mention anything about your novel?" Vicky slumped onto a breakfast counter stool.

Alicia let the novel mention hang in the air.

Vicky twirled. "Your calling him Mr. gives me the sneaky feeling he may have done something to irritate you. Maybe like Joel?"

"No, and no. He doesn't know I wrote the novel." Vicky's jaw dropped. "And, he acted a consummate gentleman. Guess, because I call him mister at the office, it just carried over."

"Wait a minute. Go back." Vicky's tightened forehead skin arched her raised eyebrows. "Whatcha mean he doesn't know what you wrote?"

Alicia delayed her response while she handed Vicky one dry toast slice and then placed the second slice next to her orange juice. Vicky was a klutz, not a blabbermouth. Alicia dragged a stool to the breakfast counter opposite Vicky, sat on it, and leaned her elbows on the counter.

"Can you understand 'pen name'?" Vicky, her mouth filled with toast, nodded. "I used one."

"And—"

"What?"

"What's your pen name?"

"Bea—" *Can't dig a deeper hole.* Alicia cleared her throat. "Lady Victoria Dash."

Vicky's lips formed a coy smile.

"You can't tell anyone. You gotta promise."

"Secret handshake?" Alicia didn't raise her hand. "Okay not." Vicky carried her half-eaten toast piece to the sofa.

Alicia breathed easier. If that satisfied Vicky's curiosity, there wasn't a need to launch into a red paper heart explanation.

Vicky scattered newspaper pages to uncover her favorite sofa cushion. "When are you going out again with "Mister G?"

Vicky's western drawl challenge to John Wayne amused Alicia. She shook her head, rose, and gazed toward the kitchen ceiling, "Oh, I don't know." She bent forward to lift and return the roaster pan and its lid to their designated kitchen cabinet.

"Didn't he ask?"

She pivoted toward Vicky. "He did." Alicia's mind swirled to sift her Victorian fantasy from Randall's date reality. "But it was sorta vague, no specific date."

"Great." Vicky's smile mimicked a Cheshire cat.

"How'd he kiss?"

Alicia cinched her robe belt tighter. "Now you don't enlighten me about Joel, do you?"

"You never ask."

Chagrined she'd mentioned Joel, Alicia withheld a further response. To not incite a fight, she pressed her mental finger on her fight or flee brain nerve to dam all Joel conversation topics.

"Bet you dreamed about your boss last night? I dream about Joel all the time."

Alicia relaxed her fingers destined for Vicky's throat. "Don't think so."

"You don't sleep quiet."

Alicia shrugged. "Don't remember." Alicia rationalized her answer wasn't a lie. Vicky didn't ask about Lady Victoria. Before Vicky did, Alicia asked if Vicky planned on using the bathroom.

Vicky shook her head.

Alicia slipped a brown peasant dress from a bedroom closet hanger, collected clean underwear and knee-high nylons from folded drawer piles, and, in front of the bathroom mirror, applied makeup for church.

The sanctuary's Biblical stained glass window subdued by winter's dullness, didn't highlight her extra foundation or her neck scar. The priest's Psalm 105 sermon enshrouded her with a spiritual pall. Her leap between the sacred and the profane loomed thinner than a hymnal page. Alicia reread the Lord's actions for those saved: "He gave them what they asked but sent a wasting disease against them."

Her Lady Dash letters from Randall offered what she wished for. Would his reaction to her red paper heart deception be akin to a "wasting disease?"

If her manuscript existed in digital bits, the enigma of the red paper heart on Wanda's desk meant what?

* * *

Alicia's quick glance saw the front door curtains of sister Elena's single-family Shakopee home part. The twenty minute southeast I-35 drive from South Minneapolis scattered her gloom amongst the leafless oak branches and the blue spruce needles.

With expectant joy, Alicia slammed shut her Contour driver's door as her sister's entrance door flung wide. Her boots crunched snow and left two-inch footprints to avoid an icy concrete walkway. Lund's apple strudel, enclosed in a cloth shopping bag, hung beneath her elbow. She greeted Elena with a hug.

"Let's shut this door," Elena said. "Jonathan's due any sec."

Alicia set her boots together on a braided cotton hallway rug just in time. Her rambunctious nephew, Jonathan Jr., almost five, jumped at Alicia with his hands extended. She hoisted him for a hug and then, by his left wrist, led him to the living room couch.

"Santa's gonna bring me a train," Junior exclaimed. "A real big one."

Weak wheel squeaks behind Alicia alerted her to Junior's sister. She turned.

"And, Nea, what's Santa going to bring you?" Alicia waited as two-year-old Nea, named after Linnea, a Swedish great-grandmother, struggled to rock her baby-surround-walker forward.

"She's getting a new Barbie," blurted out Junior. "Mommy told Santa at the store."

Alicia's right forefinger to her lips cautioned Junior. "Shush." She lifted a oaten cereal bit formed into a circle and placed it on Nea's tongue like a sacramental host.

"Dear, I'm home." Alicia recognized Jonathan Sr.'s voice.

A lanky tousled-haired man, sporting reddened cheeks, appeared in the doorway.

"These two jumping jacks wear you down yet?" Jonathan asked.

"Not yet. Long time since I've visited. There never seems to be enough time to talk when we gather for holidays at my Mom and Dad's."

"I know. I'm the kid chaser there." He laughed and his two hands smoothed his hair. Jonathan kept his hair long to hide a birthmark behind his left ear. Elena joked it was her way of telling Jonathan from a reincarnated Elvis. Alicia rescued Nea from her walker and sat cross-legged on the living room floor to play with her and Jonathan Jr. while Elena prepared lunch.

Alicia ruled out a tray to eat her sandwich in the basement recreation room with the two Jonathans and the Vikings on TV. She spoon fed Nea until Elena toted Nea upstairs for a nap. Alicia waited on the living room couch for Elena's return. "Need to ask if you can help me with my novel."

"Don't see how. Math I can do. English, well, that's your expertise." Elena stood. Listened at the top of the basement stairs and then returned to the couch.

Alicia detailed the dilemma she created by hiding behind a pen name, using their parent's address, and then the receipt of an option letter from Mr. Van Gilleran.

"Wow!" Elena's eyes glazed over.

"Hold on. There's more."

Elena's body slumped into the rear cushion when Alicia explained the red paper heart and the more recent faked telephone message. "You're in deep trouble."

Alicia nodded and seized Elena's right hand with both of hers. "Need you to be Lady Victoria Dash." The deception Alicia proposed her greatest risk yet. However, hadn't she proved Thanksgiving Day that author role-playing worked?

Elena freed her right hand. "Told you before I can't write."

"Not required. Just come to *New Romance Delights* to

163

meet the acquisitions editor, Mr. Randall Van Gilleran. Won't take but a few minutes."

"Is he one of those old, crotchety, suspender-wearing gentlemen who terrorize?"

Alicia strained not to smile. "No. He's your age, a sharp dresser, and not a bit frightening." *Well, two of three, not white lies.* Alicia tried hard to gauge Elena's reaction. "I'll try to be with you."

Elena glanced past Alicia's right shoulder as if she expected Jonathan to emerge from the basement. "When would I have to do this?"

Alicia subdued misgivings. "This next week would be perfect. I've written an outline of the story. It's in the car." Her brain in slo-mo processed the potential turmoil she intended to add to her sister's idyllic suburban life. She shivered as if the ice outdoors had migrated to enclose her heart.

Indecision clouded Elena's eyes.

Alicia grasped for the proverbial straws. "You don't have to memorize it. Pretend you wrote it a long time ago."

* * *

Alicia paced reception. The letter carrier's Wednesday submission dump cleared from her desk.

Her heart careened rib-to-rib inside her chest. Her mouth cracked a new high of dry. Blood rushed to ring her ears. The loudness a baffle against the sound of her footfalls. Goose bumps hid beneath her long cotton sleeves, exposed on her legs below a knee-length skirt chosen for this special day. Her fifth wristwatch glance within ten minutes left four and one-half minutes before Elena's expected two p.m. arrival.

They planned to say they were friends, not sisters. Elena would request Alicia to sit in.

Alicia inhaled when a shadow preceded Elena's, ah, Lady Victoria Dash's, going-out-to-dinner perfume. Alicia's brief hug didn't calm Elena's body tremble.

"You'll do fine," Alicia whispered. "Follow me and smile."

She led Elena into the inner office, waved to Wanda, and pointed to the conference room to confirm she escorted a guest to a scheduled meeting.

Alicia instructed Elena to sit on the far side of the conference room's large teak table and face the door. She stood at her sister's right shoulder. Her left hand squeezed Elena's shoulder to give them both comfort. In her calmest tone, Alicia said, "You'll be terrific. Please breathe."

Randall strode through the door in his navy blue Brooks Brothers suit, white shirt, and burgundy Windsor-knotted tie."

Alicia straightened her torso to impersonate a Buckingham Palace Queen's Guard. Her tonsils clogged her throat when she noticed Randall carried no manuscript.

"Good afternoon. Is it Miss or Mrs. Cummings?"

Elena's stare edged up from the table to Randall's nose. "It's Mrs. Cummings, but please call me Elena."

Alicia's left foot tapped her sister's right foot.

"If okay," Elena croaked, "I'd like Alicia to stay."

"If that would make you more comfortable, then by all means."

Alicia sat on the chair next to Elena. When her sister locked her hands on her lap, Alicia redoubled her efforts not to wring her own hands.

"We here at *New Romance Delights* believe we can offer new authors an exciting opportunity." Randall's gaze never strayed from Elena. "We're very happy to speak to you about your book—*A Search Fulfilled*. As my latest letter stated, we're interested in purchasing an option to publish your work. Do you know what an

165

option is?"

"Yes." Elena cleared her throat. "I took the liberty of talking to a lawyer to have him explain it to me."

Alicia tried not to squirm. *A lawyer? We never discussed hiring a lawyer.*

"Very good."

Alicia pursed her lips so as not to interrupt Randall.

"You should definitely feel comfortable dealing with us, that is, with me."

I know I do.

"What in my book captivated you?" Elena asked.

Alicia desired to massage her heart into its normal rhythm. Where was Elena going? They hadn't rehearsed the attorney or this question. Alicia tightened her imaginary seatbelt and hung on. Didn't Elena realize that the longer they stayed the more likely Randall would penetrate their ruse?

"The main character's passionate search for her biological mother impressed me. The quest twists kept me hooked. Was it from real life?"

Careful, Sis. There's a barb.

"Heavens no, although I've researched adoptions."

Alicia's right hand grasped the table's edge. *Don't go there, Elena.* Alicia's left foot kicked her sister's right ankle—their pre-arranged signal to zip it. *Randall knows I'm adopted.*

Randall hesitated and Alicia choked off her next breath until he spoke. "However, I'd be professionally remiss not to mention that a few items require tweaking."

Here it comes. Alicia's brain cells whirled. *I'm ready. Hope it's not too painful.*

"Your scene descriptions were at times too vague and at other times too dense. At times you jumbled your syntax. A few predicate phrases were out of alignment."

Didn't he realize the technique increased dramatic effect? That's right, Elena. Don't frown. Be professional, even if you don't understand. Whoa, he's not stopping.

"Certain early chapter dialogue stilted. I recall the multi-syllable words uttered by the rustic farmer to be unbelievable. His word choice suggested an Oxford University diploma hung above his milking stanchions. I expected the colloquial speech of a Midwest dairyman. This is not meant to be too negative for . . . again, the storyline or plot turned pages."

Alicia's fingers itched to clasp Elena's hand. *Has Randall stopped tossing dirt balls?*

"We're divided on whether to commit resources to publish later this year or to hold for a future date. However, we're willing to pay you an option to ease your wait."

Alicia's palms rubbed the top of her thighs to ease her skin's prickly sensation. Her vocal cords twitched. *Elena, please say something . . . NOW!*

Elena gazed at the ceiling, and then at Alicia. A silent, ready to burst Alicia stared back.

Randall rested his clasped hands on the teak table.

Alicia smothered a cough in the crook of her right elbow.

"Mr. Van Gilleran." Elena paused and then exhaled. "While I appreciate constructive criticism, perhaps you could skip that and tell me if there's a dollar figure to your option?"

You go, sister!

"Of course. We're willing to offer thirty thousand dollars. If we publish within one year, fifty percent of the option, that is, fifteen thousand, will be considered an advance against royalties. In the unlikely event we don't exercise our option within two years, you keep the full thirty thousand dollars. Does that answer your questions?"

"There's one more. When do you want my decision?"

"I'd like it as soon as possible. However, you mentioned consulting an attorney. If you haven't retained him or her, I'll have an option contract forwarded to your address. I recall New Brighton, correct?"

"Yes, please send all correspondence there."

"But the telephone number I have isn't New Brighton?"

An inward smile tickled Alicia's throat. She'd prepared Elena for this question.

"That's right. Let's me write without interruption. Keeps my Lady Victoria mail separate."

"Fine. I'll have our option contract mailed to the address we have. Thanks for coming in. If you'll excuse me, Alicia can show you out."

Alicia applied the screws to her excitement as Randall rose and departed. She hugged Elena hard. "Thank you. Thank you."

"You think I did good?"

"Call me tonight."

"You know there's no attorney, Alicia. Don't know what thunderbolt struck me to say that."

"Don't worry. You did great."

Alicia couldn't wait for four-thirty. The mere thought of Randall ignited pleasurable subconscious neurons. Nevertheless, she wished she could debate his critique.

His option-meeting words elicited the cliché of a wolf cloaked as a lamb. After her Google search uncovered a Minnesota farmer who attended Oxford, she'd anonymously feed her discovery into his e-mail inbox. Either the state Farm Bureau or the U of M Agricultural College had to sponsor a bloody Worcester dairy or hog exchange program.

Alicia squelched her budding anger. Revenge would be best served cold. She'd relish witnessing the horror on Randall's face when she introduced the Oxford/Minnesota farmer. *Boy, that would be special.* Her adrenaline level soared through the stratosphere.

She began to proof a report Wanda had left for her.

"Alicia." Randall's voice startled her. His right hand released reception's office door. It swung closed as he strode to the front of her desk.

She tugged her shorter skirt to cover her knees.

"You didn't tell me you knew Lady Victoria Dash." He surveyed the unoccupied visitor chairs as if to ensure their privacy. "Hope your friendship wasn't harmed by any of my critical comments. It's business. You have to be honest. It's all I know."

She lowered her gaze to her desk. "I'm glad I wasn't her."

"Why?" His left hand smoothed his tie as he gazed into Alicia's uplifted eyes.

Alicia pondered the words to express her true feelings without an adversarial undertow. If he prized honesty, she'd tilt that way. "I'd make the necessary revisions and submit it to a publisher willing to schedule publication, not be left to flutter in the wind for two years."

"That's a point." He again smoothed his tie. "You know it's funny, well sort of."

His oblique response caught her off-guard. Her right hand forefinger tapped her computer's mouse. The courser jumped across the monitor. Her left hand clutched her left knee as she weighed her words so vital to her secret identify as Lady Victoria Dash.

"What did you say was funny?"

"I often thought it peculiar that all Lady Dash messages got left with you and not Wanda."

Oh-oh. Alicia's heart skipped a beat. Her right hand dropped the mouse, grabbed, and then squeezed, a drawer handle to steady and hide from Randall's gaze the shakiness that coursed through her core. She pressed her lips together.

"When you told me your roommate's name was Vicky, short for Victoria, my suspicion congealed around the idea that your roommate, or possibly you, was Lady Victoria." His eyeballs searched reception's acoustical ceiling tile slower than an airport beacon.

Her anxiety leapfrogged to the throes of agony.

169

One Paper Heart

Alicia's toes curled and uncurled inside her shoes. Since a little girl, she'd always been afraid of, in fact, terrified of roller coasters. Her mind braced for the next plunging loop.

Randall sighed. "Just goes to show how wrong my intuition can be."

Whew. Close. Alicia lifted one finger from the drawer handle, then another. Her lips parted.

"Since Lady Victoria turns out to be your friend, I can see why she'd talk to you." Randall smiled. "Why you, not Wanda, wrote the messages."

Alicia desired to escape, shift the topic away from Lady Victoria. "Can you tell me what time I should be ready Saturday?"

"Let me think aloud. Swedish Yule Log ceremony begins at four." He rocked on his heels. "Parking will be tight. If it's not too early, how about I pick you up at three."

"Three's fine."

Randall touched his right hand fingertips to his mouth without keeping them there. His angled step avoided the reception desk's corner.

The office door latch clink welcomed by Alicia. She rose, interlaced her fingers and, with two slow rotations, stretched her shoulders. A tenseness remained. She scrutinized every nuance of his words, his voice, and his expressions. Randall's interest in Lady Dash extended beyond Alicia, and not to Elena. How extensive and deep would his further inquiries be? Charades, the parlor game, had an end. Not all players won.

Alicia collapsed into her chair.

* * *

From the privacy of her bedroom, Alicia telephoned Elena. "You did great this afternoon," Alicia gushed.

Donan Berg

"You're ready for Broadway."

"Don't think so. Heart still pounds and my pulse hasn't yet dropped to normal."

"Without a doubt, Mr. Van Gilleran believed you're Lady Victoria Dash." Alicia doodled a little heart and a stickman. "Did you mention downtown—"

Alicia sighed. Elena's habit to abandon the handset on the kitchen counter when distracted by one of the kids didn't annoy Alicia. She daydreamed the blazing orange sun rays that flooded her bedroom were the shafts of an Edwardian sunset. That outline without definition a rider and steed. When a child's cry faded, Alicia ceased her pen swirl at the lowest point of four drawn, nested hearts.

"Judith, my next door neighbor, acted dumbfounded when I, empty-handed, relieved her from watching Junior and Nea. Teased me about suffering amnesia because I carried no *Henry O* boutique shopping bag. Bugged me for two minutes to inspect my car trunk."

"You know, I can never repay you."

"I'll take a cut of that thirty grand. Just kidding."

"You won't tell Mom and Dad?" Alicia's finger curled the telephone cord. "Promise?"

"I'll be your silent partner in crime."

Alicia cherished Elena's hearty laugh. "You're the greatest. I owe you B-I-G."

"Just remember I agreed to the have the option contract mailed to Mom and Dad."

"I'll speak to Mom this Saturday. If the contract arrived, I'll give you a call. Love you."

"Love you, too. Are you Clyde if I'm Bonnie?"

Alicia contemplated the last receding sunshine streak. Line static confirmed Elena's connection had died. Alicia's debt for family favors grew. She'd buy Elena a snazzy new *Henry O* outfit and there'd be option money to buy Georgia, her sponsored child, a new dress.

"Alicia, you up?" Vicky's voice rose from beneath Alicia's closed bedroom door.

171

"Of course." Alicia ripped her doodle sheet into half-inch pieces and strode into the living room. "Chatting with my sister. Whatcha need?"

Vicky, sprawled out on the sofa, asked, "You game for high adventure this Saturday?"

"If it's the morning." Alicia poured a glass of milk from a refrigerator carton. "I have late afternoon plans." She leaned on the breakfast counter.

"Oh." Vicky lifted her head toward Alicia. "I'll tell Joel it'll be only he and I." Vicky's outstretched right hand pointed the TV remote. "Big date?" She pressed the power button.

"Not really. Randall invited me to the Swedish Yule Log thing."

"Good. I'm dragging Joel to it." Vicky shifted to her left side and tucked her knees to her stomach to allow Alicia room to sit.

Alicia extracted a third secrecy promise from Vicky before she updated Vicky on Lady Victoria's meeting with Randall.

Excitement radiated from Vicky's eyes, even without a disclosure of the option sum.

* * *

Alicia's two fifty-five p.m. peek out her apartment lobby door didn't spy Randall's Lincoln. *Please, please get here before Joel.* No need for Joel to pester Randall about Vikings tickets.

Alicia anticipated Randall's arms to squeeze her tight, his kiss to be soft and warm on her lips. Reality differed. She countered his chilled-lips cheek peck with a hard thirty seconds lip smack. She prayed her injected warmth survived their hurried steps to Randall's idling Lincoln. She angled her face to the Lincoln's windshield to protect against a frontal blast of defroster heat that ricocheted off the glass.

Her down coat protected her from the heated seat until Randall maneuvered his car between a state park log cabin lodge parking lot snow bank and an SUV. A hundred reddened-faced adults, half with frosted eyeglasses, milled aimlessly in the lodge's main room. Two dozen stood befuddled or exasperated with a child clung to one or two legs. Four prized folding-chair rows in front of the forty-foot floor-to-ceiling limestone fireplace rewarded benefactors and select government officials. Crackles and pops hinted the centerpiece log on the fifteen-foot-wide hearth required additional seasoning as flames flickered a foot or more.

Randall, from behind, nudged Alicia's left elbow toward a punch-bowl line slowed to a snail's pace to obtain wassail samples. "Let's pass," Alicia whispered. As they planned to eat in an hour, she didn't need the traditional Scandinavian alcoholic toast calories.

A hand, extended high above a sea of heads, waved. "Alicia," Joel shouted.

Concern battled kindness in Randall's eyes. "Who's that?"

Alicia shrugged. "Nobody." When a conversation knot drifted apart, Alicia had nowhere to hide. Vicky's tasseled knit cap inched her way. Alicia assumed Joel tagged along.

Alicia grabbed Randall's right hand. "Guess it would be unlikely to come here and not meet someone." She introduced Vicky and Joel. The men shook hands.

After weather chit-chat and how mobbed the lodge was, Alicia announced that she and Randall were on their way out. Alicia yanked at Randall's still-held right hand and only let go when she settled into his Lincoln's front seat. Alicia latched her seatbelt and tried to leave it loose enough to wiggle away from the seat's hot center.

"That was short and sweet." Randall's gloved right hand slid his key into the ignition. "Does Vicky know something about you that you don't want me to find out?"

Alicia squirmed. What did he see? "No," she lied. *He's still searching. Be on guard.* She tried to force her facial muscle tension into a smile. "And, if she does, you'll never find out."

She didn't believe her bluff worked. He didn't lift his eyes off her when he shifted into drive. His focus on vehicle navigation in an overcrowded lodge parking lot didn't account for Randall's total silence. Alicia bit her lower lip when Randall exited toward St. Paul. No accident, snow piles, or flashing lights guided them away from their agreed Minneapolis Embers Restaurant. In preparation she'd skipped lunch.

Alicia recognized the Mississippi River bluffs near venerable Summit Avenue with its turn-of-the-century railroad and manufacturing-baron mansions. Randall parked at a scenic overlook. The freshening wind swirled snow in tornado-like funnels across the frozen river ice.

"It's been a long week," Randall began. "I've missed you." Masked by darkness, Alicia imagined his sensual lips. "Hope you're not too terribly hungry."

Alicia's right hand crossed to unlock her seatbelt buckle and Randall's right arm drew them together. She shunned both her stomach and any response to Randall's question. *Lady Victoria can bask in her tropical paradise.* She pushed her coat hood off her forehead. Randall either caught her cue or didn't.

He kissed her.

Their exhaled breaths between kisses challenged the Lincoln's defroster. A fogged inner windshield and four side windows said passion ruled. Alicia wasn't distracted by the electrical current that flowed through her warmed seat.

She repressed a moan in response to his tongue's fanciful slide across her lower lip.

He reached to put his left hand inside her coat. She grabbed it with her right and suggested food. When he flicked on the dome light, she wiped her dark-wine smeared lipstick from his cheek and lips.

Alicia nixed the Embers Restaurant in case Joel might be there with Vicky. When he broached a Ground Round four blocks from her apartment, she agreed. Joyous laughs punctuated their meal. Her chicken's skin piled on her plate next to uneaten fries. They flipped peanut shells onto the floor and at each other. Alicia won the shell pyramid building contest.

Alicia wished the night would never end. The long lobby good-bye from the week before repeated with a passionate encore until Randall asked about Christmas.

"Must go to my parents. It, like Thanksgiving, honors a family tradition."

"Same here. Perhaps we can find time for a new tradition, you and me."

"I'd like that." She swiped a lock of hair that blocked her right eye vision. "How 'bout we find a Salvation Army kettle. A donation will be our first year Christmas present to each other."

"Fantastic. Let's kiss on it."

Before he departed the lobby, Randall gave Alicia his unlisted home telephone number. While he admitted he hadn't cooked in ages, he suggested she think about dinner at his place.

"I could bring Chinese takeout."

Randall laughed. "Let's not go that far. I'll do it. Wait and see."

Alicia didn't recall her finger's push of any elevator button, yet she found herself alone in front of her apartment door needing a key to enter.

Unable to fall asleep, Alicia browsed through a U of M extension course catalog she'd borrowed from Wanda. She thumbed to the Tuesday night Frazer Hall essay-writing course. If Lady Victoria Dash's novel exhibited weak characterization and confused syntax, she'd upgrade her writing skills in night school from one Mr.

One Paper Heart
Randall Van Gilleran.

Chapter Eleven

Randall sorted through the Tuesday handful of business-sized envelopes Wanda delivered.

"Did Santa come early?" Wanda asked.

"Sorta. Fax a copy of this Elena Cummings's signed option to Jackson." He handed her the option and dumped the remainder of his mail into his inbox. "Oh, and make me an extra copy."

Randall lifted his office handset, dialed, and waited eight rings for a pick up. "Jackson, old buddy, you awake?" He heard from Jackson's end what sounded like an engine backfire followed by a loud groan.

Randall rose and closed his office door. He dared not let the romance staff overhear his hunger for a second Oscar. Failure gnawed at him with each gaze at the polished replica on his office shelf.

"Andy's nervous, pessimistic your lowball thirty grand guarantees rejection."

Randall's chair springs restricted his backward lean. "Tell him not to worry. Didn't mention screenplay to Lady Victoria, and . . . her signed option arrived this morning."

"Fantastic. I'll tell Andy."

Randall watched Wanda return to her desk with a handful of papers.

"You still with me, old buddy?"

"Yeah."

"Andy's belched a second hot pepper. He thinks we can capitalize on a Hollywood's discovery of an adopted celebrity. Tabloids and The Times are racing after the story. If we bust our butts, Andy sees our screenplay cashing in."

"It's not the same."

"I know. Andy knows. You know. The reading public doesn't and a producer won't care."

"Yeah, but a dozen screenwriters will attempt to mine the same vein."

"We've a head start. While others wait for the real ending, we can make up our own if we don't like what we've got. I'll hand carry Andy's first draft to you early next week."

"What? You crazy?" Randall didn't wait for Jackson's answer. "Flights will be booked solid with holiday travelers."

"Loosen up. I'll charter Santa's sleigh if I have to." Randall chuckled. He knew Jackson would if he could. "I see movie blockbuster. HBO royalties. We'll rub a new golden statute."

"Keep dreaming, old buddy."

"Good things look better in pairs. Like women, right?"

"Good-bye. Get to sleep. You'll need your strength with those dreams."

Randall hung up. He opened his office door to confirm with Wanda she faxed the option. He locked the signed original in his corner cabinet and his elation beneath a business-as-usual facade. Wanda brought him three messages after lunch. The top message from Jackson said he'd be in Minneapolis Monday. Randall scribbled a note into his day planner. Wanda then surprised Randall with the comment that Mr. Grant asked to be transferred to Alicia, but didn't say why.

"This message doesn't say Jackson wanted me to call him back. Was that an error?"

Wanda fidgeted, glanced through his office window. Randall saw no visitor or employee near her desk. "No, but can I ask a question?"

"Sure."

"Why the lower payment to Lady Victoria?" Wanda locked her hands at her waist.

"We have to make judgments to satisfy our owners. Manuscript is the author's first. Established author sales justify larger sums." He tore up the second message Wanda delivered.

"Oh, I see. Are you going to publish her book next year?"

"I've not put Lady Dash on the schedule. And while I don't plan to, she should be happy. Our option gives Lady Victoria a bigger paycheck. Let me answer this last message."

Wanda closed Randall's office door on the way to her desk. Thirty minutes later, with two submissions in his hands, he walked past Wanda into reception. He found Alicia alone.

"Hello, gorgeous."

Alicia blushed. "Please. Someone might hear you."

"Don't worry. I checked." Randall set the two submissions on the corner of Alicia's desk. He perceived her intense interest in their titles. "Would you like to view animated holiday windows and have dinner downtown Thursday?" He believed that putting Alicia at ease outside the office would offer his best opportunity to wiggle free why Jackson wanted to speak with her.

"Sounds good. I'd love to." Her smile radiated warmth.

He picked up both submissions. "Do you prefer any

particular food?"

Alicia's right hand brushed hair strands behind her ear.

He waited as his question doubled as an inquiry to determine what he might cook for Alicia at his condo. "You look very nice today." No sooner had his words crossed his lips then the office reception door opened.

Wanda, her hand still on the doorknob, smiled at them both and winked at Alicia. "Mr. Van Gilleran, there's a telephone call for you."

He was confused. Alicia's phone hadn't rung.

Wanda nodded, a signal he should not dally.

* * *

Randall's note to remind him of Mia's memorial service the next evening fluttered beneath a police department calendar magnet. He carried a Hamm's beer from his refrigerator's second shelf into the living room. A nostalgia pang chipped at his past glory when a TV promo announced his Alaskan documentary to be re-aired next week.

Seated on his sofa, he flipped the pages of a Harlan Coben novel bookmarked by Mia when they lived together in a Bloomington house. After their divorce, a psychologist friend recommended he accept the hand dealt by God. He failed. To his mother's chagrin, no woman dated since Mia earned his callback until Alicia.

He reached for his cell phone and speed dialed Jackson.

An energetic voice answered. "Twice in a day. What's up?"

"Saw a CNN headline on that Hollywood celebrity. Andy's right."

"Sooooo?"

Randall stretched his right leg, rested its heel on a

sofa cushion. "I'll be at LAX late Friday afternoon. Tell Andy. It'll be faster if we draft and rewrite in person."

"We'll dine with the foxy twins."

Randall pressed his lips together. Why waste his breath to argue work before play.

"Anyway, know Andy's committed every Friday 'til eight."

" We'll map marketing strategy until Andy gets there."

Randall uncapped a second beer. He switched channels to MSNBC.

* * *

Randall clicked off his new Blackberry, hesitant to abandon his Wednesday office tasks for Mia's memorial service. As he informed Wanda of his departure, he asked where the red paper heart on the desk manila folder came from?

"Found it on the floor days ago." Wanda beamed with a self-conscious smile. "We're an office of romance aren't we?"

"Black mark suggests cursed. What's in the folder?"

"Letters from rejected manuscript authors. Save them for ninety days from the date our form letter reply says the review decision's final."

"Okay. See you in the morning."

Randall tuned his Lincoln's radio to the traffic news. No report of a pre-rush hour accident softened his gloom. He parked on the street opposite Edina's First Congregational Church. His black dress boots crunched de-icing salt on the church's concrete steps. The steeple bells peeled five times. He pushed aside the heavy oaken entry doors to greet his former in-laws.

"I'm so sorry," he croaked to Mrs. Johansen.

Mr. Johansen's reddened eyes glistened as he nodded

twice. His former father-in-law crumpled a moist handkerchief, which his right hand wiped across tear-streaked cheeks.

"Thank you so much for coming," Mrs. Johansen whispered into Randall's right ear as she hugged him tight.

When he entered the sanctuary, Randall's father rose to stand in the aisle and allow him to sit between his parents. Brother Charlie and his wife, Mary, sat to Mother's right.

A soprano soloist sang *The Old Rugged Cross* and *God, How Great Thou Art* to start the somber service. Scripture readings, a five-minute eulogy, and congregation responses to pray for eternal life and the repose of Mia's soul completed the memorial service. Although he'd viewed the framed 8x10 framed portrait of Mia many times on his parents' fireplace mantelpiece, Randall couldn't gaze at it on the altar. The silver ring she wore on a neck chain had been his Valentine Day spoof gift that Mia had fallen in love with.

He promised on his drive home that he would honor Mia's memory. How he didn't comprehend. The gruff Phoenix detective had left the majority of Randall's questions unanswered. Whether deliberate or not, Randall hadn't deciphered the cop's expressionless eyes. Randall received no word on Mia's child presumed abducted.

Time had chiseled Mia's physical features from his memory, but no love from his heart. His editor's world embraced romances with required happy endings. No masterpiece literary tragedies with forlorn paralyzed lovers in endless grief, if not dead. *Pure fantasy. He crumbled to heart-wrenching reality.*

He should appreciate life's little joys. Like . . . like Mother allowing him to pray for Mia without a mention of Beatrix Smothers or Christmas. Randall relished his Dad's rare hug, memorable both for its intensity and its thirty-second length.

The Bunyan Exposition Center lobby bustled for a Thursday, even if a workday's end. Randall popped two Tic-Tacs. His leftward glance recognized Alicia's white furry hood, her smiling face second.

"Never would have expected you to select a department store cafeteria for dinner."

"Why not?" Her words quick and taut. She uncurled her bottom lip. "You said my choice."

"I did." A Nicollet Mall's circular snow swirl lowered his head as he marched.

"Couldn't decide so I will watch your food selections for next time."

His chilled facial muscles refused to smile. He froze her "next time" words into his memory. Warmth beckoned thirty feet ahead. It lay hidden behind a revolving door that exposed a creaking down escalator to their cafeteria destination.

"You amaze me." Randall unbuttoned his overcoat. "You're diplomatic, logical."

Her gloved right hand unzipped her down coat. He helped her find a coat hanger.

"What if I pick the passion fruit?" Randall trusted his flirtation hadn't breached a line that his groping hand met at the overlook. Later, when he thought about it, she'd been right. He hadn't been respectful. He'd acted with the bravado Jackson claimed.

Alicia's cheeks flushed Pink Panther pink to crimson red. He could've hugged her. Yellow caution flashed in his mind and his action control light turned red. He couldn't. *Think long term.* "Sorry. I'll go first. You keep a lookout for an empty table."

Randall lifted their food-laden trays and followed Alicia to a four-top table next to a center-support column. Raised voices jerked their eyes to three tattooed young adult males three feet inside the cafeteria's entrance. Six clenched fists stood ready if stares failed to intimidate. One shoved another. A purple-snowsuited toddler with a terrified expression burst into tears.

"Excuse me." Randall strode to shield the toddler from the youths. He lowered his right knee to the floor's tile to face the toddler. "Where's your mommy?"

The girl pointed to a woman that ran toward them. Randall rose and proceeded to the coat rack. He lifted his and Alicia's outerwear. "Precaution," he whispered as he piled their bulky coats on two empty chairs at their table. He pulled out Alicia's chair for her to be seated.

"You know the child?"

"Never seen her before. Guess I crave to rescue children who might be in danger. Those juvenile delinquents could've trampled that little girl." His eyes revisited the vacated spot where the toddler had stood as his chair legs scraped black and white linoleum tile squares. Diners toted large green paper bags, often two or three, with logos of Santa, elves, and Rudolph. A store security officer arrived to escort two of the three youths to parts unknown and Randall's thoughts drifted to Alicia.

"Can I snap a picture of what you have on your tray?" Alicia teased.

He stared at her tray, all vegetarian except for a tuna fish half-sandwich. No red meat. "Should be me with the camera. Confession time, I guess." She pressed her lips into a straight line. "Had hoped to discover an idea of what I could fix if you came to dinner."

No utterance nor any eye or facial movement offered Randall a clue. Had he misinterpreted her "next time" words? Randall dipped his spoon into beef vegetable soup. Through the visible vapor he launched his fall-back position. "You could invite your roommate and her friend, what's his name?"

Alicia's smile returned. "Vicky and Joel."

"Right. Vicky and what's his name." They both laughed. He didn't press for an answer. He pondered if he should mention Jackson's name. No. His next-day trip to California cancelled Jackson's trip east. By Jackson's facial reaction he'd have a better gauge of Jackson's seriousness and possibly the reason for his buddy's request to speak with Alicia.

Randall confined his fascination to why Alicia chopped vegetables into ever-smaller pieces and never sampled more than two. Halfway through his meatloaf, Alicia reminded him he hadn't answered her question about the five points necessary to be a good romance writer. He pressed a napkin to his lips to delay his response.

"Did Wanda ask you if you'd written or contemplated writing a romance novel?"

"Uh-huh."

"Thought so. She's fixated on that question."

As Alicia toyed with her food, he maximized his opportunity to gobble his last three meatloaf forkfuls rather than invoke Jackson's memory with conversation about a Vikings's nosedive. While the atmosphere around them evoked questions of Christmas plans, he dodged the topic as he would snowplows—wide and fast.

He shivered when the outside bank sign flashed sixteen degrees. At Alicia's urging, he had abandoned his skywalk suggestion for them to stroll the mall. They weaved past, around, and between holiday shoppers. He laughed, when, at the statue dedicated to Mary Tyler Moore, Alicia touched the top of her fur-edged hood and faked a hat toss into the air. Alicia's spirit uplifted him, a glorious twinkle in a gloomy sky. She could be a Yule log spark, spectacular, yet potentially dangerous.

Randall peered from behind Alicia's right shoulder when she stopped at an animated window display. When Alicia's right hand pointed at a dancing elf, he chuckled.

"Bet I could do that." His hands-on-shoulders pose

185

mimicked the puppet.

"Good job."

He squeezed her gloved right hand. Her face radiated; her gaze toward him lengthened. Like vagabonds finding shelter from the breeze and cold, they snuggled within a recessed vacant doorway stoop, next to a wall's silver fire hydrant cap.

One chilly kiss and Alicia's shivers caused him to rotate her shoulders and to step onto the sidewalk. Hand-in-hand, they scurried to the office parking lot. His Lincoln's heater and activated seat coils warmed them to their red-cheeked faces. Her kisses stoked his passion, which he sensed as more emotional than physical. His fired insides never cooled. He grappled to transcribe the unrelenting intensity into words and could not.

Alicia agreed to his Sunday night movie offer before his Lincoln parked at her apartment's curb. "If not dinner, what about a double date with Vicky and what's his name?"

Alicia stared out the windshield. "I'll talk with Vicky. You don't have to walk me."

He wished the evening to continue, even if a short walk.

She leaned his way and he kissed her warm lips.

"I'll be okay. Not a little girl and there's no gangbangers in this neighborhood."

Randall swallowed hard. "I'll watch."

* * *

Randall's stomach somersaulted Friday evening with his plane's hard Los Angeles landing. When he exited the LAX security concourse, he shook his head in astonishment. Jackson, in a black beret, orange shirt, and dark navy blue slacks, waved a white eight-by-twelve inch cardboard sign above his head with "Van Gilleran" printed in squiggly letters. Two foxy twins draped with plastic leis and clad in fake-grass hula skirts flanked him.

"Your club transportation awaits," Jackson snorted.

The club dancers stirred the crowd's attention with their rush to lock onto Randall's arms.

"You scalawag."

Jackson bent forward to whisper into Randall's left ear that a photographer waited to splash Facebook with the twins kissing his cheeks if he didn't agree to dinner. Jackson's right index finger pointed to a lanky man wearing a nondescript dark suit. The bearded man raised a SLR camera and waved his right hand fingers. Randall shrugged in acquiescence to Jackson's blatant blackmail. He could never outdo his friend's high jinks, nor trust Jackson's future leniency.

At a Hawaiian-themed restaurant near Sunset Boulevard, Jackson hyped the twins' banter of sought after movie roles. He also needled Randall by offering the twins a film excursion to be South Pacific island explorers. Between Jackson's words, the twins' never-ending smiles, and the occasional feminine pat on his knee, Randall strained to contemplate why Jackson would desire Alicia.

The ice cubes from Randall's second drink melted as he finished his Mahi-mahi. None at the table kept pace with Jackson's Mai Tai orders, except the ever-appearing server. After the twins joined Randall to refuse an after-dinner liqueur, the man with the camera reappeared to chauffeur the foursome to Jackson's condo. Sandwiched between the twins while Jackson rode shotgun, Randall didn't dare relax.

Randall's alcohol-enhanced jet-lag grogginess not relieved when he slumped into a living room papa san chair. He didn't know which twin sat cross-legged on the floor next to him. They'd switched names off and on during and after dinner. He fought to remain alert until his eyelids collapsed.

One Paper Heart

Randall tossed aside a chintz bedspread and a Star Wars top sheet. He rubbed reality into his eyes to find himself alone in Jackson's spare bedroom. His clothes lay scattered on the floor. A strange perfume smell lingered in the flannel, galactic-crested robe folded neatly on a chair. Randall stretched his arms into the robe's sleeves. Unsure if it was the perfume, an inhaled bacon aroma, or the abrupt climate change, Randall sneezed. He inched into Jackson's kitchen. A familiar brown satchel rested on the kitchen table between two place settings.

"How we doing, old buddy?"

"Got coffee?" Randall's right hand on a counter edge steadied him. "Do I dare ask what happened to the twins?"

"Both disappointed you conked out early. One really, *really* disappointed."

Randall yanked a chair free of the table. "Which one?"

"Huh?" Jackson's eyes rolled with his belly laugh. "What difference does it make?"

Pain twinges pulsed behind Randall's eyes. He plopped into a metal-backed kitchen chair. Frayed above-the-neck nerve endings registered a hazy recollection that Andy had awakened him for a greeting and then departed after words of a screenplay draft.

Jackson delivered pancakes and bacon. "You still bent to leave tonight?"

"If Andy and I get quality time this afternoon." Jackson's lips quivered. "Don't ask. Can't survive another dinner." Randall opened the satchel to find a screenplay entitled "*A Search Fulfilled.*"

"You'll disappoint the twins."

* * *

Alicia's flared, white slacks dazzled him when he

188

greeted her in her apartment lobby Sunday evening. Not even her stylish beige Irish Aryan sweater with its rope stitch drew his eyes from her slacks. Her kiss boosted his spirits higher than an electrical line spike.

Her warmth radiated to him through their joined hands in the Cineplex darkness.

Only a short trip to the Ground Round Restaurant kept their knees apart.

"Have you seen Mr. Grant lately?" Alicia asked. Her voice flat.

Randall, in rapid-fire succession, asked, "Has he done something? Vicky agree to dinner?"

"She said she'd chaperone." Alicia's left hand formed a barrier her right hand stacked shelled peanuts against. The pile collapsed with the thirteenth peanut. After three itsy-bitsy hamburger bites, Alicia answered his first question. "Mr. Grant requested nothing. He's the only friend I know you have and I tried to make conversation and not be surprised by his next visit."

Randall opted to be vague for Wanda may have tipped Alicia on his early Friday departure. "You won't be. Visited Jackson yesterday. We're working on a new project." He leaned across the booth table. "With your literature knowledge, we may want to challenge . . . er ask you a question or two as we progress."

"I'd be happy to help."

Was that to help him or Jackson? He finished his burger, left the raw onion slice.

Alicia delicately touched her finger to his lips. She suggested his drooped eyelids longed for an evening's early end.

He switched on the Lincoln's seat warmer even though he was drowsy. Moonbeams from a Jackie Gleason Show-sized moon reflected off the glistening, crystallized snow cover outside Alicia's apartment. Her black boots separated the snow's whiteness from that of her slacks.

One Paper Heart

Randall's mind staggered between reality and delirium. Nature's idyllic scene would have made poet Henry Wadsworth Longfellow proud. Hiawatha, his Indian maiden subject, however, would've shivered in her skimpy, animal-skin miniskirt.

With Alicia's hood up, its fur edge tickled his ears. His engaged lips recited no poetic words. His levitated passion rode the moonbeams and touched the clouds of heaven when they embraced.

Poet or not, conscious or dreaming, her kisses enthralled him.

Chapter Twelve

Sunday afternoon, between church and Randall's date, Alicia couldn't coax, challenge, or cajole the writing god into action. Try as hard as she might, her inner voice failed to craft traits for a new heroine. She desired originality and wouldn't duplicate Randall's stated method by giving her last heroine a new name and a revised character location.

Alicia left her bedroom dresser ointment stash undisturbed. Was the blank computer screen an omen? No. Superstition didn't exist in her world. Nor did astrology.

Without writing to consume her time, it dragged. She filtered out fears of her one p.m. Monday appointment with Doctor Beck. Her physical, postponed when she had lost her teacher's insurance, rescheduled with her eligibility under her NRD policy.

Alicia shuffled from her bedroom into the living room. Vicky lay sprawled on the sofa in her red, oriental-patterned, silk pajamas watching *Drop Dead Gorgeous*. "Can I interrupt?"

"No problem." The television picture froze mid-tractor explosion.

"Randall offered a dinner at his place. Would you go?"

"Why? You scared to tiptoe into the lion's den all by yourself?"

"No." She tightened her jeans belt one notch. "I trust Randall."

"Must be second thought jitters. You haven't been there in a while."

Alicia perched her buttocks on the sofa arm. "You can tell?"

"Not Einstein. Comes with the third rapid-fire date." They both chuckled.

"Want to be polite, yet not eat for fear I'll bloat to my old self. End up uncomfortable." Alicia's throat choked off the self-pity. She loved her new me.

"You have qualities beyond physical. Honesty, caring, and perhaps homemaking skills rarely shown around this apartment."

Vicky's jab struck Alicia as playful. She sheathed a retort. "Oh, Joel's invited, too."

"You think that's wise?"

"Can't be just us. Joel's stopped with the leering looks behind your back."

"I'll get him for that."

"Forget I said anything. We'll revert to our old plan. You stomp his foot when I flash you the sign language signal for the letter R."

Vicky nodded. "New question. Have you expanded your office horizons? You're wearing shorter skirts when you mention Randall's absent?"

"Trying to blend in. That's all. Everyone's so fashionable."

"What about your novel?" Vicky powered off the TV.

"Hesitant to say much." Alicia distracted herself with the movie's jewel case. "I've not seen it at work." She slid from the sofa's arm to a cushion to sort through the newspaper for the entertainment section. "What about you and Joel? Things going good?"

"He's fun to be with. Like you, I'm concerned about the future."

"You want me to bribe Randall to ask him a question at our dinner?"

"No. You get him drunk. I'll ask." A smirk spread across Vicky's face.

"You serious?" Alicia tossed the newspaper onto the coffee table.

"Of course not." Vicky fidgeted with the remote. "What can I say? I'd like to see Randall's place. The vibes from the walls may help you decide."

"Don't believe in that ESP stuff. Kisses tell me more."

* * *

Alicia rapped on Randall's condo door. Her raps echoed past Vicky and Joel behind her into the hallway's Saturday stillness.

Pleasant roast beef and fresh bread aromas filled Alicia's nostrils with memories of her New Brighton home. When Randall carried their coats into a bedroom, Vicky whispered to her how cute Randall looked in his apron with its chest-high row of embroidered red hearts.

The condo's three modern abstract paintings intrigued Alicia. Two colorful pastels adorned the east and west living room walls and a stark black and white hung in the dining room. The red, orange, green, and yellow filled rectangles displayed no artist signature. She had expected a European castle or a mountain landscape or a sports motif.

"Wow, do you see that TV?" Joel exclaimed. "Has to be 50-inch. Betcha its digital projection HD." Vicky ignored Joel and walked the living room perimeter. She complimented Randall on his choice of sturdy, masculine Mission-styled furniture.

"Excuse me, that's the oven timer."

With Randall out of earshot and Joel kneeled before the TV, Vicky bent close to Alicia's right ear. "No woman lives here or visits often."

Alicia, in a low tone, replied, "Better that the fire detector works and we're not above the seventh floor."

"Want Joel to do a courtesy inspection?"

Alicia pressed her forefinger to her lips. She guessed Randall had seen them whispering before he offered all three drinks and a dining room table escort to Alicia.

Alicia passed on the mashed potatoes to dine on the fork-flaking pot roast and carrots. *How can Scandinavians stay slim eating like this?* She slid the butter to Joel and enjoyed the warm, fresh bread with dips into the pot roast juice. Vicky shrugged when Alicia requested her dessert with coffee later. Joel carried his lemon meringue pie to the cloth-covered card table stacked with board games.

Alicia, paired with Randall, defeated Vicky and Joel in the "Spy Alley" board game. When Joel groused about his third embassy loss, Vicky grabbed Joel's wrist for a team timeout in the corner. Joel's hangdog expression readied Alicia for the evening's eleven p.m. end.

As Joel finished his foamless beer chug, Vicky announced she would join Joel outside when he warmed up their car.

Alicia, not surprised Vicky planned to leave her and Randall alone for a private, passionate kiss, dilly-dallied to collect game pieces and add drink glasses to Randall's sink. She repaid Vicky's favor by striding straight into their apartment lobby without a rearward glance.

She rushed upstairs to telephone Randall from her bedroom extension. "Home safe. Thank you for a glorious dinner."

"You're very welcome. Next time you should let Joel

194

win at least once."

"He's a big boy. I love you." She lifted the handset from her ear and realized she'd ended the call as if it were her family. She hadn't planned to say, "I love you." It sounded natural.

She had heard a faint "I love you, too."

Alicia plopped herself in front of her computer. Excited, time-delayed neurons raced to her mind's euphoric center receptors.

She'd reveal to Randall her Lady Victoria Dash pen name at the *A Search Fulfilled* publication release press conference. Until then she'd hide her authorship and her weight-loss rationale, but not her desire to share life and learn everything about him.

* * *

Doctor Beck's receptionist escorted Alicia to his office and directed her not to change into a gown. Alicia tapped her right foot. Her two painful weeks of Rod Serling nightmares not erased by his nurse's post-physical suggestion not to worry. Alicia rubbed both palms on her thighs until a draft suggested the door behind her opened.

"Stay seated." Doctor Beck limped as he rounded his desk to his chair.

Alicia gazed up into his solemn face.

"Concerned about your weight loss. Have you experienced cramps or any unusual midsection belly pain or, say, across the pelvis?"

"Nothing unusual. There was that reddish toilet bowl tint."

"We can forget that. Nurse said you ate beets the day before."

Alicia felt stupid. "I made a conscious effort to lose the forty pounds."

The doctor glanced up from the papers on his desk.

One Paper Heart

"While I preach against obesity, you're the opposite. I'd be concerned if you weighed less than the hundred and twenty-five pounds you now weigh."

Alicia hadn't planned to wear a less than size six dress or corset her waist to less than twenty-four inches. Her biggest clothes purchase to date: three bra and panty sets. "I don't want to balloon up again."

"Eat sensible and record what you eat daily, include every bite."

Alicia breathed a sigh of relief.

"We need to order a CT scan."

"What?" Dizziness permeated Alicia's brain. Her hands grabbed both chair arms. "Am I dying?"

"Heavens no. We need to be precautionary. The weight loss you've experience is praiseworthy. It can also mask cell changes not so beneficial."

"Cancer?"

"Your test results don't indicate that. Best we be sure." He rose from his chair and stood next to her. "Talk to the nurse and we'll speak again after the scan results."

Alicia didn't trust her legs. She treated herself to a cab ride to the Bunyan Center.

"You doing okay?" Carol asked. She rose to relinquish the receptionist duties to Alicia.

"Routine checkup. Think I earned a gold star."

Alicia immersed herself in e-mails until she lifted the flap of the now familiar statistical report she proofread for Wanda.

"Hard at it I see."

The quick flip of her head tightened her neck muscles. Her lips parted.

Mr. Grant tossed a beige London Fog overcoat on a visitor chair. His arms cradled his brown satchel. His toothy grin AWOL.

"How . . . how are you?" The pencil in Alicia's right hand plopped onto her desk.

"Santa helped me forget that you spurned my

Christmas lunch offer."

His bulky, Nordic crème-colored sweater didn't duplicate the disheveled wrinkled-suit look reminiscent of when she'd first met him. "I'm sorry." She cast her gaze away.

"Don't worry. Spring offers a new beginning. Is Randall in?"

His formal tone showcased that more than his outer clothing had changed. "I'll buzz Wanda."

Her frequent glances to reception's office door didn't hurry the room's clock clicks. Mr. Grant's leg shifts between progressive clock clicks unnerved her. When Wanda opened the door to reception, she slumped as he passed.

It was too late for Alicia to shout he'd left his topcoat behind. She convinced herself he'd remember or learn winter's lesson. Twenty minutes later, Mr. Grant, without his brown satchel, retrieved his topcoat and gave Randall a good-bye hug. He offered her a casual good-bye.

Wanda peeked into reception, glanced four times toward the hallway entrance, and then into the main office behind her. She whispered, "Can you meet me after work?"

Alicia agreed and the two of them hid from public view in a tall-sided Donnelly's Irish Pub booth three blocks southeast of the Nicollet Mall.

"What's the big secret?" Alicia asked.

"Shouldn't be blabbing this, but I overheard Mr. Grant and Mr. Van Gilleran talking about a manuscript entitled *A Search Fulfilled*."

Alicia pressed her right hand to her shrunken stomach. *Oroville Dam.* She felt something begin to break inside her, a reservoir of emotional rejections at risk of flooding her writer's psyche. Right hand fingers stroked her sternum. Her rib cage flexed, but didn't crack. Her fingers calmed a heart ready to bound across the booth table like a Mexican jumping bean splashing her

197

diet cola. She soaked up the cola with four paper napkins from a dispenser to her right.

Wanda stared at her. Had Wanda discovered her authorship? Alicia's attendance at Randall's option meeting hadn't been an office secret.

Alicia inhaled deep and long. "What did they say?"

"Well, Mr. Van Gilleran, in his usual tirade, criticized the writing." Wanda lowered her voice. "He told Mr. Grant the manuscript would never be published by *New Romance Delights*."

"You sure . . . real . . . sure?" Alicia fought to remain coherent. A wave of dizziness erupted within her to distort Wanda's features. Alicia's left hand groped to grasp the booth table edge to steady herself. "You positive he said that?"

"Cross my heart and hope to die." Wanda sipped stout through its Guinness foam.

"Why . . . why not publish?" Alicia failed to recall if Elena ever mentioned a conversation with Randall outside her presence. She harbored no doubt he said nothing about not publishing her manuscript during Lady Victoria's option meeting. His unmixed facial nuances had soared her enthusiasm about holding her novel.

"The two of them wanted the story idea for a screenplay they're writing." Wanda followed every sip or two with a peek past her left shoulder, around the booth's corner, here and there, most often toward the pub's entrance. "Mr. Grant also said the price paid was cheap."

Alicia's queasiness bubbled into seething anger. It looped vein after vein. *Sanford Dam, Texas.* A suspicion gnawed Wanda knew more.

In a small voice, Alicia asked, "Why tell me this?"

"See you as a friend of Lady Victoria Dash. Don't know how I'd reach her. Too scared to call her lest Mr. Van Gilleran hear. Any letter might get returned to him."

"You're very kind." As Wanda's complexion reddened, Alicia figured hers must rival a street corner mime without the red lips.

Wanda's hands gripped her sweating beer glass. "Please, if you tell Lady Victoria, you can't say I blabbed."

"My lips are sealed." Alicia's neck stiffened, and then her spine tensed. She struggled to exhale. "I'm torn if I should, or should not, ignite my friend's anger. Her every word convinces me she expects her book to be published."

"I know I couldn't wait to be published and not have it happen." Wanda sighed. "I'd better go. My husband worries."

"My treat. Go." Wanda slid out of their booth. "And, Wanda—"

"What?"

"Wipe that foam mustache before you kiss your hubby."

Wanda chuckled and reached for a napkin from a nearby table before her departure.

Although Alicia desired a cosmopolitan, she asked the server for their check, and paid the bartender on her way out. She kicked a discarded blue mitten to the curb. *Randall's proclaimed honesty a total lie. A scoundrel clothed in fine tailored threads.*

She reined in her anger. If she lashed out at him, her pen name secret and their growing relationship torpedoed. She couldn't involve Elena. Alicia counted her possible options as nil, zippo, and nada.

* * *

Alicia let the four forty-five No. 34 Orange bus leave the Bunyan Center stop without her. She boarded the Washington Avenue bus to drop her off a block from the University of Minnesota's Frazier Hall. A half hour early, she found, with ease, an unoccupied front row classroom seat.

She had, four days prior, inflated a slight cough, ticklish throat, and no fever to beg off a Saturday concert date with Randall. Wanda's unnerving Lady Dash revelation had sapped her strength and devoured her desire to be alone with Randall outside the office. She didn't want to go on, or trust anyone ever again.

Her clipped verbal interactions with Randall didn't stray far from business necessity. She planted a tissue box, borrowed from Vicky, next to her office computer screen. That he'd asked her out signaled to her she hadn't embossed her inner feelings on her forehead.

Alicia stood and paced four seats left, seven right. *It's not too late.* She smoothed the sleeves of her blue wool sweater. *I should withdraw.* Her inner self convinced her not to act on anger and supposition without collaborative proof. While she trusted Wanda, any false accusation against Randall destroyed her publishing goal. And, his kisses had convinced her his asserted affection was rooted in sincerity.

She extracted a folded business-sized envelope from her purse and laid it in her lap after she sat. Georgia, her sponsored child, hadn't, at age five, written the one-page letter, nor clipped the photo to its upper left corner. Still, the news of a healthy Georgia and that Santa had brought her a Raggedy Ann doll for Christmas warmed Alicia's heart. She imagined Georgia hugging the doll close as she had her first inanimate playmate, a nondescript teddy bear with large, goo-goo eyes. She stuffed the letter into her purse when she heard someone whisper "He's coming."

A motionless Alicia stared at the lectern. Halfway through his introductory speech, Randall's jaw dropped while his eyebrows rose. He stared at Alicia. Long horizontal furrows deepened across his forehead. He clamped his left hand to his mouth and turned his back to the class. His cough echoed.

200

Alicia gazed sideways. A murmur began behind her. Randall's pivot to face the class silenced it. He apologized for the interruption, focused his gaze on the last row while he detailed the essay deadlines and his pass/fail grading.

When the attendance sheet came to her, Alicia initialed in the space provided for one "A. L. Danielson." No student interrupted Randall's half-hour lecture on simple and compound sentence structure. He spoke each point as if his soles had stepped in wet glue squeezed on the floor behind the podium. At the end of class, one man, raised his hand to say "Senor."

"Si, Jose."

"When is final exam?"

"No final. Class is pass/fail. Pass is based on successful essay completion."

Alicia stood as her classmates filed out. She said good night to a broad-featured lady who had belatedly sat beside her. Randall collected the attendance sheet before he approached Alicia.

"What are you doing here?"

Alicia had expected his question. "Trying to improve my writing." She left unsaid for who.

"You shouldn't expect to learn much in this class." Randall glanced to the lectern. She noticed he'd left his briefcase there. "It's basic remedial writing structured for the GED test. To my knowledge, you're the first college grad ever enrolled."

"Maybe the review will help?"

Randall's eyebrows rose. He twisted and stretched to retrieve her down coat from a nearby seat. Alicia pushed her fists into its armholes and he lifted the coat until its collar fit the nape of her neck. "I predict you'll be bored."

Alicia rotated right to again face him. "We'll see." She ran her right hand forefinger across her lips and crossed her heart. "Promise I won't jump up and kiss you."

"A-L-I-C-I-A!" He shook his head and retrieved his briefcase.

Alicia's cheeks warmed at his reaction to her impromptu tease. She'd never deliberately try to embarrass him until she proved he lied to Lady Dash. "Expect you'll treat me like any other student."

Randall shook his head a second time. He preceded her to the classroom's door, collected excess class handouts scattered on a nearby table, and unclasped his briefcase for them. "Would you care to walk back to the office parking lot with me?"

She nodded.

Between clouds of exhaled vapor, they spoke of upcoming community events. Alicia expended her largest exertion to avoid piled snow. Randall halted his advance when she pointed out a mongrel dog shivering beneath a street light.

"He or she's got full unmatted fur and a collar tag. Best I call the animal shelter."

Alicia hadn't seen the dull metal tag. A thoughtful Randall, rather than a Mr. Hyde, wasn't making it easy for her to dislike him. Her tangle of emotions knotted tighter as she focused her full attention on Randall's red facial pores and the white ice flecks that salted his five o'clock shadow.

She flattened her wool mittens to her face until they arrived at the Bunyan Center. Without an expressed reason, she refused his offer of a ride home. He waited with her until the half-full No. 34 Orange bus crunched exhaust-darkened gutter snow at her feet and she mounted its rubber-ribbed steps.

From a safe mid-bus window distance, she acknowledged his wave with her own.

* * *

When Alicia opened her apartment door, Vicky ran to her. "Thank goodness you're home. I thought something serious might have happened."

Alicia apologized for her failure to remind Vicky that tonight had been her first writing class. She slipped out of her boots, hung her coat, and handed her roommate a class handout.

"You got a message from a doctor's office."

"What's the message?"

"Listen for yourself." Vicky disappeared into her bedroom.

Alicia pressed the voicemail message button. The woman said she worked for Doctor Beck and that Alicia needed to make an appointment to visit Doctor Beck as soon as possible. Alicia didn't understand why. Perhaps they'd jumbled her recent visit. She had no pain.

Alicia carried a glass of water to the living room sofa. Thoughts of Randall eclipsed by medical fears. Vicky and her grasped laundry basket squished the cushion beside Alicia.

"Anything you care to unburden about the doctor call?"

It was a gamble, but Alicia couldn't bring herself to even think what a CAT scan would find. "Even if I say I'm not scared, you'll notice."

"About what? You look great."

"Don't have pain. But when I visited my parents when the first Lady Dash letters came . . ." Alicia's conscience applied the brakes.

Vicky twisted a dry unmatched sock in her hands. "So?"

"I noticed blood in the toilet water."

"You sure it was blood?"

Alicia sipped from her glass. "It was red. What else could it be?"

"Something you ate. Kidneys can turn urine reddish

from beets."

"That's crazy." In too deep, she couldn't blurt out that's what the nurse had said. "Well, maybe not if you say so." Alicia gambled on a change in subject. "You wash Joel's shirts?"

"Those smoky things, never. Why take night classes?"

Alicia regretted her tactic.

"And . . ." Vicky pulled her cupped left hand toward her chest.

Alicia fished for a new lie from her depleted storehouse.

"C'mon." Vicky kept the pressure on by a repeat of her cupped hand gesture.

Alicia dusted off a new half-truth. "Randall at work criticized my writing." She picked up the TV remote. "He's teaching this essay class at the university." When the television's glare spread across the room, Alicia prayed this new distraction would silence Vicky.

"Bet there's another reason."

"No." Alicia's raised voice to combat Vicky's tease startled even her.

"Okay, okay." Vicky's immobilized eyes returned to normal.

"Sorry. I need to understand how publishing companies want stories written. They won't tell you." Vicky shook her head. "Plus, listening to others may help overcome my recent writer's block. I stare at the computer screen, my brain blank, unable to start a new story."

"With Randall as the instructor, I think you're tempting surprises never imagined."

Alicia rose. Her only concern about surprises would be from the doctor. She handed the remote to Vicky and grabbed her purse off the island counter. "If you don't object, I'll take a bath tonight."

She pulled Georgia's letter from her purse and closed

her bedroom door. She gazed at Georgia's dimples unable to dispel or leash her medical worries. That the five-thirty, time-stamped message came after normal hours churned her stomach, haunted her subconscious. Food was out of the question. More water increased her chances of never falling asleep.

Alicia filed Georgia's letter and picture with all prior letters kept in her bedroom desk drawer. A soaking hot bath failed to dispel her ill-defined fears. With her belly button exposed and her stomach skin harder to pinch, her worthy weight loss idea no longer carried its great appeal.

* * *

Alicia telephoned Doctor Beck's office after she made sure no visitor or office coworker eavesdropped. "Can you tell me what's so urgent? Why Doctor Beck wants to see me?"

"You must speak with him."

"Is he in?"

"On hospital rounds. You'll need to make an appointment."

Alicia scheduled one p.m. Friday.

* * *

Randall's right hand tossed his condo key onto his dining room table, too late to answer Jackson's ring tone. He mentally calculated it to be four-thirty p.m. Thursday in California. He pressed his Blackberry's redial.

"Good buddy, you're slipping."

"What in blazes do you mean? Hold on a minute. Just walked in the door." Randall laid his cell phone next to his keys and shrugged off his suit jacket and topcoat. He reclaimed his Blackberry and kicked off his shoes before he stretched out on his living room sofa.

205

One Paper Heart

Randall propped his cell next to his left ear. "What starlet dumped you today?"

"Your screenplay draft sucks."

"Did a twin lock her chastity belt?"

"This isn't comedy time. Andy agrees."

Well aware the trio strived to craft and promote a spectacular screenplay to wow the Oscar voters, Jackson's attack grated on Randall. He rose to pull a comb-bound screenplay draft from his living room file cabinet.

He pressed his phone's speaker button and twirled it on his kitchen counter. "I coulda said a thing or two about Andy's draft, but I didn't."

"Don't put me in the middle. Andy said he busted his butt on the first draft."

Randall's refrigerator yielded a Hamm's.

"Your revision's female lead and two major scenes confused me big time. You then flabbergasted me when I counted thirteen, not one or two, but thirteen misplaced commas and I ain't no English teacher."

"Don't believe it."

"Check pages twenty-three, forty-six, and seventy-eight for starters." Randall hustled to dog-ear pages. "I've been schlepping through every major studio, independent producer storefront, and director's office pumping our project. That'll be wasted if you don't match or exceed your past perfection."

Randall paced his condo in his stockinged feet. He paused at his fridge long enough for his left hand to extract a second beer. He swallowed a large gulp, belched.

"You misspelled a character name. Wanna know the page?"

"Heard you say it sucks." Randall guzzled more beer. "You don't have to chastise me like a three-year-old."

"I'm your friend. Better you be mad at me now than we become an industry laughingstock." He heard

Jackson's background music cut off. "Can understand
Mia's death jolted you. Think it's another woman. In all
but the last California visit you would've tickled feminine
bodies like the twins and partied until the wee hours. You
acted bored."

"If the screenplay upset you, I'm sorry. I've spent
every spare moment on it."

"You didn't hear me. Me think a woman's messed up
your focus. Maybe the receptionist? On my last visit her
skirt hem touched knees, not ankles." Randall failed to
swig cold beer from a bottle that contained nothing but
air. "Or maybe Charlotte? She's chasing. Her intentions
all but scrolled the Metrodome football scoreboard."

"I'm no grave robber."

"The receptionist then?"

"We've gone out . . . nothing serious." Randall lied to
keep Jackson off his back.

"Good. Keep it that way until we bank our investor
dollars."

"Andy will get my revisions in a day or two." When
dead air convinced him Jackson had spent his rage,
Randall pressed his phone's end call button. He doubted
Jackson had read his script version that close. Randall
figured that more than likely a producer's assistant had
circled sentences and scrawled the harsh comments
Jackson repeated.

Bygone days of being an unknown writer showered
with rejection slips didn't seem that far away to Randall.
His efforts to break in as a mystery writer lured him to
California where a UCLA summer class in contemporary
English literature promised carefree evenings. Randall's
apartment sublet amenities included a pool friendship
with a retired screenplay writer. The veteran writer's
introductions forged an unlikely triumvirate.

Randall saved a copy of the $1,000.00 check he,
Jackson, and Andy received for an unproduced
screenplay option. To meet expenses they prepared sushi

and pizza, served meals and drinks, and lugged sound studio equipment. Lightning in a bottle struck when Jackson schmoozed an independent producer to take a flyer with their Alaskan documentary.

Randall sighed. The Oscar's radiant bloom didn't attract fresh investor dollars. Tangent work dried up. Jackson's tirade underscored his desperation. His shriveled lifestyle would die if he and Andy didn't develop a marketable screenplay he could sell within six months.

While he wouldn't harm either Andy or Jackson, the time crunch caused by his NRD work, his screenplay deadline, and his endearing relationship with Alicia put one item at risk. He wouldn't sacrifice Alicia. She inspired him to be a better person. He would've never thought of mutual, selfless gifts to charity as Christmas presents. Only Jackson kept track of meaningless hemline length changes.

First time Jackson had berated his writing and Randall pondered Jackson's ultimatum. Randall didn't relish his Hobson's choice or that Jackson's friendship hung in the balance.

His physical virility weighed a close fourth. Alicia had, more than once, expressed her desire to have a family. If the fertility specialist's opinion proved right, his choice to favor Alicia shortchanged the screenplay. If the specialist erred, he could lose both.

NRD submission and manuscript reviews provided his easiest dilemma escape. He scanned more, skipped rereads, and evaluated manuscripts with a speed never before utilized. To ward off office interruptions, he authorized Wanda to route routine requests to others in the office.

In the evening quiet of his condo, he graded his extension class essays with the attention to detail of a school teacher. His students required full explanations in easy to understand terms.

Alicia concentrated on her essays until physical exhaustion sapped her energy. She revised her first three essays fifty-two times. Randall's first assignment asked her to write about a far away location her heart longed to visit. When the class in its third week received the first essay back, Alicia froze. The extensive red ink and margin notations extended to the page's reverse side shocked her. At the bottom of her first page she had written:

> When one tires of visiting beaches and native villages, you can renew your strength in one of Honolulu's lovely parks, sitting by a lake and watching the Hawaiians at play.

Randall had marked it up to read:

> When sightseers have exhausted themselves visiting beaches and native villages, they can regain their strength in one of Honolulu's lovely parks, either to sit by a lake or watch the Hawaiians at play.

Randall's margin note cautioned not to forget the context of a recurring word such as "one."

Alicia left class without a word to Randall. The bus trip home allowed her to read and reread her essay. She touched pages to her nose to hide her "Burl Ives" tear.

She mumbled a "hello" to Vicky and closed her bedroom door before Vicky lifted her head buried between two fashion magazine pages.

Alicia sobbed into her pillow.

* * *

One Paper Heart

Alicia's flat greeting two days later didn't dissuade Randall from dawdling in reception.

"Since we're alone, do you have any first essay questions?"

"I thought you were awful harsh."

"My words weren't meant to be mean-spirited." He spoke with rare in-the-office softness.

Alicia found it hard to be polite and escape his stare.

"Honest. We can talk about it."

Without a reason except delay, Alicia shifted unprocessed submission envelopes on her desk. Her words shouldn't hint at or divulge her bottled up anger. "Found an old fiction writing book by Dean Koontz. His book gave me a better insight into the truth of what you had written."

"You should've noted your essay punctuation was perfect. Hope that helps."

She requested he check out a manuscript submission arrived that morning. He hesitated before he walked to the side of her desk and leaned toward her.

Alicia kissed him on the cheek. Randall bolted upright and stepped back.

"That's for the nice compliment," Alicia whispered.

His eyebrows fell to their normal position and his lips touched before he spoke. "Your kiss beats an apple any day." He grasped her right hand between his. "We should get back to work. And, I need to warn you. No, that's too harsh. Tip you off to the university rule that students face expulsion for bribing, or attempting to bribe, instructors."

"Yes, sir." Alicia's tone brusque in grave military fashion.

Randall shook his head as he departed toward his office.

One at a time, Alicia received essays two and three. Red correction marks appeared, however, their number less than a third of essay one. The words "good and excellent punctuation" popped up in her essay margins.

Alicia tried to model Randall's comments with each succeeding essay. Her writing god time-traveled into and out of her writing efforts, never staying long. After an aborted effort, she deleted from her computer her outline for a historical romance.

She repressed her infrequent desire to confront Randall and have him explain why Lady Dash's manuscript would not be published. His essay writing critiques hinted at improvements to *A Search Fulfilled,* if she dared expose her authorship.

Twice she chickened out. A third try never materialized.

She half-heeded Vicky's advice to live in the moment and accepted Randall's date requests. He never broached her essays and she treated the subject as taboo. After the movie *Inception*, she accompanied him to his condo. Labeled the lion's den by Vicky, Alicia enjoyed the sixty-eight degrees, although the preference order of snuggles and kisses switched. She cast aside all thoughts of a mean-spirited Randall.

They broiled salmon. She teased him about his apron and apologized with left-to-right sequential kisses on each embroidered red heart.

* * *

Alicia's weekly telephone call to her mother revealed the expected—no more letters from *New Romance Delights.* She withheld mention of her doctor-ordered CAT scan with the rationalization Mom need not worry.

A worried and elated Elena bombarded Alicia with questions when Elena received a check made out to one Elena Cummings for thirty thousand dollars, less twenty percent withholding for taxes. In a mutual decision they deposited all money in a new bank account that listed

One Paper Heart

Alicia as joint owner with right of survivorship.

* * *

Randall's concerted screenplay correction effort put him two weeks behind in grading student essays. He attacked two dining room table essay stacks. Even without distractions, a full Saturday afternoon and evening left him with four plus Alicia's two essays ungraded. He reviewed and e-mailed his completed screenplay revision to Andy at ten p.m. Sunday. To thwart Jackson's ire, Randall left him a telephone message before he completed grading all essays except Alicia's.

Randall skipped his lunch Monday to finish Alicia's essays. The sentence structure and word usage in front of him struck a chord. He inserted a 1.0 GB flash drive into his office computer's USB port. From the file menu he clicked <Lady Victoria novel>. He searched for a minor law enforcement character he remembered from the original manuscript.

Randall lifted Alicia's latest essay from his desktop. His essay assignment required students to include dialogue. His eyes darted from Alicia's essay to his monitor screen. *It's either plagiarism or the same person.* Randall deemed the dialogue to be too close to have been coincidental. He expanded his review to solidify or debunk his initial impression. Analogous sentence structures and word choices emerged.

Randall tossed Alicia's essay onto his desk. *She'd played him.* His original suspicion that Alicia was Lady Victoria Dash spot-on. Now obvious she'd enlisted a writing friend to join her masquerade.

On the pretext of needing a missing file, he interrupted Wanda's office lunch with Alicia. With Wanda out of earshot, Randall asked Alicia if she'd meet him after work at an Irish pub.

Alicia's bunched brows made him hesitate. "Need your help to give Jose a class surprise tomorrow night. If you miss the bus, I can give you a ride."

"If you mean Donnelly's, I'll meet you there."

Randall curbed his intense feeling to blurt out his discovery. "Agreed."

Four hours of manuscript rejections ached his mind; his deception anger unsoothed.

* * *

Randall sensed a stiffness in Alicia's hello and a tenseness in her shoulders when he helped remove her coat. He handed it to her and she laid it on the seat of the high-backed Donnelly's Pub booth before she slid in opposite him. He ordered a Guinness pint and her a diet cola.

"Alicia, you know I adore you."

She neither spoke nor sipped cola through the straw she inserted.

Randall gazed at the foam inside his glass recede into liquid. He raised his eyes and waited for inspiration to fill in the blanks for what he'd say next.

Alicia sat stiff, her arms folded tight across her chest. "Yes."

"Never been faced with a situation that crisscrossed work with my university class."

Long furrows creased her forehead. Her eyes widened. "Don't understand."

"I've obviously read your essays."

"And, heavily criticized them, too." Alicia hadn't once lowered her lips or raised her glass to imbibe. She extended her left arm to grasp her coat. When his fear reached its zenith that Alicia prepared to leave, she seemed to have second thoughts and touched her right palm to her glass.

"Not talking red marks." Randall exhaled a deep inhale. "I've concluded that it's you, not your friend, who's the real Lady Victoria Dash."

Alicia's entire body froze. Her gaze pierced him colder than the sub-twenty winter weather outside. He clasped both hands around his beer glass. Its condensation chilled his fingers.

He tried to sound matter-of-fact. "You've been dishonest with me." He tried to extract her inner reaction from her expression. He couldn't. Alicia's frown and gaze trapped in time.

"Mr. Van Gilleran . . ." Her low volume lacked inflection. "Mr. Van Gilleran. You have exceptional nerve to accuse anyone, especially me, of being dishonest. I never said I *was not* Lady Victoria Dash . . . or said that I was Lady Victoria."

His squirm on the booth's bench vinyl emitted an audible squeak. If Alicia kept her composure, he'd also do so. He'd been too strident to use the word "dishonest." However, his anger at being duped refused to allow him to take it back, even if he dared.

Alicia's back arched. "This country has a long and strong tradition of authors keeping their birth name identity hidden." Her loudness rose. "On the other hand, you've been totally dishonest."

He gasped. She'd parried his word into a sword against him.

"When we met with Elena, you said my novel had a chance to be published within the next two years. That was a big lie."

How did Alicia know? Perhaps she guessed? The conviction in her voice persuaded Randall to doubt this possibility. Why hadn't she confronted him before? She cornered him. He had no way to dispute her without telling another lie. Where would his path of littered falsehoods end?

Alicia glared at him. "You've never had any

214

intention, either before the option meeting or since, to publish *A Search Fulfilled*. You and your henchman, Mr. Grant, schemed behind my back. The two of you only interested in me giving up my hard work without the payment of a fair price." Gravity jiggled a tear from her left eye. "You preyed on my innocence."

Where did Alicia come up with all this? How would she know what we might pay others? Did Jackson betray him? His screenplay revision quality hadn't been that bad. He'd made corrections. Revised its pace. He hated to think Jackson wielded a sharpened dagger to deny them an Oscar or cutthroat a best friend?

"You, behind my back, considered Lady Victoria to be a fool." Alicia's voice trembled. "What's worse, you made me believe you treasured me."

Randall, unable to bear her righteous glare, bent his head forward. His constricted throat blocked his every attempt to formulate a response. Alicia's voice strengthened. Her words, laced with contempt, battered him.

"You repeatedly told me that being honest was what you were. And, all the time you're a fraud, a con artist."

Randall didn't lift his head nor utter a sound.

"Betcha, if one were to check, your Oscar's a fake."

He raised his head to observe Alicia cross and uncross her arms. She didn't otherwise move until the back of her right hand glided her full cola glass toward the booth's inner side.

Randall remained silent, speechless. Her words stung with the ferocity of ageless truth. He did treasure her. If he said so, his gut said she wouldn't believe him. Did Jackson drive a wedge into his relationship with Alicia for his own personal gain? Randall hadn't discovered why Jackson called her in December or if there had been other contacts. Maybe Jackson promised her a connection with a California publisher?

Alicia began to rise. He had to speak up without

triggering additional angst.

"I'm sorry. Publishing is a business—" Alicia cut him off.

"Is publishing a dishonest business or is it that there are dishonest people in the publishing business?" She grabbed the booth table edge with both hands. "Which is it, Mr. Van Gilleran?"

His mind generated no quick idea for his lips to enunciate. Either way he answered shoveled quicksand under his feet. Alicia's excellent parry demonstrated her debater skills and the validity of her point far exceeded his showering her with kudos. He needed to escape with as much dignity as he could muster.

"I understand this conversation's difficult. Words easily misconstrued. I don't want that."

"Please don't patronize me. Truth isn't difficult."

Randall waved the server away. Dryness invaded his throat. Neither he nor Alicia had moistened a throat with a drink swallow.

"Real life," Alicia continued, "isn't a football game where one team decoys the other to win the cheers of delirious fans in the stands. Real life, Mr. Van Gilleran, isn't a romance novel." He twisted his gaze away from Alicia. "If you'd look at me you'd see you're broken my trusting heart, trampled my true-to-life aspirations, and skewered my soul with words as searing as any heated fireplace poker. If that's what you define to be quote 'honest' unquote, then I don't know what to say to you."

"Alicia, I hurt you. I can see that." Randall coughed. "You're right . . . life's not always a make-believe romance novel. But, real life can have happy endings. You can't deny that."

Her right hand squeezed her furry white hood to lift her entire coat. "Okay."

"It takes work."

Alicia's gaze dropped to his eye level. "What?"

Randall tried hard not to stutter. "Maybe for us it'll

take extra effort. I'd like for us not to make any hasty judgments. If you want to hate me today, you can do that. I'd appreciate it if you'd be willing to talk about us at a future date you choose. An opportunity, that's all I ask."

Alicia exhibited no visible reaction. She mirrored an unchangeable expression, like the Mary Tyler Moore statute on the Nicollet Mall, absent the smile and the powerful glee. He contemplated without resolution if he should best leave without her answer.

"Mr. Van Gilleran—"

"Please call me Randall." He swallowed hard against his constricted throat.

"Randall." Alicia's soft voice broke an extended silence. "I honored your request to meet after work without informing my roommate I would be delayed. I owe it to her to leave now." He nodded. "I'll think about your request."

She fastened her coat and started to step away. "I'm not saying it's the right thing . . ."

Randall never heard her finish her sentence. He stood and his spine quivered like Jell-O. Alicia exited the pub without one glance behind.

He started to count to ten, stopped at three. Perhaps, he'd catch her outside?

Chapter Thirteen

Alicia, unwilling to chance Vicky's presence, tiptoed through her apartment's kitchen into her bedroom's privacy. Tears she'd dammed on the bus ride dampened her left dress sleeve. She stared into her dresser mirror. Mascara streaks imitated Indian war paint and a cloth hand towel smeared lipstick onto her chin. *Tims Ford Dam, Tennessee.*

Her insides throbbed and her nerves collected her thwarted expectations at the base of her skull. She blinked her eyes into focus. The ibuprofen bottle in the bathroom was too far away. She threw her sobbing self onto her bed.

Why would Randall be so dishonest? Deceitful? Thank God for Wanda.

Alicia couldn't remember one lie told to third grade students. Had her red heart switch exposed her potential? Had her red heart switch been obvious to Randall from the get-go? Her signal to him she was gullible enough to fit his design to deceive his parents and to chisel her option price. Is that why the paper heart lingered on Wanda's desk?

Alicia pushed herself upright to don a pair of faded blue jeans and a purple flower-power tie-dyed T-shirt. She padded into the kitchen. The lasagna Vicky left could wait until her stomach calmed. An American Heart Association heart-shaped magnet posted Randall's phone number to their refrigerator. She threw both into the under-the-sink garbage can.

The telephone rang. *If it's Randall, must be to inform me I'm fired.* Alicia didn't answer. It stopped after six rings, rang again—roommate code.

"Ally, do me a favor. Box of oatmeal cookies in the freezer needs to be in the refrigerator for work tomorrow."

Alicia closed the freezer door. "Done. Your ice skating ankles still strong?"

"Great. Joel asked to introduce you to a new buddy. Didn't know what to say?" Alicia cradled the handset on her right shoulder to wet a hand towel under the faucet. "Say it's okay. But . . . don't agree to anything specific."

"You're kidding? This doesn't sound like you."

"Things change." Alicia wiped her forehead. "Enjoy yourself. We can talk later."

Alicia hung up. She pawed through the mail left by Vicky on their kitchen counter. A letter from the agency of her sponsored child boosted her spirits. She carried it to her bedroom.

She slanted her body across her bed and positioned her elbows to prop up her torso. Alicia tore open the letter expecting Georgia's new letter covered by a request for a continued donation. The first two paragraphs praised her support.

As she read, new tears clung to the corners of both eyes. A visiting couple from Los Angeles had expressed interest in adopting Georgia. Regardless, the agency director explained, Georgia's sixth birthday in three months required them to transfer Georgia to a state-run Arizona foster care registry since the agency's charter

One Paper Heart

limited it to caring for children age five and younger.

When Alicia didn't find a letter from Georgia, she tossed the director's letter into her computer desk's bottom drawer atop her Georgia folder. Her heavy heart required a diversion.

On her bedroom's outside doorknob, she hung her Do Not Disturb, Writer at Work sign.

* * *

Vicky's next morning rush to depart with her cookies eliminated Alicia's need to explain why she dreaded work this day. Her bus, crowded with senior citizens, left her no seat.

Every office reception door squeak caused her to jump. Randall never appeared and Wanda didn't enlightened when they shared a yogurt eat-in lunch.

With her attention zeroed in on answering e-mails, a familiar voice interrupted her.

"Good afternoon, darling."

"Hello, Mrs. Hauser. How are you?"

"Weather's dreadful. Temperature seventy-two in San Diego last week."

"What can I say?" Alicia watched Charlotte drape her fur coat on a visitor chair.

"This darn cold caused my hat to stiffen." Charlotte extended her right arm. "See."

Alicia could not care less. "I see." *Perhaps she'll leave quick?* "What can I help you with?"

"Randall called. He wants to talk about my next book and to let me cook him dinner."

"Allow me a moment, I'll buzz Wanda you're here."

Charlotte eased into the visitor chair nearest Alicia. "You know, darling, just between us women, when I said I was going to cook dinner that isn't really true. Either I gracefully remove tinfoil from caterer containers or rely on Andrew, my cook." Alicia froze her lips into a smile while she wondered what kept Wanda. "If you want to catch a man, a woman has to do those things one does well, and finesse the rest. Me? I'd rather organize fund-raisers than chop vegetables or blend gravy."

"You make interesting points, Ms. Hauser." Alicia shuffled papers to appear busy should Mr. Van Gilleran pop into reception instead of Wanda. When Wanda entered, Alicia's invisible safety valve release permitted her tension to escape in an inaudible sigh.

She didn't see Mrs. Hauser until two hours later when she hurried through reception with Mr. Van Gilleran. Randall kept his gaze straight ahead without a word to Alicia. Thirty seconds later Wanda dashed past Alicia to the hallway door. Alicia stood silent as Wanda pulled the door toward her and poked her head into the hallway without an expected shout.

Wanda retreated toward Alicia. "Did Mrs. Hauser mention why she visited?"

Alicia blocked out all references to Randall. "A vague mention of her next book."

"Strange. She never leaves California in the winter."

"Wouldn't know." And Alicia didn't. As far as she understood, lower cost telephone, e-mail, or facsimile facilitated author consultations. Why Randall, if it was he, altered the routine, she didn't care. Neither he nor she had said one word to the other since their pub confrontation. That suited her fine.

* * *

Alicia arrived ten minutes late Saturday afternoon for her parent's thirty-fifth wedding anniversary home celebration. She ate sparingly. Since brother George was away on naval duty, no one teased her that her piece of Elena's frosted yellow cake required ice cream.

221

One Paper Heart

She shooed Mom into the living room to join Dad's romp with the grandkids. After she piled collected plates into the dishwasher, she stood at the sink next to Elena, who peered toward the living room.

In a lowered voice Elena said, "We might be in trouble with the book money."

"What?" Alicia gasped.

"Jonathan hosted a lawyer from his company two nights ago. During dinner the lawyer said something about another store manager signing a contract to sell something that the company didn't own. He advised Jonathan to be careful."

"What else did you hear?"

"Not much."

Alicia's stomach churned. "Think harder."

"The lawyer gave an example of a merchant finding a case of product mistakenly left by a delivery truck driver. The merchant signs a contract to sell the found case to another. This contract is void or voidable . . . don't recall the lawyer's exact word." Alicia stood quiet. "Anyway, the money the selling merchant received isn't really his because he didn't own the merchandise. There's no finders keepers since the product wasn't abandoned on purpose."

"Doesn't sound like a problem. I wrote and own *A Search Fulfilled.*"

"Ya, you wrote it." Elena rinsed a glass cake pan. "But I signed the option contract, which states I wrote or owned rights to the book. I checked."

Alicia back-stepped to the kitchen table. Her mind wandered. "Whatcha checking?"

"Guess this isn't time for humor. Meant to say I'm not you and think we're in trouble."

Alicia collapsed into a kitchen table chair. Her manuscript submission plan had seemed so simple. Stick on a red paper heart. Take it off. Hope for publication acceptance. No personal meeting required. When her plan floundered, Elena rode to the rescue. Elena's *A Search Fulfilled* option signature and the lawyer's words surfaced from the jumble in Alicia's head.

Elena lightly rested her left hand on Alicia's shoulder. "What you thinking?" Elena's hand squeezed. "You need to tell me it's all right. I'm not in trouble."

"I may have to own up to being the real Lady Victoria Dash."

Elena sat across from her. "What about the money?"

"They can have their stupid money."

"Come again." Elena rubbed her hands.

An unexplained thud echoed from the living room. A startled Alicia rose. Elena's face reflected a brief pallor. A kitchen clock tick punctuated the room's stillness.

Dad yelled, "No one's hurt."

Elena's son, Jonathan Jr., ran into the kitchen to ask for a drink. Alicia filled a glass half full with orange juice. Junior, with the glass, scampered into the living room.

"*New Romance Delights* can keep their money," Alicia repeated. She folded her arms.

"What? Give up your dream? Maybe you could sign a new contract. Keep the money."

Alicia felt tears swell at the corners of both eyes. Her right hand to her cheek collected the first stream. "Two days ago, I found out that Mr. Van Gilleran bought the book to use it to write a screenplay. He never intended to publish it."

Elena rose. "Sis, I'm sorry. . ." She hugged Alicia from behind as Alicia hunched her shoulders. Jonathan Jr. burst into the kitchen.

Elena released her arms. "Honey, what do you want now?"

Alicia hid her eyes and tears behind raised hands and pretended to play peek-a-boo.

"Pop," he said. "Grandpa says he's thirsty."

Elena passed a cola can from the refrigerator into her

son's hands. "Wait honey. Take this glass for grandpa."
Alicia closed her fingers in front of her eyes, then peeked
to see Elena's son dash out of the kitchen. Alicia waited
for Elena to sit.

"Maybe you heard wrong it wouldn't be published,"
Elena suggested.

"I'm positive. No mistake. Randall confirmed it when
I confronted him." Alicia's strained nerves regained a
painful ache. Her entire dream flipped upside down.
Alicia's option meeting elation receded into a catatonic
memory.

And then her unrepressed emotional hydraulics
sparked a relevation. Her simple analogy, subject to
library research, struck her as a godsend. If Elena didn't
write *A Search Fulfilled,* she possessed no legal right to
sell or option it, thus, no legal sale existed. That's what
Alicia understood the company lawyer to tell Elena's
husband. With no sale, *New Romance Delights* didn't
own Alicia's story. She did.

Elena leaned forward. "What devilish thoughts gather
now?"

"Don't worry. I'll find a publisher. You'll get the
outfit I promised."

"Forget clothes. Forget the book."

"Can't."

"Do it for today. Mom's missing us and we can't add
to her burden."

Alicia wiped her face with a wet dishtowel. Loving
parents and the prospect of a boisterous romp with her
nephew or niece, even if none were biological, tempered
her anger and self-pity. When she entered the living
room, she dismissed her petty irritation that her father had
usurped her fun. Dad lay on the floor building a log cabin
with his grandson. Mom cuddled her granddaughter as
she tilted to and fro in her favorite rocking chair.

Dad gazed at Alicia as he hoisted Jonathan Jr. as high
as he could. "You should stay over. We haven't seen you

enough these past few weekends."

"Okay, Dad," Alicia replied. The simple pleasure of absorbing Nea's smile gladdened her heart, and, to her chagrin, Georgia's dream smile faded. Aunt Agnes's not-so-subtle urge for her to be vulnerable to attract a man wouldn't happen.

Friendly parishioner faces greeted Alicia and her parents at Sunday mass. She passed on the pickled beets without comment and, after dinner, joined Dad in the living room. Mom excused herself to take a nap. Alicia settled onto the sofa to face Dad, his eyes so loving.

"You never mentioned you work with a Van Gilleran."

Alicia felt flushed. "Never seemed important." She feared to ask Dad his source.

He cranked up the sofa's end section footrest. "Couple weeks ago for my Ford department I attended an all-day new paint finish improvements seminar. One presenter was a chemist named Charles Van Gilleran." Alicia's heart skipped a beat. "Very knowledgeable. Anyway, he joins my luncheon table. During conversation he mentions his son works downtown with a romance book publisher. At the time I think nothing of it."

Mom called downstairs for Dad to lower the thermostat.

When Dad rose, shivers of relief he'd finished his story flooded Alicia's body.

Dad eased himself onto the sofa. "Later, I remember you work for a romance company. Off to the side, I ask Mr. Van Gilleran if his son works for *New Romance Delights*."

"You didn't have to."

"Why not?"

Alicia doesn't wish to explain.

"He says, yes. I mention you work there."

She murmured, "You didn't have to."

"I'm proud of you." He shifted forward and his calves pushed the leg rest under the seat cushion, and then he smiled at her. "Do you know this Van Gilleran?"

"He's acquisitions editor."

"He must be about your age, right?"

"D-a-d. Don't know his age. Looks older." She rubbed her hands, again and again. Alicia's lower lip overlapped her upper. "Let's not talk about work." She knew Dad loved her, had always been proud of her. With hundreds of thousands of people in the Twin Cities, what Fate or Muse directed Randall's father to eat lunch with Dad?

"If he's anything like his father, I bet he's good looking."

Alicia felt her facial muscles tense. "There's more to a person than looks . . . honesty, for example." Her gaze rotated to the ceiling.

"Don't get upset. I'm only making conversation."

She gazed straight into his eyes. "I'm not upset at you."

"Good. Merely telling you about an interesting coincidence."

"Know that, Dad." He reached for a Sunday newspaper section on the side lamp table. "Try hard not to think about work or job applications when I'm here." She hoped Dad would read and drop this subject.

"And Mom and I are happy to have you. How's Vicky these days?"

Alicia expounded on Vicky's department store job and, in response to Dad's question, stated she had no inside knowledge when or if Vicky would be engaged. Her visit, after the seminar detour, returned to normal. She excused herself to find brother Alan before Dad drove her home.

* * *

226

"Good morning, Ally."

The booming voice caused Alicia to twist her upper torso to face reception's hallway entrance. A beaming grin jarred her Monday morning. "Mr. Grant, you startled me." Alicia lifted her long skirt above her ankles to allow her legs to swing with her chair's swivel.

"Please. Please. We've met. I'm Jackson."

"Yes, sir. Sorry, Jackson. But if Mr. Van Gilleran appears, you'll again be Mr. Grant."

He nodded. "You Minnesotans must love waking up in a freezer. I'll bet you summer vacation in Antarctica."

"Of course not." Alicia's soft rebuke uttered without brain intervention. "Although we've learned our warm hearts require parkas." She caught her Vikings reference in her throat. There was no way she'd be coy with Jackson's jersey gift.

"How about empty stomachs?" His question's tone matched his serious expression.

Her woman's intuition sparked an inkling of Jackson's hint. "Only warm hearts."

"What say you and I find a restaurant for lunch?" *Bull's-eye!* "We could beat the noon rush. It's been a different time zone since I skipped breakfast."

"Can't leave until my scheduled time." NRD's screen-saver logo floated on her monitor.

"How 'bout I see Randall and then together we three put on the feedbag?"

His mention of Randall triggered her stomach's twist into one big knot. "No. I'd be in the way. You know, three's a crowd."

Alicia bit her lower lip. She'd said too much, and too little. The cliché vague in a way she'd not intended. To clarify required her to admit she avoided excessive interactions with Randall. Within the office, outside of reception, she ducked into the ladies room whenever he approached. She delivered submissions to Wanda after

227

her check to see if the coast clear. When at her desk, she acted polite, spoke as little as possible, and prayed that Randall caught her drift and left with the foot speed of Mercury.

Mr. Grant didn't urge her to buzz Wanda or do anything. A little-boy sadness crept into his eyes. She couldn't upset the implied truce between her and Randall that her job remained unless she bad-mouthed him. The silence cornered her. "If you wait until noon, I'll join you for lunch, but I don't enjoy group eating."

Jackson's eyes twinkled. "You be ready at noon. I'll suffer until then." He ambled past Alicia and through reception's entrance to Randall's office before she found an intercom button. Lady Victoria's novel rotated into and out of Alicia's mind as she waited for the clock hands to join at the number twelve. Unless Jackson proved to be outrageous or leveraged his longtime friendship with Randall, she calculated lunch to be a bevy of nods and inane, impersonal subjects.

No way would she get personal. Her job prospects were in shambles. She hadn't had a favorable interview response to any teacher or substitute application since Christmas. NRD medical benefits were a lifeline to escape financial ruin. Dad's advice to her when visiting Mom in the hospital was to pray. She tried and also crossed and uncrossed her chest while awaiting her lymphangiogram results. When she showered the black and blue bruise on her foot reminded her of the unknown dye injection. Were unanswered prayers a godsend? Doctor Beck hadn't summoned her to his office to tell her if the cancer had spread from either almond-sized ovary.

When Jackson escorted her to lunch, new frets filled her mind about what information Jackson might have learned from Randall about her and Randall's pub meeting. While she had exposed Randall's dishonesty, she harbored no inkling of Jackson's involvement.

While her limbs shivered during their restaurant hike,

she appreciated the distraction and the banal weather chitchat it encouraged. He echoed to the bistro's hostess her assent to a balcony's secluded corner. Although he might interpret her position next to him at the four-top table as intimate, his back to the wall in the confined space limited their being overheard and shielded her lips from anyone who stared.

Jackson floored her with his first question. "Has Charlotte been in the office recently?"

"Last week." She didn't understand why Jackson ranked Ms. Hauser's comings and goings to be important. Should she suspect Ms. Hauser enticed Mr. Grant? Or did he worry about her fascination with Randall? If so, why should she care now?

"Interesting. Not to be repeated, she flew up to LA to convince me to find a screenwriter for one of her non-NRD stories. Then shop it around Hollywood."

"Wouldn't know anything about any screenplay."

"You wouldn't."

Alicia fought off her mind's gallop to decipher his last statement as true, a dodge, or a polite Hollywood platitude. So far he'd cloaked his intentions with niceness. His ignorant screenplay comment pricked a touchy subject. She remained on guard.

Jackson ordered a pork tenderloin with sweetie fries. Alicia stayed with a chicken-topped lettuce salad, vinegar dressing on the side.

"Don't suppose you have an opinion on Jay Cutler's trade." Alicia shook her head. "Figured."

Alicia sliced a quarter-inch chicken strip into fourths.

Jackson lifted six to eight tenderloin forkfuls to his mouth before he stilled his right hand alongside his plate. "Don't know if it's me. But you're as somber and quiet as Randall was this morning. You sure you two don't have the same mother?"

Alicia cringed and loosened her gulp with a second swallow. She stretched her body upward to eliminate her slouch. "Did Mr. Van Gilleran tell you I admitted to him I'm the author of *A Search Fulfilled* by Lady Victoria Dash?" She gazed at him, expected the worse.

His eyelids widened. Furrows stretched across his forehead. "No, he didn't." His right hand forefinger tapped a table knife. "You're not joshing me?" Jackson sliced his tenderloin.

Alicia sat quiet until he swallowed. "I'm serious. Lady Victoria Dash is my pen name."

Jackson's lower lip quivered.

An anxious Alicia rued her confession. Nevertheless, if the cat was out of the bag, Jackson's surprise hinted at Randall plotting greater mischief than acquiring her novel on the cheap. "Mr. Van Gilleran didn't tell you?"

He shook his head sideways.

Alicia dispatched her dad's advice to think long and hard before decisions. Extra deliberation often confused her options. Her snap judgment said Jackson was being evasive. "Then again, since he has no intent to publish the manuscript, why would he tell you about the decisions made by *New Romance Delights*?"

"You're right. He wouldn't." Jackson left his knife and fork on his plate.

Alicia tightened her stomach muscles and her right hand rubbed her thigh. She cleared her throat. Her question scattered figurative eggshells under her inquiry. "Did he mention using my story for a screenplay adaptation?"

Moisture glistened on Jackson's forehead. Little droplets along a furrow like those strung along a spider web filament in a Northern Minnesota national park on a humid summer morning. "I don't . . . I'm not . . ."

His hesitation emboldened her. "You don't have to admit anything. Randall told me." Alicia's chest heaved with a twinge of guilt. Randall hadn't been that blunt. Her retraction was out of the question, although she wouldn't repeat her lie or go further. She decried dishonesty. With it she'd trapped herself. Randall might not find out. However, she knew. She had to live in her own skin.

"Don't know I should be the one to talk about creating screenplays." Jackson lifted a last forkful of pork halfway to his mouth. "I only find buyers after it's written."

Alicia leaned forward. "Even if it's written, you mightn't have a chance to find a buyer."

"Did you receive a sour salad? You're not eating."

Alicia gazed at her rearranged lettuce leaves and the shifted chicken strips. She hadn't realized her only action had been to twirl a fork while engrossed in analyzing Jackson.

He reached below table level and his left hand reappeared with a handkerchief. He wiped his forehead with the folded cloth.

Alicia leaned on her memory of the football lingo brother George had bored her with and struggled for a gridiron image to emphasis her point. She ignored his salad question. "Think of my situation this way: fourth down and long, Chicago Bears, with the ball, are losing by four points, there's eight seconds to go, enough time for one play before the game ends." She watched the whites of his eyes brighten. "I've learned the option contract for *A Search Fulfilled* signed by my sister, Elena, isn't legally valid."

Alicia exhaled. Her shoulders relaxed. Certain that Jackson would report this information to Randall, she gazed at the floor next to her chair to locate her purse. When her purse rested on her lap, she lifted her gaze to see Jackson's handkerchief spread to wipe his entire face. Deep inside she regretted she'd squeezed Jackson between her and Randall. What option did she have? There was no future with Randall except as a peon until she landed her elementary classroom contract.

If she harbored no feelings or desire for Randall, she wouldn't have spent an entire restless night sobbing.

When she kissed Randall, her physical lip tingle expanded to touch her soul. No relentless scrubbing obliterated his imprint. No first aid kit carried an ointment or bandage to heal her wanting. Tears would dry. Her soul's scar eternal.

"What?" Jackson collected his wits. "That can't be?"

"From all I know, it is." Alicia envisioned she tiptoed amongst the eggshells. A cherry tomato burst within her mouth and squirted juice into her dry throat. "My sister listened to a lawyer who handles business contracts. She learned that if a person doesn't own something he or she can't sign a contract to sell it." Jackson leaned forward. He appeared to hang onto her every word. "Elena didn't own *A Search Fulfilled.* Therefore, she couldn't sell it nor sign a legal option contract. Only the owner can sell the rights and I haven't done that."

"But . . . but money was paid for the option."

Aha, he knows more then he admits. "You're right." Jackson waved the server away.

"You don't know everything about the money. It all sits in a special bank account." She gazed direct into his eyes. "If you want that money right now, I'll write you a check."

Jackson squirmed.

Alicia unzipped a purse compartment. She hated to ratchet Jackson's visual discomfort, nonetheless, she would've crumbled if she had faced Randall.

"Please. You don't have to give me a check. There must be a big misunderstanding."

She steadied her gaze on his forehead. "There's no misunderstanding." She rested her checkbook atop her purse. "I have proof I wrote the manuscript. Ask Randall to show you the contract original. My name's not on it, nor is my signature because I didn't sign it."

Her teeth crushed a second cherry tomato and she gagged. Her stomach's stop sign erected.

"Alicia, this . . . this surely can be worked out." His

voice wavered before it died and required a restart. "If you seek more money, I can be on your side."

Alicia arched her back. "Money doesn't solve everything in Lady Victoria's world—nor in mine. Money doesn't help one sleep at night or find real happiness." She refused to let Jackson interrupt. "My brothers, sister, and I have real life experiences to know that an orphanage can provide food and shelter, but often nothing more. That may give us a different perspective—" A teardrop slid to her chin and plopped on her chest. She reached for her purse and a tissue, not a blank check. Emotional tears were neither her ploy nor her definition of self.

"I . . . I didn't mean to upset you." Jackson's voice quivered. "Money plays a big role in my line of work."

Alicia dabbed the tissue below her eyes and watched his lips move without a sound heard. When they stopped, her voice filled the void. "I must get back. Don't want to be in trouble."

"Don't worry. You won't get in trouble for agreeing to have lunch with me." He rose, pointed, and wiggled his right forefinger at his left palm. "It's one promise you can count on."

Jackson excused himself when they reached the Bunyan lobby. Alicia offered her thanks for lunch and saw neither Jackson nor Randall at *New Romance Delights.*

She forced herself Tuesday to ride the bus to Frazier Hall to face Randall. She carried two essays. Both addressed Randall's assigned topic entitled "What Really Matters to Me." The first was a dry and clichéd appeal to end hunger in Appalachia. While worthy, it stirred no passion in her soul. To ease an ache in her heart, she composed a second essay that detailed the joys an adopted child brings and that one hurts no less when an adopted child is lost.

From the essay's first to last word, her upcoming

sponsorship loss of six-year-old Georgia remained in her mind's eye. Her writing spurred her to send a special donation equal in value to the donation that celebrated her completed NRD probation. She included a note to specify the money should pay for Georgia's required school immunizations.

Alicia promised herself to sit up straight, be cordial, and not cry in front of Randall. The class became restless as its start time neared. She entertained no doubt Jackson had relayed to Randall her awareness of the option contract's illegality.

She waited to see the fire in Randall's eyes before she ran.

Chapter Fourteen

Randall didn't expect Jackson to stay overnight in the Twin Cities without a Bears football game the next day. His buddy's cryptic cell phone message said to be home at eight. Randall hustled home from his essay class relieved not to find Jackson pacing his second floor hallway.

Randall uncapped two beers.

"Good buddy, beer won't help," Jackson kidded.

He didn't grasp why Jackson teased. *I can outlast him.* He sipped while his friend slipped off his shoes, tossed his topcoat onto a chair, and plunked himself onto the sofa with a beer.

"We risk real problems if we use that Lady Victoria story."

"Why?" Randall leaned his butt on his sofa's armrest. "We paid for it."

Jackson gulped a mouthful of beer. "Not that simple. When I had lunch with Alicia yesterday, her repressed anger resembled a blast furnace. And, good buddy, it spewed at you."

"You're exaggerating." Randall stood and paced three

times to and from his living room window. "Her eyes, the brief time I saw them an hour ago, flashed no daggers."

"Let me explain it this way." Jackson rested his neck on the sofa back. "If our lunch would've lasted five minutes longer, I'd not be here but in the hospital with my skin the black casing one chips off a burnt bratwurst."

"Where did you get that? A pulp novel read during a long plane flight or, who's that California writer? ya, a cheap Danielle Steel rip-off."

"Don't listen. Make jokes." Jackson swung his right hand and the bottle it clasped.

"When you're calmer, you'll see there's always a readymade solution." Randall stuck his right hand into his refrigerator's lower bin for a Hamm's.

Jackson jerked his bottle's neck from his mouth and belched. "Did you tell Alicia *New Romance Delights* had no intention to publish the Lady Victoria manuscript?"

"Don't remember." Randall halted his advance and faced Jackson. "She may have garnered it from someone else in the office. Or guessed. I don't know."

Jackson slid his body forward on the sofa cushion. "Whether you said it to Alicia or someone heard you and passed it to her, is it true you've no intent to publish the manuscript?"

"Told you before it wasn't well written."

He fixed his gaze upon Jackson until his friend waved an empty bottle. On his trip to the kitchen, he remembered Alicia's passionate pub declarations about honesty. In her hiring interview, her soft answer she'd lost a teaching position because of nepotism probably not recommended, but honest. He had gambled her shy reserve would evaporate while the marionette personalities of older-women applicants would never change. Neither did he desire to hire a man-hungry woman. Alicia's college English minor granted him the flexibility to promote her should the proofreader turnover continue.

In baby steps he learned Alicia, without fanfare, tried to uplift others. His being a slave to syntax, word choices, commas, and periods blinded him to her qualities beyond punctuation. His myopic view of *A Search Fulfilled* missed the underlying universal human drama of a search for a connective blood-relative bond. Its unique suspenseful journey unlike hundreds of others. He, Andy, and Jackson's sole quest to cash in on a celebrity's anguish represented their crass distortion of *A Search Fulfilled.*

Randall strode into his living room, banged a six-pack on his coffee table, and fell backwards into a blue-fabric wingback chair. Fame, money, family, or love? What represented his quest.

Jackson cleared his throat. "What say we have Alicia revise it with your guidance?"

Randall shook his head no.

"We can offer another five grand. On second thought, that might not be such a good idea." Jackson snapped a twelve-ounce beer from its plastic holder.

Randall stood and departed in silence to the kitchen. He returned with cheese and crackers. "By the way, where's my draft? The screenplay's second revision."

"Andy has it. Before I left LA, he said he needs to time every page to make sure each represents a movie projection minute. No biggie. Until the film's in the can, Andy always claims a few pages are short or a second or two long."

Randall sat silent in his wingchair. He tipped a second beer to his lips.

"As a friend, what did you do to Alicia anyway? You said you dated her." Jackson's shoulders relaxed against the sofa back. "You put your hands someplace you shouldn't have, and rather than slap you silly, she wants to skewer you by taking back her manuscript."

"Didn't touch her." Randall's words rose in a crescendo. "At Donnelly's she told me I was dishonest in

One Paper Heart

what I said to her friend posing as Lady Victoria."

"So it's secondhand. Alicia saying you were dishonest is hearsay?"

"Not really. Alicia attended the option meeting, said to be Lady Victoria's friend. Saw no harm." Randall's right fist punched the chair's arm. "Wasn't I the grand fool?"

"Don't kick yourself too hard, ol' buddy. I'd have done the same thing."

"What'll we do now?"

"Plead with Alicia. We'll be laughingstocks. Producers have elephant memories."

"Don't know that I can." Dread congealed in his chest. "Or that she'll listen . . ."

"LAX newsstands overflow with newspaper columns devoted to the search for the missing celebrity. We need a rock solid option." Jackson stood. "You think hard, find the right buttons to push, and don't lose sight of the fact that time's not on our side."

With his coat on his arm, he bade Randall good night.

Randall reshelved three unopened beers into his refrigerator. His telephone rang. With a thought Jackson had forgot something, he checked his caller ID to find his mother's number listed. No way he had an answer to her last week's request to invite Beatrix Smothers to her upcoming book club meeting. He let his answering machine do its thing.

Sleep closed his eyes with the promise he'd speak with Alicia the next day.

From eight to four Wednesday, Randall tried to marshal the courage to ask Alicia to meet him outside the office. Circumstances shot him down. Either Wanda interrupted to ask a question, the phone rang, or lunch intervened.

He broke into a lunchtime conversation between Carol, Wanda, and Alicia. "Wanda, do you have last month's statistics?"

Wanda finished chewing. "Alicia has it."

Alicia glared at him. *How could he be so foolish? He'd reminded Alicia her manuscript wasn't on NRD's to-be-published list.*

"Bring it when you can." He slinked to his office. Impotent? *Hate that word.*

Regardless, forty-thirty came and went. He had failed to effectuate a resolution or even secure a truce table. He left two evening telephone messages with Alicia's roommate along with one unanswered voicemail.

As he uncapped his third beer Thursday night, he detested his fate. Jimmy Dean sausage biscuits cooled in his microwave. He refused to traipse from the kitchen to answer his condo's landline. *Jackson didn't need to bug him about Lady Victoria?* His cell phone chirped. Its caller ID listed Mom.

"Son, Mrs. Johnson found an author for when she hosts next month." Randall didn't need to guess where his mother's conversation would lead and he felt helpless to interrupt. "I host the month after. Beatrix's such a charming person. Could you ask her to be our book club speaker?"

Randall inhaled deep. Ever tighter slow spirals of his mother's request battered his psyche. "Don't think she's available. She's on a new book deadline. Last minute revision research."

"Surely you can do it for your m-o-t-h-e-r." Her last word jackhammered his eardrum. While it vibrated, she added sugary praise. "I know you can."

At his wits end, Randall contemplated spilling the beans he was Beatrix, but, as before, he bit his tongue until the urge melted away.

"It's but two hours," his mother continued. "No one can be that busy. Dad or I, to avoid her hassle with cabs or buses, can pick her up and drive her home."

"Give me time, Mother. Can't make any promises." He switched his cell to his right ear.

"I know you'll try your best."

Randall reached for an uncapped fourth beer, and then decided he'd drunk enough and didn't need to slur his speech. "Can't promise."

When Mother allowed five seconds of dead air, he believed he'd survived Mother's latest matchmaker attempt.

"Dad tells me he met a Mr. Danielson at one of his seminars. This Mr. Danielson said his daughter works at *New Romance Delights*. Do you know a woman writer, last name Danielson?"

Randall's cell phone slipped from his fingers. His left hand's quick reflex grabbed the cell before it crashed on the floor. *Dad has a connection with Alicia's father?* His stomach triple somersaulted. Speechless, he grappled for words to hide his anxiety.

"You still there, son?"

"Writing myself a note."

"Good. If Beatrix can't attend, could you ask this Ms. Danielson? I'll visit the library to find out what she's written to be ready for when the book club meets here."

Randall cringed. He gathered his wits. "Don't think so."

"What don't you think? Why not?"

"There's a receptionist by the name of Danielson. That's the only Danielson in the office."

"Maybe she's one to help you get over Mia?"

"M-O-M." He contemplated a punch of the cell's end-call button. Love said he couldn't.

"Okay. Call me with the good news on Beatrix. I love you."

Randall pressed the end-call button. He sank into his wingback chair as a headache blossomed to constrict his sinuses. Even if Alicia agreed to a Beatrix Smothers encore, his whole charade was ripe to blow up. How would he know whether Dad had been shown a picture of Alicia Danielson? Parents carry billfold snapshots of their

240

children. Worse, Facebook existed.

Exhausted with imagined dire consequences, he stretched out on his bed. He tossed and turned unable to sleep. Vivid memories of Alicia's kisses aroused him. Desperate to sleep, he trashed the biscuits and microwaved a glass of milk for thirty seconds. The warmed milk splashed into his stomach's beer pool and he vomited.

After seven hours of restless sleep, a poetic romance dawn didn't energize his TGIF. Neither did a pulsating shower spray. Near eleven a.m. Randall found Alicia alone in reception. He squared his shoulders and tightened his abs to wait until she faced the hallway door.

Her blank expression said volumes.

"I need to speak to you." She stared at him. "If not here, we can go after work to the cafeteria we ate at before Christmas. It's public and shouldn't be crowded." He shifted his weight from his right foot to his left. "I thought you and I had something." Her facial expression didn't change. "I won't ask to relive the past." His breath grew elongated and whispery. "This tension, I'd guess, isn't doing either of us any good." He gazed to the ceiling to avoid the contest her stare invited. He'd said what he wanted to say. The next word would have to come from her.

"If I say I'll go, you'll not be nasty?" Her flat enunciation shaded with a detectable sharp edge.

"No way." He couldn't determine by her expression whether he'd broken through. If no inroad, he'd beg as a last resort.

"You find a table." For a split second, she gazed at her hands. "I'll join you there."

"Thank you. I'll do that." Randall stepped sideways.

"I'm not making any promise I'll stay."

* * *

Randall gripped a cafeteria mug filled with bitter, if steaming, coffee. His chosen table so far removed from other patrons he believed he fostered the impression he carried a contagious disease.

Five minutes after he poured two sugar packets into the mug, Alicia walked through the cafeteria line to select a fountain drink. On her advance to his table, she glanced left and right three times.

He stood. "Thank you for coming." He sensed the apprehensiveness between them would dull the proverbial knife.

Alicia unzipped, but didn't remove her coat. "Don't know if this is a good idea. At four o'clock I'd convinced myself not to come. I telephoned Vicky. She reminded me I'd never run away from anyone as I did you that afternoon at the pub."

"Let's not go back," Randall pleaded.

Alicia bowed her head.

"You deserve and I wish to sincerely apologize for hurting you. I know I did." He sipped coffee. "If life had an eraser, I'd use it." While Alicia didn't meet his gaze, she remained seated. He deemed her staying a positive. The negative was she offered no verbal statement his apology narrowed the fractured relationship crevice that yawned wide between them.

She spoke to the tabletop. "I agree it's best not to return to our last conversation."

Randall laid both hands on the tabletop, his palms exposed. "If that's an indication to make a fresh start. I'd like to do that." He didn't expect a quick answer.

After agonizing seconds, he heard her soft murmur, "I would, too."

"That's great."

Alicia stirred her cola and sucked a straw full. "First, there has to be a few understandings." Her right hand reached into her purse.

Randall glimpsed the edge of a folded paper.

Before Alicia unfolded it, a nearby voice startled them.

"Hello, darlings."

Alicia's right hand stopped in midair. She pushed the paper scrap into her purse.

"Ms. Hauser, how nice to see you," Randall said.

Alicia smiled at her.

Charlotte's yank bounced a chair away from their table. "Randall, I arrived late at the office. It was a long shot to find you here. We need to discuss my next book."

Vertical creases appeared between Alicia's lowered brows. He held his breath as Charlotte seated herself with a flourish. It made him squeamish Charlotte mentioned her to-be-published book in front of Alicia.

"I had a question for you, too," Randall said. His words echoed stiff.

Alicia, a motionless statue, stared off into space, an outsider to his conversation with Charlotte. That didn't bode well, but he couldn't dismiss Charlotte either.

"My mother asked me to invite an author to speak at her book club in two months. Would you do it?"

"Darling, that's impossible. If I chitchat with readers, it'll be at my sponsored fund-raisers. Why not Beatrix Smothers? NRD publishes a lot of her books, and, although I've never met her, perhaps she'll be gracious and accept."

Alicia lips twitched, but she remained silent.

"Only asking, Charlotte. No big deal."

Alicia rose from her chair. "If you'll both excuse me, I must be going." She zipped her coat's inner zipper and waved as she hurried away.

He offered a weak right hand wave.

Charlotte shifted to a seat opposite him. "Lovely young lady you hired."

"Yes, yes she is." Randall sighed. He gazed past Charlotte's right shoulder to the cafeteria doors as they

243

closed behind the departed Alicia.

"You'll be too busy to remember her when you start up your new publishing house."

Randall's right hand fingers rubbed his forehead. He'd forgotten about Charlotte's previous whispered inducement to entrap him. She'd been savvy enough not to mention it with Jackson or anyone else present. No recorded telephone conversations left proof of her desire to lure him and sabotage *New Romance Delights.*

Charlotte lowered her voice. "My lawyer informed me that adequate notice to *New Romance Delights* gets their hooks out of you . . . and me. If you hire a new acquisitions editor, you can build the defensive wall to defeat NRD's claim you stole any of their authors."

"That's hard to believe."

"Why? Since authors sign contracts for specific book deals, every author holds an escape cord. You can convince the best ones to sign with you when free agents. I will."

Randall stared at the cafeteria doors. He should be seeking Alicia's forgiveness and author rights, not fending off Charlotte. "Don't know. No way can I scrounge up the money to start a new imprint."

"Let me worry about that, darling." She scanned the immediate area. "This isn't the place to discuss our relationship. Put on your coat. Let's hail a taxi to my house."

Randall's gut told him to protest. He'd witnessed Charlotte firsthand with reluctant fund-raiser donors. She didn't take no for an answer. Like a dog that chased its tail, he'd exhaust himself trying to fabricate excuses until his depleted willpower reserve petered out.

Past the cafeteria doors, Randall scanned the building lobby and the street outside for any hint that Alicia lingered. His shoulders slumped into a cab when he found none.

Charlotte bent near him. "You've never seen my new

Donan Berg

carpet have you?"

"I haven't." Nor would it be something to thrill him. He remembered his last visit to Charlotte's house for a Susan Komen fund-raiser and didn't recall the old carpet's color. The milling multitude then saved him from Charlotte's advances. If truth be told, he'd never entered Charlotte's house alone lest the temptation to consent to her wishes proved too powerful.

After eight steps to a canopied landing, Charlotte, with a waved-hand flourish, inserted a gold key and pressed the buzzer.

Escorted to the front sitting room, Randall uttered the obligatory praise. "Your carpet is exemplary, excellent diamond pattern."

"The finest imported wool." Charlotte beamed.

"Give me your coat and sit here." She pointed to a lavishly appointed wood-accented burgundy sofa. "I'll have us fixed a cranberry cosmopolitan. If you've never had one, you're in for a treat. If you've sipped one, welcome back to heaven."

Charlotte disappeared with his overcoat. Randall wished he'd never given it to her. It could be hung in a closet he'd never locate. He didn't know which dearly-departed husband owned this mini-mansion. Larger than a St. Paul Summit Avenue guest house, he estimated it to be two-thirds the size of an 18th century railroad baron's country estate house. Expensive marble-topped antique tables, gold-plated candlesticks and vases, and frilled lampshades filled nooks and crannies and gilt-framed, oversized landscapes graced the gold-leaf walls that shimmered behind and above heirloom King Louis-the-something furniture.

The actual room less distinguished than the one Charlotte described in her last novel.

"Loosen your tie, darling." Charlotte followed her voice through a doorway different than her exit. "I forgot to telephone dear Andrew. He tells me dinner will be in

245

an hour."

Randall didn't believe her failure inadvertent.

Halfway toward him, she posed, feet together, her right slipper an inch forward. To rise, his hands pressed the burgundy fabric aside his thighs.

"Stay seated. I calmed Andrew by saying we're in no rush." Charlotte, changed out of her tailored gray suit, wore a flowing, blue silk gown edged in gold, which she lifted delicately and dropped over her knees as she sat on the sofa next to him. Blue gemstones in a circle above her instep graced her gold slippers.

A stronger perfume aroma engulfed Randall. He labored to resist its choking grasp on his throat. "Talk of my running a publishing house is all very flattering." Deep down Randall believed he could succeed after the mandated relocation from the Midwest. That troubled him. He detested New York City and the required extensive travel. He feared he'd strain his future family like his father.

"I'd say practical."

Randall gazed opposite Charlotte. "With all the upheavals in electronic publishing, you're better to wait until the dust settles before you risk any investment."

"Darling, call me impetuous." He couldn't miss the glint in her eyes. "I've hired a business manager who's developed this new age publishing model that leverages advanced technology. We hire people to do the actual printing, marketing, web design, and all those other tedious things." Her hand-created cushion depression allowed her to inch her torso closer to him.

Her caterpillar crawl stopped when Andrew entered with a silver tray and two martini glasses filled with red liquid. He handed Charlotte a drink and then Randall grasped a stem. Andrew departed after a sharp, small bow.

"Cheers." Charlotte lifted her glass high. "What is needed is a sharp mind to determine what books are

saleable. Also to guide a stable of top-notch writers.
You're the person with the demonstrated insight and
experience."

Her knee bumped his and his drink rippled. Fortune
smiled as his right wrist twists prevented the tiniest
splash.

Charlotte seemed oblivious to his near disaster.
"Here, let's toast to good health, great times, you and
me."

How could Randall not toast? His glass clinked hers.
"To good health."

They both sipped. The gin and perfume whiffs stung
his throat. His nerves rallied to urge his kidneys to flush
his system before the alcohol dulled his common sense.
No pleasant memory remained of his beer bouts with
Jackson. Charlotte's upping of the consumed alcohol's
strength presented a sure path to regret.

Charlotte's tongue surrounded her drink's cherry. His
stuck to his glass's bottom.

"After dinner, darling, you and I can discuss more
details, but not too much business. Daytime is for
business. Andrew's sumptuous dinner will present an
enchanting prelude. If it's late, you're welcome to stay.
Let's enjoy the opportunity we have."

"Can't stay." His voice sounded far away. "Not even
for dinner." He jerked himself erect, tinkled his glass on a
marble side table, and faced Charlotte.

"But . . . but—"

"No doubt the allure of establishing my own imprint
tantalizes me. Fact is, I need to earn it on my own, not be
seduced by a martini on a silver platter."

Charlotte's steely gaze clashed with his stare.
Andrew's march in with a second cosmopolitan round
halted in mid-stride by Charlotte's raised left hand.

Randall requested his coat. Charlotte nodded and
Andrew retreated. In the interlude required for Andrew to
retrieve his coat, Charlotte remained seated, her head

One Paper Heart

bowed. Her fingers encircled a martini glass stem whose base rested on her closed knees.

Andrew's bass voice intoned, "Sir, let me call you a taxi."

Randall's right hand fingers inside a suit coat pocket gripped his Blackberry. His conscience prompted him to at least observe the protocol of the rich. "Thank you. Give the dispatcher the street names that intersect north of this block. I'll be standing at the west curb."

"Yes, sir."

"Good night, Charlotte. You deserve my greatest respect. Visit me Monday at the office, your convenience. We'll get your novel on the schedule."

"We'll also discuss what's best for you." She nodded to a returned Andrew.

Andrew lifted Randall's overcoat shoulders to aid Randall's shrug and his right arm extension into its sleeve. Once fitted for the cold, Randall repeated, "Good night, Charlotte."

Andrew, his arms at his side, stood in the entrance doorway until Randall descended the steps and struck out into a north wind. The air's constant slaps chilled Randall's cheeks.

He'd walked out on Charlotte in the exact hurting manner inflicted on him by Alicia at the Irish pub. Not until this moment did he realize how this act also mortified the person who initiated the abrupt parting.

He and Charlotte had traveled a long friendship road. While she may have exposed her wish for an expanded intimate relationship, and he had held back, she warranted his respect. He desired not to inflict intentional melancholy. Her fan base and its creation by her pushy egotistical personality benefited and increased his value in shareholder eyes.

Randall raised his overcoat collar, and pulled it tight against his neck's nape.

He hadn't had an opportunity earlier to say more than

Donan Berg

a greeting to Alicia before Charlotte's unannounced cafeteria arrival. Only a fool would've expected Alicia to lay bare or hint at her feelings with Charlotte listening.

That Alicia fled a second time couldn't be their defining moment. Randall's heart beat strong and evidenced the courage he needed to rely on to restore Alicia's warm companionship. He began to pace the west curb. With each crunch of snow, he lambasted his pigheadedness in not waiting indoors for a taxi. The unlit entry light at Charlotte's door didn't encourage his return.

He mentally flogged himself for asking, in Alicia's presence, Charlotte to attend his mother's book club. In retrospect, his question highlighted his willingness to deceive those close to him. His devised masquerade to have Alicia pose as Beatrix Smothers, while well intended, molded one dishonesty brick in a monument of deceit.

The arriving cabbie questioned him three times through a partially-lowered driver window why he stood on a deserted street corner without Andrew who'd telephoned. Randall refrained from a lengthy explanation and handed the driver a twenty before the rear door latch popped and he could climb in. Without the exact fare, Randall let the grizzled cabbie pocket his twenty and its thirty percent tip to the meter rate.

Randall stopped in his condo's lobby to check his mailbox.

"Hello again." Olivia stood beside him.

"Hello," he replied. He didn't know she lived above his unit's ceiling.

"I was outside. It's nice to feel warm."

"Yes . . . yes it is." Her left shoulder pressed against his right. "How's your daughter?"

"She's with her friends. My dear child visits her lonely mother every other weekend."

"I'm sorry."

"Don't be. She has her own apartment with two other

249

girls. She's energetic girl. Maybe you remember her dancing in the laundry room." He nodded. "She do that all the time."

"I better be going."

"Can I ask question?" He repeated his nod. "Man doing laundry tells me man lonely. I like to cook, but can't eat everything. Perhaps you can be guest tonight."

"I . . . I'd hate to impose."

"In America, neighbors are friends right? Friends enjoy food together. Please."

Randall, as it was that laundry room day, couldn't focus long on Olivia's face with its disturbing eye. If he were Humphrey Bogart and she Elsa, the lobby lacked the plaintive moan of the airplane's propeller in the foggy, misty night.

While he wasn't Bogie and there were no light standards or assistants clapping white and black scene boards and shouting "action," he couldn't be a jerk twice in one night.

Randall followed Olivia into her condo unit. Its ambiance enlivened his senses. Rich apple reds, azure blues, and lush tropical forest greens dominated. Spanish scrolled woodwork dominated the chairs and sofa. Metallic birds in flight on one blue wall accented an impressive walnut dining table with four chairs. White blotches on the blue ceiling imitated clouds. Randall felt serene, ready to dine on a mountaintop.

Olivia excused herself and then returned in a white blouse and black slacks that flared below her knees. He folded his overcoat and laid it on a dining room chair. Since there were twice as many chairs as people, it seemed logical. A silver heart pendant on a chain adorned Olivia's throat. Mia loved a similar two-heart ring she'd worn about her neck.

"We drink merlot, okay? You can help with the cork?"

"Excellent choice." He uncorked the pantry bottle

Olivia handed him.

She set two red wine glasses on the dining room table and he poured.

Randall raised his glass. "To health."

"To happiness and friendship." Olivia clinked his glass.

He tagged along after her to the living room. Her wispy, black hair still reminded him of a mop, even more so with her thin fence-rail body. Her breasts resembled nothing more than an untrimmed protruding knot. If a colonial fence stood as a testament to the utilitarian and the practical, Olivia didn't. She possessed an aura of fragile sensitivity and caring forged with an underlying strength of determination and character.

She pointed for him to sit on the sofa where a knitted afghan protected its velvet.

"I like nice things. Oh, you're not Jewish?"

Randall brushed his forehead with the back of his left hand. "No, no. Why do you ask?"

"Ham's baking. If you Jewish, I find chicken."

Randall laughed. "Sorry, I'm not laughing at you. No one has ever been so concerned about what to serve me."

Olivia inched her body closer. "Guest should be pleased."

"Please call me Randall."

She lifted her still full wine glass. "Here's to Randall. May he enjoy life."

"Thank you." He tipped his half-full glass toward her. "And, to you. May I ask what work you do? I believe I told you in the laundry room I work for a publisher."

"Not big job. I, what you say, manage servers at banquet hall."

"That's hard work. Organizing people to do what needs to be done is a special gift."

"Thank you, thank you." Olivia kissed him on the cheek. "I bet you have important job."

"Can't say. I help publish romance novels. You ever

251

hear of *New Romance Delights?*"

"Not read much."

Randall cringed at his insensitivity. Olivia didn't seem insulted.

"My daughter read."

"Then I saw her book in the laundry room. It's not ours."

"Sorry. Hope you not mad."

"Don't be silly."

Olivia excused herself to check on the ham.

Randall leaned his back on her sofa. He sipped slow even though he didn't have to drive home. The sweet aroma of a brown sugar ham glaze aroused his nostrils. He was sure romance novel critics would pooh-pooh his and Olivia's meeting as pure chance. Maybe so, but the proof that such things happen he could attest to.

The contrasts of his evening adventure, if one could call it that, were amazing. Charlotte lured him to her house and didn't hide her intentions and expectations. She wished to seduce him to a rich and famous lifestyle. Charlotte depended upon paid help such as Andrew, wrapped herself in expensive gowns, and served hip drinks to overpower his senses. Her house, if not in reality, then in Randall's mind, a museum dedicated to collected heirlooms cleaned daily by Charlotte's maid for scheduled and impromptu exhibitions.

Charlotte acted in her own self-interest, which included fronting the venture capital for Randall to launch a publishing house she'd eventually commandeer for her own aggrandizement and christen The Charlotte Oprah Publishing House.

Hard at work in the kitchen to please him was a woman he'd but briefly met. She perhaps motivated by the identical loneliness that often gripped him. Olivia hadn't asked him for anything except to share company and conversation, to hold off the forces of despair or to dull the middle-of-the-night internal guilt that ravaged the memories and the humanity of the depressed. He didn't think he'd descended into melancholy, but perhaps that was his delusion.

Randall's glance around the room interrupted by the realization something was amiss. There was neither a visible TV screen nor a cabinet large enough to hide one. Was it the strange eye Olivia possessed that accounted for this? He wouldn't ask.

"Dinner's served," Olivia announced.

Olivia lowered her dining room lights. A lord's dinner of ham, potato salad, green beans, and strawberry ice cream greeted him. She clicked on a light that splashed a brilliant yellow beneath the metallic birds. The mountaintop added a sunset to his imagination.

After he licked his dessert spoon, he said, "Olivia, this dinner was stupendous."

"I'm pleased. I hope you won't think badly of me if I tell you the greater joy comes with your presence. Will you sit with me a little longer?"

Randall hadn't once checked his wristwatch. He sauntered to the window that bathed the sofa in deep shadow and accepted a wine refill. Olivia's left thigh tenderly pressed his right as they sat together on the sofa. Even in the dim light, he couldn't help but focus his eyes on the silver heart at Olivia's throat. He sipped his wine and put the glass on the coffee table.

"You stare at my neck, but not my face. Does my eye upset you?"

Randall teetered at the precipice of truth. "There's no wish to embarrass you. You have a pretty face." Randall believed that. If he'd said head with her mopish hair he'd have lied.

"You're kind. My husband meet me and marry me in Europe. He was a soldier. Fifteen years ago I visited him overseas for vacation. A terrorist bomb explodes in hotel lobby. A little piece of metal hurts my eye."

"I'm sorry."

"The Italian doctors try but surgery can't connect nerve. I praise God he give me two."

"Your husband?"

"Killed. No stop him. He runs to marketplace." Tears flowed from her good eye. "Bad guy shoots him." She leaned sideways and Randall's impulsive wrapped his arms around her.

"Bad guys killed my Mia a few days ago." His tears cascaded into Olivia's hair. "I wish I could run after them."

"It not matter," Olivia murmured.

Randall's body heat mingled with Olivia's. "It's good you have your daughter."

"My life's joy. Part of my husband I can hug. I'd like to be with her, give her more, but she wants to be independent."

"Seems that at her age we all feel the same."

"How true."

Randall listened to Olivia breathe. Her rhythmic exhales were soft and endearing. She'd snuggled her body against his and his desire strained the fabric of his suit pants. Without a physical touch, Olivia wouldn't perceive his excitement if her left hand continued to caress his shoulder. His right hand gripped her far shoulder until her right hand tugged his left hand across her blouse.

He didn't know if he prompted her to kiss him when he leaned his head or if she initiated their kiss. Regardless, the results were sweeter than the dinner's strawberry ice cream or a country song's strawberry wine. His lips lingered on hers. She'd asked him for nothing tangible. His wallet, stowed in his overcoat after paying the cabbie, contained little cash and two credit cards. Not much to steal. She hadn't spiked the wine for he uncorked it.

Moreover, she lived in his building and, if his memory of encounters accurate, had for two years. Her condo didn't reflect a person ready to flee. The multiple personal items he'd noticed after her wrenching story of injury and husband loss included pictures and a heroism medal. Life's mementos, all unpacked.

Their kisses blossomed into a passionate intensity. He tried to adjust his body for mutual comfort. That proved difficult as they almost slid off the sofa's afghan.

Olivia giggled.

Randall chuckled at the incongruity of an adult woman's girlish giggle.

"Let's try bed."

He didn't resist and hugged her waist. Her bedroom lacked the kaleidoscope colors of her other rooms. A queen bed in the center dominated. Olivia drew her simple white drapes closed to darken the room.

By touch his fingers found the fluffy cotton comforter. Her kisses inflamed him.

Disrobed, his fingertips stroked her sides and traced the slight depressions in her ribs and the projections of her areolas. Her busy fingers raked across his pecs and angled towards the split of his thighs.

"Love me," she whispered. "Protect me, and I won't care if you're gone before tomorrow."

Her honest words shocked Randall. He hadn't considered STDs and any condom he owned dry-rotted in a full Trojan box covered by Fourth of July napkins with pictures of exploding firecrackers stashed at the back of a high kitchen cabinet.

"Didn't come prepared."

"Drawer. Right side of bed."

Randall extracted a condom foil pouch. Olivia's loving touch helped him stretch it. Her heels pressed into his backside and her soft moan announced his entry. When she murmured another man's name, Randall thought of her husband. The tinkle of Olivia's silver necklace ignited Randall's passion. Doc Campbell hadn't deceive him. His locomotive engine's piston able to drive his train to the desired destination whether the freight cars were loaded or empty.

He collapsed with an audible gasping exhale. Olivia supported his entire weight until he rolled off right. His arms embraced her. The salty taste of perspiration, hers or his he didn't know, wet his lip. The smell of satisfaction engulfed them. They kissed. No shame inhibited their actions. All emotion far from one-sided.

His physical euphoria complete, Randall lay between Olivia's sheets. She hadn't asked him to pronounce his love, and he knew in an emotional sense, he never would. His mental mop image erased and replaced by a matchstick with flaming hair. They'd been two souls willing to grasp the moment with the future undecided.

He declined Olivia's offer for a joint shower before dressing. With his overcoat across his arm, he hugged and kissed her without a sideways glance.

Randall clomped down one flight of stairs to his unit. His telephone answering machine blinks sparked no desire to disturb Olivia's warmth in his heart.

He counted six blinks once, twice, and then smashed a pillow against his ears to drown out the persistent beep.

Sleep evaded him.

Chapter Fifteen

Alicia, in Doctor Beck's beige, seven-chair waiting room, thumbed through a woman's magazine to hide her anxiety from three women and a man. Article words fused into unreadable gray blocks and sentence punctuation disappeared. She tossed her magazine atop two others.

With Randall out of the office the first three workdays since their second cafeteria meeting, Wanda had approved her absence. The cafeteria had also been the last time she crossed paths with Charlotte. The prior evening Vicky mentioned to Alicia she wouldn't be surprised if both were in California discussing Charlotte's next book.

Stuck on the number seven, Alicia tugged her baggy jeans belt and recounted the chairs.

A scrubs-clad brunette with wrinkled chin skin entered to Alicia's left. "Alicia Danielson."

Alicia raised her hand, rose, and allowed the woman to direct her, not to an examination room, but to a large office. Medical diplomas filled one wall. Streaky light entered through blind window slats behind the mahogany desk. She rubbed her hands on the leather arms of a cushioned chair that faced the desk. When her glance noticed her hands had smeared the chair arms with perspiration, she gasped and dried the leather with a tissue.

"Good morning, Alicia," intoned her gray-haired physician. From the office door, he limped round his desk's corner to square his swivel chair and claim it as his own. He asked his nurse to close the door and stay. A single dark brown folder before him displayed two-holed punched tabbed sheets. He continued without Alicia's response.

"The medical tests have come back. There's cause for concern."

"Why?" Alicia's voice soft. "Haven't experienced pain. Trouble eating was number one until last week's urgency to pee. Figured both happened because I've denied myself."

"You know I saw you for regular checkups when you were a teacher."

"Yeah, but there's been a problem with insurance."

"Not to criticize, but isn't your health more important than insurance?"

Alicia bowed her head. "Guess so." She'd worried about unpaid bills.

"It happens all the time. But let's get back to you." His semi-circle eyebrows flattened into a straight line. "You're been healthy. Past checkups provide a beneficial baseline history."

Alicia's torso squirmed against the restraint of both hands squeezed to her chair's arms.

"Has anyone come with you today?"

His words scared her. What monster lurked within her? "No." She gripped the chair arms extra hard. "I took the bus downtown and expect to ride it home."

"That's good. First, let me be clear that nothing I will say indicates that you won't be able to enjoy a long life."

Alicia swallowed hard. Her right knuckles lost their pinkish color.

"You wouldn't have had any noticeable symptoms for a long time. Your weight loss presented a clue along with the frequent urination. Although you didn't come in, there's a clinical file note you called a month ago concerned about a vaginal discharge."

"That happened once, never again." Alicia gazed at the doctor and then rotated it toward the nurse for a telltale sign she would be all right. The nurse's stoic mien morphed into a plastic smile. Alicia's neck throb signaled her pulse jump. "My roommate teased me when I mentioned beets and red-tinted stool water. She convinced me I'd gotten nervous for no reason."

"That makes that clearer."

Alicia found it harder to swallow. "Go back. You mentioned weight, frequent going. What clue? Symptoms of what?"

The doctor separated two folder tabs. "The CT or cat-scan you underwent showed a small pelvic or abdominal abnormality. Fatty tissue images found near one ovary."

"Oh no!" Alicia shrieked. Her hands clasped and then released her face. "You're telling me I have cancer?"

Shoes squeaked behind her. Alicia didn't have the energy to fight off the delicate pressure on her right shoulder. Her sideways peek discovered the nurse, with her left arm extended, standing beside her chair. The doctor turned a page.

"That hasn't been one hundred percent confirmed. The lymphangiogram disclosed no lymph node blockage."

Alicia's voice cracked. "That's good then?"

"A strong positive. However, a more experienced colleague pointed out your blood test results suggest, with eighty percent probability, the possibility, and I must stress the word "possibility," of a germ cell tumor in your left ovary."

One Paper Heart

Tears streamed across Alicia's cheeks. Her head slumped forward until her chin rested on her chest. Tears dripped and darkened her skirt's fabric. The nurse handed her a box of tissue. Alicia twice grasped four. Her constricted throat muscles transformed her wails into muffled sobs.

"You need not decide today." Her cloudy eyes perceived the doctor to lean forward, his forearms at rest on his desktop. "Since your lymphangiogram procedure gives us insight if or what staging is present. We're holding back on a laparotomy."

Alicia raised her head. This was happening to a person she didn't know. It was a character sketch. Lady Victoria Dash hadn't lived a romance. Dean Koontz had hijacked her.

The dark figure in her mind asked, "Do you understand what I'm saying?"

A weak "no" escaped Alicia's lips.

"The lymphangiogram injected dye into your feet. It's a process to determine if—"

Alicia's brain recognized Doctor Beck. "You can say the C word."

"Okay. It's a process to determine the tumor's staging or spread."

"And . . ."

"If, and you must understand I'm emphasizing the "if there is a tumor," it appears contained. We could do surgery to wash the abdominal cavity with fluid and capture it and determine under a microscope if the C you speak about is present."

She felt so helpless. "What am I to do?"

"Since I like to be conservative, I'd recommend we draw additional blood today and compare cell counts with your first test. Abdominal surgery, as would be a hysterectomy, represents major surgery with its own risks."

"Whatever you say. I'll do it."

"Can Nancy bring you a drink of water?"

Alicia nodded.

"I can't overemphasis that as a healthy woman you have an outstanding opportunity to enjoy an active life for years to come since we're attacking sooner than the normal diagnosis."

"But children . . ." Hoarseness and fear restricted her words.

"That's hard to say. If we need to proceed to a hysterectomy, I can't hide it would foreclose your ability to bear children. But we're not there yet." Doctor Beck stood. "Please call this office with any question."

Alicia's weak nod repeated as the doctor departed. She released her hands from her chair arms after she stood. Nancy directed and followed Alicia to a blood draw station. After a Band-Aid covered her right elbow blood-draw needle puncture, Alicia swallowed a gulp of water and asked for directions to the restroom. She stared at the mirror's reflection as she scrubbed off her streaked makeup. Her reddened-skin and sunken eyes would go away, but not the small birthmark under her chin. Until then she'd believed the mark and the fire had represented the worse things to have happened. Her shoulders quivered.

She wobbled until her gait steadied upon nearing the waiting room.

Nurse Nancy spoke soft encouraging words: "You'll be all right."

Alicia folded the double-sided ovarian cancer fact sheet and accepted the nurse's words as a question. She replied, "Yes."

While she questioned whether her numb skin would feel the sharp wind gusts, Alicia nonetheless bundled up and dismissed both a walk and a Bunyan Center office return. She took advantage of her explanation to Wanda that her absence could drag out the entire afternoon, asked the bus driver for a transfer, and waited for Orange

No. 34. Broken clouds allowed the sun to wash her face with chilled warmth.

Her earlier bus with its extra mid-day stops boarded a man with a walker and older women who struggled with collapsible canes. She removed her CD earplugs and gazed at the people the bus passed. How many harbored or spawned undiscovered illness? Did all women agonize when faced with having their stomachs cut open and their reproductive organs removed? Would she still feel complete?

What about the *Sixty Minutes* exposé on unnecessary hysterectomies? Hadn't Doctor Beck sought a second opinion? Was it reliable? Alicia's thoughts traveled to her mother. Mom raised and loved her without having given birth to her. Men married women to beget children, especially bloodline sons. Dad must be a saint.

She tugged her hood tight for the short, brisk walk to her lobby's warmth and the elevator ride to an empty apartment. Alicia inspected refrigerator shelves without the urge to eat, paced the living room, and turned the television on and then off before she threw herself face down on her bed. When red LED lights changed her alarm clock digits from a three to a four, the telephone rang. She choked back sobs to answer. Alicia hung up the telemarketer's charity pitch before he finished and willed herself to do something positive to drive out her nauseous worry.

She thought of calling Mom. No. She couldn't fake cheery or dispel Mom's fear that a mid-day call meant something dreadful happened. Alicia pulled out her desk drawer with Georgia's folder. She reread the letter that presaged her sponsorship loss. *Perhaps an option exists the form letter hadn't detailed.* The Arizona agency letterhead contained an 800 telephone number. The lady that answered placed Alicia on hold for the agency director.

"Ms. Danielson? Mr. Shirley here. Thank you for

calling. I understand you're perplexed by the letter you received."

Alicia sat cross-legged on her bedroom floor, her back pressed against her bed. "Why can't I sponsor Georgia?"

"Our charter limits us to care for Navajo children, and even then our role is limited. We must respect funding restrictions. Any child six or older has to be transferred to foster care. With her endowment and your generosity, Georgia was an exception."

"I recall a counselor's explanation two years ago that dyed black hair and a part-Indian heritage assertion tricked the agency." Alicia wiggled her toes inside her slippers. "What happens now isn't fair. I'm willing to continue my contributions, even increase to the extent I'm able."

"You've been extraordinary. We praise God everyday for persons like you. Yet, Georgia's needs include more than money. She requires a home. A family."

"I tried to explore her living with me."

"The agency doesn't mean to be cruel, but single-parent adoptions aren't permitted."

Alicia couldn't, nor did she want to, understand how God brought her to find Georgia among all the world's needy children. Nor could she fathom how an agency, controlled by well-intentioned men and women, fashioned rules to deny her the ability to form a family bond. And now, Georgia wasn't to be hers to love daily and visit twice a year.

"But can't you continue her exception? Let me be a trial?"

"The simple answer is no. What further complicates matters is that a couple has expressed an interest to adopt Georgia."

Hoover, Hoover Dam. Alicia calmed her urge to fire her rage at Director Shirley. "That wasn't said in the letter."

"That there's been no completed background check is one explanation."

"Will I be able to see Georgia? At least say good-bye."

"Certainly. You're always welcome."

Alicia thanked the director through her sobs. What if someone had blocked her adoption by Mom and Dad? Or George's? Or Elena's? or Alan's? She piled an unlit self-pity stick upon her heart's cold hearth. "Holter Dam, Montana . . ."

She shuffled toward the living room while she muttered three Holter Dam repeats. *It wasn't fair, wasn't fair, wasn't fair.* Alicia propelled her body to land stretched out and face down on the sofa. She clicked the nearby remote. How could soap operas rule viewers' lives? Her weary eyelids and tear-laded lashes closed involuntarily. No surreal images of Victorian manors or horse-drawn carriages invaded her dreams.

A hand jostled her right shoulder. Alicia muttered, "I'll make the school bus."

"Wake up, wake up."

Alicia's eyes admitted flickering TV light through narrow slits. Vicky, with hands on hips, towered above Alicia. Vicky wore her outdoors jacket.

"What time is it?" Alicia asked. She eased her rotated body upright, the small of her back against the sofa's end cushion, her legs crossed.

"Almost six. Why?"

"No reason. This day's been horrible, absolutely horrendous." Alicia waved her right hand to request Vicky join her on the sofa. With multiple halts to phrase her words, she explained that day's doctor visit.

Vicky slid close and wrapped her arms around Alicia's shoulders. She whispered, "You're strong. You'll beat this. I'll help all I can."

When the telephone rang, Vicky answered and lied that Alicia wasn't there.

Alicia telephoned Wanda early Friday to tell her she'd caught a twenty-four bug and wouldn't be in. After Vicky left for work, Alicia laid on her back atop her bed comforter. She pressed her hand to her abdomen.

She imagined her stomach muscles collapsed without inside support, organs removed to create a hollowed Halloween pumpkin that in time would rot and collapse into itself. She powered on her computer. Its monitor screen faded to black as Alicia failed to lift a finger to enter a keystroke.

Alicia struggled to find a comfortable spot on the sofa. Sprawled face down with her nose in a library medical book, she peered toward the breakfast counter when Vicky's key clicked in the apartment's front door.

"Randall wanted to talk to you last night," Vicky reported. "He's the one I told you weren't home, not a telemarketer. Wanted to protect you. Hope you're not mad."

"No. Met him last Friday. Haven't mentioned it because it was so frustrating. We had little time to talk before Charlotte Hauser pranced in with her irritating 'hello, darlings' greeting."

"You mean you and Randall are still mad at each other?" Vicky rubbed her arms.

"Guess so." Alicia had given little thought to Randall in the last forty-eight hours. Once Randall found out, he'd never want to have a long-term relationship if she couldn't physically measure up to be a normal woman. She grimaced with the remembrance of how his mother at Thanksgiving doted on the joy of biological grandchildren.

"Hold on. Either you're mad at each other or you aren't. Which is it?"

"He apologized. Suggested we start fresh." Vicky

bobbed her head. "Before I could retrieve my notes from my purse, Charlotte appeared. Realized there was no use to stay after Randall hinted at my impersonation of Beatrix Smothers."

"What impersonation?" Vicky's eyes widened. Her lips parted.

"Oh, oh. Guess I didn't tell you." She sat up to allow room for Vicky on the sofa.

Vicky perched on a cushion's edge. "Nooo . . ."

"Well, last Thanksgiving when I went with Randall to his parents. At his request I pretended to be Beatrix Smothers, a writer for *New Romance Delights*."

"Where was the real Beatrix?" Vicky slipped off the cushion to sit cross-legged on the floor.

"She doesn't exist. Randall uses Beatrix as a pen name for the books he writes."

"So . . . all you writers use false names? Is that what I'm hearing?"

"Sorta." Alicia excused herself to fill a glass with kitchen tap water and return.

"And, you wonder why—with all your deception—you have problems with relationships. I'm staying with Joel. Firemen fight fires, not each other."

"You going out with Joel tonight?"

"In two hours. I can wait downstairs. Say you're sick."

Alicia rose to return her water glass to the sink. "You can finish the lasagna. I have to edit the final paragraphs of my final class essay."

Vicky pushed herself erect. Before she reached the entrance closet she pivoted. "We'll finish this tomorrow."

Alicia carried her medical book into her bedroom and faced a blank computer screen. To avoid an incomplete, Randall required a final essay, although she doubted the university registrar had bothered to add her adult education pass/fail registration to her undergraduate transcript. Until this past week, after a cancelled class because of a Frazier Hall boiler breakdown, she'd been confident Randall wouldn't fail her if she completed all assigned essays.

With student choice announced as the last essay topic, Alicia retrieved her unsubmitted Georgia essay. Its words infected Alicia with uplifted memories of Georgia's smiles, her giggles, and, most important, her hugs. Alicia's joy lit up her monitor. Her words flowed with the hopes, dreams, and struggles of an orphaned female infant. She infused her own soul and left out Georgia's physical details to protect the five-year-old's privacy.

For the first time in weeks, words danced on Alicia's computer screen. The writing god's return announced with a flourish of energetic verbs and colorful nouns. She finished her essay's final proofread minutes before Vicky returned without Joel after their date.

Vicky tuned in a late, late night TV talk show. Alicia folded her essay pages in half and sank into the living room's chair.

"You call Randall?"

"No." Alicia turned her gaze from Vicky.

"Why you being so hardheaded?"

"Because . . ." She faced Vicky. "Just because."

Vicky pressed the remote to lower the program's sound. "You're punishing him?"

"Opened myself up by agreeing to the cafeteria meeting." Alicia let the silence grow.

"You could meet again."

"Wouldn't help. When Charlotte Hauser barged in, Randall could've told her he'd see her later. He didn't." Alicia reached for a small pillow, sat upright, and squeezed it between the small of her back and the chair.

"You said that earlier. Sounded like no big deal. You trying to make up excuses?"

Alicia stared at her roommate. They'd had soul-searching talks before. More often than not about men. She hesitated to go there, but Vicky demonstrated an ability to be nonjudgmental.

"Let's go back to what you wrote in your book. I remember reading in an early chapter where your determined heroine refused to take no for an answer. Does that sound familiar?"

"Yes, but . . ."

"Crystal, or whatever her name was, strove relentlessly to find her lost son and win the man she loved. Dauntless, you wrote. How many hurdles did she overcome?"

"Three or four. I forget."

Vicky stood and strolled around their breakfast island. She rejoined Alicia with a writing tablet and knelt on the living room floor to face Alicia and use their coffee table as a desk. "We'll make a list. You've grumbled these past several days about deception. In the right column will be real deception. In the left column will be events without deception."

Vicky drew the vertical column lines on her tablet. She labeled each column.

"Don't know about this."

"What? You want to mope forever in your current funk?"

Alicia shook her head. She understood a determined Vicky wouldn't be deterred.

"Okay then. Let's get on with it."

"It's not that easy."

"Quiet. If you suffer, so do I. First, you impersonate this writer, Beatrix, at Thanksgiving."

Alicia nodded.

"You know why?"

"Something about his mother wanted him to bring her to the family Thanksgiving."

"Right. No real deception." Vicky jotted words in the left column. "You got a mother who wants to see her son have a girlfriend. I think lots of scared sons make their mothers happy with the same be-my-girlfriend-for-a-day routine. Haven't your parents or close relatives like your Aunt Agnes tried to interfere." Vicky waved her right hand. "Wrong word, tried to graciously suggest that you walk past an open church door and pray the magnetized altar would attract?"

Magnetized? What magazine did Vicky steal this from? "Guess that's happened."

"And how did you feel or react?"

"Prayed they'd stop it, let me chose my life."

"Right. And I'd bet Randall figured the impersonation would do more than prayers."

Alicia watched Vicky scribble a note into her right column. "Hiding from you that your book wouldn't be published. That's real deception. Hurtful. Mean. But, if we examine it, his action wasn't directed at you."

"Help. Slowdown." Alicia adjusted her pillow. "You've lost me."

"When Randall said that, he didn't know you were the writer. Correct?"

"Well, yeah." Her brain fog lifted. Still, Vicky's direction wasn't clear.

"Surefire deception, but not directed at you." Vicky picked up her pencil. "Do we have any other deception episodes?"

"Not really?"

Vicky's eyes fixed their gaze on her. "Has anyone ever wronged or cheated you and you forgave them? Think hard, Alicia."

"Guess so." She waited to determine if her soft-spoken words reached Vicky.

"Who and why did you forgive?"

"Brother George long ago took my favorite teddy bear from my room, hid it, and then lied about it. The longer I stayed angry with him, the worse I felt. I wanted us to be like we were."

Vicky's left hand brushed a stray hair strand from her left eye. "Right. You forgave your brother because you

269

believed his one action didn't represent the real him. You trusted him to be a better person if he understood his change made you feel better. So what about Randall? Do you know what Lady Victoria wrote so poorly? Not generalities. Give me specifics?"

"Couldn't ask him. Nor could I expose myself as Lady Victoria."

"Why was that?"

Alicia wished Vicky ended her probe. "Well . . . I put my paper heart on someone else's manuscript with knowledge Randall would reject it because of the one paper heart."

"Oh, so now we have your deception. Is that what I hear?"

"I had to . . ." Alicia watched Vicky draw a third vertical line on her tablet.

"New column titled counter deception. Can you put Randall's actions into this column?"

"Not that I know of." Alicia squirmed against the pillow. It didn't relax her knotted stomach. A pain emerged at the base of her throat—heartburn or guilt?

"Does Randall know you switched the heart?"

"Told no one except you right now." Alicia's eyes released a tear trickle. She bowed her head. "Oh, Vicky, I'm the worst of all."

"Listen, you're not a bad person for making a mistake or acting in your own self-interest. Haven't I been trying to tell you that?" Vicky tossed her tablet to the floor.

Alicia's voice croaked. "Don't know what to do."

"Focus on correcting the action, not vilifying individuals. Prop up the other person. Radiate confidence you know the person won't repeat his or her misstep."

Alicia curled her lower lip. "Don't have the strength."

"How did Lady Victoria's heroine conquer her obstacles?"

"I'm not her."

"C'mon. How did Lady Victoria's heroine conquer

270

her obstacles?"

"She stood up. Said what needed to be said without personal regard for the outcome."

"You're saying she believed in her own self worth." Vicky retrieved the tablet and started to draw a fourth vertical line, but lifted her pen when Alicia spoke.

"Guess so. You're suggesting I tell Randall what? That I want to know why he thinks my novel wasn't well written?" The back of Alicia's right hand wiped at dried tear trails.

Vicky smiled. "And, if you disagree, tell him so." She winked. "Be nice."

"Can't."

"Why not? You have an idea of what he'll say if you've been reading his essay comments."

"Never thought of that."

The telephone rang. Neither moved to answer it.

"Randall did say," Alicia continued, "that he reached the conclusion I was Lady Victoria when he compared my essay to the manuscript."

"Talk to him about the manuscript. Act like you want to become a better writer. Massage his ego. It's not personal. Dangling a participle doesn't make you a bad person—just a violator of some stupid, sorry, some well-respected English grammar rule."

Alicia savored Vicky's courage infusion. Grounded in life's realities, her roommate often cut through the chaff. Her word "stupid" suited one or two grammar rules.

* * *

Randall fumbled with his key as he staggered into his condo. The red message light blinking on his answering machine irritated his eyes. *Who's calling me on a dateless Saturday night?*

"Hello, Mr. Van Gilleran, this is Sergeant Lopez,

Phoenix Police Department. Please call me Monday after
seven p.m. Pacific time. Number is 602-555-1302.
Thanks."

Phoenix, the city, registered in Randall's alcohol-
hazed brain, nothing else.

* * *

Alicia garnered no opportunity to corner Randall at work
either Monday or Tuesday. She first laid eyes on him
when he strolled a minute late into her Tuesday evening
essay class. They didn't speak, not even when she handed
him her final essay.

Wednesday afternoon, Alicia spoke up when Randall
walked through reception. "Mr. Van Gilleran. May I have
word with you?"

He stopped and pivoted on his heels to face her. "Yes.
What is it?"

"I'd appreciate . . . no, I would be honored if you
found time for me to learn what improvements you would
recommend for Lady Victoria's . . . I mean my *A Search
Fulfilled* manuscript."

His lower jaw dropped. He recovered to press his lips
together. "How about tomorrow after work, in our
conference room. Check with Wanda to make sure it's
not booked."

"That would be fine."

"Unless told otherwise, I'll assume the room's free.
Please excuse me. An appointment beckons." Randall
swung the hallway door closed.

Alicia sighed. Step one completed. She swiveled her
legs to the right, rose, and sought out Wanda at her desk.
Alicia balanced herself on her right leg as Wanda flipped
an appointment book page to confirm the conference
room had nothing scheduled after four p.m. She wrote in
Alicia for two hours.

"You two talking again?" Wanda asked.

"Why?"

"It's been real apparent that you two have something going on. Either you're actually angry with each other, or you want everyone here to think so and are meeting secretly to do whatever affair lovers do."

"W-A-N-D-A! How could you think such a thing?"

"Saw it on 'As the Planet Revolves' last week when home sick with the flu. You could write that into a romance storyline. Pretty slick deception if you ask me."

"Mr. Van Gilleran and I aren't engaged in any . . . deception . . . as you call it. We plan to talk about a manuscript. That's all."

"Yours? Randall had your essay on his desk."

"Another writer." Alicia didn't wish to pile up gossip tidbits. That Norma stopped her conversation the other day when Alicia approached now made greater sense.

"Okay, but watch out for a hidden camera."

Chapter Sixteen

Randall shouted in vain for the blinking light on his telephone answering machine to burn out. He paced his condo to search for the solitude he couldn't command. Every second circle he swigged an O'Doul's rather than a Hamm's to savor the beer taste without the alcohol. Coupled with repeated messages from Jackson and Charlotte, alcoholic hangovers had compounded his novel and screenplay writing distress.

That Olivia re-invited him to dinner when they crossed elevator paths added to his anxiety, as did his half-truth he'd need to get back to her.

Randall struggled for the right descriptive words to portray Beatrix's latest sweet, headstrong, and ambitious heroine. He jettisoned a Southwest desert bat cave prologue because Beatrix devotees voiced vociferous objection when jolted into unfamiliar first chapter settings. Dare he alienate readers by editing out his endless descriptions of crinoline-enhanced skirts, embroidered silk blouse initials, or poodle appliqués?

He hung his vintage clothes on racks in a make-believe second-hand store. The heroine wouldn't be his typical sultry, twenty-eight-year-old, frilly, airhead. She'd experience deep tumultuous emotion, struggle with real businesswoman competitive decisions, personal fears, and heartbreak before her summoned inner strength propelled her to the required happy ending.

He scribbled his thematic breakthrough into a journal while hunched at his dining room table and thought of Alicia. It pained him he didn't apologize to her when she stopped him in reception. His not speaking to her at the final essay class had been the epitome of rudeness. Beatrix's heroine had once remarked to a muscled weightlifter that an honest apology didn't brand the gym rat a sissy. Alicia's final class essay, inches to his right, awaited his grading. Her timely assignment completion sufficient for him to pass her without his grading her last essay.

Randall reached for his Blackberry and disconnected it from its charger. He dialed Sgt. Lopez in Phoenix. "Sergeant, any luck locating my child?"

"We're working on leads. Nothing definite."

Randall chafed at the vagueness of police detectives. "You being straight?"

"Found a domestic who might've seen a young girl at the vic's house."

Randall gulped. This was his Mia, not a generic victim. "Can I help? Is this person cooperating?" He laid his journal on Alicia's essay.

"I'll be interviewing this witness tomorrow."

"I'll telephone in a day or so." Randall pressed his end-call button. He might have a daughter. He might not. *Damn.* He should've ignored AND canned his divorce lawyer.

Randall stretched out on his sofa to forestall lightheadedness. Too early to pop another Advil. He bypassed his "A Search Fulfilled" screenplay to retrieve Lady Dash's original manuscript. If critical, he owed it to Alicia to be conversant and fair.

He should've chuckled when he reread the stilted farmer dialogue but didn't. His red pen drew a large question mark in the margin. He read on in earnest and strived to twist his prior editorial criticism into positive encouragement.

* * *

Randall laid his two manuscript copies on the conference room table. He was alone. The NRD clock said 4:29 and he was certain it was Thursday afternoon. Alicia would have sufficient breathing room to be comfortable if he sat four chairs away from the table's far end.

"Mr. Van Gilleran . . ."

He pivoted to face Alicia. She asked to sit at the table's end closest to the exit.

He carried Lady Dash's manuscript to be across from her. His hands, six inches apart, rested on the tabletop. "Please call me Randall. Even literary villains are addressed without the mister."

Alicia didn't smile. She gazed at the comb-bound pages next to his hands.

"I've had two copies of your original manuscript printed for us." He slid her one. "Let me first say my apology expressed last week should be expanded to include Tuesday night."

"Thank you." Her acknowledgement was stiff and stilted.

"Now," he cleared his throat, "this manuscript has a realistic and strong plot. Punctuation exceptional. We need to look at other things."

"What things?" Alicia's tone defensive.

His praise and the use of the collective pronoun had been ineffective to enliven her expression. He flipped several pages of his retained copy.

"Long-winded character dialogue encourages a reader

to lose track of who's speaking." Alicia raised her eyebrows. "Turn to chapter two. Start at page 56. A detective and the main character speak for ten pages. Gobs of information, but the reader will struggle to follow who says what and in the process is likely to forget who knows what."

"I carefully put in quotation marks and paragraphs to show alternating speech."

"Yes, but the author needs to help the reader. One way, add a name. For example, the detective can say: 'Michelle, do you understand the question?' That alerts the reader the detective is speaking."

Alicia lifted her chair around the table's corner. She gazed at his manuscript copy. "Randall, you love red ink, don't you?" The hint of a repressed smile emerged at her mouth's upturned corner.

"Yes, and you illustrated my dialogue point." Her smile remained undeveloped. "Your essays also lacked this technique of character identification. Sometimes your indirect speech failed to clearly indicate who said what." He pointed to page 78.

Alicia peered over his left shoulder. He highlighted at page 132 where a character told another not to speak and then proceeded to ask two questions.

Alicia appeared receptive to his comments, especially when she grabbed her manuscript copy and dog-eared two pages.

"If you wish, we can exchange copies."

Alicia set aside the manuscript copy he'd given her. "Okay."

Randall searched for his next entry with the knowledge it would be positive. Their hands accidentally touched; he noticed her stiffen. He shifted his gaze from her to the open page.

Her question broke their silence. "If there were good parts, why not send back to the author and request a rewrite?"

"That's possible, but not practical. Because of the submission volume we can't become a writing coach. If we expend the effort to suggest improvement, we have no guarantee we'll get the revision back."

"Never thought of that." Alicia's gaze traced the ceiling perimeter before she spoke. "Why offer money if you won't publish?"

Alicia edged her body farther from the table's edge. Her clasped hands reminded him of her riding in his Lincoln. His conference room hot seat ready to riddle his mind as his front car seat roasted his butt.

"Bear with me while I struggle to condense and not mess up a complex explanation. Jackson, Andy, and I were searching for an idea on which to base an Oscar-worthy screenplay. *A Search Fulfilled* struck me as the answer. We're not devilish rogues bent on usurping a writer's work without paying for it. That led to the search for Lady Victoria Dash."

"You almost threw it away?" Alicia bit her right hand forefinger.

A pang in his chest failed to repeat. "You told me that at the Irish pub." Should he be consumed with guilt because he missed a key point when enthralled? There was no balance with women in his profession. They were either haughty and distant or like Charlotte, pushy and suffocating. None understood he too had personal troubles and Jackson's friendship ready to crash. His gaze swirled until it met Alicia's stare.

"You . . . you don't understand what my throwing it away reference meant. You may fire me. Don't know." Her shoulders slumped.

"I'm not going to fire you. Your job is safe if you're not admitting you stole money. And, I doubt that since you don't handle cash or checks."

Alicia rubbed her hands and began to cry. She hunched forward and became as small as the chair would allow. Randall scrambled to grab a tissue box from the room's far corner. He offered her the box, and then sat down.

She pulled three tissues, dabbed her eyes and cheeks.

"Alicia, listen. I said I'm not going to fire you, repeat, not going to fire you."

"It's not money . . . it's the red paper heart." She balled her moist tissues into her palm. Her fingertips and forehead muscles fought to stretch her eyelids apart. Her eye movements searched for his face. "You probably don't remember. The day my large envelope submission arrived it had a red paper heart on it so I could easily identify mine from others."

Randall's arms ached to reach out. He couldn't and didn't.

She continued between sniffles. "You surprised me. Said any wannabe author who would put a heart on a submission should have the manuscript rejected without even being read." Alicia's forehead touched the conference tabletop.

Randall waited uncounted anxious seconds for her head to rise. "I remember the heart." He rested both hands on the table. "While I may have said that, you convinced me to read the submission regardless." He fiddled with his red pen.

"Didn't trust you. Removed my paper heart and pasted it on another envelope."

"You did what?" He clamped his lips tight, ready to temper his voice and reconsider the propriety of his reaction. He didn't believe what she'd said and asked her to repeat.

"Feared my synopsis and my submission would be tossed out no matter what you said. I peeled my red paper heart from my envelope and stuck it on a similar envelope."

"Wait here."

Randall stood and scampered to Wanda's desk. He returned to the conference room with the rejection response folder. He remained erect, inhaled until it hurt, and exhaled before he slapped the folder on the conference table. "You mean this red paper heart?"

Her head tilted forward. "Yes," she whispered.

"You can look at me. I don't have Medusa's head. I did read the submission that had this heart on it. You caused no harm." He refused to remind her she'd accused him of deception. He strained not to utter the cliché of the pot calling the kettle black.

Alicia rose and hugged him. Her head pressed his right shoulder. His instinct advised retreat. He didn't. They stood there. He tried hard not to slam his fists into her shoulders. The wall clock ticked two minutes. His right hand lifted her head and he gently kissed her lips. That her lips didn't respond in kind didn't upset him. His cheek didn't smart from a slap.

"I'm so sorry," she murmured. "Felt hurt. Held you personally responsible. Overlooked my own actions. I'm sorry."

"I'm sorry, too." What else did his heart command him to say? "Could we start fresh?"

"I'd like that." Alicia stepped back and her chest heaved with a deep inhale.

While he noted Alicia's real life reaction, Beatrix Smothers had jettisoned all reference to heaving bosoms in her last two novels without one reader protest. *Forget Beatrix.* He had to live his life. "I'm going to keep your red paper heart."

"Why?"

"My Oscar statuette gets lonely." Alicia grinned for the first time since her conference room entrance. "How 'bout I say that science has proven that less direct light will protect this precious paper heart from fading. You can visit it often."

"What about impersonating Beatrix? I recall Charlotte turned you down."

He gazed at his feet. Mom's book club landmine he

didn't wish to detonate or even discuss. "Let's talk about that over food. Take both manuscripts and call your roommate. I'll meet you in the lobby."

"Agreed."

"One more thing."

Alicia's hands quivered. "What?"

"We're not eating in any cafeteria. I'm taking you to a private dining club."

* * *

Randall bowed as he opened his Lincoln's passenger door to escort Alicia into his parents' house. They were early, in fact, a month early. Mrs. Johnson, scheduled to host, lost her author friend to a family emergency. Randall's mother, in a gesture of friendship, advanced her hosting.

"Beatrix, it's so nice of you to come," Randall's mother gushed. "Randall has told me how busy you are. The book club ladies will be impressed. I know I am."

Alicia followed Randall to the kitchen where his mother flitted around like a butterfly—from coffee pot, to cookie bars, to flatware. "How have you been since Thanksgiving?"

"Fine. Like Randall said, busy. Thanksgiving here was fantastic."

Alicia sipped Chamomile tea at the kitchen table while Randall assisted his Mother greet and seat eight club members in the family room. He checked Dad's study to find it empty.

Mother introduced Beatrix to enthusiastic applause. Alicia's white Nordic sweater, in sharp contrast to the dark fireplace brick behind her, accented her stiff posture as her tailored black slacks blended in.

"I hope you'll grant me one request," Alicia as Beatrix began. "I understood and see that your club is all

281

One Paper Heart

women, but Randall by the kitchen passageway does a great job of keeping me out of trouble." Randall felt the escalating warmth in his cheeks. "In the event I dangle a participle, I'll look for him to interrupt and offer assistance. For all present I've brought a copy of a recent book by an author standing in your midst. And, with Randall's help, all copies have been personally autographed."

Randall edged to an empty chair inside the archway. He listened with pride as Alicia/Beatrix recited the memorized presentation they'd practiced. No participle's dangled as she referenced Beatrix's two most recent novels. Alicia even convinced him her blush was authentic when he interrupted to help expand upon one character's motivation. Unfettered, but unexpressed, pride at Alicia's demonstrated poise and engaging personality swelled within him. He harbored no qualms Alicia would handle any posed question with skill, grace, and the required evasive candor.

Mrs. Hitcher raised her right hand. "You're so pretty, but you don't put your photograph on your books like other authors. You shy?"

Alicia's Beatrix stood rigid. Her lips frozen into a line. Randall battled an icy void in his kidneys. The women waited. Beatrix in stilted, halted language repeated the story she'd told his parents at Thanksgiving.

One woman's gasp startled the club woman to her right when Alicia offered an enhanced version of her terror as a stalked college female. As a group, the assembled women clung to Alicia's every word. Their eyes fixed on her.

Mother whispered to him: "If she were married, she wouldn't have to worry so much about an evil stalker."

Randall didn't answer, nor did he turn his head toward Mother. He desired this meeting to reach a quick conclusion to be alone with Alicia.

After dessert, all the book clubbers, many of whom

clasped Beatrix's hands, expressed individual and collective thanks and, with pride, carried her novel on their exit.

His mother beamed and approached Alicia in the vestibule. "I can't thank you enough."

Alicia excused herself to return to the family room fireplace to retrieve one novel copy that rested on the brick hearth. When she straightened her body, she hesitated and gazed at a photograph on the mantelpiece.

Randall ambled up behind her. He gazed at his photograph that included Mia. Her neck displayed her cherished two-heart ring on a silver chain. He called out to Mother. "Is this a new photograph on the mantelpiece?"

Mother wiped her hands on an uplifted apron as she walked across the family room to where he and Alicia stood. "Yes. Beatrix, that's Randall, as you can see, and Mia, his ex-wife. Poor darling, police discovered her murdered several weeks ago."

"Didn't know," Alicia said. "I'm so sorry for your loss."

"It was tragic. Randall grieved, first, the divorce . . . and, now, this murder."

"Mother, Beatrix doesn't need to have you recount all the gory details."

Alicia gazed at Mother and said: "You should excuse Randall. As a man, he likely doesn't realize the grief extends also to the parents and the parents-in-law."

Randall sensed that, at his expense, Alicia had strummed the right chord to have Mother worship her. He expected he'd never hear the end of Mother's urging him to marry a woman who extolled the compassion that sprang from Beatrix's vocal cords.

"You're so right," Mother gushed.

Randall shrugged.

Chapter Seventeen

After her encore portrayal of Ms. Beatrix Smothers, romance writer extraordinaire, Alicia squirmed on the front seat of Randall's Lincoln. Her teeth chattered until the warmth from the heated seat radiated throughout her torso. Her leather gloves protected against the cold metal seatbelt buckle until clicked into place.

She invited Randall into her apartment with the knowledge Vicky wouldn't be home for another sixty to ninety minutes. They shed boots and rubbers into a drip tray by the entrance door and Alicia hung their coats in the front closet.

"You were fantastic," Randall crowed. She'd have kissed him without his compliment. Their relationship continued to sail calm seas ever since her conference room red paper heart confession. "Glad your eyes twinkle again."

"Do you think your mother's still convinced?"

Randall's right hand rubbed his chin. "There's no need for you to worry. However, I do need you to do one thing for me?" He retrieved two envelopes from his topcoat. "Would you keep the office auditors happy and

284

sign this reprinted option?"

"Let's have a seat on the sofa." Alicia removed three pages from the thicker envelope. She read the first page and scanned the last two. "Can't."

"Huh?"

"Be back in a minute." Alicia shut her bedroom door to hide her bed's pile of granny dresses destined for Goodwill. No longer could Vicky tease they belonged in a museum. She found her pen and struck out the inked in $40,000 option amount and signed its signature block. She heard Randall hum as she entered the living room. "Here you go."

A quizzical sheen glazed his eyes. "What did I do now?"

"In my anger I was willing to latch onto anything. Jackson no doubt told you I blasted him that money wasn't everything. That hasn't changed. There's still thirty thousand dollars in the bank. That's enough."

"Give me your pen." Alicia squeezed it tight in her right hand. "Please, give me the pen."

Alicia extended her relaxed right hand.

"I won't threaten. I'll beg if you make me. Please initial the forty thousand. Jackson's threatened to kill our friendship if you don't accept. Call him on my cell phone if you don't believe. I've the ten thousand dollar check in this second envelope. You're a generous person. Give it to whomever. You won't surrender your principles if you initial." He pouted. "Please."

"All right."

"Please put this check someplace safe."

Alicia carried it to her bedroom. She slipped it into her purse along with two notes written earlier that day. The first a reminder Doctor Beck's office had scheduled her laparotomy surgery in three weeks. The second a reminder to telephone her parents to apprise them of her visit in a day or so to soften the shock of her surgery news.

One Paper Heart

If a silver lining, the extra ten grand served either as a medical expense cushion or to pay for her plane flight to visit Georgia to urge Mr. Shirley to reconsider Georgia's fate.

Randall massaged her shoulders as they sat on the sofa. "You're tense, really tense. I won't mention the option again. It isn't still my mother?"

"Of course not." Alicia worried about her Mom and her reaction to Alicia's news. To distract Randall and herself, she kissed him until the door buzzer interrupted. "Vicky's home."

Vicky bounded in. "Hi, you two." She carried a foot-wide carnation bouquet.

"What we celebrating?" Alicia asked. She bounced up to give Vicky a hug.

"Joel asked to go steady." A school ring on chain dangled at Vicky's neck. "I said yes."

Alicia heard sofa cushions suck in air. Randall's hand touched the small of her back. "Congratulations," he offered.

"Must find a vase." Vicky's grin dwarfed her face. "Aren't they beautiful." She darted to her bedroom.

Randall locked his hands at the front of Alicia's waist. "I'm sure Vicky has more to share. Give me a good night kiss and I'll find the way to my car."

Alicia pivoted and hungrily smooched Randall's lips. She broke away to retrieve Randall's coat as he slipped on his rubbers. Her lips smothered his again. When the knob on Vicky's bedroom door creaked, she blew a kiss into the hallway before he closed her apartment door.

Vicky laid the carnations on the breakfast counter as she filled a clear glass vase at the sink. Alicia buried her nose in a bloom before the two roommates giggled. Alicia blotted out her unpleasant Joel memories and extended Vicky a sincere wish for her continued happiness with her fireman beau. As a writer, she volunteered, "I'd say he lit your fire."

286

They both groaned and then laughed.

* * *

Alicia timed her Saturday New Brighton arrival to speak
with Mom before Dad finished his weekly grocery
shopping trip and arrived home at eleven a.m. She parked
her Contour at the curb, checked her composure in a
compact mirror, patted on makeup powder, and greeted
Mom at the front door. The two of them settled at the
kitchen table with cups of coffee. Alicia waved away her
Mom's chocolate chip cookie offer.

"Save them for Alan." Alicia calmed her nerves.
"Mom, I need to tell you something."

"Anything, dear."

Alicia's hands rubbed her blue-jeans-covered thighs.
Her sweater's collar itch didn't register as important.
"I've seen Doctor Beck and tests indicate there's a
problem with my ovary—"

"Noooo." Mom screamed. Her overlapped hands hid
her eyes.

Alicia expected Mom's tears, not unbridled terror.

"Can't relive this again," Mom screamed and ran
from the kitchen to her sewing room.

Alicia tried the doorknob—locked. "Mom, let me in.
Please, let me in."

Emotion launched Alicia's tears and gravity tugged
them from her chin. She tried the knob a second time
with no luck. Her repeated pleas went unanswered. She
leaned her ear to the wood and picked up no interior
sound.

Alicia slumped to the floor, her back against the door
when the kitchen door squeaked its familiar tune.

"Precious, where are you?"

"Here, Dad." Alicia rose and stepped into the kitchen.
Dad had placed three cloth grocery bags next to the sink.

He rushed to her. "What's the matter? Where's mother?"

Alicia pointed to the sewing room. While Dad pounded his fist on the door, she swallowed a sip of her lukewarm coffee. "Dad," she said when he returned. "I did it. Hurt Mom."

"What do you mean?" He plopped into the chair next to her.

"I've had appointments with Doctor Beck. Dye traces, scans, and blood tests discovered a growth or tissue on my left ovary. Doc Beck has recommended exploratory surgery."

"Oh, Precious. It'll be all right." His eyes reddened and he hugged her. When he released her, he said, "Mother will be all right, too. It's the shock. I'll be back."

Dad departed. Alicia heard less frantic sewing-room-door knocks and Dad say "I'll shut the door."

Alicia rewarmed her coffee. Dad didn't need to cope with two women in crisis. To relieve the tension that gripped her entire body, Alicia rose and paced the kitchen floor, checked the refrigerator for juice, and closed its door when she found none. She stopped to splash her cup's cold coffee into the sink.

She clasped her jittery hands when Dad entered the kitchen.

"Mother's resting in her sewing chair," Dad said with a sigh. He collapsed into the kitchen chair he previously occupied. "Guess you've never been told Mother's complete story."

"Dad, you don't have to." This crisis presented new dimensions for her and she didn't know exactly how to respond. Her right hand on his left shoulder steadied her until she sat in a chair next to him. As a child she'd have been directed to leave the room.

"You're old enough. Mother and I agreed never to mention this to any of you. We figured heredity brought no fear since we adopted."

"Dad . . ." Anxiety caged her words inside her mind as if prisoners.

"Our first child was aborted when tests disclosed potential Down's syndrome. It wasn't enough for us to agonize a deliberate rejection of our Catholic Church's teachings. Hospital doctors diagnosed stage two ovarian cancer."

"Oh, Dad . . ."

"In her grief of having lost a child, she faced what I'd guess would be what you're facing now. Perhaps you'll do as we did, adopt."

"I've tried. Single-parent adoptions are frowned upon."

"There's an obvious solution to that obstacle."

"You don't have to explain."

"As long as we're alive, your mother and I will be here to support you."

Alicia stood as Mom appeared at the kitchen entrance. Her Mom's face patchy with red marks and a twisted towel clutched in her hands. When Mom approached, Alicia hugged both her parents. It was easy to feel blessed with the world rosy. Harder when challenges loomed, but doable. Greater blessings abounded with the unqualified joy of loving parents.

Mundane concerns eased the tense emotional high when Mom asked Dad if he'd put the ice cream in the freezer. He replied, "I'll get it out of the bag on the counter."

The soft ice cream never reached the freezer. Alicia enjoyed her scoop. Her Dad clutched her Mom's hand as Alicia did the best she could to explain in non-emotional terms what Doctor Beck had said in his office. She explained no pain and her frequent bathroom trips.

Mom laughed when Alicia spoke of how rattled her nerves had been after eating Vicky's jar of pickled beets. Dad asked if Alicia planned to still bring her boyfriend the next day.

One Paper Heart

Alicia felt her cheeks warm before her affirmative head nod.

* * *

Alicia, on their Sunday drive to New Brighton, filled Randall's brain with her family's background until the green awning D quickened her heart. Mom met them at the door.

"It's so nice to meet you, Randall. Come inside quick."

Dad waited until Alicia arranged her and Randall's snow-covered boots on the rubberized vestibule drip mat. He welcomed Randall with a handshake. "Let's get settled in the living room before Alicia offers introductions. It's this way."

Alicia went through the formalities of introducing Randall to Elena, husband Jonathan, and their two kids. Her two brothers weren't home. Aunt Agnes beamed.

Randall and Alicia sat upright and rigid next to each other on the knitted afghan that adorned the sofa. Alicia expected Mom, who'd slipped out of sight during Dad's handshake, to re-emerge with bars and coffee, even if dinner scheduled to be served in a half-hour at noon. With Aunt Agnes in Dad's recliner, Dad relaxed in Mom's rocker, kiddy-corner to the sofa.

"Your father is Charles Van Gilleran, correct?" Dad asked.

Randall's lips twisted and his eyes bugged out. "Yes."

"I met him at a coatings seminar related to my managing the Ford Plant's paint department. He said his son worked for a romance book company downtown. That fit with Alicia."

"You have good intelligence."

Alicia adored the double meaning to Randall's words. Aunt Agnes listened with a stenographer's attention.

Donan Berg

While Alicia yearned to help Mom in the kitchen, protecting Randall from Dad's questions ranked more important.

"Is the book business having it as hard as the automobile industry?"

Alicia interrupted. "Dad, let's not discuss work." She asked Elena about the latest Nea and Jonathan Jr. pictures. Elena obliged.

When Mom entered with a tray of lemon and raspberry jam bars, Dad rose to bring in the coffee cups and the carafe. Alicia mentioned sports and the male conversations blossomed: first football, then baseball. Mom retreated to the serenity of her kitchen. Randall expressed his partiality for the Chicago Cubs.

"You're lucky they aren't in the American League or they'd be farther under .500," Jonathan Sr. said.

"Dear," Elena said, "shouldn't we leave the cheers and boos at the ballpark."

Elena's husband sank into his chair. He released his hold on Jonathan Jr., who then raced into the kitchen.

"Grampa, Grampa," young Jonathan shouted.

Dad rose from the rocker and stumbled on his first step to the kitchen. His second step restored his balance. Alicia reached the kitchen door behind Jonathan Sr. and gasped to see Mom face down on the kitchen floor. Dad knelt next to her.

"I'll dial 9-1-1," Elena shouted.

"Hold off," Dad said.

Randall steadied Alicia's shaking shoulders. "Call Elena," Alicia urged. "The red splatters near Mom's head look like blood." She escaped Randall's grip to step near her mother's shoes.

Dad's eyes flashed. "Hold off, I said. Mother appears to be all right."

"What about the blood?" Alicia asked.

"Pasta sauce from the hot dish," Dad replied.

Jonathan Sr. and Dad lifted Mom to her knees and

291

then onto a chair.

Randall cradled Nea and it pleased Alicia to see how contented Elena's daughter appeared.

"Don't none of you fret," Mom said.

All, except Mom, Dad, and Aunt Agnes, retreated to the living room where the only conversation emanated from the television speakers. A half hour later, Dad invited everyone into the kitchen. After a somber hot dish meal, a side-by-side Alicia and Randall walked to his Lincoln parked in the home's driveway. She waved good-bye to family as Randall backed into the street.

"Hope your mother will be okay."

"Accidental slip. She'll be fine." At least that's what Alicia prayed for, not a dizzy spell relapse spurred by Alicia's surgical announcement shock of the day before.

"Do you think your parents liked me? I shoulda kept my mouth shut about the Cubs."

"Don't worry. They did. Forget sports." Alicia didn't wish to talk about sports teams for fear it would lead to the Chicago Bears and Jackson. "Elena privately told me she liked your shorter hair and that you impressed her as a better person than the serious editor she met downtown."

"That's nice."

"You also hold little girls with ease."

Randall blushed. "There's one thing though—" He braked for a red traffic light.

"What's that?"

"How will I explain to the paramedics they need to be present when my mother meets you as Alicia Danielson and not Beatrix Smothers?"

"Mothers have a natural resiliency."

She gazed out her side window, clear except for the frost mantle across its lower edge. Brother Alan last month griped that Mom nagged him about college, girls, and a part-time job. Alicia assured him Mom strove in her own way to motivate him to be his best, and, on days

Donan Berg

when her medication and body rhythms weren't in sync, could use his love and understanding.

Randall smiled. "If you say so. I'll still bring smelling salts."

"Enough all ready." Alicia tapped her right foot on the car mat. "Would you like to visit awhile at my apartment?"

"If Vicky doesn't mind."

Alicia had prepped Vicky to hide out in the building's laundry room. "I'll bribe her with pizza." As Randall hung their coats in the front closet, Vicky emerged from her bedroom. The laundry basket she carried bumped into Alicia.

"Sorry. I'll knock when I return."

Alicia tried to return Vicky's smile without Randall's intercept. "If you want."

Vicky departed and Alicia escorted Randall to the sofa.

"Can we shelve all talk about mothers?"

"Let's also forget pen names." Randall's gaze meandered to the TV and closed his circle at her. "Have I mentioned your final essay was excellent. The story's underlying emotion drew me right in."

She didn't think he had read it for there were no red marks. "Thanks. I adore Georgia." *Oops.* "Could I get you coffee?"

"Later, maybe. Is Georgia the essay's little girl. Some details seemed mismatched."

What's the big deal? He'll find out sooner or later. "Wait a minute." Alicia returned with Georgia's latest picture. With a parent's pride, she handed Randall the snapshot and fell backward onto the sofa.

As Randall, his back to her apartment door, scrutinized Georgia's photo, there was a knock on the door. Alicia shouted, "Door's open."

Vicky appeared. "Forgot bleach. Any important news? You guys planning the full house of kids Alicia's

293

always dreamed of?"

Alicia gasped and bolted to her feet. Randall squirmed and laid Georgia's photo on the coffee table. His left hand smoothed a tie he didn't wear. Alicia glared at Vicky as she hastened to the cabinet under the sink and thrust a blue box at her roommate to short-circuit her further embarrassment.

"Sorry," Vicky whispered. She departed, Clorox in hand.

Alicia sat on the sofa to face Randall.

"Were we being teased?" Randall asked.

"I know I one time said 'I love you' and, while I haven't repeated the words, I do love you." A lump formed in her throat. "I also recall saying I wanted a large family." Alicia hadn't expected to discuss her upcoming surgery. "To achieve that goal, I might have to follow my parent's example."

Randall's impromptu hug startled Alicia. "My parents expected kids," he began. "I was the medical roadblock. My body couldn't produce the required sperm quantity." A single tear escaped his right eye.

Alicia squeezed him tighter. "Your problem isn't insurmountable. There's *in vitro* fertilization. I saw it on *Sixty Minutes*. All a doctor does is capture one of your little soldiers in a test tube." He laughed. "I have a higher mountain to climb."

"Huh."

"Grab your seatbelt." Alicia exhaled. Her heart pounded his chest. She eased away. "After what I say, if you leave I won't hold it against you." Alicia gazed deep into his eyes. "My doctor discovered my weight loss wasn't all diet. It hid a potential cancer."

Randall trembled until his right fist relaxed.

Alicia kissed his cheek. She figured her cryptic comments would've scared even her.

Randall's eyes radiated fear, not hurt.

"I'm scheduled for surgery in a couple weeks." He

stared at her. "My parents know about my doctor visits, preliminary tests. I'm getting past my denial it's happening. I'm facing a surgical procedure for ovarian cancer."

Her gentle kiss lingered on his forehead and her tear dropped onto his cheek. Her words struggled to emerge. "My fear is I'll never be able to give birth to any man's child."

Randall stroked Alicia's hair. "Didn't you tell me you had the greatest family? Never loved Mia based on a medical report. Nor did I ask her for her doctor's opinion."

He cupped her face in his hands and kissed her lips.

"You don't have to explain." She didn't solicit, nor want, pity. Alicia reassured herself with a dozen kisses Randall's words were devoid of deception.

"I want to. This is too important. I love my parents. You've made me understand my parents' values or desires aren't wrong, but other values exist just as valid. My heart's expanded. You've demonstrated that the love a person gives returns many fold. I'm not . . . not . . . giving you up."

"You're truly special."

Randall's fingers released her face. "If doctors can capture what you called my little soldier, then a surrogate mother could help create our large family."

Alicia squeezed her arms around Randall. "I have another suggestion. We could adopt Georgia. She responds to me and needs a family. Little girls adore you. I saw you and Nea."

"Would you consider two girls . . .?"

Chapter Eighteen

A silent scream zigzagged through Randall's body when Sgt. Lopez informed him that a telephone survey of sixteen home care agencies failed to locate the sought after domestic. Phoenix squad room desks foreclosed his urge to fling his coffee cup.

Randall pleaded: "Please tell me her name at least."

Sgt. Lopez shook his head. "Civilians muck up investigations. Won't go there."

Randall conceded temporary failure and let the sergeant escort him to the street.

"Do yourself a favor, sir. Board the next flight to Minneapolis."

Randall cultivated his anger against Sgt. Lopez into a harbinger of good things. He converted his saved two hundred dollars flight-change fee into a night's lodging and a cab ride to Mia's apartment building north of downtown. Within a four-block radius, he buttonholed strangers.

"Do your recognize this woman?" No matter their response he inquired if they'd seen the woman in his photograph with a little girl or knew a maid who visited

296

El Rancho Apartments. He expected no quick success and kept at it.

Randall bristled at a long-haired convenience store clerk who sported a teenager's acne and whistled at Mia's photo. His right hand fisted, Randall pressed its knuckles to his blue jeans.

"You haven't seen her?"

"She work at El Rancho, too?"

"Lived there. You know any woman who works there?"

"Older woman. Wears blue dress."

"You see her today?" Clerk shook his head. "What about yesterday?"

"She stop to buy her Payroll bar. Does that."

Randall extracted a twenty-dollar bill from his billfold. "Tell me about her."

"Know her name's Rosa. That's all, amigo."

When the clerk convinced Randall he would get nothing more than a sketchy description, he laid his twenty on the counter. With a second twenty, Randall purchased a cola, two Payroll bars, and snack cheese crackers. He located a shady bench in a park across the street from the canopied entrance to the El Rancho apartment building. His patience paid dividends. At mid-afternoon, a woman of Rosa's description dressed in a blue uniform carried a pail and cloths toward the apartments.

Randall reacted like a panther to intercept her. When he called out "Rosa," she scurried toward the canopy.

Randall caught her fifteen feet from the revolving door. He grabbed her right arm. "I won't hurt you. Need to ask a question."

With mottled fear in her eyes, Rosa stared at the photo of Mia.

He released his grip of her arm with the hope it would accent his words he wasn't there to harm her. "I need to find my child. Please help me."

Rosa shivered. "Me no talk."

"I'm no cop. Not sent to harm you. Did . . . ?" The words stuck in his throat. "Do you know this woman? She . . . Mia was her name . . . she was my wife."

Rosa's lips barely moved. "Si."

He asked, "Did Miss Mia have a child?"

"Little girl."

Randall's heart pounded. "Do you know where she is?"

Rosa bent her head and shielded her face with her pail. "Must go. Be Late."

"Please, Rosa." He grabbed her right arm. "I'm trying to find my daughter."

"Southeast Phoenix, 2459 S. Lomax Street, Cecilia Running Bear. I go now."

"Thank you, thank you." In what he deemed to be an insignificant gesture, Randall handed her the two Payroll candy bars, his business card, and left. *Damn.* He raced through the park and hailed a taxi that had discharged a couple on a church's steps.

Randall asked the cabbie to wait in front of four bungalows that sported brown-grass lawns, peeling white-painted siding, and uncluttered porches. From his pocket he extracted Mia's photo and knocked on the house numbered 2459. The low sun blazed strong on his neck's nape.

A thirty-something pregnant woman answered the door as a child cried within the house behind her. The woman's right hand gripped the doorframe. Randall hurried to explain he was neither the police, a detective, nor a bill collector. He sighed when the woman's skeptical eyes eased with his mention of Rosa.

"Does the girl live here?"

She shook her head and elongated the time between rearward glances when the cries ceased.

"Where then?"

"Maybe five years ago. Husband left me with three

kids. Rosa offered me money if I agreed to take an infant girl to my Navajo Reservation people. We dyed the girl's hair black."

"When's the last time you saw her?"

"Two, three months ago at the Indian School."

"Thank you, thank you."

A reservation security guard blocked Randall's cab. He pleaded to no avail. Forced to leave a message for Sgt. Lopez, Randall abandoned his Phoenix efforts and plotted what he could do from Minneapolis. His search for his name on an Arizona birth certificate yielded no hits.

When Sgt. Lopez hadn't responded in four days, Randall tried with his cell phone from Alicia's bathroom. "He'll have to get back to you," the dispatcher said. Randall returned to Alicia's living room.

"You okay? Could I get you water?"

"I'm fine." Alicia snuggled into his arms while they sat on the sofa. "Let me tell you a story." As coherent as he could, he repeated his Phoenix search story and included his conclusion that the disguised infant girl sent to the Indian School was his daughter.

"Omigawd. That's tragic and you couldn't find out for sure?"

"Let's be upbeat. Wanda mentioned you received news about your sponsored child. Is that the same little girl you wrote about in your final essay?"

"Yes, it was."

"And, you referenced a Lakota Indian School in North Dakota."

Alicia gazed up at him. "I did, but that was to protect Georgia's privacy. She lives at a Mission School in Arizona."

Randall gulped. "Near Phoenix?"

"Yeah."

"When you wrote at the essay's conclusion about a silver ring, was this a ring with two little, intertwined

299

hearts?"

"Why? What's so important about a kid's play ring worth less than three dollars?"

"Remember that fireplace mantelpiece photo at my parents?"

"Sorta."

"The ring matches in description one I'd given to Mia. Concerned the cheap ring would turn green on her finger, she strung it through a chain, wore it as a necklace adornment, and cherished it as a keepsake."

"Then Mia had it with her in Phoenix?"

A logical question to which Randall had no answer. "I'll try not to bore you."

Alicia snuggled closer. "With what?" Her warmth penetrated his shirt.

Randall explained his pre-Thanksgiving Day travel trip to Phoenix upon learning of Mia's murder. He detailed his reluctance to examine Mia's belongings and, when he did at Sgt. Lopez's urging, did not find the silver heart ring. When he telephoned Mother, she said she did not know of the ring's whereabouts.

"I've never relayed to Mother the police finding drug paraphernalia in a drawer in Mia's apartment nor the coroner's examination conclusion that Mia may have borne a child." His gaze confirmed Alicia remained awake. "I've already mentioned I unearthed a Navajo woman who helped Mia find care for a little girl. Best I can determine is that the girl today is near age six."

For a second time, Alicia shrieked, "Omigawd." She pulled away to face him. "That's Georgia's age. That's why she's being sent to a foster home, or by now may have already been adopted." Alicia ran to a bedroom. She returned in two minutes with several pictures.

"These are all the pictures of Georgia I've received from the agency. I don't remember seeing any ring, although Georgia wrote about having one." Alicia knelt at the coffee table to sort her pictures. "Those rings exist by the thousands, if not millions."

"I know." Randall stared at the pictures one-by-one.

Alicia shouted, "Come in." She raised a finger to her lips as Vicky plunked a full laundry basket on the breakfast counter.

"Don't you guys ever tire of little girl photos?"

Randall shrugged. Alicia's cheeks darkened to a pink-red tint. He lacked the ability to decipher if it was anger or embarrassment and didn't wish to ask.

Alicia crossed her arms. "No, Vicky. Someday I may fill my house with a hundred picture albums of children and add a few more with a dog, two cats, a canary, possibly a gerbil. However, I'm not telling you anything until the National Inquirer pays me first." Alicia's glare cold enough to freeze the scrotum off a brass monkey.

"S-o-r-r-y." Vicky picked up her basket. The lock's click from her roommate's bedroom door echoed throughout the apartment.

* * *

Wispy smoke seeped from the airplane's economy cabin sidewall into Alicia's face. She screamed. The drop of an oxygen mask failed to activate her muscles. Her thoughts froze on Joel, two thousand miles away, unable to rescue her at 30,000 feet. She stared straight ahead as Randall fixed an oxygen mask tight to her nose and mouth.

We'll never make Phoenix.

Randall's tight right hand grasp of her left wrist strained to dislodge her fingers clamped on the armrest that separated them. Glued-together shrieks, in front of and behind her, insufficient to be the escape route knotted bed sheets provided. Outside her window no lights nor stars twinkled. The panic inside the cabin drum-rolled. Afraid to see flames, Alicia closed her eyes.

"Please stay calm," the flight attendant shouted. *Who*

except us within two rows can hear? If the attendant defined calm as frozen in place, she was. Alicia's brain whirled. Would her blond hair strands be washed and combed by angels? Had the weight she lost been saved in heaven ready to be wrapped in place as an asexual cummerbund.

Joel had rescued her from asphyxiation once. Could Randall? It was all so surreal. *Thy kingdom come. Thy will be done. Or was it: Thy will be done. Thy kingdom come.*

Alicia's ears popped. Her head hurt. She peeked and couldn't see the overhead aisle seatbelt sign or the bald spot of the passenger who had sat in front of her.

"Alicia, breathe," Randall whispered. "Slow and easy."

He sounded so far away.

* * *

Alicia's first ride on an airport's luggage cart lacked the road-warrior glamour of the carnival. She signed forms in duplicate to refuse transport to the hospital for medical observation.

This close to her Georgia meant the world to her. Alicia coughed no worse than after the high-rise fire. No doubt, each mile flown—minus the condenser midair burnout—ratcheted up Randall's anxiety although he seemed to hide it well as he pampered her.

Alicia clapped her hands to divert the dark-skinned, muscular taxi dispatcher's attention from Randall's hop out of their reserved rental sedan he had double-parked in a taxi-loading zone. She clicked her safety belt. "Do we need a map?"

Randall floored the car's accelerator. "Got GPS or a police escort."

Alicia contained her smile until the Navajo

Reservation security guard waved them along. She pointed Randall to an area of slides and swings.

"Hi, mommy," Georgia shouted when Alicia emerged from the car. They ran to each other. Alicia dropped to her knees on the grass and Georgia clung to her. Alicia whispered to Randall, "Georgia calls all older women 'mommy'." The agency director, Mr. Shirley, joined them at the playground swings.

"So happy to see you Ms. Danielson. And, your friend's name is?"

"Randall Van Gilleran."

"After I received your telephone call Tuesday, I found a silver ring in Georgia's case and it's in my office. She needs to return to her classmates until noon. You two can visit later."

The threesome walked to the director's office. While the room's window air conditioner drone hampered normal conversation, Alicia didn't object. She enjoyed the welcome comfort of cool air unaccompanied by smoke.

From a small, manila envelope, Randall dumped a ring into his left palm. Alicia maneuvered for a look as he assessed the ring. Alicia longed to reach out from her visitor chair next to him. Director Shirley, his shoes silent on the carpet, paced the bookcase wall to the left of his desk.

"This resembles Mia's ring. The vibes are strong it was hers. With no initials or special marks, I can't be positive."

"I think I understand," Director Shirley said. "However, the ring came with Georgia and I can't give it to anyone other than her."

"That's fine," Randall replied.

"When is Georgia leaving here?" Alicia asked.

"Four weeks from now," the director said. "I can put a temporary hold on the transfer for there to be a paternity determination."

303

"For how long?"

"We try to be flexible. If I understand correctly, Mr. Van Gilleran may be Georgia's biological father. The agency does not, and cannot, pay for any paternity testing. Under the circumstances, we will not traumatize Georgia by sending her to a foster home while testing to establish you as her biological father is underway."

"Sir, I'm trying to find a reputable testing lab. I believe she's my daughter." Gravity tugged a tear toward his chin.

Alicia's right hand traced the puffiness of her own eyes. "What about the adoptive parents?"

"Their background check is incomplete. I can't say more. We've had to proceed with foster care arrangements, but any transfer hold applies equally to an adoption."

His words pleased Alicia.

"Mr. Van Gilleran, for all my students including Georgia, it's a glorious day when a child finds a parent. However, at this junction, I can permit only Ms. Danielson, her sponsor, to spend time with Georgia. It's not beneficial for a child to form an attachment that might not last. I trust you understand our position."

"For Georgia's sake I will."

Alicia witnessed the hurt in Randall's eyes. She couldn't excise from her mind his excitement on first seeing Georgia. A father's concern, a father's love, a father's caring, she'd seen it all in Randall's first glance.

She cradled the memory and waved as Randall drove off in their rental car for a drive around the countryside while she played with, talked to, and repeatedly hugged Georgia. Late in the afternoon, Randall returned to pick her up and drive them to their motel. The reserved suite provided them with separate bedrooms.

* * *

Alicia adjusted the suite's sitting room curtains to block the morning sun. The emotional high Georgia infused into her handcuffed Alicia's return flight smoke fear.

Randall's mood dip perplexed her. The Wounded Warrior TV ad shifted her thoughts to PTSD. Wasn't that a war injury? Randall never wore a military uniform.

"Alicia," Randall's resonant tone broke the room's stillness. "Please join me."

She sat across from him at the window's table and ignored the tree branch scrapes on the outside glass.

"If the doctors say Georgia is my daughter, you can't imagine how happy it'll make me. That you helped puts me in your debt forever."

"Randall, you're not the only one to be extremely happy. I was fearful Georgia would be sent off to who-knows-where and end up in an abusive family environment. I hope she's your daughter. Then I know she'll be well cared for, and provided all the love every child needs." *Can't cross line to hint I desire to be Georgia's mother.*

"This is hard for me. I heard and remember Vicky's comments last week where she said you want to have a large family. I wouldn't want to deprive you of your dreams?"

"Don't understand. You . . . you can't forget my situation?"

"Mia and I tried to have a child. Until the last few months I didn't know there existed the reality she gave birth to a child. I figured she blamed me as the medical roadblock."

"Still don't understand. Can't in the foggiest fathom why Mia gave away her little girl to be raised on the reservation. To my knowledge she never visited."

"Rosa said Mia couldn't care for her daughter. There were tell-tale signs in Mia's apartment she used illegal drugs. That may have had something to do with her death."

"Let's not speculate. Keep the positive memories you have of Mia."

Randall clasped her right hand. "You're an angel."

"Keep that thought. We need to hustle to make our flight."

* * *

Randall kept his early Monday morning office appointment to have Doc Campbell's nurse perform a DNA mouth swab.

"Please hold on, sir. The doctor would like a brief word with you."

"About what?"

"Please. This way."

Randall tagged after the nurse to an examination room. She instructed him not to disrobe. Left alone, Randall paced the longer distance between opposite walls. Two minutes later, Doc Campbell knocked and entered.

"Thanks for waiting. Do you handle a lot of cash register receipts?"

"Two or three per week. Gas pump, grocery store, mall."

"Don't look so perplexed. What about soaps, shampoos? Your bathroom have a shower curtain that gave you a headache when hung?"

"No. Not that I remember."

"You drive a Lincoln, right?"

"Yes." Randall shifted his weight from his left foot to his right. These questions were silly.

"Like your heated seats?"

"What Minnesotan doesn't?"

"I think we've discovered a potential cause for your sperm problem."

"Huh." Randall didn't believe it. "If I didn't understand your first questions, I'm now flabbergasted by the blame you heap on heated seats."

"Latest issue of *Infertility Clinics Newsletter* listed several sperm slayers. Chemicals mainly, but heated car seats, believe it or not, are also culprits. That toastiness you feel can damage your sperm quality. Higher testicular temperatures caused by direct heat cause the problem."

"Don't believe it."

"Since my prescription didn't work, I suggest you turn your car seat heat switch off. Also, keep any home heating pad plugged out. We'll do a sperm test in sixty to ninety days and see what happens. You game?"

"Of course."

"Good. We'll send your DNA swab to a St. Louis laboratory. We've sent a swab to the Indian reservation along with a mailing label to the same lab. All costs will be forwarded here."

Randall flashed a thumbs up to the nurse as he departed Doc Campbell's office. His left hand reached low after he slid into his Lincoln and switched off the seat warmer. His chilly buttocks squirmed his entire drive to the Bunyan Center ramp. He burst through reception's door and throttled his enthusiasm when he encountered a woman seated to Alicia's left.

"Mr. Van Gilleran this lady has been expecting your return."

He turned to the visitor. "Good morning. Isn't it a great day to be alive?"

Both Alicia and the woman smiled.

The visitor rose. "Mr. Van Gilleran, I represent two authors whose work fits well with *New Romance Delights*. I should like to speak with you about them."

He gazed at Alicia and then focused on the visitor. "I'm sure they're fine writers, but I've already scheduled this time to confer with an exciting new author. If you have submissions, I'll take them now and you must excuse me."

The woman handed Randall two envelopes. He departed to his office and requested Wanda to report to him the minute Alicia had no one in reception.

He stood in front of Alicia's desk. "Great news, I think."

"Phoenix police discovered evidence Georgia's your daughter."

"Too early for that. But the DNA process has begun. Doc Campbell believes he's isolated what's caused my man problem and we'll know in a couple of months."

"That's great."

Alicia's tone didn't match the elation that coursed his veins. Then it dawned on him. He'd been selfish not to consider what obstacle lay before her. He'd already approved her medical leave with his signature on a blank form that let her fill in the dates. Perhaps Wanda hadn't given it to her yet.

"Alicia, please stand next to me."

She inched herself erect, glanced at both reception doors, and eased herself around her desk to stand in the room's center. She shuffled to face him as he walked to the hallway door and flipped the lock and then braced a visitor chair under the office exit door handle.

"Done." His right hand reached into his right suit coat pocket and stayed there. Her guarded stance as unmoving as the Mary Tyler Moore statute she once mimicked. Her quizzical eyes fixed on his right suit coat pocket.

He dropped to his right knee. "Alicia, will you marry me?" His extended right hand held a ring box flipped open.

Her facial muscles froze.

"Please Alicia, say yes, I don't know that I can hold this position forever."

She burst out with a laugh followed by a stern mien he remembered his third grade teacher had displayed when she brandished a ruler above his knuckles.

"Randall, please get up."

"Not until you say "Yes."

"Yes. Yes."

He hugged her tight. Kissed her neck first and then her lips.

"I do love you, but we should wait with any engagement announcement until my surgery. You'll do that for me, won't you."

"I told you before and I mean it. My love isn't conditioned on a medical report."

"Sir Galahad you are, but I've got to think about my Mom and Dad, Aunt Agnes, and the shock to your mother and father. You told me you'd have to bring smelling salts for your mother."

"They adore Beatrix Smothers and perhaps your father already showed your picture to my father and they've joined the grand conspiracy against mothers and wives."

"You've got to be kidding."

He kissed her again. "Okay, I'm kidding. But with any joke there's an underlying rational that may hold a germ of truth."

Alicia shivered.

His mind raced uncharted roads to a dead end. He didn't understand the chill he inflicted.

The frown at the corner of her lips slipped away. "Let's wipe my lipstick off you. Keep the ring until we go public. This is, after all, a business office."

Randall was all too ready to wipe his errant quip from history. With his handkerchief stuffed in a rear pants pocket, he unlocked the front door and shifted the visitor chair to its carpet indents. He squeezed Alicia's hand.

"Telephone Elena and Vicky. I'm treating the three of you to dinner tonight. If necessary we'll pick up Vicky at your apartment and drive to Shakopee."

"Why?"

One Paper Heart

"If anyone is going to tell them and request secrecy, it'll be us together."

"Okay."

"And, for your information, my heated car seats went on the fritz today. So I'll not be blamed for your cold butt until the heater or defroster warms the interior."

* * *

The stainless steel operating table chilled Alicia's entire backside. She recited a descending number count until the anesthesia kicked in and she floated into unconsciousness.

The ceiling fluorescent light hum when she awoke didn't distract her from the intensifying dull pain below her waist. She hesitated to lift the white sheet and the thin blanket that covered her from chin to toes. She feared the worse.

A nurse bent over her face. "How you feeling?"

"Okay, I guess."

"If you're talking, you're doing great." The nurse's face disappeared.

Alicia's left hand hovered above her abdomen. When her hand rested on her blanket, it didn't fall into nothingness. She sighed in relief that her worst nightmare hadn't blossomed into an actuality.

A low-frequency buzzer tone resonated around her. *Monticello Dam, California.* A rolling cart attended to by a flurry of persons surrounded her bedside.

"Alicia, you're post-op IV disconnected. Did you jerk your left arm?"

"Maybe."

"Please lie still for the next hour. You're doing great."

"Okay." She imagined herself in a white full-body cast. Her expanded imagination visualized her writing god grinned at her inability to rub her VapoRub on his chest. The images didn't distract her from Randall's marriage proposal she'd asked him to reconsider in light of her physical reality.

If what she feared existed, she expected him not to ignore his parents' wishes, especially his mother's. If Randall wavered in the least little bit, he wouldn't match what she appreciated in her Dad. The black clock hands on the distant wall blurred. She groped for an unfound call button.

She screamed until her brain saw no clock and she heard her words: "I want my Dad."

"You're safe." A mellow voice behind her head repeated, "You're safe."

"My knee. Dad said he went for a Band-Aid. Where is he?"

"He's waiting for you," the soothing voice said. "The anesthesia gave you a bad dream. You're out of recovery. Any nightmares will fade away, faster if you let them."

"How do you know?"

"Twenty-five years tells me you're not the first."

"Where are you?"

Alicia focused on a gray-haired woman in scrubs so close she could've kissed her. "Lift your head." The nurse added a second behind-the-head pillow. "Is this better?"

"Thank you. Is my Dad here?"

"He's here, your mother, and a man who says his name is Randall."

"When can I see them?"

"Rest a little. Your higher anesthetic dose may take longer to wear off. Don't worry. It didn't hurt you. You're out of recovery, and waiting here in ICU until we can clear a regular room."

"What if I fall asleep?"

"You do that. We're watching."

Alicia closed her eyelids.

"You all right?"

Two shallow breaths filled Alicia's lungs. Her hard squint blurred the large figure.

"Precious, you all right? You haven't moved for ten minutes."

"The heat, the flames. Lost your picture . . . my novel."

"Precious, you're safe. And, your mother's here."

"Dear, I'm so happy. The doctor said modern medicine has spared you what I had to endure. Praise God."

As additional soft light gathered on Alicia's retinas. No firemen strutted past. No Joel. No Darth Vader masks. A mist of tears enclosed her world. She had no inkling of what her mother meant, except that it must be good. "You've always elevated my spirits."

"The doctor says rest's best. Dad and I'll be near if you need us."

"What about Randall?"

"He's in the waiting room. He promised not to leave until he can see you. We're happy you met such a fine man. We're sorry he had to lose his wife for you to have a church wedding."

Alicia gulped. "He told you he wanted to marry me?"

"He didn't. But mothers can tell. You'll come to know that."

* * *

Randall pushed Alicia's hospital wheelchair as Vicky carried cards and two plants. A sparkling blue Lincoln awaited them outside the hospital's main entrance portico.

Vicky left a glass of water next to Alicia's bed. She radiated a coy smile. "I've got laundry."

"I should leave." Randall's words more of a statement

than a question.

"Pull out the computer chair," Alicia suggested. She hoisted her shoulders higher to rest on her bed's tufted violet headboard. "It's my only chair."

Randall focused his seated gaze upon the quilted comforter that covered her feet. "This seems odd. You've never allowed me past the living room."

"Why? If you know about Lady Victoria Dash, you should visit where she lives."

"Don't care about any Lady Dash. I love one Alicia Danielson."

"Kiss me."

Randall rose bent forward.

When their lips met, she kissed him. "Do you know what the doctor said?"

Randall knelt on the floor next to her bed. His elbows sunk into her mattress. "Your mother tried. Since my mind was made up, can't say I listened."

"Remember when I said to fasten your seatbelt?"

"Sorta."

"Doc Beck yesterday told me the surgery found the dreaded C in my left ovary." She forged ahead undeterred by Randall's tears for she knew that, if she stopped, she'd never finish. "Hope reigned when the microscope showed the bad cells hadn't broken away from the primary tumor, which Doc Beck explained as smaller than normal. No cancerous cells had migrated to the ovary's outside surface. While performing the laparotomy, the surgeon's try failed to excise the bad cells without removing the entire ovary."

"And that's why they kept you four days?"

"One reason. The surgeon wished to keep an eye on the unremoved right ovary. It may or may not ovulate, however, the silver lining is my uterus remains viable for egg implants."

"That's great news."

Alicia hesitated. "Does you mother know why you

found the hospital to be a second home?"

"She told me she doesn't care what your name is. She wants you to be in my life. If I disappoint her by not capturing your heart, she threatened me she'll never buy another Beatrix Smothers book as long as she lives."

Alicia laughed until her abdominal stitches ached.

"Don't you dare stop bringing joy into my life."

"Have you any news about Georgia?"

"The process drags on. I'm hopeful, as you should be."

"I'll pray every day Georgia is your child. And, whatever happens, I love you."

"And I you. I'm happy to kneel near you."

"Lady Victoria Dash in her day and age would approve, but let's not let Vicky see you."

Randall aborted his laugh. He reached into his right pants pocket. "Before I stand, it's time you wear this diamond ring."

Epilogue

Georgia, age six and a half, with a crimson bow in her hair, sprinkled red rose petals the entire church-aisle length she walked. When she reached the altar, she hugged Randall's right leg. To their right stood Best Man Jackson and Groomsmen Andy and Jonathan Sr.

Ring bearer Jonathan Jr. carried the wedding rings on a red satin pillow as he joined his father. Matron of Honor Elena led Bridesmaids Vicky and Wanda.

When Alicia lifted her white-gloved right hand from her Dad's left forearm, she hugged Georgia and Jonathan Jr. before she reached for Randall's right hand.

After they exchanged vows, Randall and Alicia greeted family and guests in the church's downstairs fellowship hall. DNA hadn't confirmed Randall as Georgia's father, but his and Alicia's administrative petition for her adoption continued its snail-paced advance. Their temporary custody foreclosed Georgia's detour into foster care. Randall swore off heated car seats.

Jackson whispered to Randall: "Best screenplay I've ever read. We've investors clamoring. Dust your shelf for

another gold statuette. We should give novel credit to
Alicia."

"Don't go there. If there's to be a credit, it goes to
Lady Victoria Dash, no one else."

"Who stole the bride and groom figurines from the
cake?" Joel asked.

"Hush," Vicky said. "Don't put your finger on the
frosting."

"What Randall and Alicia did is so heartfelt," Wanda
said.

"So romantic," Vicky replied. "Even with the black
mark, it's one beautiful red paper heart."

About the Author

Author Donan Berg landed four times in the romance winner's circle of the 2014 Ninth Annual Dixie Kane Memorial Contest. In 2013 he garnered three awards in the Eighth Annual Dixie Kane Memorial Contest. His vibrant writing talents, honed as a journalist, corporate executive, and lawyer, are displayed in his three Skeleton Series Mystery novels entitled *A Body To Bones, The Bones Dance Foxtrot,* and *Baby Bones. Adolph's Gold,* a police procedural mystery, has many attributes of his Skeleton Series Mystery novels while *Abbey Burning Love is* a fast-paced, novel-length, small city murder mystery/romance e-book.

A native of Ireland transplanted to the United States Heartland, he's also authored a collection of short stories entitled, *Bubbling Conflict and Other Stories*, where the lead story highlights the never-ending sectarian violence in Northern Ireland.

His novels have earned the praise of entertaining mystery, heartwarming romance.

If you've enjoyed *One Paper Heart*, don't be bashful, write a review. Also join Sheriff Jonas McHugh, first introduced in Author Berg's *Baby Bones,* in an upcoming 2016 mystery adventure entitled *Into the Dark.* Here's a taste:

Into the Dark

Donan Berg

Chapter One

Crinkled and faded $100 Federal Reserve notes tumbled out of a shiny-silver Republican ballot box. A bewildered Silver County Sheriff Jonas McHugh, this first Wednesday after the Tuesday Iowa caucus, poured fifty more into a second pile before he tilted the box upright.

Sister Luann, who'd kicked his houseguest butt out to repaint, wouldn't believe what he'd found unless he knelt next to the cabin table piles for a selfie. No picture needed for retired Sergeant Ronald Oelschleager due to arrive any minute from a recon of the frozen lake fifty

1

yards west. The unexplained cash now jeopardized Jonas's fishing vacation.

His boot stomps failed to dispel the forest's high-altitude chill that prowled beneath the cabin's planked floorboards and slithered upward through splits and cracks.

When his curiosity exceeded caution, he started a third pile of C-notes, peppered with crisp twenties. He manuevered the ballot box to keep the bills from falling off the backwoods cabin's three-by-five-foot sanded-board table. The unbuffed edge of the unclasped, slotted lid swung free to sting his ungloved right-hand.

"Damn." A full-lung-capacity blast launched Jonas's curse past his chilled lips into the wintry twenty-degree cold of an unheated cabin. His overtaxed memory failed to pinpoint a date when he'd seen so much unbundled cash.

Behind his back, the cabin door latch clink preceded the louder hinge creak. Jonas dropped the ballot box and his black calfskin driving gloves to lift his parka from his right hip. Only when he'd completed his pivot did he remember he'd locked his service revolver in Sgt. Oelschleager's Suburban's glove box.

"What critter scared you?" Sarge asked. His body filled the doorway, his left thumb hitched to a front pocket of a non-regulation orange flotation vest worn over a dark-blue parka. The vest, a fishing relic devoid of law enforcement initials, bespoke of the trip's intended purpose and Sarge's retired status.

"You." Jonas's tensed shoulders slumped.

"Holy-moly. Maybe you're the one scared now that I know about your money?" Sarge's left hand pulled the door closer to its doorjamb. "Trouble is all that cash won't catch fish. Nor does the half-inch lake ice, spider-webbed with cracks, help. 'Fraid the trout are safe. The lake's ice cap isn't thick enough to support a toddler's weight."

Jonas peered into a table shadow and squatted to retrieve the ballot box and his gloves. A straight-line draft through two punched-out knotholes chilled his forehead perspiration beads. His torso muscles and toes, warmed by a dark-red parka and insulated hiking boots, warded off half the penetrating cold. Upon standing, he laid the box on the table and his left hand fingers rubbed his cheeks to stir capillary blood. "Don't know where this came from." He winked his left eye. "Sure it isn't yours."

From inside the fur oval of a hooded blue parka, Sarge's eyes narrowed and his lips contorted into a twisted grin.

Jonas didn't equate Sarge's stare with forthcoming wisdom. "It's cold enough." Jonas's teeth fought off an urge to chatter. "Don't let more in."

"Don't be a pantywaist." Sarge spit out his words. "It's been a warm winter. Can't dare tiptoe on the lake's bubbled ice nor toss bait to open water for there ain't any."

While Sarge stepped inside and re-latched the door in non-record-setting time, Jonas inverted and aligned the tin box six inches above the tabletop. With the box gripped tight in his now-gloved left hand, he thrice banged his right gloved palm against its bottom. One folded white sheet of bond paper in a stream of green arrested Jonas's scanning eyeballs. His left forearm muscles tensed as he watched it flutter and come to rest atop the cash.

Sheriff McHugh stifled his crude comparison of how the cash carpeting the table resembled the overabundant and thick juniper underbrush his boots crunched from Sarge's Suburban to the cabin's front porch. Faint sun rays, filtered by the dirt splats on the windowpanes of the one west window, pooled into a ragtag striped-yellow design at his feet. The stack's top bills rippled as Sarge strode closer. Jonas gazed left to spy a dozen airborne bills. Three landed in an unlit hearth on seasoned and cobwebbed two-foot long stacked logs.

"We gonna count that?" Sarge asked. His words accompanied by a frosty mist. "Must be thousands." His wide eyes pushed his trimmed brows upward to a brown crew cut. "Ever thought of how it might be to be rich?"

Jonas doubted his infrequent two-dollar lottery ticket purchases would enhance his odds for an early retirement. "Only when Powerball hits $200 million."

An out-of-season gunshot rattled the grimy windowpanes.

"You hear that?" Sarge asked.

Jonas nodded. Even though the frozen ground wouldn't muddy his new hiking boots, to check it out would be a waste of official energy since Jonas was six hours outside his Silver County jurisdiction. "I'm not gung-ho enough to jog twenty minutes to your Suburban for your police radio."

"At least, shouldn't we check the cabin's perimeter."

Jonas shrugged. Without January snow around Andrew Lake for the first time in his thirty year recollection, he still wasn't enthused enough to abandon the loose bills.

Sarge hugged the cabin wall as he sidled to the fieldstone fireplace, its black cat andirons toppled horizontal to crisscross on the mortared brick hearth. Stretched cobwebs, the lattice for a quarter-inch fuzzy dust layer, obscured the finer andiron detail but not the three stacked unlit hardwood logs, one resting in the hollow of the two beneath it.

"Help me layer these bills back into the ballot box." Jonas stated his request matter-of-factly. "No use messing with it too much. That is, if it's evidence." It irked him that the money saddled him with filling out an incident report on a trip born of Luann's threat to throw him, a live-in tenant, out of her Kanosh house. He was certain he could've slept on the living room sofa while painters brightened the second floor bedrooms. Luann's Christmas present of new hiking boots, a special tread design for hilly terrain, didn't mollify him. He hugged her anyway for he could wear them on the rolling hills of his Silver County jurisdiction.

Jonas continued to flatten and stack bills without separating denominations.

Sarge shuffled around the table. "Didn't expect we'd find this cabin."

"Now you tell me." Jonas pressed his lips together. He shouldn't be sarcastic, even if he uttered a little white lie. "Had faith in you. You know this state better than most know the back of their own hand.

"Keep telling others that." Sarge opened the two doors in the cabin's cabinet that, besides the table and three pressed-back chairs, represented the one room's only furniture. "You know, a person's reputation is a perception not always reality unless they hear it three times. That's my goal. Triple repetition equals respected reputation." Sarge's deep-guttural laugh surfaced after he slammed the cabinet door shut. "No beer. How inhospitable."

Sarge's steps halted at the edge of a braided and liquid-stained cotton rag oval rug that stretched its longer dimension eight-foot length in front of the fireplace.

Jonas set the ballot box down, tugged his right-hand glove off finger-by-finger, and reached for the folded white paper.

"Whoa," Sarge shouted.

Jonas glanced toward Sarge. "What?" If certain the cold wouldn't have engraved lines at the corners of his mouth, Jonas would've frowned. "I'll be careful." He separated the twice-folded sheet by its edges. Scribbled at the top of the page, on the fill-in-the-blank line after the printed word "county," were the words "Balder" and

"West School." On the next line, two half-page columns were headed by the words "Candidate" and "Votes Received." He pinched the sheet at the edges and held it upright for Sarge. "Didn't Balder have one of the eight missing Republican primary precincts?"

From the opposite tableside, Sarge leaned forward and squinted at the paper sheet held upright by Jonas. "Think so. But don't trust me. Don't waste time with national politics. Found it better suits me to spend my time with state leaders." Sarge unzipped his orange vest and then his parka to lift a cell phone from his plaid shirt's breast pocket.

Sarge's claimed detachment from federal politics tweaked Jonas's skeptic bone. Iowa's first in the nation caucus blended national into state politics. His eyes scanned the candidate column, and the numbers written alongside the listed names: Roper, 435; Sandman, 239; Gingham, 123; Derry, 91; and Packman, 48.

Jonas tried to equate the numbers with the official GOP Iowa Caucus results publicized at the prior week's humble-pie news conference. New official vote totals that didn't include the eight missing precincts erased Roper's caucus night victory. Sandman's eighteen-vote presumptive win justified by the state GOP policy decision that the missing votes were irretrievable. If the votes on the sheet in Jonas's hands weren't tabulated, Roper bested Sandman. "Sarge, you think these votes were counted?"

Sarge raised a right hand index finger. Jonas nodded in response. The February north wind gust rattled and unlatched the cabin door. A freezer-blast of cold iced Jonas's cheeks. He buried his lower face in the crook of his right arm as he strode through swirling currency toward the door. After eight choppy strides, he used his left-hand glove to insulate his shivering fingers as he grabbed the door's iron handhold. He dismissed the crack

6

heard beyond the tree line as an animal or a wind gust detaching a weak branch. Jonas yanked the metal bar tongue above the latch before the wind wicked further warmth from his body.

"Central committee friend tells me Balder and Cooper Counties had a missing precinct," Sarge said. "Don't know which one. With charges and counter-charges flying, the Republican state chair and the party's official spokesperson are being tight-lipped."

Jonas added twenties to the hundred-dollar bills he squatted to retrieve. "Didn't one official go missing?"

"If you mean Sandman's campaign manager, consensus is he's hiding from the press."

Jonas circled the twenty-by-thirty-two-foot room as he and Sarge gathered bills from the floor. They squared the money into small piles before a gloved Jonas laid each stack inside the ballot box. His tranquilized mind rippled with no answer to his $64.00 questions: who paid the money? and who was paid off?

"Would you agree this is a caucus ballot box?"

Sarge let the fireplace rug he had lifted drop to the floor. "Seen Democrats use one similar."

Yet, the vote-total sheet confused Jonas. While it indicated the box may have contained ballots, the names listed were Republicans, not Democrats. Moreover, the first nationwide caucus last week didn't elect national convention delegates. How much did it matter? A headline? The proverbial light bulb glowed. Campaign contributions. The winner guaranteed to rake in hordes of cash. A caucus victory rallied a campaign cha-ching.

"Know what's strange?" Sarge pocketed his cell phone and rubbed his hands on opposite elbows. His horizontal forearms, indicative of a powerful man, rested on his protruding teddy-bear abdomen until he arched his back to stiffen his six-foot-two frame.

"What?" Jonas asked.

Sarge's taut jaw skin a sign he was ready to speak.

"With no bed, I'd say no one's slept or even stayed here for ages."

Jonas nodded. The faded drywall stains, the dirt-caked windowsill, the one west window either painted or nailed shut and the undisturbed fireplace dust all an unspoken testament to verify Sarge's observation. Jonas recalled neither scattered wood chips, a chopping block nor an outside woodpile. The logs inside all within the hearth.

"There's one oddity." Sarge plopped onto a chair, his legs sprawled. From his front pants pocket he extracted matches to light the Coleman propane lantern he'd carried in with him.

Over its hiss, Jonas asked, "You mean the lack of dust and dirt on the floor?"

"Exactly."

"Sleeping bag?" Without an answer from Sarge, Jonas added to his question, "Or blankets?" Even if there was a right answer, Sarge's lack of a response gave Jonas no reason to pick a quarrel. The place sure didn't have maid service. "Who owns this place?"

"Wendell O'Dell did 'til he died a couple years back. Would assume Catherine, that's his wife, you know, inherited." Jonas didn't, but he nodded anyway, confident Sarge didn't need encouragement to continue. "With her need to use a cane, she probably never hiked here."

"Don't know her." Jonas, convinced he had stacked the last of the bills, closed the box's lid.
Sarge twisted to gaze at the now dark curtain-less west window. "Sure you do. Runs the B & B in Elba. That's still your neck of the woods, ain't it?"

"Yeah, but I gotta think. Elba? Isn't but a grain elevator and half dozen buildings. B & B, you say?" Jonas rubbed his jaw. "There's one old Victorian house. Don't recall a sign."

"Maybe Catherine got remarried."

8

"She an older . . . dull-haired redhead, sorta stocky, standoffish?"

Sarge chuckled. "On the money."

"Introduced to her as Cath Weeks." Jonas paused to pull out a chair. "She a Republican?"

"While the caucus possibility explains why the money's here, doubt Catherine left it." Sarge fiddled with his lantern's flame. "Wendell was knee-deep in Democratic politics for decades."

"Another explanation stares us in the face. A B & B is a cash business. These bills are well worn. Drugs and money laundering high on my distinct-possibility list."

"Been a lot of that in Silver County?"

"Don't remind me."

Two loud knocks rattled the cabin's door. Their echo enhanced the cabin s claustrophobic effect. Jonas glanced at the stuffed ballot box and then at Sarge's quizzical mien, partly hidden by his upraised hands. They both stayed quiet. Heavy footwear squeaked porch planks outside their field of vision.

Sarge hadn't spoken about inviting anyone other than Jonas.

"Come out. Hands up," a voice boomed. "Come out, whoever you are."

Into the Dark

Look for Author Donan Berg's newest entertaining mystery, *Into the Dark,* in early 2016.

Don't be surprised if you find skullduggery interlaced with heartwarming romance.

If you've enjoyed **One Paper Heart,** post a review at wherever you obtained your copy and elsewhere.

Thank you.

Acknowledgements

The author wishes to acknowledge the invaluable assistance rendered by friends, family, and the members of two book clubs who encourage with insightful zeal, softened with unending compassion. Special mention is given to the late Nicholas A. Genovese Jr., Dixie Kane Memorial Contest Coordinator. He never offered a contest advantage. He just wanted you to try your best and learn from your own decisions.

Cover by James, GoOnWrite.com.